THE BLACK HILL

Also by Mamang Dai

Fiction
Stupid Cupid (2008)
The Legends of Pensam (2006)
The Sky Queen (2003)

Non-fiction
Mountain Harvest: The Food of Arunachal (2004)
Arunachal Pradesh: The Hidden Land (2003)

Poetry
Midsummer: Survival Lyrics (2014)
The Balm of Time (2008)
River Poems (2004)

Children's books
Hambreelsai's Loom (2014)
Once Upon a Moon Time (2003)

THE BLACK HILL

Mamang Dai

ALEPH

ALEPH BOOK COMPANY
An independent publishing firm
promoted by *Rupa Publications India*

Published in India in 2014 by
Aleph Book Company
7/16 Ansari Road, Daryaganj
New Delhi 110 002

ISBN: 978-93-82277-23-1

13 15 17 19 20 18 16 14 12

Printed in India.

'Oh that thou wouldst hide me in the grave, that thou wouldst keep me secret, until thy wrath be past, that thou wouldst appoint me a set time, and remember me!'

—Job 14:13

'Song thief, my heart,
how shall you capture them? You suffer.
Like a painting
take the black ink
And lay in the red.
Perhaps by the time you have done your task
You will no longer suffer pain.'

—Irene Nicholson, *Firefly in the Night*

Contents

Prologue / ix

1847 / 1
1848 / 12
1849 / 17
1850 / 25
1851 / 43
1852 / 74
1853 / 153
1854 / 205
1855 / 257

Author's Note / 290
Acknowledgements / 295

Prologue

I once knew a man whose shoulders touched the sky. He was a very brave man. Everything came to him as if he was appointed by the gods to go where no man had gone before. Everyone who met this man wanted to turn into someone else. They wanted to exchange their old selves for a new life. This is the story of that man. No—it is the story of two men, for now, after all is done, I can tell you that they were one. I can still see them, walking together in the high mountains. So silent and endless, this story—who can tell it all? I only know that I will remember, and never forget...

These are the words of a woman telling me a story. If anyone were to ask me where I heard this story, how I found it, I would have no answer. Every dawn I think all the stories of the world are connected. At night another voice tells me—no, there are more stories yet that are silent and separate. There are many lost stories in the world and versions that were misplaced yesterday or a thousand years ago. Perhaps this is one or the other of them.

I have books in front of me. They tell me things about this land, and a priest who walked across these hills carrying a cross and a sextant. They tell me what he saw and thought, but these are words fixed on yellowed paper. There is another story from an unwritten past hidden beyond the mountain wall. I journey for many days to find it, and one day I come upon a black hill. It is a deserted site, so bleak and sad, and it is here that my eyes fall on an abandoned hut, half burnt, where shafts of light pierce through the roof like golden arrows. There is no one in the house, but in the deep silence I sense a presence, as if someone has come in and lit a candle. A closed book is opening. Someone is speaking to me from the past and the words are clear as day: A man, a woman, and a priest. This is their story.

I can see them now, vivid as the red flowers of the coral tree against the pillars of smoke rising up on the far side of the river—just as it was one March evening in the nineteenth century when the events that I am going to relate take place. The reader can decide whether this story be true or not. The reader can decide whether to believe, or not, what I believe: that after everything is laid to rest, all that matters is love; and that memory gives life, and life never ends.

1847

The Arrival of Strangers in Mebo and The Man from the East

A woman is standing on a hill. Her name is Gimur. It is the name of the month she was born in a village called Mebo. It was a cold day, her mother had said, but red flowers were ablaze on the beautiful tagat—coral tree. The tall and thorny tagats that surround the village are in bloom again, and Gimur has to rear up to look beyond the treetops. In the last light of the sun she is a sculpted silhouette poised on a rock at the edge of the hill. What are those pillars of smoke rising up from the flat land across the river? Are they fires? She wonders, staring hard as a thick band of fog begins to spread over the river like a screen, shutting out the distant plains.

'What are you looking at?'

Gimur turned around. 'Are you following me?'

The young man who had addressed her raised his hands. 'I was passing by and saw you here,' he said. 'Everyone is looking for you.'

Looking for her. They were *always* looking for her, thought Gimur, her friends, relatives, uncles, aunts. Her mother most of all. What did they want that they were always looking for her?

'It's late,' said the young man.

She cocked her head to one side and nodded without saying anything. He waited. The sun had sunk behind the steep cliff and except for the dark hill and the red band of light above the horizon, everything had been swallowed in a milky blue haze. She stood in silence for some time then abruptly jumped off the rock and turned swiftly in the direction of her house. The young man stood aside to let her pass. His name was Lendem. He was some ten years older than Gimur, and his father was a village elder just like Gimur's father had been before he died quite suddenly when she was still a child.

What a girl! I must be her only friend in this place, he thought, as he watched her walk imperiously ahead of him.

Gimur did everything that young girls in the village were expected to do, in fact she was better than most at household chores; but, as her mother always said, she was uncontrollable and daring, more like a boy, whistling and climbing trees and getting into scrapes. At the time this story begins Gimur was seventeen years old. Of late her impetuous nature appeared to have toned down to an uncommunicative silence, and now she liked doing nothing better than to spend her time sitting alone on the veranda at the back of her parent's house staring at the hills all around. She wondered if there were other villages hidden in the hills and if there were people living across the river.

'Of course there are,' Lendem had told her many times, but she would not believe him.

'Where, where are they? I don't see them.' She would narrow her eyes and say, 'I see only you!'

'Hoh Ho Hoiee!' A long shout ricocheted off the cliff and Gimur and Lendem began running back to the village. It was a signal. Here was proof of others living beyond their village! Night was falling and every man, woman and child in Mebo was on alert for the return of a group of men who had left Mebo at crack of dawn to meet some strangers at the foot of the hill. It was what Gimur had been on the lookout for. 'Hoh! Hoh Ho!' The men were approaching swiftly. They were coming up the hill. Gimur felt the ground reverberating and suddenly their village came alive with the brightness of bamboo flares, the pounding of feet, and cries of welcome. Everyone was talking at the same time: 'They're here! Are they here? What news? What news?' She caught a glimpse of the men at the head of the column and her heart raced at the sight. They were like gods, with their spears and shields and their war helmets resplendent with the feathers of the hawk and the curved tusks of the wild boar. The men were bare bodied and shining with sweat. Right in front was Lendem's father, his chest like a bull's and his calf muscles twitching in the eerie light.

'Hide your face, girl,' her mother tried to pull her back but Gimur was thrusting forward and craning her neck to look at the warriors. She was not interested in the men. She wanted only to see if she could detect any change in their eyes—something new, something different—after their contact with the strangers from faraway worlds. Who were the strangers? Everyone had heard about the British, the white men—the miglun—who were coming upriver towards Mebo in long boats. They wanted a meeting with the villagers to talk about establishing a trading post a few miles downstream from where the river turned in a wide loop hugging bare rock before it flattened out and flowed away below the sloping hill of Mebo.

'But they want something more,' Lendem's father had said. 'They want to protect those pathetic fishermen and gold washers who worked for us and have now fled to the Assam plains. The miglun want us to make peace because it is their territory now and they want the gold. That is why a miglun officer is coming to meet us from Assam, from Saikwa Ghat.' Lendem's father had been angry and restless for many days. It had fallen on him to decide what was to be done about the meeting. He was a village elder, but like all the older men he did not trust strangers. In the end he had decided: 'They want to talk. We will talk, but we will not show them the way here. We will meet them at the foot of the hill by the river. We will travel at dawn, all the men of the village. One look, they want one look. We will also see who they are. One look matters.'

On that warm March night, who was to know what eyes peered out of the darkness and saw the curtain of time lifted by the light flickering in the night wind? There was the British camp by the river, the men and the guns, and Captain Hamilton Vetch standing like a tall shadow, staring at the dark hills. The British troops could not reach Mebo, not yet—the bend in the river cutting into the steep hill prevented anyone coming by boat from reaching the village. The captain thought the meeting with the villagers had gone well. Vetch was an able and experienced officer, who had been in Assam for many years serving in both civil and military capacities until his appointment as Political Agent of Upper Assam. His mission was to keep an eye on the restless tribes inhabiting the hills and protect British interests. The Abor have been told about our laws. We'll see what happens, he thought.

Prodded by her mother, Gimur rushed back into the house only to emerge on the veranda at the back used for drying paddy. It was empty; she sat, wrapping her arms around her knees, concentrating on the voices, trying to hear what was being said. A half moon was rising above the trees and she stared at it, willing it to rise faster. She tilted her head back and closed her eyes. 'Come, come to me,' she said softly. 'Shine on my face. Enter my body, float in my blood and settle in my heart like a golden swing.' Thump. Thump. She was concentrating so hard she thought the moonlight had covered her face when a shadow passed before her. Without a sound she opened her eyes very slightly, just like a clever animal giving the impression they were closed, but able to see everything in front of her. A man was staring at her. She thought he was standing on a big stone as he was craning forward to look at her. She did not move. She did not open her eyes fully, but she could see his face clear and white in the moonlight like a rising spirit with burning eyes and a hard, angry mouth. He wore a black cloth wound round his head.

'Who are you?' she whispered with her eyes shut.

The man did not move away.

'I am Kajinsha,' he said in a harsh, grating voice. 'What are you doing?'

'I'm talking to the moon,' she replied.

He did not say anything. She opened her eyes a little and saw that he was not standing on a stone as she had thought. He was a stranger, and he was alone. She opened her eyes wider. He stood firmly in front of her with his black eyes fixed on her face. He looked like a tiger, solitary, self aware, as if ready to face anything. She waited. She wanted him to say something more.

'Where is your village?' She wanted to hear his voice again.

But the man had slid away without another word. Gimur continued to sit there facing the breeze. Moonlight flooded the village. Everything was calm and peaceful but suddenly, for no reason, Gimur felt strangely bereft.

◆

'We will not come this way again'

Kajinsha had come from the east. He had travelled a long way summoning every ounce of stamina to cross the big mountains. He had never come this far before, but he was satisfied that he had made the journey and reached the Abor village of Mebo. 'It is there that the white men are going.' He had heard this being discussed by other travellers one night, and he had decided on the spur of the moment that he would track the miglun and follow their boats and men as they moved upstream. He had kept close to the bank. Sometimes he was ahead of them, hidden among trees that sloped straight down to the water's edge. He left no trail. He did not know how many days he had been shadowing the white men but he knew that the moon was yet to be born when he had started his journey. Now it was full. He thought of the girl he had seen standing on a rock. And then he had seen her again with her eyes closed talking to the moon. He remembered the blue tattoo on her chin. Who was she? He wondered if it had been a vision. I'll find out later, he thought. He had memorised the route. He could return.

Now something else was on his mind. He was lying face down on a flat rock overlooking the land below. The mountainside fell away into a green plain. He saw the river glinting and turning like a giant snake as far and wide as the eye could see. As he stared at it the river changed shape. Now it was like the trunk of a giant silver tree, spreading its shining arms and limbs across the body of the earth. It had crashed into the earth from the mountains, and now it wanted to hold the earth in a vast embrace.

'It goes away into the land where the sun sets,' his father had told him, speaking about the river and a nether world somewhere between their villages and the great sky beyond. Kajinsha stared at the smoke pillars spiralling upwards from settlements that he knew belonged to the white people, and something, a memory, an old ache, made his face bitter.

Kajinsha had been born in a village beyond the Dau River in the Mishmee Hills. The village is no longer in existence and even back then it had been a nameless settlement not recorded on any map. What was a village in those days but a house or two, a family— father, mother, children and a few clan members? If they moved, that was the end of their village. In the 1800s what was known as the Mishmee Hills was a sparsely populated region of towering mountains and swift flowing rivers where three great clans of the Mishmee tribe lived. However, the people of Mishmee country called themselves the Kmaan, Taraon and Idu people and the term 'Mishmee' was an alien word to them. If anyone had asked Kajinsha who he was he would have said he was Kmaan, distinct from the Taraon whom the Kmaan knew as Tah-wrah or Chimmu, and the Idu clans whom they called Mindow and who occupied the territories further south and northwest.

When Kajinsha was seven or eight years old—the year was 1826—his father had told him that a race of white men called the British had conquered the Ahom kings of the east and were now the rulers of Assam. Perhaps this would unite the warring clans of their land, he had said. But he did not believe it would; for had he not tried hard to make this happen for years? Kajinsha's father had performed rituals for a peaceful existence in the shelter of the snowy mountains but the gods had not answered his prayers. Kajinsha had grown up in an environment of war and death. Steeped in isolation, the tribes living in one valley across from the other viewed their neighbours with suspicion and dread. Claims over land, possession of rivers and streams and ownership rights to hunt and fish, regularly erupted into bloody, inter-tribal feuds and no one knew when the fighting would end. One summer night Kajinsha had woken to the cries of men and women fleeing like helpless spirits even as attackers of a neighbouring clan cut them down.

'Run!' his father had shouted. And Kajinsha was running through the forest like a deer, crashing into the undergrowth, crawling under leaves like a naked worm. Hush. Hush. Keep still. All night he lay on his belly choked by the fumes from their burning village that spread over the trees like a black cloud. He did not know how long he lay there. In a silent, blessed conspiracy more clouds piled up far above the trees and sent down sheets of rain to douse the flames and save the lives of the Kmaan clan as the attackers retreated, seeking shelter from the sudden and furious downpour.

It was then that Kajinsha's father had decided to move further north to the Dagum mountain range on the border with Tibet. He was a big strong man but peaceful at heart. He did not want war. His relatives and friends taunted him. 'You are running away,' they said. His father did not reply. Instead, he asked, 'Who will come with me?' When no one answered he said, 'You are afraid. You cannot fight, and you cannot find a new place to defend. Stay here then and hide! How long will you hide? I am leaving and anyone will know where to find me. I will not hide.' He turned to Kajinsha and lifted him in his arms. 'You are my son and I will let no harm come to you. One day you will marry and bear sons and daughters in a new place far away from here.'

They had left, accompanied by Kajinsha's father's brother and his wife. They had found rest in a high valley of the Tho Chu. But rest, even young Kajinsha knew, was momentary. Soon enough word reached his father that the white men were travelling far and wide in their territory. What did they want? They were looking for a way north and heading towards them. They were being aided by men of rival clans along with some people of the plains, who acted like servants and carried the white men's food and clothes. 'The others may be eating their salt but we will never allow them to come here,' his father had said. Since the British had occupied Assam their hills had been disturbed by these strange, foreign men who crept deeper and deeper into their land carrying gifts of salt, iron, tobacco and opium. Many chiefs had succumbed to their overtures but Kajinsha's clan had remained aloof.

To stop their advance his father and uncle masterminded a strategy that was to have far reaching consequences. His uncle travelled north and enlisted the help of their Tibetan neighbours who lived in the Zayul valley. 'First, it is important to teach our own brothers a lesson,' he said. 'They are giving up our land and showing strangers the way to come here.' In return for the help of the Tibetans he promised them that their clan would defend the land and allow no stranger right of way through their territories to cross into Tibet.

In 1836 Kajinsha's father and uncle had led a group of Tibetans from the Zayul valley to meet the powerful Mishmee chief of Ghalum who, along with his brothers, controlled the southern part of the territory. The purpose of the meeting was to tell Ghalum of their decision and ask him to unite with them to stop any stranger from entering their land. Many years later Kajinsha's uncle was to say that all that happened on that night was the work of evil spirits, but by then his words had lost their meaning for the young Kajinsha. All he knew was that the meeting had turned bitter. The alliance offered by the Tibetans had been spurned by the Mishmees of Ghalum. Kajinsha's father had stood up to leave. 'So be it,' he had shouted. 'We will not come this way again.'

Kajinsha's father had thus turned his back on his Mishmee brothers in the south. But there were other tribes who shared his hatred of the British and feared being brought under their control. In 1839 news reached him of a plot by the Khampti clans of Suddya in Assam to rise up against the British. Their chief, who went by the title of Suddya Khawa Gohain, had been stripped of his title and dignity by the British authorities and removed from his position. He sent out a call for help. It was a chance Kajinsha's father could not miss. In the dead of night he led a group of men south to the Khampti villages dotted around the banks of the Burhampooter River. They joined hands with 500-armed Khampti warriors who advanced on the British station from all directions. In the surprise attack the British Political Agent, Colonel Adam White, and his forces numbering some eighty men were butchered and all but two sepoy lines burned to the ground. In the fighting Kajinsha's father had been fatally wounded. 'I saw the white people running,' he had said. 'A woman and two small children were hiding in a boat. I was hiding near Gurmura creek until help came.' He had returned with a deep wound in his stomach tightly bound in rags smeared with the juice of jungle herbs. He was close to death. His feet were swollen and bleeding but aided by his brother he had reached home. The shaman saw him and muttered, 'I have seen the weapons of war falling from a great chief. There will be misfortune.'

Misfortune and death. That was how it had been. Since his father's death Kajinsha's life had not been easy. It was war, always war. Even now he was looking down at a country still at war. He was looking at the Suddya country of Upper Assam in the extreme eastern end of the Burhampooter valley. Extending from the mountains in the east it was a densely forested area of some ten thousand square miles with its northern and southern tracts divided by the mighty river stretching into the plains as far west as the Dhunseeree river that separated it from Central and Lower Assam. The mountains in the north were home to his people and independent tribes like the Abor people he had just visited, and the lower eastern end was occupied by the Moamaria, Khampti and Singpho tribes who controlled the routes in the eastern Patkoee mountains between Assam and Burmah. For centuries, hordes of Shan invaders had poured in through those passes and the plain below had run red with the blood of fugitive kings and ministers. In recent years, some local rulers had fled to Calcutta and begged help from the East India Government to oust the invaders from Assam. That was how the British had gained a foothold in this country. In the last days of the Ahom monarchy, the raja had escaped to British territory abandoning Assam as a province of the Burmese empire.

Now the British were strong; they had gunboats and hundreds of soldiers. Kajinsha raised his elbows and cupped his chin in his hands. He had only stopped to see if the landscape had changed. One side of the sky was dark with black clouds but to the west the sun was beaming down. All was still. The country seemed to be

Mamang Dai

at rest. But Kajinsha never forgot anything. And now, as memory returned afresh he stood up to continue his journey. Rest… There was no rest. 'Be ready, my son,' his father had said. 'Prepare yourself. Be ready!' But the old man had died without telling him what it was that he had to be prepared for. All Kajinsha remembered was his father's perplexed gaze and the way he had lifted his hand as if trying to point to something beyond.

1848

Far Away, Another Life

Far beyond the mountains sloping down into the Assam valley, further away than Kajinsha could imagine, across a great ocean where the rise and falls of the waves was like time rolling its dice, a young French Jesuit priest would soon set out on a journey from an island shore, and never return.

His name was Nicolas Michel Krick, son of Michel and Elisabeth Dubourg Krick of Lixheim, in Lorraine, France. Born in 1819, he was the second of five children. His parents were pious, hardworking people who lived each day in a simple routine without thinking too much about things like Fate and Destiny. 'This is destiny, the way we are living now,' his father might have said. He was a tailor, a good, kind man who worked with his hands. It was a happy household. The children spent their time between home and the village school and the young Krick grew up in an atmosphere of love and security. It was when his mother died soon after his youngest sister was born, that Krick, who was then seven years old, first encountered the shock of death and the loneliness. His father married a middle-aged widow soon after—a decision that was apparently supported by his father-in-law, Jean Pierre Dubourg—so that life in the tailor shop could continue as before with the children growing up under the care of their stepmother and the aging grandfather. Two of Michel Krick's brothers were also tailors and the shop buzzed with activity. Customers plied in and out and perhaps it was during this time that young Krick acquired his eye for detail, and his love of nature, which came from his grandfather, who was a gardener. These interests were to later guide his correspondence and notes he would make when he was alone and very far away from home.

And it is in faraway places and events that we must look to understand Krick's journey, his life, even though facts do not explain the twists and turns of fate. In 1839 at the age of twenty, Nicolas Krick entered the Seminary of Nancy. He was ordained in 1844, and three years later he was appointed as second curate in Phalsbourg. It was a time of sweeping changes in France—the Revolution had come and gone half a century ago, but bloody feuds still raged in the narrow streets of Paris. When Krick arrived in the parish of Phalsbourg it was just three weeks before the fall of the monarchy in 1848.

The climate of change also affected the spiritual life of Europe. There had been a time when the Roman Catholic Church had thriving Christian communities in far-flung corners of the world. In Asia, Jesuit priests had enjoyed the patronage of the Ming rulers of China and were the first Europeans to obtain permission to establish permanent residence on the mainland. French Jesuits had played an important role in the imperial court, working on scientific projects and teaching mathematics, astronomy and cartography. In 1658 the Société des Missions Étrangères, the Society of Foreign Missions of Paris—often called the MEP—had been founded with the appointment of the first Vicar Apostolic to Asia, followed by the setting up of a seminary in Paris which sought to convert non-believers and impart training and preparation for missionary work in Asia and countries around the Indian Ocean. All this changed with the downfall of the Ming dynasty; the Manchu emperors began to expel foreigners from China. In 1724 Christianity was proscribed and missionaries in the provinces were deported to Canton and Macao. Since then evangelical and apostolic activity in the distant corners of Asia had all but ceased.

Now, there were signs of hope. If change was sweeping across Europe, so it was in Asia and the Far East. Britain had risen as the dominant power in the nineteenth century, and the British East India Company with its merchants, soldiers and naval fleet was playing a pivotal role in restoring Christian communities in China and other eastern lands. The turning point was the defeat of the Manchu by the British in the First Opium War and the Nanjing Treaty of 1842 that ended the isolation of China with the cession of Hong Kong Island paving the way for the opening of the Chinese market to western nations. In 1844 the Treaty of Whampoa (Huángpú) granted commercial privileges to France with access to certain ports and free travel and missions in China. After protracted negotiations France also secured an edict of tolerance from the Chinese emperor that would permit Christian missionaries back into China.

Church leaders began to look east again. They saw the island kingdoms of the Far East and Laos, New Japan, Indo-China and Korea, but what drew their gaze most were the unexplored mountains of the high Himalaya and the mysterious kingdom of Tibet. Remote, mystical, Tibet was the land of reincarnate god kings, the source of great rivers, the destination of caravans, immense riches, magic and miracles. In an age of Christian martyrs, Tibet lured explorers, merchants and priests as if it was preordained that men would leave everything and fall to a spell blowing like a fierce wind from a distant world that called with such insistence that they could do no more than submit, set sail, struggle to find a route through the glittering pinnacles of ice into the secret heart of that world, or perish in the attempt.

Nicolas Krick might have felt this pull like many young men who were leaving their French parishes to serve in remote foreign missions. His scholarly, contemplative nature would not be satisfied with easy answers. His first sermons of this time preserved in the Archives of the Paris Foreign Missions, 'Existence d'une autre vie', testify to this. He wanted a faith that would be unshakeable and for this he had to question the very nature of reason and faith and the meaning of freedom of conscience. Day by day, every hour of prayer was a preparation for voyage, a tidying up of things, a constant farewell to the grounds, tender flowers and green grass of his home, a strengthening resolve to travel out in the name of God—to live another life 'over there'.

Where?

Sometimes, at night, the thought crossed his mind that no one would care nor remember where it was that he was going or what happened to him. All summer he had thought about this. There was his parish and his peaceful life in a familiar countryside. He was well loved, and he could dedicate his life to service here, but deep inside, his honesty of purpose and his liberal temperament recognised that traditional ways of preaching had perhaps served their purpose only too well in these quiet parishes of European towns. His parishioners were a flock safely nestled under undisturbed wings, so much so that church attendance and rituals had become routine and almost meaningless. Father Krick wanted meaning back. He wanted to abandon oratory and speak to an assembly in the language of the heart. He could not rest until he felt every prayer and sermon was imbued with the original, passionate conviction of his vocation in the service of God. More than the challenge of carrying the gospel to unknown parts of the world Krick was seeking an experience of the passionate union with the divine. He knew this union would come only through the path of love and service. And for that he would have to leave his safe habitat and take flight into the wide sky. What lay beyond, he did not know. There was only a promise of a love that glowed in his heart and crowned his thoughts with a hope of something beyond the self. It was a search that would take him across seas and continents to the utmost ends of the earth and into the belly of the darkest, bleakest mountains of the world. In October 1848 at the age of twenty-nine, Nicolas Krick took the first step of this long journey when he completed the formalities of a candidate and arrived at the Missions Étrangères de Paris, Rue du Bac, Paris.

1849

A Fire

'Get up, will you!' Gimur's mother was stomping around making a lot of noise. She tugged at her daughter. 'Hai! What is this! Did I make this blanket for you to sleep in like it was your cocoon?'

Gimur woke up with a start. What had happened to her? She was returning from a land of dreams.

Why is the village so quiet today, she wondered.

'Lendem is waiting for you', said her mother.

Aah! Everything came back in a flash. There was no time to lose. She jumped up and rushed out to the veranda. Lendem was sitting there with his back to her.

'Has everyone left?' she asked. Lendem nodded.

'Wait,' she said, hurriedly turning back into the house. She appeared again in an instant in a yellow ga-le hastily tucked in around the waist. Lendem looked at her and thought she was still half asleep. She looked rumpled and her eyes were puffy and sleepy. 'Let's go,' she said.

They followed the path leading out of the village. It was a bright, clear morning but Gimur could feel the heat rising up from the trees. Everything came back clearly now. The migluns had set fire to a nearby village. It was not far beyond Mebo, but to get there they would have cross a wide swathe of forest skirting the river and the trek would take a full day even if they walked fast and did not stop. All the villagers had escaped into the forest and were now holding a meeting in another village where Lendem had relatives and where the men of Mebo had already gone. 'Why should you go?' Lendem had said when he had heard of Gimur's intention.

'I want to see,' she had replied. She had heard the shouts of runners arriving in the dead of night shouting that they were now at war with the British. Gimur had heard about wars with the Tayu Tage and Dangga tribes north and east of their village. But a war with the migluns, this was a new thing. The news had filled her with a fierce joy. In her mind the British were a fearsome race of people who had appeared suddenly from nowhere. They travelled up and down the country trying to enter other people's land without any respect for anyone. They possessed firearms and punished anyone who tried to stop them. When they reached a place they ordered everyone to obey them. Someone should teach them a lesson she thought.

Her thoughts were fuelled by the stories surrounding the death of her father. Among warlike tribes, they said, he had been the greatest warrior of the Lego clan. He was a quiet, self-effacing man, who spoke little; in physical appearance he was short and stocky, there were others taller and bigger built than him, but when it came to fighting, no one could outrun or overpower him. He carried a secret power that made him the best tracker in the land, and in a hunt no animal or human enemy could escape him. The shaman who travelled into the realm of animals and spoke their language said that tigers trembled when they heard his name.

Gimur was six years old when her father who had been fit and healthy had suddenly collapsed on the village road and died. 'It is the work of the white devils,' someone had cried. Her father, they said, had fought a war somewhere, the British had forced him to help them, and now they were getting rid of him. 'Wherever the

Mamang Dai

migluns go they bring death and outrage!' Other men had taken up the cry and the village was seething with shock and rage until another man, Lendem's uncle, had said, 'No! It was not true. The migluns had not killed him.' He, Gimur's father, had been ill. 'I do not know what illness was eating him,' the uncle had continued, 'but he told me he had been struck by visions. He said that a bad time was coming and that this dread followed him in his dreams.'

'What did he see?' a man had cried.

'I don't know!' the uncle had replied.

And there the matter had ended, with no one any wiser about the reason for a great warrior's sudden death.

And now people said the British were so strong they had gunboats and hundreds of soldiers and they could scheme and plot without fear. 'They are armed with an evil wind that starts blowing the moment they set foot anywhere,' Gimur thought. She crunched her feet down hard on the river stones as if to avenge all that had happened. If I feel strongly enough perhaps the strangers will take off and leave us in peace, she thought. She was so engrossed in her thoughts that Lendem, turning to look at her, thought she was in a trance, walking without looking where she was going. The sun was directly overhead and the heat and glare of the white sand along the river was becoming unbearable.

'We can stop for a while,' he said, mopping his face.

'No, let's walk,' she replied.

They hurried on without another word.

When they reached the village where the refugees from the burnt village had gathered, the sun had already dropped behind the mountains. The men were all assembled in the moshup, the barrack style longhouse for men that was a prominent feature of every Abor village. Gimur could see the glow of a fire through the gaps in the bamboo walls. Lendem went in to join the men and Gimur walked on to his aunt's house. The old lady was waiting. 'At last!' she cried. 'I was worried about you. This route is very dangerous because of elephants.' Gimur wanted to laugh. How innocent this aunt was, talking about wild elephants when there were men with guns attacking their homes. Everyone called the old lady Moi, and now Moi sat Gimur down by the fire where Lendem's sister Nago and a group of other young girls were talking excitedly.

'The villagers raided the migluns' camp. They killed three guards!' Nago told her.

'They should have killed everyone!' someone else added.

'Hush, hush,' said Moi. 'It won't be so easy to drive away the migluns. I know them.'

Gimur craned her neck to look at Moi but Moi was moving about beyond the circle of firelight, picking up baskets and bundles of leaves. Her voice echoed from different corners of the house.

'They are very clever and careful people. When they want something they will never leave until they get it. Mark my words. I know them.'

Everyone believed her. A long time ago, when Moi was a skinny young girl, her father had travelled south to settle in Mebo village. The year was 1822. Just like Gimur's father and his clan they had come from Bor Abor country, from a place called Damroh in the north. No sooner had they settled in Mebo, when a case of abduction disrupted their lives. A young woman of their clan had been carried away by someone from another tribe. No one knew how it had happened. At the time rumours were afloat that the woman might even have run away willingly, but the man was from an enemy clan and the Mebo people were honour bound to react. Word got around that fearing reprisal from his own people, the man had fled with the woman to Assam. It fell on Lendem's uncle to give chase and bring the woman back.

A year passed. There was no news. Another year, and still

nothing. Lendem's uncle never found the woman. Something else had happened instead. At one point in his search, Lendem's uncle had met the British and presented his case before them, demanding that they punish the plains people for sheltering the runaway couple. But where were they sheltering? No one knew. And the British were not interested. A war was looming and their primary concern was to enlist the help of the hill tribes in capturing Assam from Burmese invaders. The uncle was one of the first Abor tribals they were meeting. They thought he was a smart fellow whom they could put to good use—and sure enough, more Abors came to fight on the side of the British in the maan-mimak, the first Anglo-Burmese War that broke out in 1824. Lendem's uncle was wounded in battle and left for dead but he lived and made his way back to Mebo. He had been away a long time and he wondered if he would find welcome and rest in his home village, but he did. And a year after his return he and Moi were married. He never spoke of his meeting with the miglun again. It was Moi who asked questions, curious about the white-skinned strangers who crossed vast oceans to—to do what? What was it that they wanted, so far away from home? What hungers drove them?

In 1836, when a group of two hundred Abors went down to the plains to meet the British and stake their claim to settle on the banks of the Dibang River, Moi went with them. It was an unthinkable thing at the time, for a woman to join what was a mission only for men, but her husband had been unable to dissuade her—'I want to see the place where you lived before you met me. I am your wife, your past is my past.' Perhaps it was guilt that made him give in. And so Moi accompanied him to the plains.

There was no enmity with the British at this time and the Abor delegation was well received in a place called Suddya. Perhaps because she was the first woman from the tribes that they had met, the migluns were intrigued by her. A miglun woman and her husband became very fond of her, and they gave her food and clothes. One day the miglun lady brought out a book and a pencil. 'Here,' she held out the pencil, 'hold it like this,' she said. Moi was a grown-up, married woman, just like this woman before her, but she had never held a pencil before. 'Like this,' the woman's plump hand was over hers and Moi cringed. She drew away her hand and sat silently. 'Oh ho,' laughed the woman. In her hand she held another book and suddenly, bending close to Moi, she opened it and began to sing.

Moi had moved away instinctively but the miglun lady was undaunted. She raised her right hand and began gently beating the air. When she stopped, slightly flushed and out of breath, she looked straight at Moi and smiled at her, showing big, white teeth. Moi only stared back at her and every time she told the story, even now, she wished she had returned that smile. The woman had vanished from her life leaving only that smile. Who was she, really? Moi did not know her name. Only some years later would she learn that the lady was a miglun priest's wife, from a land called America. The priest was one of two who had set up a school in Suddya. Moi remembered seeing children there. The lady had also given her books, but just when Moi thought she was beginning to understand the alphabet, her time in Suddya had come to an abrupt end. In 1839, a group of Khampti rebels of the Suddya Khawa Gohain, aided by the Singpho and Mishmee tribes, attacked the British stockade. Moi was in the Mission compound. 'We had nothing to do with it,' she said 'We were onlookers.' She had not known that her husband was there in the thick of battle, defending the garrison against the attack and fighting his own fellow tribes. The rebellion was crushed, but the man whose life had been marked by his first meeting with the miglun strangers, was killed in the fighting. Moi returned to Mebo but soon moved away to her present place, living the life of an energetic widow who never stopped talking about the past.

And that is how we know why things happen, thought Gimur listening to Moi's words among the refugees from the burnt-down village. She had a stake in this long, blurred history because her father's early death was associated with that incident. And one day soon after, Moi gave her another legacy from that time. 'Keep these things,' she had said, handing Lendem some books and giving Gimur a book and a pencil. 'It might be interesting for you later on.' When Gimur got home, she had thrown the pencil and book into a basket.

It was late and Gimur's eyes were beginning to droop when she heard voices. The men were coming out of the meeting house. She left the fireplace and peered out. Lendem was holding a bamboo flare and talking to some men. In the orange light she discerned a vaguely familiar figure and stared hard at the man. 'It's him!' she whispered to herself. She recognised the black turban. The shadowy figure turned and she saw his white face. He had told her his name. Kajinsha! Gimur was so startled that she jumped when a pig suddenly squealed beneath the house. The man moved away and she saw Lendem approaching her.

'Who was that man?' she asked him.

Lendem looked around. 'Which man?'

'There was someone standing near you just now. He looked like a stranger.'

'Oh, there are some visitors,' said Lendem. 'One of them is the son of a Mishmee chief who died after the Suddya attack. The one that Moi keeps talking about.'

How strange! thought Gimur. The past was not so distant from the present after all. It was as if they were all bound by the name of a place she had never seen. 'Where is he from?'

'His village is quite far away,' said Lendem. 'He was here visiting the Idu clans of Anuda village. They came together. Everyone is interested in what has happened, you know. And don't worry,' he said, looking at her frightened face, 'no one wants the British to come into the hills. The elders have decided, and we, all the tribes, we are together in this. If the migluns want to use force, just let them try!'

1850

Kajinsha and Gimur

In the days following the meeting, Mebo became a centre of feverish activity. Tall men dressed in heavy woollen coats and carrying long swords arrived from Damroh, and then there was a stream of visitors from near and far. The men all gathered at the moshup. The British had some knowledge of the numerous Abor clans occupying the territory between the plains of Assam and Tibet, but if they could have seen the Mebo moshup they would have been surprised to see it crowded day and night with men of the great Padam clans and visitors who had travelled from villages beyond the Pari mountains and the confluence of the Siang and Yamne rivers.

'A fire draws people together,' said the elders, and it was true. At the time there were more than twenty-four recognised meroms— fireplaces—burning brightly in the Mebo longhouse, each merom for a particular clan. All the talk was about war.

'Our numbers are many,' they said. 'Who can threaten us? The British may conquer the world but they will never take our land. The words of the migluns are like a fleabite.'

At the heart of this anger was the issue of runaway 'slaves' who had taken advantage of the tribes' engagement as allies of the British during the Anglo-Burmese war. These 'slaves' were the offspring of men and women captured by the Abor in tribal wars who had been absorbed into the tribe to perform domestic and agricultural services. Now they had run away from their masters down to the plains, where they sought British protection. The British had not actively encouraged their desertion, but they did not respond to Abor demands to return them, either. Around the same time, the British began extending protection to the saniwals and beheeas, the gold washers and fishermen, who came up from the plains for profit and traditionally surrendered some payment in kind to the Abor and other original residents of the hills. Provoked by this, some Abor men had mounted a raid on a British garrison and kidnapped three saniwals. It was in retaliation that the British had burned the offending village and demanded the return of the saniwals.

And now there was feverish activity in Mebo, the village of two hundred homes overlooking the Siang River, which was called the Dihong in those days. Right from the start—and no one could tell with any certainty when that was—Mebo had been an important settlement with its strategic position on a range of hills that guarded the route to the Abor villages in the snow mountains to the north. The word Abor was not of these parts; it belonged to the plains. The word conveyed something that meant both 'barbarous' and 'independent' in Assamese, and was a term applied to all the tribes occupying the Siang valley in the mountainous country between Assam and Tibet. But no tribe living here called itself this name. The people of Mebo were the Padam, just as the other Abor groups were known as Bori, Bokar, Minyong, Pasi, Pangi, Tangam, Ashing, Komkar, Shimong and Milang.

No one could tell how or why the village came to be known as Mebo, but it was generally agreed that it was a place of nostalgia. What they actually mean is that this was a place of desire, Gimur would think sometimes. And who is to say this wasn't true? Maybe this is how it happened: when the first wave of tribesmen came south from the harsh mountain passes, looking for new land, they found this clear space in the middle of dense forest. 'What is this?' they cried. 'It is a desirable place! This is where we will live and build our homes.' Then many clans lived together, but soon the founding fathers were afraid there would not be enough water for everyone, so though they liked the place and wanted to continue to live there, family groups eventually dispersed to settle elsewhere. But the name 'Mebo' stuck, meaning both desire and nostalgia for the long-ago time when brothers had lived together.

And now, so many years later, men were coming together again. Every night the Abor from near and far held meetings in the moshup. Sometimes Gimur heard their footsteps at dawn, when they were returning from their night-long discussions. Usually she slept like a log—her daily duties were arduous. The village woke early and for young girls like her there was little rest. On any given day Gimur was up before daybreak. She lit the fire, let out the chickens, threw a stick at the pigs and as squeals and grunts mingled with the crowing of roosters, she started pounding paddy on the veranda of the house. Other girls would come out until every household was awake and the village reverberated with the rhythmic sound of mortar and pestle against grain: hssah! hsssah!

Gimur lived midway between the topmost houses facing the Siku stream and the girls' dormitory building, the rasheng, where all young, unmarried girls of the village met every evening to socialise and chat. Beyond this stretched the Kumku forest that no one liked to venture into. It was a dark and silent patch of giant trees rising out of a bed of dense, green undergrowth where unlucky victims had died with their heads twisted by malevolent spirits. Gimur skirted this strip of forest every day to reach the cultivation clearings where she and her mother carried out their subsistence farming.

It was only in the evening after Gimur had delivered meat and rice beer to the moshup that she had some time to herself. She sat cross-legged at the back of the house from where she could see the steep flank of the hill falling away into the bed of the river below. An old jackfruit tree stood in front of her. Its rustling leaves made her feel restless. She stared at the thick trunk and wondered how long it had stood like that. Some of the trees in the village were older than the oldest grandfathers, they said. Did the tree know its age, she wondered.

'What are you doing? Did you deliver the things?' her mother's voice disturbed her.

'Yes,' she shouted back. 'I have done everything.' She was sometimes mean and smug with her mother, she knew that. But then, why did the woman fuss so much? Always a worrier—'Will it rain today?' 'What should we do about the paddy?' 'Have you stored the ginger?' 'Where's that packet of fish?' Gimur wanted to hold her by the shoulders and say, 'Calm down! Relax. I have everything under control.' Sometimes Gimur pitied her mother for her slow, shuffling gait, for her shallow breath, for wasting so much of her life worrying about little things—such little things, when the world was so big and life was waiting to be lived.

One evening Gimur pulled out a basket from a corner and found the book and pencil that Moi had given her. It was a spelling book in the language of the Khampti people. The migluns had given them a script and taught them to write, Moi had told her. Gimur had opened the book a few times before and stared at the pages, but the black letters had meant nothing to her. This time, however, the letters danced irresistibly before her eyes. She drew her hand over the thin page and pointing the pencil sharply downwards, wrote a letter—a slanted line, then another, like two sticks joined at the top—and then a quick slash across. She laughed loudly and tried to rub it out with her hand. The letters looked like strange tattoos. She felt such pleasure trying to guess the meaning of these symbols, almost as if she was performing magic. She closed her eyes and tried to imagine the face of that woman who had smiled at Moi. Who was she? Moi did not know her name. 'So,' she thought, 'among the migluns, too, a woman's name is forgotten so soon.' She made swirling movements in the air with the pencil, swaying left and right, as if in a faint trance, while the big tree spread its shadow over the veranda and swayed over her until night fell suddenly, wiping out the tree and the outline of the hills.

The clear days of winter passed quickly and Mebo settled into an uneasy calm. Many of the visitors had left, saying, 'Call us when the time comes.' They knew, just as well as the British did, that nothing could happen now during the rainy season from March till September. Everything was subservient to the weather. Now it was planting time, working time. A gust of wind brought the first drops of rain and Mebo had a deserted look as men and women hurried to prepare their arik—fields, before the weather broke. Small shelters called ippo dotted the cleared slopes—shacks of thatched bamboo raised a few feet off the ground in the middle of the fields. Men and women stayed here during this time, sheltering from the rain, passing the night in blessed sleep after a long day's work in the fields; living here allowed them to start work early in the morning—much earlier than if they had to walk from the village. A notched log served as a moveable ladder and a small square of packed earth in the centre of the shack served as a fireplace. As the planting season began in earnest Gimur spent more and more time in the fields and stayed overnight in her shack. It was back breaking work, but her friend Nago worked in the adjoining field and all day the two girls called out to one another while they weeded, turned the soil and dibbled their precious seeds.

At nightfall Gimur climbed into the hut, pulled up the ladder after her and thrust it to one side. She lit a fire and sat back facing the bleak southern face of Kumku. It was from this scarred mountain that the Siku stream flowed out of a narrow cleft in the hills. She was not frightened. No matter what everyone said about evil spirits lurking there, she felt drawn to that patch of forest, a secret place, hidden most of the day behind a thin mist that crept down the hill and engulfed the land as if the ravine and the river had dissolved into the air. She closed her eyes and slept peacefully. One such night, thunder that woke her—a thick rumble that rolled across the sky and burst with a thunderous crack over the hut. Rain was hissing down like a spray of stones and a fierce wind was whipping the trees and blowing ash and sparks from the fire. I wonder if Nago is awake, Gimur thought. What a storm! She was bending towards the fire when she heard someone cough. She froze. Silently as a cat she moved her face back into the shadows, while her hand closed over a burning log. With her other hand she felt for her knife. She waited. Nothing. The night was pitch dark. She seized the burning log and holding it aloft thrust her face out into the wet night under the low thatch and shouted, 'Who is out there?'

A bright flash of lightning dazzled her eyes. In the white light her startled gaze met another pair of eyes looking up at her. A man was standing pressed up against the shack, smoking a pipe. It was Kajinsha! The name came back to her in a flash. But her reaction was to shout louder. 'Who are you!?'

'Don't be frightened,' he said. 'My name is Kajinsha. I saw your fire and came to check… it is very windy.' He spoke with a strange accent. As she stared at him he made as if to take the log from her hand. Gimur felt like hitting him with it. Her heart was thudding. She had expected to see a wild beast or a ghost straight out of the Kumku forest. Instead it was this man standing drenched in the rain under her roof. She threw the log back into the fire and moved aside. Let him stay out in the rain, or let him find the ladder if he wants to come up, she thought. She prodded the fire and waited. She heard him lever himself up—he did not take the ladder—and in an instant he was inside the hut.

This was the beginning of their meetings. Kajinsha would appear suddenly and say, 'Can I join you?' He sat quietly by the fire and smoked his pipe—'kacung,' he told her, tapping the long brass pipe. He was never without it. Sometimes he dozed, but not for long. 'I have to go,' he would say, and then he would be gone, melting into the darkness as soon as he left the hut. A few days later he would be back. Gimur didn't know what to think. One day he brought her a gift of fish and sour green fruit. He must be prowling around these fields day and night, she thought, but just when she had framed words to ask him about it, he failed to appear. This agitated her. He was always before her eyes. If she looked up, she saw him, where the outline of the mountain was emerging through the mist, advancing towards her; sometimes he was there sitting by her fire but gone when she looked hard, like a leaf carried away by a hard wind blowing in darkness and rain. He was a dream, an illusion. That was what she thought sometimes.

She did not tell anyone about him. Only Nago knew, but that was because one afternoon she had come looking for Gimur, climbed into the hut and seen the packet of fish. 'Hai! Where did this come from?' she exclaimed.

Gimur looked at her friend. Nago was a down-to-earth, sensible sort. She was the ponung rutum, the one who looked after the younger girls who slept in the rasheng and Gimur remembered how they had giggled like mad to see the older girls receiving their boyfriends in the darkest corners of the house. Now it was happening to her. The only difference was that it was not happening in the village rasheng but in a lonely hut perched on the flank of a mountain. So what? thought Gimur, it is the same thing, is it not? And *he* had not done anything—yet. There was no intimacy. He was a visitor. She decided to tell her friend everything. At the end of it she asked, 'What do you think?'

Nago was calm. 'What is there to think?' she said. 'He wants to sit by the fire, poor man!'

The only other person who could have any inkling of what was happening was Lendem. Gimur knew him well enough to know that he would miss nothing. Of late whenever they met—when she was carrying in vegetables or water to the house—his behaviour was unfriendly and tight-lipped. She knew he was suspicious. One day he broke his silence. He met her near the rock where she used to stand looking down at the river and said, 'Gimur, what are you doing?'

'Doing? What?' she pretended to have no idea what he was talking about.

'Aren't you afraid?'

'Afraid of what?' she said, laughing, recovering from the shock of being confronted so suddenly; but already she was angry.

'You are alone in the fields all the time. Your mother was telling me.'

'Nago is there too. We are working.'

'Nago was home last night,' he said. When she looked at him he added quickly, 'I didn't ask. She said she was off to the rasheng. She told me you were sleeping in the arik.'

'Yes, and so I was,' replied Gimur.

'It is not a good thing, you know,' said Lendem, looking away from her.

Now he's trying to lecture me, thought Gimur. Just because he can speak Assamese and read a few words he thinks he knows everything.

'What is not a good thing? What do you mean to say?' she challenged him.

'Why does he visit you?' said Lendem.

So he knew! Gimur stepped back and tossed her head. 'If you are talking about Ka-jin-sha,' she said his name slowly, 'you know him better than I. He is a visitor.'

'Yes!' said Lendem, showing anger now. 'I know Kajinsha. He is not from our village.'

What is the difference? Gimur wanted to say. And what is so great about our village? The words were on the tip of her tongue but she kept quiet. She would handle it her way, she thought. She had many things to think about and she needed time.

Just to allay suspicion Gimur decided to spend more time in the village. She found her spelling book and returned to her favourite spot in the back veranda from where she could watch the mountains. Every day she thought about her meetings with Kajinsha. Who was he? Why did he appear so persistently? She looked at the book in her hand and pretended she was recording words and events. 'My language is Kmaan lai,' he had told her. New words were leaping into her heart: awang—rain; lai—moon; minung—nose. It gave her pleasure to sit alone in the house and think about the reasons for his presence in her life.

Her mother, fussing around the house, barely glanced at her but seemed to be aware of what was going on in her daughter's head. 'Lazy,' she said. 'What kind of magic are you expecting by doing this?' She lifted the book and shook it in Gimur's face. 'What are these things? Words! What are words?' she cried. 'Speak the words you mean and say no more. Go out and work! See how the leaves and shoots grow. Do they speak words or make a sound? No! If you work you will have no time for this idleness, wasting time with these white, dead leaves!'

Gimur was infuriated by her mother's sharp words. Poor woman! What did she know about the human heart? What did she know about words and books? She had aged rapidly after her husband's death and had become mean and cantankerous. She worked day and night planting, weeding, washing, fetching, digging. Her hands were black with charcoal, wood, fire, paddy, husk, pigs, fowl. Gimur pitied her.

She left the house in a huff and returned to the shack carrying her book and pencil. The planting season was almost over. There would be less and less people staying overnight in their fields away from the village and Gimur knew that she would be afraid to stay out alone in the forest. Her mother would not allow it, and if she insisted it would draw suspicion. She wondered if Kajinsha would come. Perhaps he had gone away to his village during her absence. She needed him to visit her again, especially now, after her angry exchange with Lendem. She would ask him questions and find out everything. That would teach Lendem what she was capable of. Aih! Where are you? She waited anxiously and prayed that he would return.

And he came to her, like the wind. She sat in the hut facing the dark mountain and watched a darker shadow detach itself from that background and begin moving towards her. A smile turned up the corners of her mouth. She stayed silent, controlling her breathing. She saw a flash of light on his face, his gleaming chest, limbs, and the movement of his arms. She saw his searching eyes, impatient, because he had been waiting for her. He climbed up swiftly and removed his head cloth. She narrowed her eyes when he sat down beside her.

'Do you have anything to say?' he asked her. He was so close she could hear his heartbeat.

'Yes, look. There…' She pointed and they both stared at the mountain in front of them. There was no movement, no one following him or coming to look for her. It was so still they might have been the only people in the world. Kajinsha made a movement and suddenly she was in his arms. Her wrap was being unwound and his hands were on her breasts. She did not make any movement to assist him but allowed him to strip her naked, silently, without words. She knew this was what he wanted. This was what he liked, this silent and open mating when he could explore every inch of her body with his hands, his eyes, his mouth. He cradled her in his arms and she did not cry out even when she felt a searing pain as her body arched up and she saw the slope of his shoulders as he pressed down on her as if he would devour her.

All through the summer Gimur and Kajinsha met in the little shack perched on the flank of the mountain. She did not speak his language but he had some knowledge of hers, and it was enough. He was a warrior of the skies who travelled across the great forest in the deepest night. He was afraid of nothing. The land was there for him to explore at will. The trees were a swathe of green that revealed its secrets to this man who knew their hidden paths and the frozen routes over the mountains that kept tribes apart. 'We are afraid,' he told her, 'because we do not travel.' These had been the words of his father. On a moonlit night his father had stood with him on a high mountain, looking at the river, and said, 'It is the silver vein that embraces us all. It goes everywhere.'

'If we follow the river we will reach my home,' Kajinsha said to Gimur. 'And all animals and birds have a map. We can follow in their path.'

'What do you want?' she asked him, when he lay on his back, half asleep with one arm flung out and the other curled around her.

'I want life,' he said. 'You and me, and no secrets.'

He was always trying to unravel secrets. Sometimes, Gimur thought, he was like the shaman, the miri, who talked to the gods. 'We call him kambring,' he told her, teaching her a new word. 'Why does the kambring say the other world will be like this one?' he asked her, laying before her his thoughts to be examined. 'I say it will be bigger, better. There will be no forests. Only river and grass, and you and me. Like this.' He shifted his face down towards her, with his eyes closed, and clutched her tighter.

She peeped at him just like she had done the first time when he had appeared before her. She felt rested, content. She touched his cheek. She tucked herself against his body and was still peeping, watching his chin, his nose, his mouth, until her eyes too shut suddenly and they were both sound asleep.

◆

Over There

Thousands of miles away from the lonely shack on the mountain, the priest Nicolas Krick was awaiting his assignment orders at the Missions Étrangères de Paris. The assignments were not disclosed until a few days before departure, but since his arrival two groups of missionaries had already left and his name had not been on the list of those leaving for India and Hong Kong. Maybe I will be sent to Tonkin or Korea, he thought. He felt ready to go anywhere, wherever his superiors might decide to send him to take up his apostolic work. The days passed. It was October and still there was no signal for imminent departure. The delay was due to strategic considerations regarding a prized mission that beckoned and then closed its doors, that was as remote as it was tantalizing, and obscure and cruel as it was enigmatic and ever desirable—Tibet!

In the seventeenth century Portuguese Jesuit Fathers had established a mission in Tsaparang and preached in Shigatse. Italian Capuchins had also had missions in Tibet for a while, before their expulsion in 1745 during the anti-Christian movement in China when Tibet, administered by the court in Peking, retreated into its icy fastness and closed its doors to the outside world. In 1846 two French Lazarist missionaries, Evariste Huc and Joseph Gabet, had reached Lassa only to be picked up by the emperor's resident representative and sent back to Canton. It was evident that despite the new treaties of 1844 legalizing the practice of Christianity in China, the court in Peking did not take kindly to foreigners visiting

Tibet. Chinese magistrates were established in Tibet and the road to Lassa was lined with military posts, ostensibly to keep the Mongols out and protect the Emperor's mandarins from brigands, but anyone recognised as a European was also picked up, interrogated and sent back. Tibet, like the Holy Grail, remained unattainable.

In France the expulsion of Huc and Gabet and the publication of their travelogue which included reasons for the failure of Christianity in Tibet, caused a stir in Catholic circles. It was received with some misgivings but the account of their travels also had the effect of rekindling missionary zeal that had been extinguished for a century. At the time Krick joined the Mission, the Apostolic Vicariate of Lassa had been established by Pope Gregory XVI in 1846, and the responsibility of the Vicariate and the exclusive right to preach the gospel in Tibet had been entrusted to the Missions Étrangères de Paris. The Directors of the Paris mission were galvanized into action. Thousands of miles separated Europe and Asia and the dilemma confronting the Directors was about geography. The data they had was insufficient and information from the two missions in Szechwan and Yunnan in southwestern China that they depended on took weeks and months to arrive. To overcome this obstacle the Mission had sent one of their best missionaries, Charles Alexis Renou, to Szechwan to assess the situation and prepare the ground for the Tibet Mission. It was a time of renewed hope, enthusiasm, frustration, and feverish anticipation. Surely, there must be a way, a gap in the mountains, a breach in the wall, a passage, no matter how hard and narrow, to those gleaming citadels of ice on the roof of the world?

Renou sent optimistic letters favouring entry into Tibet by the western route from China. However, the Directors at the Paris Missions were cautious. Renou had failed to enter Lassa from Szechwan and it was evident that it would be impossible for any European to enter Tibet through China without the permission of the Emperor. The Directors decided there was no gain to be had in antagonizing the Peking government and jeopardizing their mission in China. The only alternative was to find a southern route across the Himalaya through India. This was an area equally distant and untried, but India was ruled by the British and there was greater opportunity here—if not to find a route into Tibet, than to discuss the matter with Thomas Oliffe, coadjutor of the Vicar Apostolic of Bengal. The response the Directors received from Oliffe was warm and generous. They had requested permission for a landing point in Bhootan where they could practice the holy ministry before crossing into Lassa, and Oliffe offered them the whole of the province of Assam. This offer was ratified by the Vicar Apostolic of Bengal, Bishop Patrick Joseph Carew, who further proposed that the Paris Missions add Assam to their mission in Lassa. The Directors were surprised. They had no knowledge of Assam other than that it was an Indian province of mountains and rivers that the English had taken from the Burmese in 1826. But it was an offer they could not refuse. The Missions Étrangères de Paris was regarded as the pioneer in Asian missions. In the atmosphere of ecclesiastical rivalry surrounding the evangelization of Tibet all that mattered was the success of their mission. If the only accessible route into Tibet was through Assam in British India, so be it.

The Directors agreed to the suggestions of Carew and Oliffe. Rome approved their decision and on 16 February 1850, ratified by a note from Pope Pius IX, Assam was officially added on to the Apostolic Vicariate of Lassa. All that now remained to be done was to send out a team to establish a south Tibet mission. The missionaries selected to take up this task were Julien Rabin, Louis Bernard, and Nicolas Krick. When Renou heard the news he was quick to send words of advice from Szechwan. The whole of Tibet, he wrote, was under the scourge of a terrible disease. It was the small pox, feared even by the monks. He suggested that knowledge of medicine and vaccines would endear the missionaries to the indigenous population. This would pave the way for the spread of the holy gospel. Renou also alerted the mission to the necessity of learning Tibetan and the three missionaries started Tibetan lessons at the École Pratique des Hautes Études and studied medicine at the Necker hospital.

On 23 December 1849 the group left for Portsmouth to board an English vessel heading for Madras. For Krick it was the end of a long wait. He had no idea of his new destination but he was willing to learn. The preceding months had been but a preparation towards this end, to go and carry out his apostolic work wherever it was his destiny to be sent. It was farewell to the quiet hours of study in the seminary. Farewell to his dear friends, the chapel and the green garden of the rue du Bac in the heart of Paris. At last he was on his way to 'over there'.

It was a voyage of four months. They set sail on 1 January 1850. On 7 February, they crossed the equator when the captain and crew celebrated crossing the line in ancient naval tradition with the riotous Neptunus Rex rituals for dominion over the seas. The missionaries were exempt, but sitting in his cabin Krick also prayed for succour as they sailed into tropical waters. Safe passage—it was what everyone wanted. What would they find in Tibet? But first they would have to reach Assam. What would it be like over there? On board there was plenty of time for study and reflection. How great was the gift of prophecy, he thought, and the gift of vision. What had he been chosen for? Other brothers going to their missions were received by colleagues who spoke the language and understood the customs of the country they were in, but for their mission Krick could envisage no such help. Tibet was different. The Europeans who had entered the country had left no established mark in that kingdom. All of them had been speedily expelled, and explorers who had reached Lassa had done so with armed escorts or by ruse and stealth. This made him smile. He was big man, blond and blue-eyed, who could, perhaps, dress in Tibetan robes, but it would be impossible for him to travel incognito, least of all into Tibet disguised as a monk or an oriental merchant. They would have to trust divine providence. He listened and prayed, hoping for a hint from God. In his heart he carried a deep desire to love and serve in God's name, but there was no answer. Over him, over them all, brothers on long and separate journeys, stretched the high vault of heaven, and their ship was a mere speck on the waters bobbing up and down as they ploughed on and on.

They reached Madras on the evening of 26 April 1850. They had been at sea more than hundred days and Krick had turned thirty-one on the ship. It was with mixed emotions that the missionaries set foot on Indian soil. This is going to be home from now on, thought Krick, reeling under the scorching heat that hit them all like a blast furnace the moment the ship dropped anchor. They carried no letters of recommendation but their arrival had been announced in the English press and they were warmly welcomed by Archbishop Farrell. They were, after all, in coastal south India where the Catholic faith had been introduced very early. According to local tradition it was here that Saint Thomas had been martyred in AD 72 when he was speared to death while praying, kneeling on a stone on a hill now called Saint Thomas Mount, near the ancient town of Tirumailapur, the town of peacocks, that the British called Mylapore. Several French families living in the settlement of Pondicherry also visited them. Krick's fellow missionary Julien Rabin wished they could spend more time with their colleagues in Pondicherry but time was short. They had to reach their destination, Assam, which, by all accounts was still a long way off.

Their first days in the subcontinent passed in a haze of sleeplessness and fatigue, the bustle of arrival and a terrible rash of prickly heat.

Two weeks later they reached Calcutta where they found a large Christian community, both Eurasian and native Christians, that had grown in the early sixteenth century with the arrival of Portuguese merchants in eastern Bengal. Now it was the residence of Archbishop Patrick Joseph Carew who had come from Mylapore to take charge as vicar apostolic of the entire province of Bengal. Carew received the French missionaries warmly, even organizing a special collection on Pentecost Sunday for what was reported in the *Bengal Catholic Herald* as 'the new mission in Assam'. It struck Krick then that the closer they got to Tibet the further away it seemed to recede, for now the name of their mission had erroneously been changed from Tibet to Assam! But there was no time to dwell on these issues; there were more pressing practical activities to be attended to. The British represented the only opportunity for a passage to Tibet and he knew they would have to bide their time. Once we reach Assam everything will be clear, he thought.

The missionaries left Calcutta on 14 June, sailing up along a big river that the British called the Burhampooter, to a place called Gowhattee. The journey was long and circuitous, with a brief halt in Dacca where they met Oliffe whose meeting and correspondence with the Paris Mission Directors had finally persuaded them to send the missionaries into Assam. When they reached Gowhattee the first impression was one of disbelief. 'There's nothing here!' cried Julien Rabin. It was the middle of summer, the Burhampooter was swollen in summer flood, and standing with their baggage on the bank of this great river Krick also felt as though they had entered a strange and desolate place at the end of the earth. The only consolation was that they were now within striking distance of Tibet. But despite having come so far, nothing was clearer. In Paris the missionaries had studied English and Tibetan but they soon realized that this would be of no use to them here. The people they met, their helpers and houseboys, belonged to different ethnic and linguistic groups and spoke different dialects and languages that the missionaries had never heard of before. They would have to engage language teachers and learn a new tongue all over again—at least Assamese. Krick also noticed that despite the friendly reception from the British authorities and the Protestant clergy, the response to questions about Tibet was always the same: 'Do not venture out,' they said. Beyond the Assam plain was terra incognita and anyone who went into those wild hills did so at their own risk. It was the land of 'savage mountaineers'.

1851

Colour my Heart

For Gimur far away in her small hut, the steep mountainside was a landscape of beauty. Every day she had cleared the ground, stooping and planting, moving a little higher terrace by terrace until now she could look over the treetops and see the wide plain below her to the west. Kajinsha had gone somewhere there for a few days and she was awaiting his return. It was a time of rest. Rain swept the land and brought fertility and life. The fields were green with maize and paddy. In sheltered corners, wild yam sprouted in dense clumps and creepers grew rapidly covering the slope with their spreading foliage. She was pleased with the work of her hands. Her mother could rest. They need not fear for a shortage of food this season. One day she was staring at the big leaves of yam when she experienced a strange sensation. The sunlight spun dizzily, making her shut her eyes tight. The moment passed. But a few minutes later she felt a terrible urge to eat the leaves and thick stalks of yam that were generally cooked for pig feed. She told Nago about this.

'Why not?' said her friend, imperturbable as ever. 'We cook them all the time. It will make you itch but nothing else will happen.' Then she looked at Gimur and said, 'You're not...?' She patted her belly and giggled.

'Hai!' Gimur flushed. 'Are you mad? Look! ' She stretched out her legs and sat up straight. She was as slim and firm as a green bamboo.

'Well, you can never tell,' said Nago. 'But your mother will know. Maybe it's time for you and Kajinsha to be married—but then,' she cried, 'you will have to go and live in his village! Hai!'

'Never! I will be here,' said Gimur, but now she was worried.

Gimur watched and waited. She tested herself by stretching and turning to see if anything about her body had changed. No one in the village had said anything to her yet. She drummed her fingers on her belly and felt curiously elated. One morning she woke up convulsed with waves of nausea rising up her throat. She splashed water on her face and breathed deeply. Perhaps Nago was right. She was with child! She couldn't believe it. She ate ginger and craved the taste of salt in the orange clayey mud that women sometimes dug out in thin strips from the hillside. Nago helped her. She seemed to know all about food cravings and Gimur, in her present, excitable condition, thought Nago's manner was calm and even other-worldly. 'Hush, hush,' she told Gimur. 'Now you better let the elders know.'

But first Gimur had to tell Kajinsha. She waited impatiently for his return. What would he say? What could they do now?

Lying in the ippo, she lifted her head and faced the black hill. The sky and the mountains had merged but she could see in the dark, like this. She sensed his presence and smiled. 'Are you back?' she murmured.

'Yes!' His dark face was very close to hers. 'What has happened?'

So he knew! But how could he, thought Gimur. Maybe it was her manner that had given her away. She moved away and folded her hands in her lap. He was staring at her.

'Nago thinks I'm pregnant,' she said. She waited with her eyes fixed on him. He was still staring at her—then he scrunched up his face, clapped his hands and hugged her. 'My sweet woman,' he cried, 'God has blessed us. I worship you!' He was shaking his head and laughing. Then he said, 'Blow into the fire, blow into the fire!' The big coals glowed as she puffed up her cheeks and blew. Ash flew up and she smiled at him, slapping back her hair. He picked up the bamboo tube and delivered a good blast leaning close to her and the flames hissed to life. They were two illuminated figures bending close together by the fire. Ah, how sweet was the breeze on their faces that night! How comforting the small enclosure of the shack! They could smell sky and trees and with her eyes closed Gimur could see time like a cascading stream passing right through the hollow of her curled hand. 'Let it continue to flow like this,' she prayed. 'If we are not afraid there can only be joy!'

'I will speak to your mother and your uncles,' said Kajinsha. 'And I will take you with me to live in my village.'

'Shhh…' Gimur put her hand on his mouth. 'No, no, shh….' She shook her head vigorously. 'I will speak to them first. Let me speak to them first.'

Gimur knew that what she had to say would not be well received. She remembered how Moi's husband had gone to look for the woman who had run away from the village with a lover so many years ago. Her uncle and relatives were respected elders but they were taciturn men who talked only of Abor pride. She knew what they would say: an Abor girl should behave according to custom. Every girl is an asset to her family and a man taking her away in marriage must compensate her parents for depriving them of a daughter. This was the customary bride price called a-re gelik. Just for a moment Gimur wondered how many heads of mithun she might have been worth… But in her case she knew Kajinsha's gifts, even if he brought them, would be rejected. Abor villages were secure enclaves where the rules of tradition were never crossed. Inter-tribe relationships were a betrayal to the community and girls marrying outsiders were spurned, useless like mustard seed scattered to the winds.

Kajinsha did not say anything but he guessed what was going on. In his village the reaction would be the same if a woman was marrying a man from another tribe. Still, his pride was hurt. He would have given a big feast and brought her people a line of mithun if they wanted that, but Gimur's behaviour alerted him that in their eyes he was unacceptable. So be it. There were only two ways to deal with this. It was either war or abduction. He sighed deeply. There were more things on his mind. He felt a presentiment of danger but he could not pinpoint the cause. Perhaps it was the threat of white strangers coming their way, or the other, deeper things—he had some secrets that he had not told Gimur yet. One night he said to her: 'There is a young boy in a village...' He raised his arm to indicate a place and stopped. She stared at him. He was speaking very slowly with his head bent. 'He is my son,' he said suddenly. Gimur jumped up but he clutched her wrists. 'It happened a long time ago,' he said. 'It was my father's wish. The boy's mother is a sick woman and lives alone. I beg you, come with me. You are my wife now!'

When she did not answer he said, 'I have a plan. But first there is something I have to do. I will come back.' he said. 'Be ready.' She nodded, unable to resist. The days of anxiety had taxed her and she was grateful for any respite from the pressure to reveal everything and seek her mother's advice, face the village, or even face Kajinsha now, or try to persuade him to live in Mebo until the outcry she anticipated had died down. Whatever happened now, she knew there would be no celebration for her and Kajinsha whose village and family status were unknown in Mebo. If her father had been alive, she thought gloomily, he might even have killed them both. She decided to talk to Lendem.

'You remember that man...' she said to him one day.

'Yes,' he said. 'Kajinsha. I recognise his face.'

'I have something to tell you…' she stopped and Lendem said, 'Ho. What, is he going to marry you?'

'Yes, I…we are thinking about it. What do you think my mother will say?'

'What is there to say *now*?' He stressed the word as if it was too late and he was accusing her of a terrible crime.

'He wants to take me to his village,' she replied.

'Then go!' Lendem shouted suddenly. Gimur was taken aback. She had expected that Lendem would help her and act as mediator. Instead he was waving her away, saying, 'Why should I be bothered with your problem? You know what you are? You are a torn branch hanging from a tree. That's what you are. You want to be part of our society but in your heart you have always been pulling away from us. Go with whoever you want, go! How can I stop you? Here we are struggling to fend off strangers to protect our territory and you want to be the lone arrow flying over the hill. You don't know anything!'

Lendem's words spoken in anger and scorn enraged her. 'Yes! I am that arrow,' she shouted back. 'You watch what I do. I will never stay in this wretched place!'

No sooner were the words out of her mouth than his open palm struck her across the face. Gimur's head snapped back but she held her ground. She faced him with burning eyes and said, 'I hope I never see you again.' Then she spat on the ground and walked away from him.

After this meeting Gimur gave up all thoughts of talking to her mother. The old lady would weep and scream and the whole village would know everything. The village kebang, the council, would give their verdict and everyone would agree. If she was with child then the man responsible must pay with work in their fields and live in their house. Her romantic life would be brushed aside.

It was something Gimur could not think of. She knew instinctively that Kajinsha would not agree. He was a visitor who had come to their village because he was shadowing the movement of the miglun among the Abor villages; in his own territory he was a chief with a place and a people. He would demand her cognizance of this and say, 'My child must be born in my village.'

What could she do now? She thought of killing the baby—there were herbs and roots that she could take, but she would have to tell someone, and everyone in the village would know. This was what held her back.

At this time Moi came to see her. 'Oh, Gimur, Gimur, I have come all this way, it is too much for me,' said Moi, crawling into the hut. She drank some water and sat down heavily. Gimur waited. 'See how beautiful it is,' said Moi, like a clever hunter tracking prey from an unexpected angle for a surprise attack. 'Why are you planning to leave us?'

'Hai! What...who said?' Gimur cried involuntarily.

'No one has said anything,' replied Moi. 'I just know. Your mother has also not said anything. But I am saying if the young man is good—why, he can have all this and stay here with us. No, no,' she said when Gimur tried to interject. 'You can go away when you are older. I guarantee you that. But now, now...' she sighed, 'it's not the best time. There is war. You know how the migluns burnt our villages when you came to my house with Lendem. It is not the right time to do anything or go anywhere. Be patient. Tell me about this man.'

Moi's words were a foretaste of what was to come if she remained in the village. 'A woman must obey,' she told Gimur. 'If a woman looks after the house, prepares food and feeds her husband and her children she will be loved, and she will be happy.' Moi had no more words of the time when she had travelled to Suddya with her husband and stayed with the miglun lady who gave her books and a chance at a new life—if only she had taken it. Gimur felt that she herself would have—she would—if she could just get away from this place that bound you to...what? She could not be sure.

But I, I have to know, thought Gimur. I will go beyond. When the chance comes for a life beyond, what other choice is there for anyone but to take it? Gimur's only ally at this time was Nago. 'So what if he has a son? There is no shame in it. You did not know. You did not ask. At least he has told you. Now it is up to you.' She promised not to say anything until Gimur had decided, and she did not breathe a word. Lendem was equally silent and ignored her as if she were dead. So be it, thought Gimur. She busied herself with housework and waited. A small voice inside her head told her that nothing stayed exactly the same, not even for one season. Life was a tumbling race of moments like a swing, up one way and then suddenly down another before it suddenly ended. She knew this from all the stories about her village that she had heard as a child, from the way a man could slip from a bridge, or a villager have his head twisted by an invisible attacker on the way to the fields, all preys to evil spirits who roamed these hills. Mebo was also a place where many children had disappeared. They had gone into the forest and never come back, leaving the village haunted with the wailing cries of their mothers. But most of all Gimur knew this from the words of the shaman who told them that in every life there is a turning point when, suddenly, the records of past deeds—all the words, thoughts and dreams and everything else that moved a person along a certain path—all of these would one day be placed before them. This is time standing still, the moment of choice. And after that, felt Gimur, there remained only one thing to do—fly.

The warm days of summer were nearly over. Soon the harvest would be done and the fields abandoned. It was the time when everyone worked hard before the lean period of winter set in. Gimur was as busy as anyone else. But her preparations were not for the rituals and festivals associated with the season, but for flight. It was what she had decided. Foolish, she thought, putting her clothes into a small basket. Foolish girl! But her heart was singing. She cooked food for the pigs and stacked a pile of maize in one corner, but all the time she was laying out her plans for permanent departure. She could barely contain her happiness.

'Why are you fiddling with your things all the time?' her mother asked her.

'I'm tidying up,' she said. 'We will have to move these things around when we are ready for the new thatching, won't we?'

Her mother looked at her sharply and said there was plenty of time for that. It would not be necessary until February. There were other things to be done first. Gimur nodded, watching her mother slyly. Was there any sign that she knew what was going on in her daughter's head? No one had said anything yet. She did the day's work and by sundown the chickens had been fed, the fire lit, and her mother would be sitting outside with her friends, waiting for darkness to fall. In the middle of the night she felt free and happy. Foolish. But I am leaving nothing behind. Nothing! She told herself, lying awake and listening to the wind stirring the leaves of the old jackfruit tree. There are people here, families, but I will find new friends and families in the other place too. And Kajinsha and I will be together. That was the prize. Love! She rolled over on her belly and was lost in thought staring at the fire. An elderly relative was asleep in the space across from the hearth, facing the door. In the adjacent corner her mother was asleep too. Everything was quiet. But Gimur was careful. Her mother was a sly woman, who sometimes pretended not to hear or see, but Gimur knew better—it was only a ploy to find out things. The relative too, despite being old and bent double, had the uncanny knack of noticing things just when you thought he had forgotten the missing knife, the dead chicken or the plantain ready to fall under its ripening weight. She strained her ears. Her mother could be reading her thoughts in the dark. Gimur pretended to close her eyes. Foolish! She cupped her hands over her mouth to hide her smile and fell asleep dreaming of a secret jungle path that stretched into the darkness.

◆

Strange Pilgrims

Far away the priest was also dreaming of a journey. He was in Gowhattee, the headquarters of Kamroop district, Eastern Bengal and Assam. Everything here was different, indescribable. Krick had to admit that he had embarked on this journey not knowing what he expected, but his spirit responded to the newness of everything. Despite the enervating weather this was a pleasant place surrounded by a chain of low hills in the form of a semicircle through which the Burhampooter flowed in a wide arc. About two miles to the west of the town stood the famous shrine of the goddess Kamakhya and in the centre of the river stood a rocky island crowned with a temple called Umananda, believed to have been created from the holy ash on the forehead of the Hindu god Shiva. He had been reading what he could find about the place. Once called Pragjyotishpur, Gowhattee had been the capital of all Lower Assam with a viceroy, or Bor Phukan, and seat of the Ahom kings when the district was absorbed into the Ahom kingdom. But years of internecine struggle and war had reduced its former splendour. Its monuments, brick fortifications, water tanks, wide ramparts and fine masonry gateways that had once marked the entrance to the city had been decimated by flood and fire. In 1826 with the occupation of Assam by the British following the First Burmese War, Kamroop, along with the rest of the Burhampooter valley, became part of British territory and Gowhattee was now the seat of the commissioner of Assam and Agent to the Governor-General in the North-East Frontier, Major Francis Jenkins, successor to T.C. Robertson and David Scott before him.

Krick and his fellow missionaries had moved into a rented house. Rabin thought it was too small, but at least it was home. They could store their books and equipment and explore their surroundings. This was what Krick wanted most of all to do. To begin. But where, and how? Gowhattee was a town with offices and a bazaar but the rest of the Assam valley was an unknown territory of jungle and rivers and scattered villages hidden among clumps of bamboo and rice fields. The only mode of transport was by boat, following the river, or by elephant, if one could be procured from the British authorities. Another more pressing problem was language. The East India government had changed the prevalent use of Sanskrit in native primary schools and introduced English as the medium better suited for imparting 'useful knowledge'. But the majority of the native population spoke Assamese or Bengali. The missionaries employed two language teachers for six hours of lessons every day but there was a dearth of language books and progress was slow and frustrating. What is the origin of the word Tibet, wondered Krick. Why was it so difficult to find out anything about the place? No one here called it Tibet—it was either Lama Country or Za Gd, or Jam, and some tribes called it Thelong. He was full of questions but there were more questions here than answers. He found no Buddhist monks and very few Christian converts. The few Europeans he met, around thirty odd families, responded with incredulity when he mentioned his hope of entering Tibet from the Burhampooter valley. 'What!' they cried. 'Is your pope a tyrant to send you to a place where no one has gone before? Who will take you there?' This made him laugh. He was friendly and courteous, and someone at the time had commented on his modest, blue eyes. He got on well with the British and the protestant clergy who assumed that the French missionaries would be paid well and that, considering the risks, they were assured of a good position and a large government pension following the success of the Mission.

'Oh no,' Krick would correct them. He was a Catholic priest treading this path of his own free will. Neither pope nor bishop had obliged him to take this step. It was because he believed that the servant was not above his master and that there was no hardship or danger so great that he could not face as a servant of the Lord. He felt closest to his goal when he was away from Gowhattee. No doubt they were made welcome here by the English community and the commissioner, Major General Jenkins, was generous with his support of missionary agencies, but for Krick it was always the promise of Tibet hidden beyond the mountains that drew his gaze. Despite the trials of arrival in a new place so far away and so different from his life in the parishes and the seminary, in his heart he carried a landscape of hope. His mission was Tibet and he knew that God would open the way. He looked at the hills surrounding the town like an amphitheatre, and he wanted to break out and follow the river into those mountains.

The first summer passed in fruitless ventures of travelling to Upper Assam and Bhootan. The missionaries were still struggling to acclimatise themselves to the tropical heat and Rabin and Bernard were in poor health. For Krick it was a year of waiting. All their plans for expeditions were thwarted by the rainy season and lack of means to travel through miles of country without interpreters and guides. But it was not this that daunted him. What was disquieting were the changes taking place within their group and in the man who had been nominated superior of the group by the Directors in Paris. Julien Rabin was disintegrating. Perhaps it was the weather or the slowness of things, but Rabin had never recovered from the initial disappointment of finding himself in a remote colonial station with no support. As the harsh summer battered them with heat, rain, and mud, Rabin sank into delirium and bouts of homesickness. He had been Director at the Couets School in Nantes and now he changed the dream of a Tibet mission into a grand vision of a Catholic centre in Gowhattee. 'If we have Gowhattee all the rest will be easy,' he said. He outlined feverish plans for a large bungalow on a hill that would be the founding of a great seminary. It would be a centre of rest, and learning. Young missionaries would come here to regain their strength and other missionary brothers would join them from all over Assam, Tibet and Bhootan. A church would rise up, overlooking the river and the trees... Clearly the superior's mind was wandering. Krick saw this, but there was little he could do. He and Rabin were the same age and had been ordained at the same time, but Rabin had been appointed Superior of the Mission and the hierarchical structure had to be maintained, or all their efforts towards the Tibet mission would be wasted. Rabin had become suspicious and prone to nervous outbursts. It was best to remain silent. They were three men thrown together in the most trying and unfamiliar circumstances, and he knew no one could do anything now to change what had been started.

In the winter of 1850 Krick had the chance to travel to North Bengal at the invitation of the coadjutator of the Vicar Apostolic in Calcutta, Thomas Oliffe. It was a happy period for him, a respite of four months during which time he also worked on a mission for the English in the diocese of Calcutta at the request of Archbishop Carew, but soon a letter arrived from Rabin asking him to return as soon as possible. Both Bernard and Rabin were bedridden with fever and recuperating in a place called Goalparah, west of Gowhattee. When Krick returned he found Rabin more paranoid and desperate, fussing over administrative details and despatching letter after letter to the Directors in Paris to send more men to help them in Gowhattee. As days passed their mission was bogged

Mamang Dai

down in indecisions and inaction. Krick had no wish to contest Rabin's authority but his strong personality chafed under the vague and hesitant efforts of their leader. In their cramped quarters of three rooms—one kept as the dining or meeting place, and only two rooms to sleep in—life together for the missionary team was becoming impossible. A wild plum tree leaned heavily against the back wall of the house before curving out again towards the sun. On many nights Krick stood outside looking at it and wondering when the time would come for him to be of service to the mission.

His chance came in May when Rabin announced that he was going to make an attempt to enter Bhootan. He chose Bernard to accompany him and the two men set off, only to return a few weeks later. It was another failed attempt. They had been turned away at the border by sentinels of the Deb rajah and ordered to return to Assam. Krick took the opportunity to make a bid for his long awaited excursion into the mountains. He sought Rabin's consent for an exploratory journey, going through the Assam towns of Tezpore and Nowgong, to the Mishmee and Abor tribal areas at the foot of the Himalayas. 'Perhaps,' he told Rabin, 'another route to Bhootan and a road to Lassa could be found through those hills?' The two men looked at one another. They had come such a long way in pursuit of a dream. What was to be done now? Rabin gave his consent. Though they did not know it then, it was to be the last time that the two men would be together, for their journeys now would take them in very different directions and reach very different ends.

Father Krick left Gowhattee on 26 May 1851. He was a priest travelling alone in British India, in a strange land among people whose language he was painstakingly coming to grips with, but he was happy. He carried a letter of recommendation from Captain Dalton, the magistrate of Gowhattee, and soon he was in a boat with two oarsmen moving upstream along one of the many rivers that flowed through the Assam plain. For the first time since his arrival he was suffused with a sense of liberation and well-being. How expertly the men guided the boat. How beautiful was the countryside with its luxuriant growth of grass and trees. The landscape made him think of music—he played the flute and carried it with him wherever he went, and now he laughed, recalling notes of music and nodding happily at the boatmen who grinned back at him.

Wherein the difficulty of entering Tibet? he wondered. It was a question that bothered him all the time. How to reach the land of lamas? He had a suspicion that the tribes living in the hills between Assam and Tibet might hold the key. But he did not know the tribes. He had never met an Abor or a Mishmee—Michemi, as he'd heard them being called sometimes—and that was what he secretly planned to do now. Tibetans themselves had never been hostile to visitors. In the case of the French Lazarists, Huc and Gabet, he recalled reading that the Tibetan Regent had held them in mutual regard and that they had been expelled, not by the Tibetan, but by Chinese authorities who feared Tibet might be seized by a foreign power. It was the case with Rabin and Bernard too, he thought, who had been turned away at the Bhootanese border by officials working under the order of higher authorities who had ruled that they must bar entry to outsiders on pain of death. And the case might be the same with the tribes living along the Assam frontier. They were hostile because they were afraid that the British would capture their territories. That was why they had placed guards wherever there were dwars or entry points along the frontier and shut their doors fast. It was his hope that he would be able to dispel this fear. He was alone and unarmed. He carried only his cross and his flute, and most importantly, he was not English.

His first stop was in the small town of Mungledye, a few miles north of Gowhattee. He wanted to revisit Rabin's aborted Bhootan expedition and find out if there was a connection from here with Bhootan and Tibet. Yes, he was told. There was a route to Lassa used by pilgrims and merchants passing through an Assamese trading mart at the foot of the Bhootan hills, but it would be impassable now. He would have to wait for the dry season at the end of October. That meant another five months. It was too long a period for Krick to remain inactive, even though the British representatives here offered him the services of a Bhootanese lama being held in the English prison to teach him the language. He decided to head for Nowgong town where they had been asking for a priest. He was received by Dr Pingault, a man of French origin who introduced him to the only Catholic community known in Assam outside of Gowhattee and numbering barely a dozen adults. The rest of the Christian community were largely of the American Baptist Society who had established one of their bases here and ran a school and an orphan institution founded by the Reverend Miles Bronson in 1843. Everywhere there are men of God, thought Krick, struggling against untold dangers and terrible isolation. For his part, his vocation as a Roman Catholic priest was the avowal to share the gift of holy ordination and practice an active spirituality. He began by organising morning prayers, study, Mass, and catechism for children. He gave Holy Communion, prayed and sang with them, blessed and baptized two children, and at the end of a month, though they lacked services and books, Krick felt he had succeeded a little in his duty to the small Catholic community by restoring a feeling of warmth and closeness of a real parish. Now he had to turn his attention to the Tibet mission and find a route through the mountains. But as if unwilling to relinquish the visiting priest, the sky sent down fierce rain that pelted down on the land so hard as to make all movement impossible and keep Krick in Nowgong for another month.

Fortunately Krick had access to the library of a friend who

commanded the garrison of Nowgong and he spent his time reading the accounts of British travellers who had travelled up and down this country and tried to cross into Tibet from the same eastern frontier where he was now. They were British officers, soldiers, surgeons and plant hunters, but one by one all these travellers, despite having gathered all the best possible conditions for success—protection, power, money, guides, soldiers and retinue—had failed. In Paris Krick would never have imagined what it would be like here, and it gave him a strange feeling now to read their words. He was drawing closer to Suddya and another place called Saikwa Ghat that he had read were the last British stations in Upper Assam. They were the gateways into the wild mountains. These were names that beckoned him now. He knew that American missionaries had entered Suddya in 1836 when the Serampore branch of the English Missionary Society needed evangelists to work with the hill tribes in Upper Assam. The American Baptists had opened a school and run a printing press in Suddya. This was known as the Shan mission of Reverend Nathan Brown and Reverend Oliver T. Cutter and the latter's wife, Eliza Cutter. They had come from the Burmah mission.

Mrs Cutter was the woman who had given a book to a tribal girl from the Abor hills a long time ago. It was a spelling book that was now in the hands of someone called Gimur. But Krick would never know this. Their lives would intersect—his and Gimur's—but nothing would be spoken, no secrets shared, no pasts explained. Life works in mysterious ways.

Krick only heard Pingault's account of that terrible January morning in 1839 when a band of Khampti and Mishmee warriors had attacked the European barracks in Suddya and how the political agent of Upper Assam, Adam White, and eighty sepoys had been killed. Pingault had been there as apothecary and the missionaries had barely escaped with their lives, hiding in a boat and floating downriver. In retaliation, the commissioner, Major General Jenkins had ordered Captain Hannay's Assam Light Infantry to burn the Khampti villages and deport their population to other parts of the district. But no European could feel safe again in Suddya. The place had been abandoned and the army cantonment shifted to Saikwa Ghat on the opposite bank of the Burhampooter. Since then, said Pingault, the Reverends Brown and Cutter had relocated to other towns nearby.

At this time the British evangelicals had also relinquished their operations in Assam in favour of the American Baptists, and the entire Burhampooter valley had been opened to them. The missionaries had moved to Sibsagor, Gowhattee and Nowgong and in 1846 they had started the publication of the first vernacular newspaper in Assamese, the *Orundoi Sambad Patra* from the mission's press in Sibsagor. Suddya was behind them forever. That was the story. But Pingault's account and the names of places and people haunted Krick. Suddya, Saikwa Ghat, Abor, Khampti, the Shan mission, Singfou, Mishmee, Tain, Mizou. That was the territory where he wanted to go. There is an unseen country that lies before us all, he thought. Perhaps it is bigger and deeper in our imagination. I think it is desolate and that I will discover many things, but ah! If I look closer, bend down, I will find faint lines, traces of a presence, and someone else's thoughts there before me—equally ardent, equally captive.

'You have not seen the place,' said Pingault. 'The first danger is the river. It is terrifying.' Then there were wild mountains and hostile tribes and the jungle teeming with wild beasts; and as if that weren't enough, there was the damp air and the swamps breeding malarial fever that killed men like flies.

But the river is the only mode of transport, thought Krick. If not the main channel, then the tributaries that criss-crossed the land. He would take country boats and walk the rest of the way, if only he could find guides and interpreters! Every night he looked out from his small room waiting for the weather to improve. Once he imagined a glow behind the trees. It was moonrise, a bright, full moon. But dark clouds were always blowing down from the hills. The Himalayas were prone to sudden thunderstorms and, sure enough, late that night another storm burst over the town. At first it was a sound like a shower of hailstones rattling in the wind. Then the roar of water came down so hard it seemed the room and Pingault's quarters would be broken into pieces. When the storm abated Krick peered out, fearing the worst. Many trees might have fallen, he thought. He saw the straight stem of an areca palm glistening with a glowing greenness. Amazing! So calm, so straight and clear, so tender. He knew then that it was time for him to go.

At last! he thought, staring at the silent landscape. For how long have I waited to look on those snow covered mountains! They had crept into his dreams. He felt the pull of this fascinating part of the country. Step by step words and stories were appearing on what had been a blank slate and he could not turn back now. He decided to go to Saikwa Ghat.

◆

Journey

In Mebo, Gimur was poised for flight. It was a hot day, and she was in her shack in the fields, waiting for darkness to fall. I may never pass this way again, she thought, looking around her. In these last few days her mother's silence had weighed heavily on her. One word, one word and I might be able to explain something, she told herself, but her mother had not said anything. Instead, when Gimur said she was going to the arik she had nodded silently and quickly looked away. What could be done now? Kajinsha would arrive any moment and then she would go away with him forever.

Suddenly Gimur saw a figure approaching the shack. She

watched carefully and recognised her aunt Moi. In an instant Gimur jumped down and ran towards the stream. She stopped and crouched among the ferns. 'Gimur, Gimur!' she heard Moi's voice and crouched lower. She knew what Moi had come to say and she did not want to hear any of it. Gimur would later regret this moment with all her heart, but now, now her heart was thudding with impatience as she watched Moi wipe the sweat off her face and look around. 'Go away, go away,' she hissed silently and waited. When she looked up again Moi had gone. There was no one on the hillside.

Kajinsha and Gimur left at nightfall, striking out from the hut where Gimur had already stashed her things. They hurried along the narrow path that skirted the village and climbed over a hill. Below them was the river, wide and restful. Everything was calm. They would be following the river, Gimur knew that. She was familiar with this part of the journey, but when they left the stretch of forest surrounding Mebo an unexpected panic seized her. She hesitated. Kajinsha stopped and looked back over his shoulder. 'Come,' he said. He held out his hand. And she followed.

It was a journey out of a dream. They were fleeing in the dark. Like a forest animal Kajinsha seemed to sense invisible paths, but sometimes he crashed against branches and cursed when he stepped on a sharp stone or a tree root. Sometimes he barred her way: 'Stop, be careful!' He knew where a path was laid with trip lines that could trigger a poison arrow set at a specific height to pierce a man in the neck, shoulder or heart. These were Abor traps and Gimur had heard the warning call many times in Mebo telling people to be careful. Kajinsha moved stealthily. She could hear his loud breathing. She followed him without question.

In that dark, unknown world a torch was burning in her heart. This is everything, she thought. This is what I wanted, and it is happening. I am free! Her life, she felt, was rushing like a stream in her veins, in the stretch and bend of her legs as they climbed hill after hill and the air flowed in and out of her, burning her lungs and her throat. She lifted her head to look at the man in front of her. Through a break in the canopy she glimpsed Kajinsha's dark shape and saw his shoulders touching the sky. Nothing else matters, she thought. Not this string of beads, this bundle of cloth, this knife that I am carrying with me. Anyone can strip me of these poor possessions. This bright light in my heart—this is is all that matters.

How long did they travel? She did not know. Kajinsha was always pointing—ahead, beyond. What was beyond? Where was he leading her? They were two small figures in the immense solitude. The rivers and streams they would soon cross were hidden from view by fields of glinting sun-grass growing taller than a man. High mountains towered up on their left. When she slowed down, he came up close to her and stretched his hands out, pointing north. Ahead. She was sweating and panting. They were both sunburnt and powdered with white sand. He mopped his face with his head cloth and stood waiting, looking into her eyes without another word. She stared back at him, struck by the power of his will. They spoke different languages, yet at this moment Gimur understood everything.

She saw a house on a hill, his house, standing against towering snow peaks. It was a high, faraway place where she could see the sun splintering into bright streaks of light. When night fell she heard the wind moaning, crying for daybreak. Her soul was in flight, soaring high above this unknown land and Kajinsha was an eagle, watching her flight and calling her to enter the freedom of the sky. She felt weightless, lifted by a strong gust of wind. Her head was spinning and when she swayed he stepped forward quickly and held her. He put his hand on her head and pressed his cheek against her face. Everything returned then, as she heard his heart speaking. And she knew that now there was no turning back.

Many years later, people who knew Gimur were still wondering how she had dared to make this journey. Her father had been a brave man, a leader of the tribe, but he was always level-headed and calm. Her mother had been obedient and superstitious. Where had the girl's wild streak come from? Who could say? In the long line of forefathers perhaps there had been one who had broken taboos, hurled insults at a life lived in fear. Someone who had broken out of the dark trees into the light of the sun. Her ancestors had emerged from a land of caves and rocks imprinted with extinct birds and beasts. Maybe that was where Gimur wanted to return—who could say? Sometimes she thought about her mother, the women of the tribe. What had they desired? What secrets had they buried in their hearts? Women were anonymous, forgotten in the story of blood lines. But every once in a while there was a sudden bend in the road, a separate heartbeat that made someone into a wild woman; a wild gene embedded in the marrow, like destiny waiting to be nudged into an all or nothing passion.

The wind and the sound of water accompanied them as they crossed one stream after another, walking miles and miles every day. At night Kajinsha dug a pit in the sand and struck a flint to the bundle of dry grass and twigs. A fire flared up and they sat together staring at the small pool of light. They fell asleep on the reeds flattened by their bodies. Her hair was matted and their bodies were covered with mud and sand. Still they trudged on and on and as each day passed Gimur felt they were becoming invisible in this wild expanse of boulders and sand.

Late one evening she sensed Kajinsha's steps slowing. They were approaching something. What is it…? They were climbing downhill and she was walking behind Kajinsha, blindly following him and she could not see anything. She heard a soft splashing sound. More water, she thought, or maybe a herd of elephants. With each step the landscape was changing right before her eyes. They had entered a forest of twisted trees and she had to bend low to crawl under their branches which were like arms stretching towards something above and beyond. She pushed through the web of trees and suddenly saw where the sound was coming from. It was a river, but nothing like the streams they had crossed. This was a flat, wide sheet that lay before her under a steep bank of mud and boulders. The splashing sound was eddies of current sloshing against the mud bank. They reached a narrow strip of sand covered with tall reeds. Kajinsha stretched his arm to signal her to stop. He was crouched low and was peering all around him. Then he whistled softly and signalled for her to come forward. She sensed he was smiling and she bent down close to him and peered over his shoulder. She saw a small canoe moored up on a sandbar. It was a narrow dug-out, black and with a tattered canopy of reeds roughly lashed together. He must have hidden it here. Where did he get it? Did he make it? He grinned at her and held up an oar. Get in, he signalled. She stopped dead in her tracks. Her ears were aching with the hum of insects and the croaking of frogs. 'Are you mad?' she said, gesticulating wildly. 'No, never!' She faced him and shouted into his face, twice. She would never get into that thing. A woman was supposed to avoid water and she had already broken enough taboos wading across streams and river beds in the middle of the night. Where did he want to go? She tried to grab the oar from his hand. He held her off saying, 'Sa-Di-Ya.' He pointed ahead along the river.

Suddya! It was a place that everyone talked about and watched day and night. It was the stronghold of the British, but it was also the place that tribal chiefs along the frontier condescended to visit sometimes, to trade and to talk to the white sahibs about territory and slaves. Her father had been there, and so had Lendem. Moi had been there! She was thinking about this when Kajinsha put a finger to his lips. He could hear voices in the wind. He strained his ears. Gimur also heard them now and stayed motionless. Voices, and the sound of water, but different from the noise of the flowing river. These were splashes, punting, the dip of oars and someone calling out softly. The voice reverberated in Kajinsha's ears. Quick! He pushed her down pulling the canoe back at the same time. He lifted the canoe into the marshy bank where the water sloshed against it and settled it into a screen of reeds. He pushed her head down and crouched beside her, still holding the canoe with one hand. Time passed. They saw a reflection of light on the water. The light spread, rippling and shaking in a widening circle ahead of a long, dark shape that suddenly loomed up like a ghost in the middle of the river.

Gimur bent her head lower and held her breath. She saw a man with a light on the prow of the boat, standing straight as a tree and looking ahead. Just as suddenly as it had appeared the vessel glided past and disappeared from view. Still they did not move. Kajinsha's hand was on her head but she felt his grip relax. Unknown to them on board the boat that they had seen moving upriver towards Mebo was Krick, the French priest, who was, listening to Captain Hamilton Vetch's account of his service in this part of empire. Now their voices were fading away in the night wind. Kajinsha wondered if more men were on their way.

The river at this time of year was shallow and broken up by numerous islets of sand. They would come by land if there were troops and elephants, he thought. He decided to skirt the sandbank and travel downstream in a complex circuit. They could not risk this route. He would have to stay very close to the territory of other tribes. It was what he had wanted to avoid, but there was no other way now. They began to float downriver. Kajinsha steered strongly towards sandy flats that seemed to emerge whenever they needed to stop. He was very careful because of Gimur's pregnancy, even though she had showed no distress beyond her unwillingness to get in the boat. But when they had to leave, she suddenly stopped protesting and climbed into the boat.

Gimur shut her eyes tight as they began to glide on the wide river, and when she opened them again she was looking at the sun blazing down on them. There was no shelter except for the tattered palm that hung over her face. Sometimes she saw small shacks—a few thin poles pitched on the furrowed sand. Were they fishermen's huts or just tussocks of grass sprouting on the banks? Occasionally Kajinsha would hail someone, and a man would appear, say something, and then Kajinsha would pole the boat away. But most of the time it was sand and water. Sand. Wind. Sun. They rarely stopped anywhere. Gimur dozed in the boat. At night she stared at Kajinsha's silhouette on the edge of the boat holding the oar. Above his shoulders the night sky rose like a giant mantle dotted with stars.

On the third day they drifted past a bank of trees pressed against towering cliffs. Kajinsha pointed at a big rock. 'Once,' he said, 'a man and his wife had no children. So they went to a powerful kambring who performed a puja and then a daughter was born to them. But in the tug of war between man and spirits, the girl was claimed by the spirit of a bird and she had to go and live with him. Before going away forever she returned once, accompanied by a tiger, to pay the bride price, and her spirit husband helped to clear the fields in the form of a mighty wind. Her parents were sad, but there was nothing they could do about it. Their daughter told them that every day she would spread her red garment on that rock, there,' Kajinsha pointed, 'and every morning a cock would crow to let her parents know that she was alive and well. For four years the old couple looked at the rock and saw their daughter's bright cloth spread out on it. Then one day the rock was bare.' Kajinsha stopped. 'So we disappear. Who remembers?'

'Who told you this story?' Gimur asked him. Kajinsha shrugged. It was a sad story. Perhaps someone had dreamt it, she thought.

There were enough dreams floating along this stretch of the river, waiting to be caught. The shaman was the catcher of dreams. Only he could read the dreams and tell stories to reveal something to us about our lives and feelings. Gimur looked at the rock for a long time. Kajinsha rowed on. They would be passing Suddya, he said, curving the boat outward into the centre of the river that was now widening as far as the eye could see. She drifted in and out of sleep, her thoughts swinging this way and that, flowing with the river: Where do we come from? What is beyond? Sometimes she sat up with a start and cried, 'How far, how far?'

Kajinsha would smile at her and say, 'Not far now. We're almost there.'

One afternoon Kajinsha veered the boat towards the left. He was rowing hard and then paddling and poling with all his might. Soon he jumped into the water and was wading waist high in a brackish pool, pulling Gimur and the boat into the reeds. They left the boat and walked across a long strip of sand. Just when Gimur was going to say that she could not walk any further Kajinsha told her that they were entering a place he pronounced as Ch-un-pu-ra. Gimur was surprised to find that Kajinsha had friends here. One of them was a man called Chowsa who offered them his hut at the edge of the forest. Chowsa was the son of one of the Khampti chiefs of the Gohain family who had mounted the 1839 raid on the British garrison in Suddya that Kajinsha's father had joined with his Mishmee warriors. Chowsa's father had died in the fighting and the Khampti rebels had dispersed to different settlements after their villages around the Tenga Panee were burned. But after their initial reprisal against his village the British were now looking for ways to engage with the tribes and Chowsa, who had moved to Chunpura, was left to ply his trade and even approached by the British to act as their messenger to the rebellious tribal chiefs of Suddya country.

He was a big, handsome man, dressed in a checked lungi of

Burmese cloth and his slow, ponderous manner belied his keen survival instincts. Chowsa spoke fluent Assamese and was familiar with the mixture of dialects used by the local people. He knew everyone in the area, he kept a close watch on British movements, met and received various local chiefs and he had messengers and informants who told him of any new arrivals, be it a white stranger or some intrepid trader of the plains trying his luck and looking to make some profit in this godforsaken region. When he saw Gimur with Kajinsha he must have guessed her condition because he left them and returned late in the evening with tobacco leaf, a bundle of salt and a piece of cloth for her. Then they ate a meal of rice and fish. The fish was cooked wrapped in a leaf and thrown into the fire. Kajinsha turned it now and then with a long bamboo prong. It dawned on Gimur that she knew very little of Kajinsha's life. It was apparent that he travelled, that he socialised, otherwise how would he know people like Chowsa? And how could he converse with these people with such ease if he hadn't been here many times before?

'After the Suddya attack my father sheltered in a nearby village,' Kajinsha told her. 'Many of the Khampti rebels were also hiding out together and they took care of my father who was badly wounded. He might have lived if he had stayed with them, but the old man was determined to return home. The journey killed him. Later I came down to see with my own eyes the place where my father had received shelter. I met Chowsa and we still meet like this, sometimes.' Gimur listened, trying to piece together the untold parts of the story. She remembered Moi and her account of the 1839 raid. She had been in the Suddya garrison too and had lost her husband in the fighting. Everyone had been in it together, but they had not recognised one another. 'How strange,' Gimur thought, 'that we should be all tied together like this, like floating pieces of thread suddenly caught and entangled by the same wind that has blown around us for a time long before any of us were born.'

Gimur lay awake listening to Kajinsha and Chowsa talking in low voices. What could they be talking about? Thoughts crowded into her head. At one point she heard Chowsa saying that the boat that they had passed was going towards Mebo. The British were stepping up movement in the area and trying to establish a trading post near Mebo. 'Yes,' she heard Kajinsha's reply. 'They're trying to make the Abor settle down and stop disturbing them. That is what I was told by Lendem...' Hearing Lendem's name gave her a jolt. Kajinsha and Lendem! They had been together in all those meetings. How well did they know each other? She felt excluded.

It was a restless night and she lay tossing and turning on the bamboo cot thinking she would get no sleep, but she must have slept because Chowsa was gone when she awoke and Kajinsha was sitting by the door. He had made a bundle of everything and put them into his knapsack. He was smoking his pipe. She liked the smell and inhaled deeply. The small hut was cosy, with the pale light of dawn filtering in through the thin bamboo wall. It was a fine morning, she thought, wishing to fall asleep again, but there was no time to linger. They might be followed, and they were not home yet. They had to travel while she was still strong and reach Kajinsha's land as soon as possible.

They left quietly, walking into the forest. From here it was a route that Kajinsha knew by heart. They struck north. They were entering Mishmee territory, moving upstream following the Thlo Brai, the Lohit River that led them higher and higher into the mountains. The wind slapped against their faces and Gimur had to look down to shield her eyes against the cold gust. Sometimes they could cover only a few miles a day, wading across numerous streams by holding on to fishing weirs of villagers they never saw. 'There are villages of Haimsong, Teme and Keasong and other Taraon clans around here,' Kajinsha told her. They had not reached his Kmaan Miju territory yet. They passed an abandoned village gutted by fire—

the scattered debris of fire-blackened bamboo projecting through the remnants of thatch and overgrown fern and vine. Someone had set it ablaze before they fled. Kajinsha slackened their pace into stages, each stage involving a walk of three to five days before they reached small settlements in small clearings in the middle of the forest. 'Look, that is chief Lamet's house,' Kajinsha pointed out from the high ridge they had climbed to avoid passing through the village. He told Gimur that a long time ago his father had broken off relations with Lamet for opening the way to white men. These were old enmities kept alive by succeeding generations, and the root of conflict, it seemed to Gimur, was always about land.

What is this land? Men spoke of land as a possession. 'From this stream to the limits of the jungle and up to that hill with the white rock is my land,' they said. Every piece of earth was claimed. The big trees, the high mountains, the rivers rushing down crevasses, the steep cliffs and jagged rocks. Waterways changed course and dried up. Men fought and killed each other. Blood flowed. Brothers became enemies. How could the mere features of a landscape ignite such love and ferocity, Gimur wondered. The shaman said: 'The land belongs to us. It is the soul of our ancestors. Where would we be, what would we do, without this land?' Maybe there was something that she did not understand. Because she did not doubt that there were unseen spirits lurking in the trees and watching from the mountaintops. Perhaps one of them was her own, or her father's and his father's fathers'. Perhaps.

But the question lingered: What is land? Why is it so precious? Even her mother had agreed that land was everything, throwing up her hands at her daughter's insistent questions. 'It is where you were born!' She had said. And how important was that? Gimur had wondered.

It would be years later, when she was standing sick and lonely on a black hill that the answer would suddenly come to her. Weeping, and clutching handfuls of grass and mud, she would tell herself: 'This is what it is. This is the secret that has hidden itself from me for so long. I was so blind and foolish. I could not see! All this time my heart and its longing have been tied up with these features—these hills, this sunset, this cold dawn and icy wind. The land has bred this. We are one. This is my desire. My life!' But that day was far away yet, to be reached after long journeys of the body and the heart. For now, she was in flight.

One day they came to a high, windy place strewn with enormous boulders of granite worn smooth by wind and water. Kajinsha said they were approaching the bed of the Dau River. 'This is the territory of the chief, Zumsha. He's a clan uncle. I've sent word that we are coming.' He stood and pointed. 'There, look!' A mountain shone before Gimur's eyes like a golden pyramid. 'Hai! What is that?' she cried. It was mica, the ore of the mountain reflecting the sunlight.

They stopped to rest before beginning a steep climb to reach Kajinsha's uncle's house. At dusk they broke through the jungle and entered a circular clearing. A longhouse stood at the far end behind a strong stockade of bamboo. They were approaching it quietly when Kajinsha stopped dead in his tracks and stretched out his arms, keeping her back. 'What is it?' She saw what looked like a lump of earth in the middle of the path. 'Sssh…' he hissed. Gimur stopped breathing. It was a black krait. Kajinsha's right hand was slowly moving towards his knife slung across his chest. The snake was beginning to move when the knife whizzed through the air and pierced its head. Gimur heard a soft thumping sound and then Kajinsha was moving forward and looking at the snake die. He picked up a big stick and held the snake down while he retrieved his knife, taking no chances. Everything was very quiet. Gimur felt it was a sinister place. She felt unseen eyes were watching them. Where was everyone?

'Yahai! Where is everybody?' Kajinsha shouted. A white face

peeped out then disappeared immediately. There was a sound of scurrying feet, a cough, and then a man emerged. He was a big man with piercing black eyes. He carried a sword in his hand. 'Ho!' He smiled when he saw Kajinsha. 'It's you! I heard you were on the way. What's this? Ril! a snake!' He flicked it up with his sword and flung it into the jungle. He turned and looked at Gimur. Kajinsha said something, Zumsha nodded, and they entered the house together. It was a long, well constructed house divided into several rooms. They joined a group of men and women sitting around the hearth in the first room.

'Here, Kajinsha is here!' said Zumsha. 'Ah!' the men smiled and the women made way for them to sit by the fire. Gimur sat a little to the corner, in the shadows. The house was dark and smoky and big chunks of meat, still raw and bloody were strewn on the smoking rack above the fire. Gimur felt tired and ill. A young girl brought her water. No one said anything to her. Out of the corner of her eye she saw that Kajinsha and Zumsha had moved away into another corner. Kajinsha was talking animatedly while Zumsha listened, his head bent, his big arms resting on his knee. Now and then he looked up and glanced swiftly around the house, his eyes taking in everything and alighting on Gimur for a mere fraction of a second.

'We'll stay here tonight,' Kajinsha told her. 'You must rest. Tomorrow we'll reach my place and Zumsha will visit us there after a few days.' He bent close to her ear and whispered, 'Everything is all right. Don't be afraid.'

Gimur nodded. She was not afraid. It was in the faces of the women in the house that she saw fear, she thought. Except for one. She was a young woman who had been staring at her and Kajinsha with unabashed interest. Gimur noticed her because she was dressed differently, wrapped in a black cloth knotted over one shoulder. She had no ornaments except for one silver hairpin that held her thick, matted hair in place. Kajinsha said she had come on an errand from chief Lamet's house. She was a slave woman kept by Lamet; he had bought her from the plains people, perhaps, or from Burmese traders across the border. Her name was Yenjee. The other women were wives of chief Zumsha. They had borne him many children, sons and daughters, and enhanced his name throughout the land as the owner of land, cattle and many sons. Now they were all busy preparing meat and rice while the men drank rice beer and smoked their pipes.

It was a strange, uneasy night. The household fell asleep around the fire with their heads and limbs resting on each other. At crack of dawn Gimur was awake. She wanted to be on her way and reach her new home. She tapped Kajinsha on the shoulder to wake him up. He grunted. She rose swiftly and stepped out to wash at the water point. Footsteps sounded behind her and when she turned around she saw Yenjee following her. The woman looked fresh and strong and gestured that she was also leaving; she was going back to Lamet's village. Gimur saw Kajinsha coming out of the house and Yenjee waved to him.

Then she turned to Gimur. 'I will visit you sometime!' she called softly in Kajinsha's language, and was gone.

1852

The Black Hill. Life by the Dau River. The Zayul Valley

High in the mountains near the headwaters of the Dau River, Kajinsha and Gimur settled down to their new life together. It was a secluded place on a ridge, surrounded by wooded slopes of trees that Gimur thought had no leaves. Kajinsha told her they were rukg trees. They glinted in the sun and filled the air with a sharp odour. They were conifers. Gimur, who was now very far away from the rainforests of Mebo, was now close to the border with the Zayul valley of Tibet and had never seen such trees before. Her new home was a thatched bamboo longhouse raised high on stilts that were planted deep into the hillside, and one part of the house jutted over the precipice. A ring of snow-capped mountains rose to the north and a deep ravine cut off the western extremity of the valley. Far below the gnarled trees clinging to this vertical chasm flowed the Thlo Brai, the river she now knew as the Zayul Chu that flowed south from Tibet right through these mountains and into the plains of Assam. A small stream flowing in from the east came close to the house and flowed on to join the Dau River which was beyond the tall trees that hid Gimur's new home from view.

'Do you like it? What do you think?' asked Kajinsha. He pointed to the rows of skull trophies of mithun and wild oxen that lined the walls of the front room called the manthang, traditionally reserved for guests. 'These are from my father's time,' he said. Gimur had never seen a house like this; it was different from the houses of Mebo because the entire building was divided into compartments. 'I built this,' Kajinsha tapped the thick wood of the projecting veranda in the front of the house called the hado. 'I made that…' he pointed to a low wooden cot that gleamed, brand new. 'The baby can have it!' he laughed. He had also built a small thatched hut pressed up against the trees overlooking the valley below. A wonderful light poured in when Kajinsha opened the door of this hut. Gimur saw stacks of corn, red, yellow, deep-brown, hanging in bunches from the rafters. A sack of salt and a pile of trimmed logs lay in one corner. 'It is better than your Mebo houses, is it not?' said Kajinsha. Then he added, 'It may not be much but everything here belongs to you.' He pointed to himself and contorting his face into a snarl, cried, 'And this one, too, this one!' Gimur laughed. She did not realise yet that Kajinsha stocked up on food and material like this because he lived in such isolation. In the days following she would learn more: about advance runners, for instance, who would arrive to ask if someone could visit him. Most of the time Kajinsha was away, travelling, yet no one dared enter his territory without permission. It was a solitary place, but Gimur was happy.

Kajinsha pointed to the mountains in the north and told her that beyond them was a wilderness that his father had travelled into and reached the land of the lamas to stake his claim to settle in this valley. It had been a period of war and rivalry, men lived like wild animals hiding from their enemies and struggling to survive. But his father and brothers together had triumphed, and this was where Kajinsha had grown up. He told her that he had travelled everywhere.

'What about your mother?' she asked.

'She died. She never came here,' he said.

She stared at him and felt a little frightened by his air of certainty and his solitary nature.

'There are villages nearby,' he told Gimur, as if to allay any fear that she might have about being cut off from the rest of the world, but she knew the nearest would be a few days' walk away. And unlike Abor villages of two hundred houses or more, here a village could mean a single family unit with but a dozen houses, or even one or two houses.

But she had no need to see other people. Not yet. At night a cold wind blew down from the mountains and Gimur, remembering her lonely hut in Mebo, would curl up closer to Kajinsha and he would press her to him and hug her tightly. This was love-time, when the heart of every flower smiled and all the trees and leaves and the wild grass glinted and sang in the light of the sun and the moon. This was before-time, when enchantment could well out of a stone, when ksha—ghosts and evil spirits, sowers of poison and seeds of mist, hadn't yet crept into their garden.

One morning Kajinsha awoke long before daybreak and lay still, thinking. A dream had broken his sleep and he was trying to remember what it was. A river came to his mind. He and Gimur were swimming and her skirt was ballooning out in the water some distance away from them. They were both laughing as it floated away and he was watching her when something splashed in the opposite bank. He saw two people, too far away to be more than indistinct shapes, and they were tugging at a long piece of cane floating in the water. But then he realised it looked like a snake. He thought of calling out to Gimur to swim out of the river, but his voice would not come. He tried to swim towards her, to hide her, but he felt the current pulling him back. She was still laughing and trying to splash water at him. He felt a gust of wind and a bird whistled past him calling in a fearful staccato song. It was the loud cry of the unseen bird that had awakened him. His heart was beating. The cry of a bird at night was a bad omen. Kajinsha seized a piece of burning wood from the night's fire and stepping out of the house, he hurled it into the open. 'There!' he thought. When he came back in Gimur was watching him through half opened eyes.

'What are you doing?' She asked.

'I had a dream about a river. I was trying to hide you because some people were there.'

'Even in your dreams!' She lifted her arms. 'You are always hiding—everything!' It always surprised her how superstitious he was. He believed in signs and omens and sometimes he would not to go out because he had had a bad dream.

'The water was muddy. There was also a bird.'

'What kind of bird?'

'It was invisible but I heard the sound. It was not good.'

'You heard the roosters,' she said.

The angry, grating cry of the bird still lingered in his mind but it was daylight now. The morning sun was pouring down on the land and Gimur was laughing and shaking her head at him.

Chief Zumsha came to visit them accompanied by clan members who brought roast meat and fish. Kajinsha had warned Gimur that Kmaan wedding rituals were complicated and cumbersome. Their case was a little different as Gimur's relatives were not present, but as a grown man Kajinsha would still have to reciprocate all the gifts that his relatives brought for him. This was called the flow of the commodity basket where the groom would seek the help of his relatives who, in turn, would approach other relatives until everyone was involved in the marriage celebration in a system of delivery and payback that could sometimes be very costly. For now he had killed a pig and honoured his guests with rice beer. Zumsha smiled. Meeting him again Gimur realised that he was a strong, proud man who reminded her of her own uncle who had come to Mebo when the big meetings were being held to fight the migluns. Zumsha echoed the same sentiments. 'There is a man,' he said, 'who has been asking for a way to reach Tibet.' This was the first hint of the French priest Krick's approach into their territory but it did not mean anything yet to Kajinsha and Gimur and the men and women sitting together in the group that day. 'They say he is a different menil,' continued Zumsha, using the Kmaan word for an outsider that Gimur understood now. 'He is not a soldier. But we have to be alert.' Zumsha's voice rose. 'He is still a white foreigner—a kla kamphlung! Who knows about these people? To us they are all strangers.'

Before he left, Zumsha pulled out a silver pipe from under his robe and handed it to Gimur. It was a big gesture. It was a nod of approval, and Kajinsha looked happy as a boy as they laughed and waved goodbye to this famous chief who had the reputation of being a fearsome bulwark against outsiders and ruthlessly ordering the death of his enemies

Now there remained one more thing to be done. Before he left Zumsha had told Kajinsha that he should visit the woman who was the mother of his son. Zumsha had already told her family about his return with a new bride and they would be expecting him. Kajinsha agreed. It would be a last meeting, he told Gimur. She could accompany him and see the village beyond the mountains where his first wife and his son lived. Gimur knew that the marriage had been arranged by the woman's uncle when Kajinsha was still a boy grieving for his dead father. It was an alliance to cement the promise of his father's clan to guard the entry into Tibet from intruders coming from the south, and Kajinsha had told her many times that the marriage was over. Still, she felt a twinge of doubt when they set out on their journey in a northerly direction towards the Zayul valley on the other side of the towering mountains.

'How old is she? What does she do now? Will there be lots of people?' she asked.

'You will see, you will see,' was all that Kajinsha said in reply.

The landscape was changing into a broad, open valley of cultivated fields and fruit trees. They walked through a thick forest of pine and soon, through the trees, Gimur glimpsed some houses. Tall flags of coloured cloth fluttered in the wind. 'There,' said Kajinsha, pointing, 'the village of Sommeu!' It was actually a small provincial town with houses built of stone clustered together along a steep and winding path. A number of people stared at them as they entered the small street. Some of them greeted Kajinsha. He nodded and said something to a few of them but he kept walking and did not stop. Gimur could hear the barking of dogs and children shouting excitedly as they passed. If she had looked about her she might have noticed a tall, sharp-featured man in a black woollen Tibetan robe and wearing a brown fur hat watching them intently, but she kept her eyes down and followed Kajinsha into a dark, two-storeyed building. They entered a large room that was a barn used for storing fodder, food grain and ploughing implements. A bright fire from a large stone hearth heated the room and a narrow cot piled high with woollen blankets was wedged against the wall at the back. They climbed a short wooden staircase to the room above. A woman lay on a bed. A young boy with his back to them was wiping a low wooden table. When he heard Kajinsha's voice he dropped the rag and turned around. 'Pai!' he said. 'Father!'

'This is Awesa,' Kajinsha said without emotion.

Gimur stared. The boy had lurched forward. He was twelve or thirteen and he was saying something but she could not understand a word. His mouth was slack and he was blubbering. His head appeared disproportionately large and he wore a dirty white woollen cap that he now twisted in his hands as he stood in front of her with a dark blush on his face. She moved back a bit.

'It's all right,' said Kajinsha, nudging her past Awesa towards the table that he had been wiping so hard with his filthy rag. Awesa ran forward and placed a small carpet on the floor beside the table. A feeble yellowish light filtered in through the narrow windows. The place was like a cell. Gimur shuddered. The woman on the bed raised herself up to a sitting position. 'I am always sick with one thing or another,' she said, addressing Kajinsha and speaking Kmaan lai which Gimur thought was for her benefit. Then she reduced her words to gestures. 'My name is Auli. Ever since my boy Awesa was born I have been ill like this,' she said, sinking back and gazing about the room with sad, wandering eyes.

Kajinsha was pacing up and down. 'It's alright, it's all right,' he kept repeating.

'Go and tell Chhomu to make tea,' the woman ordered Awesa, who immediately scrambled down the stairs. Kajinsha followed him. Now that they were alone, Gimur could see the face of the woman better. Her eyes were tired and puffy and her face was very thin, with a deep flush of colour on her jutting cheekbones. What was she suffering from? Kajinsha had said it was an incurable illness. She had the falling sickness, he had said, a sickness that everyone believed was the work of an evil spirit who, when it took possession of her, pushed her down and sat on her body. At such times she fought back clawing and foaming at the mouth. These attacks had become more frequent and violent and now everything about her was old, faded and tired. Gimur was relieved when Awesa returned with a white aluminium mug that clattered as he placed it before her and lifted the lid. She tasted the tea. It was full of salt! Awesa was watching her and she burned her tongue gulping down the hot liquid before it choked her. She had never tasted anything like it before. Her mouth was filled with oil. Had she swallowed poison?

'If we don't leave soon the rain will stop us,' shouted Kajinsha from below.

'You must come again,' cried the woman.

'Yes, yes,' Gimur said as she left hurriedly, almost falling down the steps with Awesa following close behind her. She could feel his breath on her neck.

A young woman with braided hair stood aside as she came down. She was the woman's sister and she was carrying another mug of tea. Gimur stared at her but the girl did not raise her eyes. Instead a deep blush seemed to suffuse her face. 'She's Chhomu,' said Kajinsha. 'They,' he flicked a glance towards Awesa, 'the two of them, they look after the place.' And what a place, thought Gimur. How ugly it all was, like a house of the dead! In her heart she was torn between disgust and pity, and rage against Kajinsha for putting her through this.

As they emerged, the tall man with the brown fur hat came up to them just outside the door. 'Are you leaving already?' he asked.

'Yes,' Kajinsha replied. He introduced the man to Gimur briefly as Ugyen Marpa, the woman's uncle, and marched ahead. A thin mist was drifting in and the street was empty and ghostly.

I will never come here again, thought Gimur, hurrying away from the place, not knowing then how her life was going to be tied to this lost village with its prayer flags flapping in the wind, and how one day it would be resurrected for her as a tiny place of meeting, of death and rebirth, like a mysterious universe emblazoned in her heart.

After the visit to Zayul, day by day Gimur took over the duties associated with the woman of a house. Kajinsha had agricultural land—tei-nyal—and separate spots for hunting, fishing, and catching rodents and birds; as well as forest land where chal, the beloved animal Gimur knew as mithun—eso in her native Mebo— were allowed to roam freely. Gimur began to recognise the families living in the area, and she learnt to smoke in true Kmaan fashion, puffing at the kacung with visitors and people who came to help them to plant maize and millet and a variety of hard mountain rice that could withstand the force of the strong winds. One regular visitor was Awesa. Ever since their meeting in Sommeu, the boy, his name meant just that—boy—had followed her with a dog-like devotion that had become a source of irritation. She felt repulsed by his dirty, sloppy presence, but he was strong and eager to help with all the chores that she could not manage on her own. He brought wild yam for the pigs, chopped wood, carried water and scouted the jungle with a cane rope, keeping an eye on the mithun herds that belonged to Kajinsha. Gimur noticed that father and son had little to say to one another.

Kajinsha was often away on short journeys, Gimur never knew if he travelled north into Tibet or east into the hills of Burmah, but by now she knew his habits. He was a nomad, hunting and fishing or trading in mishmee tita, the medicinal coptis, and bih, aconite, which was used as poison on arrow heads and spear blades. He returned with brass vessels, Burmese knives and swords, tobacco and salt. Once he came back with dyed yarn from the Singpho people. This made Gimur set up a loom in the small hut. She was a good weaver and she wanted to make a gul-khana jacket for Kajinsha. The hut began to resound with the thump of the baton as she spent many hours bent over the intricate Kmaan designs. Awesa lurked in the background, fetching small things for her, like the plantain leaf whose white powder she used to smooth the thread. She received these gifts with a grim face and when he had left quietly she relaxed, wondering what was wrong with him and how she could stop his unwelcome presence. She had arrived here in the winter and now the days were already too hot for her to work in the fields. She did not know when it would be time for her, but she could feel the baby growing inside her and hoped she would be a mother soon.

One day when she was in the hut fetching salt out of a big bamboo tube, Gimur felt a sharp, shooting pain in her lower abdomen. She doubled over, gasping, and the salt spilled from her hand. Some fell on her foot.

'Hai!' she thought. 'It is a bad sign.' She was more worried about the salt than the pain, and straightening up slowly she carried the salt out to the two mithuns. One of them, the one she loved best, had a large white marking on his black body that made him look like he was wearing a vest. He was a big animal who roamed far, but he always returned home for salt, his nose and eyes glistening with sweetness and trust.

'Where did you go? What did you do today?' she murmured to the mithuns. Their rough tongues scraped her open palms. They licked her hands clean and then snorting and stamping, slowly began to meander off, crunching over the stones on steady feet. Gimur felt happy when Kajinsha called out from the house and said maybe they could go to the river. They would not check the fish traps now, it was taboo in her condition, but they could find a spot to sit quietly and enjoy the good weather. 'Yes, I'm coming,' she shouted.

They crossed the jungle and reached a patch of white sand. Here the water was wide and flat. Gimur buried her feet in the sand. There was not a soul around. The far bank was shadowed, and not a leaf stirred. Kajinsha was sweating. His arms glistened and his eyes swept the area.

'We can go upstream,' he said.

'No,' she cried, sitting down. She was hot and tired. 'I cannot move another step.' She tapped her belly.

Kajinsha squinted up at the sky. 'You sit in the shade. I'll look around,' he said.

She sat still for a long time, staring at the river that seemed to be barely moving. Everything was still and ageless, and already she had forgotten what direction Kajinsha had taken. Behind her the green wall of jungle buzzed and sang. She looked around her trying to find the source of strange cries, the scrape of wings, the creak of wood. All the sounds mingled to form a dizzying note inside her head. A hot wind filled her ears and her scalp tingled. Idly she wondered where Kajinsha had disappeared. I'll wait a bit, and then follow him, she thought. She stared at the water again and seemed to fall into a trance watching the river rising in a green loop then falling flat again. The surface of the water was like glass, opaque green and heavy. She remembered stories from her childhood about water serpents that lived in big rivers. The Kmaan also believed there was a snake as long as the river. There is always a serpent spirit lurking in deep water waiting to pull someone in, she thought. The snake is angry because her children have been killed by men and she wants revenge. Who is the unfortunate passerby she will claim…?

She must have fallen asleep because when she opened her eyes again she saw Kajinsha moving towards her. The sun was behind him, almost sinking. For a moment she was confused. She wondered whether it was night or day, and was aware only of a strange heaviness that seemed to pulse from her gut down along her thighs. Later, when Gimur allowed herself to remember that afternoon, the images came back very easily to her. There was a shout from Kajinsha and she remembered her struggle to get on her feet. Then Kajinsha was carrying her and running. Her teeth were clenched in pain and she saw only the tops of trees whizzing past as her head was flung back while Kajinsha continued to run clasping her tightly in his arms and looking straight ahead. They reached the hut. Distant voices approached her. She felt a burning weight on her abdomen and sighed. There was a bustle of activity near her and a woman was holding her and telling her to push hard. She thought it was her mother. Her heart pounded and she struggled to tell her mother that there was nothing wrong with her, that she was still alive, and now she wanted to go home.

In the middle of the night two babies were born in the small hut on the hill. The first child was stillborn, but the other was alive. They were twin boys. Weeping with pain Gimur was aware of all that was happening, but even though she was shouting no one seemed to hear her. Everything passed in a daze. Later that night—or was it early morning?—she awoke to the touch of a hand on her brow. She opened her eyes and saw the face of an old woman bending over her.

'I am well,' she said, and immediately felt the prickle of tears behind her eyelids. A pain such as she had never felt before was welling up in her chest and she thought she would choke. Where were her babies? 'Oh gods! Where are you? What has happened?' She looked about her slowly.

'Sssh, ssshh,' the woman whispered. 'Your boy is alive. Here he is, look!'

She saw the tiny bundle near her, the shape of the small hands floating in space, and she heard the little heart pumping for life and breath, just like her own. Her son! But from the silent faces watching over her she could tell that nothing would be the same again.

Gimur knew that if the birth had happened in Mebo, among her own people, the reaction would have been the same. The birth of twins was unlucky. Her friends would have avoided her and no one would have woven cloth with her for fear of giving birth to twins. Among some tribes twins were killed at birth. And it was believed that the souls of children who died at birth went to a middle world under the earth. Sometimes these children joined hands and danced and when they did this it caused an earthquake.

In her thoughts Gimur blamed Kajinsha for the misfortune. 'You brought bad dreams into the house,' she accused him silently, remembering his dream about a wild bird. Her mind wandered back to their visit to Sommeu. 'We should never have gone there. Those people are unlucky. We should have taken precautions and performed rites,' she thought.

When Kajinsha tried to touch her she stiffened. Then he would leave the room and sit outside smoking his pipe. 'Do you want anything? Some water?' he would call out after a while. And she would answer 'no' in a small voice, feeling sad and contrite, wishing she could speak to him again like in the old days, clearly and openly. She also began to feel that Kajinsha might be asking himself questions: 'Why had this happened? What spirit had marked them for bad fortune?' Everyone knew that twin births and death at birth happened to many women, but it had never happened to anyone in his family. It was unnatural. Their surviving son was small and weak. The old woman said maybe he had a crack in his spine. How did she know that? 'It was the struggle to be born,' she had said. The baby had arrived kicking, with his feet first. Kajinsha and Gimur heard these whispered comments and they both felt sensitive and raw. Gimur defended herself with silence. Kajinsha recalled ancestors and wondered about the future, feeling lonely and crushed beneath this misfortune.

The only person who remained unaffected by all that was happening was Awesa. He moved around in the compound clearing his throat loudly. Sometimes he came close to where Gimur was sitting, mumbling something in his incoherent way that made her want to shout, 'Go away! It is you and your house that has brought this misfortune!' She was thinking this one day when suddenly a terrible fear gripped her. She remembered the sad house in Zayul and saw how she, Gimur, would become like Auli if she did not recover.

In that instant Gimur promised herself that she would defeat this curse that had befallen her. She knew joy was not given just like that. A voice had always warned her that joy could be snatched away from anyone at any time by something unnatural like a strange bird swooping down from the sky. But whatever had happened was done and finished. She had left everything to come here and build a home. Now she had to make it worthwhile. She must live. 'Save me, spirits of the sky and stones of the great mountains!' she prayed. 'Come to my rescue. Help me to endure and nurse my baby. Make him strong.'

◆

Endurance

Across the river, in the plains below, the priest was writing something in his thin, slanting hand.

Behold! What is this river rushing like a fierce beast towards me? He had achieved his goal of reaching Saikwa Ghat and every time he looked up from his notebook all he could see were the waters of the mighty Burhampooter stretching from bank to bank like a raging sea. He had narrowly escaped death by drowning when his boat had capsized before reaching this place. Had it not been for some fishermen of the Deori tribe he would have floated away with the current. These men had leapt into the water and grabbed him. They had given him food and shelter in their hut on a sandbar in the middle of the water and at daybreak they had rowed him back to Saikwa where he had received the kindest attention and help from the British authorities in the person of Captain Reid, Captain Smith and the political agent Hamilton Vetch who was camped in Saikwa at the time.

So many things had happened since Krick had left Gowhattee. His senior Julien Rabin had left the mission. The news had been conveyed to him by Father Bernard who said that Rabin had fallen ill during their second attempt to enter Bhootan and had to be carried back on a stretcher. Subsequently he had left for Calcutta and from there had boarded a ship to go back to France. Now Bernard was alone but Krick did not want to return to Gowhattee... Not yet.

'We are going up to Abor territory,' Vetch had told him. 'You might like to come with us.'

'Oh no, my journey is to Tibet,' said Krick. He felt he did not want to be part of what he thought was a military mission but Vetch brushed aside his doubts.

'Ah, but I am going to try and make peace with them,' he said. 'Of all the tribes along this stretch the Abor are by far the most amenable to engage with. And the Padam Abor might know of a route that might be better than passing through Mishmee territory. We are going with troops but you and I can take the boat a few miles upstream on the Siang River to a point near a village called Mebo.'

That was how in late September Krick had found himself on a boat travelling upstream on the same route that Gimur and Kajinsha were following in their flight towards the Mishmee hills. He had found no guides yet to take him to Tibet and under the circumstances he could think of no better way to familiarise himself with the country than by travelling with Vetch. He could meet the Padam Abor tribe and make a personal assessment about their culture and habits that would not be possible otherwise. It was an opportunity, and Krick took it—never imagining that he would soon pass this way again, but under the most severe and changed conditions.

But that was yet in the future. At this moment he was enthralled by the scene unfolding before him. Krick, wearing his black cassock and the cross around his neck, was mounted on the back of an elephant with Vetch. They had left the boat and were moving slowly along a bed of rocks in a line of eight, with more of the magnificent beasts leading a detachment of two hundred soldiers. They were met at the foot of the mountain by three young men in war helmets who stood in front of a group of Abor warriors. One of them was Lendem. Vetch began to address the gathering in a loud, confident voice. There was no other sound except that of the river gushing over the stones. The Abor, all carrying long spears and swords, stood poised on the boulders like statues.

Krick felt the tension in the air. The Abor said something and he saw movement among the thickets. The thought flashed through his head that if they were killed now he would be dying with the

English, for the English, when he would have preferred to die for his own cause. Vetch, however, had not stopped talking. Krick listened intently and felt a surge of excitement when he discovered that he could understand what was being said. Vetch was speaking a patois Assamese that was the lingua franca among the different tribes of the area. Krick felt grateful for the long hours spent in studying Assamese in Gowhattee. He heard Vetch announce, 'Here is a priest who wants to go to Tibet. Can the Abor help him?'

There was silence. Then the one called Lendem said, 'No, we do not know a way.'

'Do you know a way through the Mishmee Hills?'

The mention of the Mishmee brought back memories of Gimur and her flight. Lendem thought: a daughter of the village had caused uproar, running away to a place near Tibet, and here they were, these migluns, asking about a path to Tibet. Why should we even entertain their questions? 'No, we do not know of any route,' he replied angrily. Father Krick looked at him closely. Something else now claimed his attention. He noticed that this man and other Abors were all tattooed. They had marks on their faces, on their brow and chin, and most amazing of all the marks were all in the shape of a cross. 'What is the meaning of these tattoos? Why do you wear them?' he had ventured to ask, only to be told that they did not know. It was a custom that they had inherited from their forefathers. While Vetch conversed with the men Krick stayed to one side silently taking in the scene. He was intrigued by the cross tattoos. They were quite clearly the Maltese and Lorraine cross. How amazing! If only he could spend more time here with the Abor. But he knew they were suspicious and would not receive him into their village when he was travelling like this with men carrying guns. He would return some other time. There must be a way, he thought, to win the trust of these people, just as there must be a way to reach Tibet. He was prepared to travel up and down mountains until a chance presented itself.

And this was what he was doing now, back in Saikwa Ghat after the brief journey with Vetch and his men, waiting again, looking for someone to guide him across these rivers and mountains into Tibet through the Mishmee hills.

'There is a man who knows the route,' Vetch told Krick one day. 'I have sent for him.'

The man he was talking about was Chowsa, who, of course, knew the route since he and Kajinsha had travelled together to Tibet and back many times. 'Here is a priest,' said Vetch making the introduction, when they met Chowsa. 'He wants to go to Tibet. I believe you know the route through the Mishmee hills?'

Chowsa was cautious. 'I know the route, but it is dangerous,' he said. He was thinking how Kajinsha and Gimur had passed through this way a few months ago and the news of strangers arriving now, almost as if following in their footsteps, might kindle suspicion and provoke an incident. How would Kajinsha react? He needed to send word and warn the couple. He played for time.

'We will need porters. We will need to carry rice for the journey. The harvest is just beginning. I can collect rice in ten days,' he said.

'Do it quickly then,' said Vetch, dismissing him.

Chowsa stayed away for two weeks, hoping the priest would give up. Then Vetch sent him a letter and a present as inducement to act as guide. 'We will look after your son,' he said, 'while you travel with the priest.' Chowsa stayed quiet. So they were using his little boy, who was in school in Debrooghur, to force him to take the stupid priest into the Mishmee hills. 'The priest will pay you.' said Vetch.

Hah! You can keep your money, thought Chowsa. What good is money if we are killed? Kajinsha was unpredictable. In fact, Kajinsha was the most secretive and dangerous man he knew. He had seen him tracking animals and men, appearing like a ghost in

Mamang Dai

the middle of the night to take away whatever it was that he wanted from terrified traders living along the border who had broken their promise to pay him his due in trade goods. And why did this priest want to go to Tibet? Even if Kajinsha and chief Zumsha allowed him passage, what did he plan to do in Tibet? Was he a spy?

'Please,' the priest beseeched him suddenly, speaking in Assamese. 'I come with no soldiers, no guns. I am alone. My wish is to travel to Tibet. I will not disturb anyone on the way. I only seek passage through the territory of the Mishmee chiefs.'

Chowsa thought about it. The priest looked the same as the British but maybe he was different after all. He sounded genuine. If Chowsa refused they would find someone else. In these times of warring tribes, there were other Mishmee chiefs who would show him the way into Kajinsha's territory and then there might be trouble. He, Chowsa, on the other hand, could escort him straight through into the first Tibetan village. He knew the way. That would be his duty done. After that they would be rid of the priest and he would have an opportunity to meet his friend Kajinsha.

'I will need time to prepare a few things,' he said.

At last, on a bright, sunny afternoon, on 18 December 1851, Krick found himself with Chowsa and some seventeen porters and guides on the banks of a river near Chunpura, ready to start their journey into the Mishmee hills. The British officers had been very kind to him and Vetch had presented him a good sextant which Krick had accepted, saying, 'with these I can make myself useful to science, geography, history.' Chowsa led the way. The priest had said he was travelling alone but he had a companion, a black dog that ran in front of the party yelping with excitement. The priest called him Lorrain. It was the name of the place in the faraway country where he came from, the priest tried to explain to Chowsa, who was busy clearing a route before them, hacking and crawling through the tangle of thorny bamboo and giant rattan that grew thick as a man's arm and curved over them like a green tunnel. Bah, the dog was just some stray that the priest had been too sentimental to turn away.... Strange man, he thought, eyeing the priest slyly who was dressed in a cotton blouse with black trimming and pants of the same woven fabric tucked into big boots. He carried a rifle and a satchel containing his Bible, the breviary, his medicine box, sextant, and a supply of ink and paper. An enormous topi like a Tylorean hat was crammed down on his head. Only his beard was visible. Krick, catching sight of his reflection in the water, wondered what people in France would think if they saw a priest in such accoutrements. His missionary cross, in odd contrast to his overall unlikely appearance, was the only indication of the religious nature of the mission. But these thoughts had flown away with each step of the journey. They were on the same trail now that Kajinsha and Gimur had taken travelling out of Chunpura along the bed of the Burhampooter, but while Gimur had seen everything as a familiar landscape, for Father Krick everything was new and extraordinary.

His first meeting with the Mishmee happened very suddenly. Chowsa fired his gun into the air.

'What are you doing?' he exclaimed.

'Wait,' said Chowsa. 'There are Mishmee here. I am warning them.'

A man, two women and their children appeared out of the jungle. Chowsa spoke to them, and then told the priest that their homes had been burnt down in an attack by a neighbouring tribe and now they were living in the forest like animals. The women wore thin plates of copper like a bandeau on their heads over knotted hair that was fastened with bamboo pins. One of the women wore a necklace of black seeds. The man had large copper rings in his ears, and all of them, even the young children, were smoking pipes. It was a brief, furtive first meeting. But it was a beginning.

Krick had always dreamt of a journey like this; he felt a deep and happy solitude. They were still in the foothills and he was enraptured by the beauty of creation unfolding before him. Here there is nothing to awaken passion, pride and jealousy in the heart of man, he thought. Everything around was peaceful, as it must have been in the first days of creation. At night they camped in the open, amidst boulders and tussocks of wild grass that sprang up on sandbars and he was happy to lie down for the night under a mound of branches to protect him from the night wind. It was a green, pristine and silent world. If Voltaire had spent time here he would have become a servant of God, he mused, for in these wild hills the work of an all powerful God was truly made manifest under the transparent veil of nature.

But the path was not strewn with roses. Soon enough Chowsa told him that a mountain had collapsed up ahead blocking their route and they would have to make a detour. They were now walking along a narrow stream bed cutting through a hot, airless ravine. There was no shade. The path was steep and the hot stones hurt their feet as they trudged on with the sun beating down on their heads. The foot of the mountain was a wilderness of blocks of granite piled together and at night Father Krick slept wedged in between boulders with his arms flung out on the hard rocks. The next morning being a Sunday he put on his surplice and cassock, placed his crucifix on a block of granite along with his Bible and breviary. 'Go ye and make disciples of all men...' He recalled the blessed words and falling on his knees bowed his head in prayer. When he opened his eyes he saw a group of Mishmees standing silently around him, leaning on their spears and smoking their pipes.

They had been warned of the stranger's arrival and had come down from a village on the mountain. They presented him with some fruit from the forest and he in return gave them tobacco and salt. Everything was conducted in silence with Chowsa muttering only a few brief words before urging them onward. He, alone among the party, felt the eyes of hidden tribesmen watching them. He knew word of their approach had spread far and wide. Yet there was no message for him from Kajinsha. Chowsa wondered about this. Perhaps it is because of the way things have turned out in Kajinsha's house, he thought. He knew about the birth and death of one of Gimur's twin boys. But there was time yet. They were still many days away from the Zayul border and word would come soon enough, he knew it, from Kajinsha or from chief Zumsha.

He stood waiting while Father Krick tried to gauge the elevation but they were surrounded by a forest of trees so tall and thick that he could not see the sun. The climb was getting steeper. Krick gauged the elevation to be about nine to ten thousand feet. On some days he felt unable to move a muscle. Day by day they crept upwards until one day they emerged on top of a peak and Krick saw the mountains of mica ore just as Gimur had seen them, shining in the sun like mountains of gold and silver. I have seen the gardens of Paris, Saint Cloud, and admired the art of Versailles, he thought, but nothing, nothing can compare to the beauty of God's work in these mountains. The work of man was but a lamp of coloured glass compared to the sun! How could he describe what his eyes beheld? He was surrounded by mountains that made him think that the Himalayas were frozen waves of an enormous ocean that dominated the world. He would have lingered but Chowsa was impatient. 'Hurry up, hurry up', he cried, forging ahead. The way was becoming more dangerous.

They were descending along a slippery path to the Tidding River when all the men disappeared from view. Father Krick looked around. Where had they gone? He was afraid to call out and his legs were shaking with the strain of keeping a foothold on the slippery stones. For a moment he lost his balance and slipped straight down a slab of rock that jutted down into the trees. When he looked about him he saw the men standing there waiting for him. What kind of place was this, he thought, staring at the men who made no move to help him up. Instead Chowsa seemed even more impatient to be on their way. They too had clambered down the same rock face, after all.

They were approaching the village of Khroussa; whether they would continue on their journey or be forced to turn back, he told Krick even while the priest was recovering from the shock of his fall. Another shock awaited him when they reached the Tidding River. High above them Krick saw a rope of cane suspended over the abyss. 'What is that?' he cried. 'It is a bridge,' Chowsa told him. What a bridge! He gasped in amazement. He had heard that when the water was high the Mishmee crossed the river by means of cane hoops that were propelled along this rope. Nothing would persuade him to fly through the air like that, Krick thought. If that was the only way to cross the river he was ready to turn back. Luckily, the river was shallow enough to wade across. They crossed the river on 24 December but once they reached the other side, they found that another mountain had collapsed, blocking their path to Khroussa's village. On Christmas day it began to rain and suddenly the forest turned pitch black. There was no place of retreat. Everyone slipped, fell, and carried on, somehow crawling and feeling their way through the darkness and the rain. They spent the night in the forest drenched and shivering in the biting cold. The men were cursing and ready to turn back. Even Krick felt if he had not been a missionary he would have said: 'Let us go back.'

But the next day they were pressing on again. Chowsa ordered absolute silence as they moved like cats along a precarious, ledge hardly daring to breathe in case they dislodged a boulder and triggered another avalanche. Here there was no chance of holding on to anything. The rock face was a steep ramp littered with slippery stones where one misstep could plunge a man straight into an abyss. It was a test of nerves but they made it across. No one had spoken.

Only once a woman porter had cried out, imagining that she could hear a rumble and that she saw the mountain moving.

Chief Khroussa was a fresh-faced, athletic-looking man who had had dealings with migluns before. He spoke Assamese and in a calm voice informed the party that the route to Tibet was closed. They would have to go back.

'Others have tried before you but no one has succeeded. They carried presents and came with soldiers and servants. You are alone. What will you do?' he said to the priest.

'I have come here to go to Tibet and I will succeed,' said Krick quietly.

The hut they were in was filled with smoke as Krick put forward his case while Khroussa and five other men sitting with him around the fire argued with him. 'Sabe, sabe, the road is horrible,' they told him. 'And there is a famine. Even if you came with a hundred servants they would all run away.'

But Krick was resolute. He carried rice, he said, and as for the road he would depend on his legs and take his chances.

'Your servants will rob you and then leave you.'

'Then I will travel alone. My load will be lighter,' he replied.

A woman laughed. Krick caught sight of a young woman looking at him with bright eyes. 'She is from Lamet's village,' Chowsa told him. 'Her name is Yenjee.'

Krick understood that Lamet's was the first village he would encounter on the high pass into Mizhou territory. But Lamet was away in Tibet, he was told, and the other Mizhou clans would not let him enter. He might be attacked.

'I will defend myself. Death is nothing to me.' Krick shouldered his gun to show a resolution he did not feel. The men scrutinized him and then stood up muttering that if he wanted to go alone and get killed then so be it. They were turning their backs on him. It was a standoff. Chowsa tried to intervene, saying that the Mishmee were giving good advice, but Krick was in no mood to talk anymore. 'You can also leave if you want,' he told Chowsa curtly. 'I will find my way.'

In his heart he was praying for guidance when Chowsa called him from his bed late that night saying the men wanted to talk to him again. They had regrouped around the fire and were drinking rice beer. Khroussa now ruled that since Krick was a priest who wanted to stay in Tibet forever, his brother Kanigsa would escort him there. In return Krick was to leave two of his baskets in Khroussa's house in return for a pledge of two cows for them in a letter to Captain Smith that Khroussa would carry with him to Assam. It was a hard bargain but Father Krick agreed to the conditions, unmindful of everything else except the relief and gratitude that his journey was not over and the road to Tibet was still open.

Two weeks after leaving Chunpura Father Krick and his party crossed the hamlet of Hayuliang. It was an astounding feat for a foreigner. He was deep inside Mishmee territory, further than Wilcox and Burlton or any European had been on this route. But the achievement had come at a price. All the porters had demanded their pay and had gone back to Assam. Except for Kanigsa and a Khampti servant who had agreed to stay with Krick until they reached Tibet and carry his mailbag back to Assam, Krick's team was reduced to just a few men. Chowsa and he had parted ways in Khroussa's village. 'Now you have no need of me. Kanigsa will guide you,' Chowsa had told him, not revealing the real reason for his sudden decision to return to Assam with Khroussa. He had received a message from Kajinsha: 'Go back to Assam. I will need you there.' That was all that the message said. He had pondered this but other than an awareness of Zumsha's anger at their approach he could not make out what was happening in the hills near the Tibet border. In any case he was happy to leave.

He sincerely believed the priest would manage without him. There was an air of innocence about the man that disarmed strangers. He was also tremendously strong and determined. Chowsa was a devout Buddhist and he prayed that Kajinsha and chief Zumsha would stay their hand and let the priest pass unmolested. And maybe they would. Chowsa had heard all the chiefs talking about famine in the region—this would put pressure on everyone and tempers would flare, but on the other hand the clans would be too busy searching for food to expend energy in stalking a lonely priest. At worst someone might rob him of his baskets of rice. The last sight of Krick he had when he left the group was of a big white man in a crumpled shirt and muddy boots turning round and waving once before he disappeared into the jungle path that would lead him straight to the bleak mountains that marked the frontiers of Kajinsha's land.

◆

The last days of December were bitterly cold. In Hayuliang, Krick's escort Kanigsa had disappeared and more porters had decamped with a basket of rice and some presents that Krick was carrying in anticipation of his meeting with Tibetan authorities. All he had left now were his books, a blanket, his medicine box and a few other personal effects. On 30 December Krick met the Mishmee chiefs who were returning from Tibet. One of them was a small, dark man who looked askance at Krick. His name was Lamet. He pursed his lips and gave a military salute. 'Salam Sabe!' he said. The interminable arguments against his travelling to Tibet and negotiations for payment began again. So far Krick had resisted depression and defeat. He had overcome physical hardship and fatigue but now, step by step he was beginning to feel less willing to accommodate the depredations he was facing. 'How is it,' he shouted, 'that when you go to Assam the sahibs receive you well and give you presents? Yet when a sahib comes here you make his life miserable? Is this the way for a gambra—a chief, to behave? Shame on you! I will not give you anything. And I will go on my own!'

The men fell silent at this outburst. Krick turned away feeling he might have lost his chance of reaching Tibet. At last the one called Lamet said Krick could follow him. He would lead him to Tibet. It was an uneasy truce and Krick had no more illusions about the journey. He was hostage in an unknown wilderness where the tips of trees eclipsed the sun and he knew he could be facing death anytime. On the last day of the year as he prepared to continue his journey he wondered: Where will I be at the same time next year?

'Be very careful, Sabe,' his Khampti guide whispered to him. They were stooped against the wind on a high plateau overlooking the churning waters of a dark river far below. The man had a premonition that they might be attacked and killed in the night. He had heard some talk, he said. But Krick was too exhausted to pay any heed. The year had begun with a hard climb up the face of bare rock to reach this plateau and he was panting for breath. A man needed wings to travel in this country of precipices, he thought, sitting down heavily and looking around for Lamet. Two women appeared like ghosts and stood silently staring at them. One of them was Yenjee, who had, perhaps, come from Lamet's house. She pointed: 'Look! This is where the baba sabe was killed. Here, his body was thrown off from here.' She stamped her foot and moved her hands dramatically and laughed. Krick shuddered. From what little he could understand of the woman's words and wild gestures he guessed that this was the spot where Permanund Acharjya, an Indian fakir, and his servant had been murdered in 1848 while trying to make their way from Assam to Tibet. They said his body had been horribly mutilated and thrown into the abyss below. No one knew who had done it. A reward to find the culprits had received no response though it was claimed that Tibetan authorities had already found and punished the murderers.

He looked at the woman. Yenjee was still laughing but she stopped when she felt the priest's eyes on her. Her young face closed into a pale, inscrutable mask and as suddenly as they had appeared the two women turned around and melted away into the shadows. How strange, thought Krick, looking around to see where the women had disappeared. I have come to spread the good news of the holy gospel. Where are the people who will hear my words? The wind was blowing in his face and he felt a strong sense of danger. He could be murdered here. Look at the empty landscape! He looked around again for Lamet but there was no sign of the man.There was no one to protect him except his Khampti guide, but the man was more frightened than he, and Lorrain, the poor dog, crouched close to him as if he too was afraid of the chill wind that brought the scent of wolves, or maybe men. Ah, what does it matter? He thought, if death comes it will come. Does not God know my name and the motive of my journey? 'Into thy hands I commend my spirit Oh Lord!' He prayed.

At night they huddled close together and Krick tried to keep vigil staring at the outline of a black hill that seemed to draw closer and closer as his eyes drooped in fatigue.

◆

Tibet! The Mishmee Connection. Hunger

There are faces that you remember because you have looked at them for long, for a lifetime—a face in a photograph or in a picture on the wall, or the face of a friend whose eyes change colour as the light changes on a day of silent companionship. And there are faces that are memorable in an instant, striking you in a flash. These faces haunt you for the very reason that you know you may never see them again. There is only the most fleeting of glimpses, yet out of the hundreds of faces that you have seen, and will see later, this one stays with you, following your thoughts and dreams as if the wind, a strange wind that is always moving all around us and through all creation, had suddenly come to a halt in your heart and thrown down this image to be lodged in your memory forever.

This is was what happened when Gimur and the priest came face to face. She was sitting by the small stream nursing her baby who was about to fall asleep when she heard Awesa shouting. Bah! Awesa was always making a noise, she thought angrily. A loud whistle followed. Gimur got up and peeped through the trees. She saw a man passing by to stop and sit down on a fallen tree trunk. A stranger! For so many days Kajinsha had been talking of strangers heading towards them, this must be one of them! She held her breath, watching him. He was but a few metres away. She saw him pulling out a book from under a big hat. His head was bent and he held in his hand something that she recognised—a pencil! She was moving back slowly when the man suddenly looked up. Quick as a flash Gimur pressed her baby to her breast and faced the stranger with a hard stare, as if to dispel any harmful effect that his look might have on her child. It was a meeting they would both recall many times in the days ahead, and they would meet again, but now another piercing whistle from Awesa startled the man and gave Gimur the chance to turn around and flee.

'The strangers are here,' she told Kajinsha when she was back in the house.

'Yes,' he said, 'Zumsha told me. He sent Sosey and Khugum to warn me and stop the stranger, but I told them to let the man pass.'

If Gimur felt hurt that she had not been informed about this beforehand she did not show it. 'Who are they?' She asked

'The foreigner is a white priest. That is what Chowsa told me. But who knows? 'Maybe Lamet and Khroussa sent him here.'

'What does he want?'

'He wants to go to Tibet,' Kajinsha said. 'Everyone wants to go to Tibet and walk through our land to get there. They want to see us, you, me, our homes and our houses and...' He spread his arms taking in the valley and the hills, 'and they want to see all this... who knows what they want! What do you think?'

Gimur did not answer. She remembered the sight of the priest bent over his book. What had he been thinking at that moment? His face had been so quiet and intent as if he were about to fall asleep right there in the forest. Then she said, 'I think we should not talk to them. The moment we speak our breath leaves us and the strangers can take our hearts away with their words.'

Kajinsha nodded and made a clicking sound on his pipe. He smoked constantly these days and was silent and preoccupied. 'Is something wrong?' she asked him.

'No, what would be wrong?' he said, turning to look at her. Gimur said nothing. Instead she pressed the palms of her hands against her face and they stood together in silence looking down at the wooded valley. A pole tied with special leaves arched across the entry to their house warned any visitor that the household was observing taboos. The kambring had prescribed taboos that they were now about to complete at the end of more than six months. So much had happened since the last summer. Gimur was a changed woman. Her face was thinner and there were shadows around her eyes. Her hair, once worn straight and short just above her ear lobes, was now long and dressed in the style of the Kmaan women, except that she did not wear a silver bandeau but fastened it up in a loose coil with a long silver pin. The baby was sleeping inside. They had named him Siengbow after a legendary ancestor, but Kajinsha still shied away from holding him. Siengbow was always covered up in a blanket and once or twice when he had tried to remove the heavy clothing saying the child was too hot Gimur had snapped at him and pulled the clothes back from his hand. She had a silent and resolute manner, as if waiting for something, and it made Kajinsha frown, for he felt there was something hidden in her eyes. They were the same people, yes, standing together like this, but deep in his heart Kajinsha knew something had happened to their lives. A curtain had fallen between them.

He turned his gaze away. The wide, scooped-out valley below them now appeared more desolate than the deep ravine. It had been a bad year. Their crops had failed and many villages were living on wild yam and their last harvest of millet. This land of my ancestors was a place of ownership and rest, but now it is turning into empty space, he thought. And who was this man that they called a priest who was entering his land when they were all hungry and troubled like this? Kajinsha stared harder at the grove of pine trees along the edge of the ridge. It was the only way north and they would know if any stranger was passing through. Sure enough a frenzied barking of dogs announced the approach of strangers. There was a shout, more barking of dogs, someone whistled and the noise dwindled into half-hearted staccato barks that finally fell into a hush. Kajinsha's eyes narrowed. He could not see anyone. But in the valley below Krick was marching through the trees in a daze of wonderment.

After the terrible night spent on the cliff Krick had awoken, surprised to find that he was still alive. Maybe we are finally out of danger, he had thought. But that same evening they had been joined by two strangers. Two Mishmee men armed with long spears and swords had come up straight to their camp fire.

'Who are you?' he cried.

The men did not answer. One of them prodded Krick's satchel with the tip of his spear.

Krick felt a prickle of fear. 'Sabe, sabe, give them the bag, give them everything,' his guide was mumbling, but the sight of the guide's terror-stricken face roused Krick to snatch his rifle and jump to his feet shouting, 'Who are you? What do you want?'

At this moment Lamet had reappeared suddenly. He said something and the two men listened without saying a word, never taking their eyes off Krick. Then they had raised a hand, as if to say—'Well then, carry on with your journey,' and departed as silently as they had come.

Who were they? Krick sensed they were chief Zumsha's men sent to threaten him, but when he turned to Lamet and demanded to know, Lamet avoided the question. Instead he said, 'Look, sabe! Now you will see Tibetan villages.'

And it was true! Up ahead to their left Krick could see the top of a huge mountain, and Lorrain was running ahead, yelping, barking and wagging his tail as if expressing all that his master was feeling at that moment. After so many days of walking through dense forests where it was impossible for a man to contemplate anything except the narrow, vertiginous path ahead, the darkness was opening out into a fresh green grove of trees with a crystal-clear stream. The weather was mild, as it would be in the month of May in Europe, and most amazing of all, Krick saw tall, sturdy conifers, trees that he recognised! Where was he? For one breathless moment he was transported back to the forests of Lorrain. He was walking in the Vosges Mountains and chasing chamois in the valley! Suddenly he spied some black dots in the distance. Huts! 'It is a Tibetan village,' said Lamet. Tibet! He could not believe it. At last! Tibet! Tibet! He grabbed a stick and fashioning a cross planted it into the ground. He fell to his knees. To you, Lord, the first fruit of my joy! At this moment all his fears and doubts were swept away. He forgot the loneliness of the journey and the dangers he had faced.

If he had drawn his last breath in the Mishmee jungle his bitterest regret would have been that he had not set eyes on Tibet, but now, he thought, he would be happy to die here, in this very spot where he first heard the sweet words that he had reached Tibet!

On 5 January 1852 Krick was at the entrance of Oualong, a small village surrounded by sloping forests of pine and well cultivated fields dotted along the banks of a river. As he approached the first houses men and women peeped out and stared at him with their mouths open. Father Krick also stood agape, leaning on his rifle. How he longed to talk to them and share the joy welling up in his heart! But one by one everyone disappeared and suddenly he was alone. He waited, but there was no belated welcome. The admiration of the Oualongiens, Krick noted, seemed to have depleted faster than his. Only a few dogs barked, and then they were silent, too.

All along the way Krick had felt the presence of the Mishmee—they had argued, talked, walked together and surrounded him with threats of imminent attack, insult and robbery in the same way as they also gave him food and shelter and showed out the way to go north towards Tibet. Now it was as if he had been cast off. The pleasant valley he stood in was an empty and indifferent place. The people here had seen him, a stranger in their land, and they wanted nothing to do with him. Krick's spirits were suddenly low, but he had endured worse; he decided to trudge on along the path through the mountains that led, he had been told, to the village of Sommeu in the Zayul valley.

But not everyone was indifferent to his presence in the valley. If Krick had looked up he would have seen the top of a huge peak to his left where Kajinsha and Gimur were standing in silence. Time was still rolling its dice as the wind carried the sound of men's voices and the barking of dogs swirling up in faint echoes towards them.

'It will take the stranger two days to reach Sommeu. I will go there,' said Kajinsha.

Gimur leaned back. She knew that Kajinsha had let the priest pass so that he could follow him. 'Go, if you must,' she said. She would be happy to have a little time to herself. The taboos had kept her housebound but now she could go and sit by the stream. 'How many days will you be away?' she asked.

'I don't know. But I will carry only a few things,' he said.

'Will the priest stay in Sommeu forever?'

Kajinsha stopped to think. Sommeu was a quiet, sleepy village but recently, he had heard there had been frequent visits by the dzongpon, Tibetan officials who came from a place called Rima, a large town north-east of Sommeu. Kajinsha had travelled through Rima and he had seen the house of these officials. A dzongpon, he knew, was the head of an administrative unit called the dzong, but what he didn't know was that under the Qing dynasty this Tibetan system of dzongpon had been reformulated and brought under central government jurisdiction in the person of a resident Chinese representative of the Imperial court in Tibet with the title of Amban. A few years ago in 1843, the Amban in Tibet had pressurised the Tibetan regent to expel the French missionaries Évariste Huc and Joseph Gabet from Lassa and force them to return to Macao. It was Marpa, his first wife Auli's uncle, who had told him that the Zayul region was designated as a sub prefecture in the Manchu empire and that everything that happened in Rima and Sommeu was now under the authority of the the Amban.

'For us, what does it matter?' Kajinsha had thought at the time. 'We are people who belong to these valleys and rivers. We can wander at will travelling behind a wall of mist, find shelter with a friend, and disappear with the wind like invisible men who have no regard for boundaries laid down by any authority.' For Kajinsha and his people, and even the residents of Sommeu, empires and borders meant little. Their worlds could not be divided up, for they had lived in these lands for centuries, while empires had come and gone.

'We'll find out,' Kajinsha said to Gimur now. 'I will meet Marpa and ask him. He will know the government order from Rima.'

Early the next morning Kajinsha and Awesa set out to follow

Krick and the rest of his caravan into Sommeu. Both of them carried their tapai–satchel that Gimur had filled with maize and pieces of fresh yam. In addition to this, Awesa carried a bearskin pouch filled with bundles of roots of manjeet madder dye and medicinal coptis teeta. For all purposes they were going into Tibet as traders. The moment they reached Sommeu, Kajinsha and Awesa were caught up in a milling crowd of excited people. They had arrived just in time. Kajinsha saw the stranger standing in the middle of the narrow street surrounded by a group of bold, rosy-cheeked women.

The priest was enjoying a reception markedly different from the one he had experienced in Oualong. Warned of his approach the villagers of Sommeu had poured out of their homes to look at the stranger. Someone screamed. A dog barked. He said something in his language and the women responded with loud giggles. Their hands delved into his pockets, they touched his hair, his clothes, admired his beard and examined him from head to toe. The man submitted good-naturedly and when a big dog confused by the commotion tried to fling itself at the stranger Kajinsha watched in amazement as the man leapt on to the ledge of a building, hung in the air for a second and clambered up on hands and feet onto the balcony of a small house. This delighted everyone. Awesa clapped his hands and an old woman shouted for everyone to treat the stranger with respect. Kajinsha looked around to see who else was accompanying the priest. He had information that Lamet was with him, but he saw only Krick's guide hurrying away from this commotion. Lamet must have turned back from Oualong, he thought. A man in a red woollen jacket appeared with a pitcher of tzu—beer and when the stranger drank it in one long gulp everyone surged forward to see this wonderful, brave stranger who had appeared in their midst like someone from the moon and whose beaming face and manner gave every indication that he was prepared to share everything and refuse nothing.

Kajinsha was a silent onlooker, watching everything. His eyes were moving over this happy scene when he saw Marpa pressed up against the wall of a house. Their eyes met and the expression on Marpa's face said that they should meet, somewhere away from this street full of people. The two men moved with the crowd, walking apart like strangers until their steps converged when the priest was led away into the house of one of Marpa's friends and they walked on, straight to Awesa's mother, Auli's house. No one was in the house when they entered but a fire was burning in the iron stove. Marpa pointed to the room at the top and made a gesture for silence. He walked towards the table at the kitchen end of the big barn-like room piled with blankets and saddlery equipment and sat down. Someone had placed a tall jug of tzu on the table and strips of roasted meat on a plate. A half-open container in the centre was full of flattened, dried maize. It must be Chhomu, thought Kajinsha, wondering if she was in the house, but the door of her room at the end of the kitchen was shut fast.

'Everyone is running to see this stranger,' said Marpa. He placed his prayer beads carefully on the table, lifted the jug and poured tzu into two cups, all the while letting his eyes drift lazily around the room. He pushed a cup towards Kajinsha and said, 'Who is he?'

Kajinsha frowned. 'Are you asking me about the man they call priest?'

'Yes. Why has he come here?'

'Why? Why are you asking me? I don't know anything about him.'

'I thought he was following you. You know, since you came back with the Abor woman... Now maybe you've brought this man,' said Marpa. He was hunched forward across the table with a conspiratorial look in his eyes.

'What!' Kajinsha almost jumped up in disbelief. '*I* am the one who's following him,' he cried. 'How do I know where he came from or why he's here? He may have come following the route I travel but it was not I who showed him the way!'

'Oh Kajinsha, kisiro, my friend, please don't be offended,' said Marpa. 'I was only thinking of what is happening now and wondering…' He looked down at the cup in his hand and sloshed the thick tzu round and round. Then he said, 'Just between you and me, do you think he's following the woman?'

'Who? What…?' Suddenly Kajinsha realised the meaning of Marpa's words. 'What woman?' he shouted. 'She's my wife! The Abor woman is my wife and you know it!' Kajinsha slapped his hand down hard on the table.

'I know, I know. She's a fine woman. I'm not saying anything against her, please don't misunderstand me. But do you remember the time the Abor helped the British? I was only thinking of that,' said Marpa, leaning back and raising his hands as if everything he was saying was a simple matter of history and common knowledge. He looked calm, resplendent in a blue brocade jacket with his black plaited hair and turquoise earrings dangling from his ears. The man was slippery as a fish, thought Kajinsha, remembering the time of his father's death. Yes, it was the war against the British that had killed him and what Marpa said about the Abor was true. In 1839 they had helped the besieged British garrison in Suddya, but it was a few men, not the entire Abor tribe.

'Don't tell me what to remember and what to forget,' he said, leaning forward towards Marpa. The firelight threw strange shadows on the wall and the two men stared at one another, Kajinsha's eyes glowing with anger and Marpa's half shut and impenetrable.

'That is all right. Don't be angry, my friend,' Marpa said softly. 'I trust you.' He stood up and began tightening his waistband, carefully adjusting the knot of his sash and taking his time over it. 'Your father made peace with us and gave his word that your people would not let strangers enter this valley. Now a white man is here and he says he's a holy man, hah ha! A lama guru!' He dropped his voice and added, 'It is the authorities I'm worried about. They will be angry if they come to know that the Mishmee have broken our agreement. Ah...poor man, your father,' he sighed, 'we hope you will continue in his footsteps.'

Kajinsha stared at him. He would have liked to throw this man out of the house. 'How dare he talk to me like this,' he thought, 'this man who is a thief and a liar, carrying prayer beads to hide his wicked heart!' But Marpa had followers and he was in charge of the Zayul-Sommeu villagers. If Kajinsha provoked him it could bring war on their heads. Gimur would not be safe and the priest—he did not care about the priest, he could be killed easily by anyone and his body thrown into the jungle... who would find it there? But a war on the border would shatter the dream of peace that his father had cherished. It was something Kajinsha could not afford at the moment.

'I will keep an eye on him,' he said. 'But if he is a man of God then you, lama guru, should know better about such things.'

'We'll all play our part,' said Marpa, putting on his hat and picking up his prayer beads. 'Stay here. We'll meet again and find out about this man.'

After Marpa left Kajinsha sat alone in the room thinking of the conversation they had just had. He heard soft, shuffling sounds above him and wondered if Awesa's mother was awake and listening. He realised he had lost Awesa in the crowd, but it was no cause for worry. The boy would turn up, and even if he didn't, Kajinsha knew Awesa would always find a bed somewhere and be content. He poured himself more tzu. How tired he was! He remembered the days when he used to travel with his father as a boy, when he first met Marpa, here in this village. 'Your Marpa pong,' his father had said. Uncle Marpa. But everyone knew him as Marpa the Brokpa, a reference to his work as a herder of yak and sheep. They had stayed in this house a few times and Marpa had brought them salt and woollen cloth in exchange for the musk pods that they brought. 'It is very good, very good,' he would say, his eyes lighting up as he tenderly scooped up the dark, purplish pieces and tucked them away into the folds of his robes. They were the size of a walnut and weighed almost nothing. 'But they are more precious than gold,' Marpa had said. 'It is strong medicine and everyone wants them in China!' Kajinsha's father had been one of the few who could hunt and trap the elusive tlah, the musk deer, and as a boy Kajinsha had helped his father dry the sacs in the sun, sometimes placing them on a warm stone until they were shrivelled. The pods had an indescribable scent that Kajinsha was to forever associate with those days spent with his father.

It lingered, even now, Kajinsha thought, in the beams of his house, in a sudden draught of cold wind from the mountains. A faint whiff still clung to the air in this house. In later years his father began to spend more and more time in the mountains. Sometimes he took Kajinsha, but most of the time he went alone. He was gone for many days and these were the times when Kajinsha thought his father had left the village, that he did not want to be a leader of men but wanted to lead a quiet life in the mountains he loved. One day Kajinsha's father told him, 'Marpa pong has made an offer for you to marry his niece. I told him I would tell you and then we will decide. But not now. Later, later. There are many girls in our own village for you to marry. In the meantime wear this,' he had said, removing his necklace of a single white tooth of the shy deer that he hunted, and putting it around Kajinsha's neck. Then he had smiled and hugged Kajinsha. These were the vivid moments Kajinsha remembered of the short, happy days spent with his father.

It was only after his father died that Kajinsha found out what his father had been trying to escape. Since the time he became the head of his clan Kajinsha had faced many challenges, but the biggest of them all was claim over land. It was a problem that neither he nor the head of any other clan could resolve. In Kajinsha's father's time there had been no villages in this valley. It had been a beautiful, open stretch of land with clear streams and forests of reed bamboo and rhododendron and dark swathes of pine forest covering the high peaks. Beyond this were snow-covered passes and frozen lakes—the territory of wolves, of the snow leopard, the musk deer and the heavy, surefooted mishmee takin who seldom trespassed into the territory of men. Only men did not honour territorial claims. The trespassers were the nomadic Brokpa herdsmen who wandered across borders in search of grazing ground. They slept in the open, in tents in the high pastures. In winter they came into the valley bringing their tents, their pots and pans and their cattle, accompanied by guard dogs, the ferocious Tibetan mastiff of which breed it was said that they had four eyes because of the distinct brown spot over each eye.

Kajinsha had seen Brokpa camps in the hills around the valley but they always drifted away in the spring. It was the settlers who followed in their trail that posed a threat as they began to stake claims to land. As more and more of them arrived there had been a flashpoint when the Mishmee attacked them. It was a fight for land. 'Land is a place of ownership and rest,' Kajinsha's father had said over and over again. 'If a man clears the forest and builds a house and harvests his fields the land belongs to him. If a man owns land he owns rest. He can live his life with nothing to worry about. He can plant crops and fish in the river, and he can raise his sons and daughters and live on from generation to generation.'

Ownership and rest. These were the words Kajinsha recalled now. There was ownership because Kajinsha's father and his clan brothers had fought so hard to win this land. But there had been no rest. People eyed each other with suspicion and fear and this was what Kajinsha now thought his father had been running away from.

His father had been tired. He was looking for peace and friendship when he made a compromise with the Tibetan settlers of Zayul in the north. But if he had bought a tenuous peace he had been unable to remove the age-old feuds in the region. The border was never settled. Maybe, Kajinsha thought, his father had known something that was only now beginning to dawn on him. This wedge of land that he had so passionately defended was impossible to defend. The land had a heart of its own, a voice and language that beckoned men. Otherwise why would strangers like the white priest come here, pushing across mountains and rivers, when all the signs were there that they were not welcome? When strangers like the British explorers had first appeared the people of Zayul depended on the Mishmee, people like his father, to turn them away. This they had done, but nothing could stem the approach of these strangers. Instead, a rift had been created among the Mishmee, with some families willing to aid the white man for salt and money, while others spurned their offers, until open hostility broke out between brothers. The alliance with the Tibetans had also become a trap because his people were now in the frontline of border defence for Tibetan territory, while Tibetan settlers moved closer and closer into Mishmee lands.

When Kajinsha's father stopped hunting and went away into the hills Marpa had cried, 'Oh! What a pity! He is turning into a woman, hah! Hah!' A rumour spread that his father was losing his power. They called him eunuch; a man who had turned into an effeminate being and had lain down his weapons to collect wild herbs instead, pretending he could cure the sick and even see the future. Yet his father had gone to fight in the Khampti rebellion against the superior force of the British when no one else had responded to the Khampti call for help. In the end it was what had killed him, thought Kajinsha—that desire to keep ownership of his land and live in these high valleys free of strangers.

It was the sight of his father dying that had stiffened Kajinsha's resolve; that and the moment when Marpa had come to their village and cried, 'Poor man, poor man!' Kajinsha had vowed he would bury the slur on his father's name by inflicting such wrath on his enemies as they had never experienced. He would burn their houses to the ground and take men and women as slaves. This anger had turned him into the ruthless and feared chief that he had become.

And it was his pursuit of power, his desire to be a stronger and more successful chief that had been the reason why he had agreed to marry Marpa's niece, his first wife, whose family had travelled down from the interiors of Tibet to settle in the Zayul valley. In her house now, his mind went back to the past. I took this woman, the sick woman lying upstairs, not for love but to keep my father's pact with her people, Kajinsha thought. In the beginning it had helped him rise to power among the different Mishmee chiefs because with the support of the Tibetans he held the route to Tibet, and it was an important trading route. But it had been a joyless union, everyone could see that. Even Marpa, who had pressed for the union, avoided mention of the sick woman in Kajinsha's presence. Instead he had sometimes hinted that Kajinsha should take another wife, but Kajinsha had vowed never to let Marpa trap him into another liaison. It did not prevent Marpa now from talking as if it was his, Kajinsha's fault that a white stranger—a kla kamphlung!—had found his way into this valley. That he could be suspected of this astonished Kajinsha, even more than it angered him. What did he care about these strangers, priest or soldier or Brokpa herdsmen?

What did he care about lands beyond his own? All he wanted was his life, his life with Gimur and their newborn son. He had his house and his fields. It was his piece of earth and that was that. He would live and die where his house stood on the black hill, where his life was his own and where a man could fall asleep at night without guilt or fear.

He put a horse blanket on the bench and was just settling down when the door opened and a blast of cold air swept into the room. It was Chhomu, followed by Awesa and a red-faced youth. They were talking loudly and laughing but when they saw Kajinsha they stopped. He could still see the vapour escaping from their mouths as they stood rubbing their hands and breathing hard. He waved as if to say, don't mind me, carry on. Chhomu walked quickly to her room followed closely by Awesa and his friend. The door shut with a bang but in a moment Chhomu was out again asking him if he needed anything. She kept her face down. Kajinsha shook his head. The girl left, her head still bent, and went up the stairs.

A few paces down the road, Krick was caught up in the new impressions assailing him from every direction. His host, Norbu, was a big, beefy man whose red woollen robe made Krick mistake him for a lama, but Norbu was a merchant-tax collector. He offered the priest a meal of rice and a red chilli sauce mixed with cheese in a wooden bowl. Krick had finished three mugs of salty butter tea when a loud bark from Lorrain waiting outside reminded him that that he had to think of shelter for the night. Norbu appeared to be an affable man and his house was busy as a wayside inn with people coming in and going out, every visitor helped himself to mugs of tea from huge kettles that were constantly filled by the lady of the house. Krick seized the opportunity to step out quickly and returned with his baskets and Lorrain in tow. If his host was surprised he did not show it. No one said anything and he settled into a corner of the room. Here he would stay, he thought, until… until what? He did not know, but for the first time after days of struggle and deprivation he felt at peace.

After the excitement of his arrival had died down Krick took the opportunity to take long walks through groves of conifers and small cultivated fields that formed a natural border along the river. When he passed an isolated house an old man invited him in and offered him a meal of red rice and hard cheese. How kind and simple they are! he thought. A young woman with a baby smiled when he proffered a blessing and he was suddenly reminded of the woman he had seen in the forest on his way here, that white face with the tattoo on the middle of her upper lip. Where did she live? Maybe she was here in this village, but of all the faces that he had seen here there was none with a tattoo. Who was she? He found that the Tibetan he had learned in Paris was of little use here. The people spoke a local variant of the language with a different intonation.

Norbu agreed to teach him and Krick kept his Tibetan grammar book with him all the time and also started a phonetic dictionary. He conversed in Tibetan with Norbu who always responded with a hearty laugh. He was a kind man and Krick was impressed by his pious Buddhist nature for he saw him lift his arms, bend his knees and prostrate himself in prayer every night before he went to bed. They exchanged gifts. Norbu offered him food, and some nuts and raisins, and Krick gave him a lock, a spoon and some thread and needles.

The days passed. Krick had been in Sommeu almost a month when one morning he was awakened by a great din above which could be heard the sound of hoof beats ringing on the stony street. 'The dzongpon! The governor is here! The governor is here!' Norbu was tugging at his sleeve. 'Come! Quickly!'

There was no time to dress. Krick pulled on his cardigan and went to meet the governor. He saw a tall Tibetan official whom he recognised as the visitor who had come to Sommeu a few days ago and interrogated him. Then he saw a man seated on a carpet spread over a stool set to look like a pedestal. He was the dzongpon who had come from Rima. A low wooden table with two bowls of rice and maize was placed before him.

'He is a very important man. His voice is like thunder and his words strike like lightning,' Norbu whispered breathlessly into his ear. 'He has the power to cut off the hands and the legs of criminals and liars.'

A crowd had swarmed into the tiny room and among them were Kajinsha and Marpa. Norbu was in charge of the meeting and a Singpho douania, a slave of mixed parentage stood at attention to translate the words of the priest who was speaking in a mixture of Assamese and Tibetan.

Kajinsha stood back and watched as the priest was pushed forward to face the governor. Father Krick bowed three times. The governor responded with a surprised smile and looked around at the audience. Then he leaned forward.

'What is your name?'

'Nicolas Michel Krick. Missionaire.'

'Where are you from? What is the name of your desch?'

'The name of my country is France. My village is Lixheim en Lorrain, department de la Meurthe, arrondisement de Sarrebourg, canton de Phalsbourg…'

Krick's words and accent were unfamiliar and the governor turned many times to the Singpho interpreter and shouted, 'Katchire? Katchire?' as if he were hard of hearing. 'Are you a soldier? Who sent you? Why have you come here?' In his frustration the governor rapped out his words like bullets and a tremor passed over the crowd as they pressed forward straining to hear the priest's reply.

'No. I am a priest, a lama,' the man was saying. 'I am a man of religion. I am not British. I am French.' Krick was speaking very slowly and loudly, enunciating every word carefully and kept repeating the word 'lama'.

The crowd fell back with a sigh. A lama guru! They could understand that. There was excited murmuring but the governor had not completed his interrogation. He wanted to know if the priest's country was great, and what the name of his king was.

'Louis-Napoléon,' said the priest.

'Ah! Lou-ee Na-mp-o-l-e –o-ne…' Everyone tried to repeat the name.

But why, asked the governor, had he chosen to come here and not go to another country?

'Because I heard that you are a religious people,' replied the priest.

'And who told you that?' The governor leaned forward a little.

'Another lama guru in Tibet, who stayed in Lassa and met your Regent.'

'Aah…' A thin smile gleamed in the governor's eyes as he looked around the room. 'Do you have a wife and children?' he asked.

'No, I am a lama.'

'Ah, yes, yes. You will stay here a year or two and then go back to Assam?'

'No, I will stay here until I die,' said the priest. There was a gasp of consternation at this reply. The governor's eyes flicked over the rapt faces turned towards him and then he cried out, 'Hah! Then you must be a criminal! You have done something bad in your country and you are running away to hide here!'

'No, no, I have done nothing wrong.' Kajinsha saw the priest shaking his head and making a gesture of writing something, but his voice was now lost in a rising din of voices.

'Do you have money? How will you stay here?' The governor shouted.

'No, I have nothing. But I pray that I will be granted the hospitality of the Tibetans. And,' the priest raised his voice now, 'if this is too much, then I beg to take refuge in a monastery of lamas!'

There was a pause after this exchange and the meeting ended abruptly as the governor called for tea. Kajinsha saw the priest looking about him. Norbu was fending off the excited throng with

Mamang Dai

short jabs and punches and signalling to the priest to come forward. He whispered something in his ear. He must be asking the priest to give something to the governor, thought Kajinsha. He noticed Marpa looking for him and stepped back, pushing his way out into the street. He had no wish to be seen by anyone, not yet. It was bitterly cold outside and he pressed himself against the wall and stood waiting by the door. He heard someone saying, 'The dzongpon is asking him to leave!' Then he heard the priest protesting and the loud voice of the governor saying: 'You will go back! Now the time is not good. There is war and fighting. Stay in the village of the Mishmee and I will let you return when the time is right. I will give you food and my seal of protection. The meeting is closed.'

The next Mishmee village… thought Kajinsha. That is at my doorstep. And what kind of fighting did the governor mean? Perhaps there was war in the country beyond but here everything was peaceful. He moved aside as the crowd came pouring out and made way for the governor who was followed by Norbu carrying the presents of a piece of Assamese muga silk, a pen stand and some steel nibs, a music box, a cotton umbrella and a bottle of tzi—wine from the priest's country. The horses were ready and the entourage cantered off. Fearing for the fate of his dog Lorrain, who was starving, the priest had also presented him to the governor, but the poor dog was twisting and pulling back while Norbu whistled and tried to push him along until Marpa lifted the dog bodily and ran after the departing men followed by the rowdy cheers of the onlookers.

'Thank God that is over,' said Marpa when he returned, sweating after his exertion. The town was quiet again. They were sitting by the big stove and Kajinsha was wondering what the fate of the priest would be now.

'Let him find his own way,' said Marpa. 'He will retrace his steps and go back to Assam. The governor was being diplomatic.

You watch there will be no return for him.'

The two men were silent. Marpa pointed to the room upstairs. 'Now we have to think of the puja for the village, he said, and the ritual for Awesa's mother.' 'A gelong—lama will be here in a few days.' His voice was dropping lower and lower. 'I have something to say to you,' he continued. 'I was thinking of Awesa. He's your firstborn. Now your Abor wife has borne you a son. It is the will of God if a child is born weak, but he's your son. I am not saying anything...' Marpa drew his hand across his mouth and dropped his eyes.

'My son is healthy,' said Kajinsha. He let his eyes travel slowly across the room until they rested on Marpa's face. 'I know what I have and what I want. Do not advise me on these things.'

'I know, I know. My dear friend, I was only going to suggest something. You must be feeling it too, sometimes,' he coughed softly covering his mouth with his hands. 'You should have more sons,' he said. 'Awesa's mother is sick, but her sister...' he stopped and Kajinsha felt his heart jump. What was Marpa saying? He pretended not to hear. 'Her sister is young and healthy,' Marpa continued with his proposal. 'Take her. She is a beautiful woman. Everyone will be happy. What is a man without sons?' Marpa looked up slowly but Kajinsha dared not meet his eyes. He had heard these insinuating words of Marpa's so many times since his first wife's illness and Awesa's birth that sometimes he thought they were his own words. From far away he thought he could hear thunder rumbling across the sky but the house was empty and still, like a house of the dead. Was anyone listening? Why was the fire flaring up as if a gust of wind had blown in? Marpa's words hung in the air.

'In a day I will be returning to my village,' said Kajinsha.

'Oh no! Stay a while,' said Marpa, deftly changing his manner. 'The priest will be here and we have to watch him while Norbu is away. You must also take action and drive the stranger out.'

'I will, I will,' said Kajinsha, eager to change the subject and close the conversation.

A broad smile creased Marpa's face. 'Ah, my friend,' he cried. 'Let us drink!'

Sometime during the night Kajinsha woke up and lay still wondering if he was still asleep and dreaming or awake. A heavy silence surrounded him and he felt the weight of the blanket pressing down on him. He tried to shake himself out of sleep. He saw the fire burning and when he wiped his eyes he thought the flame was a red cloth bending and twisting like a woman's garment. It burned silently and he was aware of a heavy scent slowly permeating everything. What time was it? A dizzy sensation made him close his eyes again. Where was everyone? Marpa had plied him with too much wine. His throat felt dry and parched. As he tried to get up his foot touched something. What was that? His gaze fell on a sleeping form. Slowly, hardly daring to breathe, he realised it was the girl Chhomu. Why was she here? He sat up and looked all around the room, perplexed. Perhaps someone was sleeping in her room. But who? And she generally slept upstairs, with her sister. He looked towards her door and saw it was fastened from the outside. The front door was also bolted. Where was Marpa? When had he left? He could not remember anything.

He placed his hand on the girl to wake her up. She sat up with a start. Kajinsha moved back. She stared at him and drew the blanket up around her shoulders. Her hair was undone and her mouth was open in surprise but she made no sound. He was equally silent, his eyes fixed on her. Then she seemed to smile with half closed eyes and tilting her head back she slithered down, as he bent forward with his face closing down on hers. It seemed he was reeling under fumes of opium. He slipped off the bench and clasped her tightly around the waist. He thought she was naked under the blanket but now his hands were tearing madly at her woollen dress and pulling her blouse down. Her breasts were round and white. They were struggling in silence and breathing hard. He thought someone was watching them. Perhaps Marpa was upstairs, or his wife was listening, but he did not care. Instead, the thought inflamed his lust and he wanted to wallow in this creature and rock her soft white body under him back and forth like this forever. He took her roughly, pressing her down on the mud floor. When she uttered a grunt and he saw her mouth contorted, baring her small white teeth, a sensation such as he had never felt before made him want to cry out like an animal. Was he drunk? Had someone poisoned him with a powerful drug? His body was trembling and he did not know how long he held her as she lifted and swayed with him. It is a fire, he thought. A fire, hissing and breathing and bruising his arms and entering his belly, heating his loins and streaking this creature beneath him with moisture and warmth. Every breath filled his lungs with the fire until he was blind and everything erupted into a sweet, unbearable pain as he fell away into a deep, velvet darkness.

When he opened his eyes again it was light. A yellowish glow was shining on the dark walls of the hut. What had happened to him? A wave of dizziness made him close his eyes again. Aah… He turned his head slowly and peered down over the edge of the bench but the floor was empty. Everything was peaceful. Day was breaking and a new, soft fire was burning in the hearth. His thirst had returned and with it a craving to eat something sweet, anything, like a piece of jaggery or a handful of sweet, fermented rice. He walked to the table and gulped water from the jug. He saw the door of the girl's room was open and he peeped inside but no one was there. A sound upstairs caught his attention and he climbed up the stairs calling out loudly, 'Anyone in this house? Where is everybody?' There was no answer but the door was open and Awesa's mother was sitting by the window dressed in a black gown and combing her hair. She was alone. Her cheeks were flushed when she turned to him.

'I am getting ready to meet the gelong,' she said in a loud, unnatural voice.

Hai! He had forgotten about the lama's visit. But he thought that was still a few days away. How strange! He must have miscalculated his stay in Sommeu. 'Is it today?' he asked.

'Yes, it is today,' she replied.

'Then I must go. I have not seen Awesa. Tell him I've left,' he said and, turning abruptly, left the house.

The cold air revived him. How long had he been asleep? He shook his head and looked up and down the street. He saw a black dog running towards him and suddenly recognised it as the same dog that the priest had given Norbu to carry away as a gift for the governor. Hah! The dog was back. Good for him! He whistled and stretched out his hand but Lorrain was making straight for Norbu's house. What instinct, thought Kajinsa. Following the dog towards the house, he pushed the door open and left it ajar for the dog to slip in.

'Hah! There you are,' cried Marpa. He was standing near the fire and stirring something in a big pot. 'Welcome, my friend. Come in, come in!'

The place was already crowded with people and there was barely room to move. Kajinsha saw the girl Chhomu at the far end behind Marpa churning butter tea with a group of women. He pushed his way forward and Marpa handed him a mug of tea. 'Here, here, come, kisiro, you must be thirsty…' These words were said with the utmost friendliness, and there was nothing in Marpa's face and manner to indicate anything but affection. Kajinsha realised that he would never be able to find out whether this wily man knew anything about what had happened between him and the girl.

So be it, he thought. He did not feel shame or regret. But looking at the people and Marpa's face and the girl who was working silently with her head bent, he wanted to get away from this place.

It is a bad place, he thought. It is a trap. What has happened is over. There is nothing to it. I must get back to my house and to Gimur.

'Stay, stay,' cried Marpa. 'Attention everyone, the gelong will be here any moment!'

There was a loud boom and the room reverberated with the sound of a drum. 'He is here! The gelong is here!' There was a mad scramble for the door and in the melee Kajinsha and the priest were pressed against one another, he with his sunburnt face staring at the eager, white face of the priest. A look of recognition seemed to pass across the priest's face. Hah, he has walked through my territory and recognises a Mishmee, thought Kajinsha. They were standing shoulder to shoulder and the thought flashed through his mind that in a way they were both strangers in the land of the lama. He was a Kmaan in the southeastern tip of Tibet and the priest was a stranger who was but a few paces inside the same vast country. He was far away from Assam and his homeland and Lassa too, for here people only knew of Rima, and Rima was but a provincial capital lost in the basin of towering mountains.

What colour are those eyes? Kajinsha wondered, as he caught the priest's tentative smile. He was startled to see that the man was maybe the same age as him. He looked old because of his clothes, his manner and his voice, and because he was a stranger! And he looked thin and shrivelled, as if he was ill.

'Make way! Make way!' Someone shouted and the two were pushed forward as the crowd parted and the lama was led into the room with a great fanfare of drums, hand bells, the horn flute and cymbals. Marpa was bowing low and leading the man to his seat. The room began to rock and sway as inch by inch the crowd rolled forward like a wave longing to reach the feet of the holy man. The lama adjusted his flowing robes and faced the crowd. In the deep silence that followed the lama breathed words that made the audience gasp. Some women had tears in their eyes. They placed bags of corn and rice before him and the lama laid his hand on their heads while his fingers moved rapidly over his prayer beads.

For Krick it was a great opportunity to actually witness something that he had only read about in accounts that drew ritualistic affinities between the catholic religion and the religion of Tibet. He watched the ceremony intently, but he saw nothing here to make him believe this. The lama's prayer beads could, perhaps, be compared to a rosary, and the chanting construed as the equivalent of ten Hail Marys, but for Krick these seemed more like exorcism spells to cast out unseen sorcerers and house demons. The words rose and fell in a long litany that turned into an aggressive murmur as the lama chanted louder and louder to provoke a burst of emotion amongst the audience. Krick had never seen the people of Sommeu so animated. A bright light was burning in the eyes of all the onlookers. Such is the nature of faith, he pondered. The longing to believe is our desire! Every creature of God wanted to yield to logic and reason to understand the riddles of life and find happiness, he thought. But reason had no explanation for an incurable longing, for the mystical passion to unite with the divine and say 'I believe!' Such things could only be understood through magic and constant prayer. This was the impact of the lama and the magical properties of his cure that consoled the poor and the desolate.

Kajinsha also watched the scene of faith and devotion; he saw Awesa's mother prostrate herself before the lama and clasp his hands. Kajinsha did not move when the crowd rushed out and fired rifles to accompany the sacrifice of a calf. The meat was cooked with rice and everyone was offered a portion of this meal. Kajinsha saw that the white priest refused his share, though he accepted two small statuettes made of wheat and butter that were venerated as sacred objects. 'I must get away from here,' he thought, 'before the house ritual start for Awesa's mother. Awesa could stay or leave but I must go now. He was pushing his way out when Marpa caught up with him. 'Oh, stay, stay,' he begged. 'It will be a final ritual. The gelong may not come this way again and it will be worthwhile to stay and see his performance.'

'I know what the gelong will do,' said Kajinsha. 'You can take care of it. I have other business.'

He felt his spirits lift as he set out. It was already dark but Kajinsha felt prepared to walk all night to reach home. His return was overdue, but it was not so far, just over the spur of the mountain and across the river. He walked alone. He had not found Awesa. Where could the boy be? His mind was still full of the images of the past few days and he felt he could see everything happening in that village as if he were still there. The thin face of the priest huddled in a corner rose up before him. After the novelty has worn off no one cares for a stranger, he thought. Life was hard and no one had time or food for another person. It was the middle of a bleak winter and the stranger was a speck who had suddenly fallen into their midst. Worse luck for him, thought Kajinsha. But he felt a twinge of anger at Marpa who he knew would spitefully starve the man. Since Norbu had left with the provincial governor it had fallen on Marpa to run his house. Kajinsha knew Norbu was a religious man but Marpa, he was different. Marpa had political ambitions. He would not hesitate to starve the man to death if he knew it would please his Tibetan or Chinese masters. Kajinsha had seen the priest gulping down a bowl of watery rice and looking around furtively to see if there would be anything more. Once Kajinsha had seen the priest heading towards the stream and followed him. He had caught a glimpse of his body, white like a fish, and covered in fleabites.

That is our life here, he had thought. Hunger, danger, solitude, and the man should have known that, but still, he wished Marpa would give the man proper rations until Norbu returned. Right now the man was living on crumbs. He spoke very little and since his Tibetan grammar book had been taken away during the governor's visit he wrote words in a book that he kept under his hat. Some people said that these were religious words that protected the priest from evil and Kajinsha had seen some men and women bowing down before the stranger asking him to place the book on their heads and bless them. A cold wind was beginning to blow and Kajinsha walked faster. He did not know what he would tell Gimur about the priest and all the things he had seen in Sommeu. And about the strange night with that girl—no, there was nothing he could say about that, but there were other things. Deep in his heart he had been saving some words for Gimur about how they, the two of them, should be happy together again like before. He did not know if he would say them, but the important thing seemed to be to reach home as soon as possible. Then everything will be alright, he thought, forgetting for a moment about the wind that was always blowing and watching from the tops of trees, waiting to test him and all men, at some time or other.

◆

The Weight of a Stone. The Music of Heaven and Earth

In the house Gimur was awake, sitting by the fire. She was remembering a story she had heard a long time ago—about a young bride who was leaving her parents' home to attend her marriage feast. She was dressed in all her finery and everyone was waiting for her. On the way the girl saw a big stone and sat down to rest. The sun blazed in the sky. By evening the girl still had not arrived at the groom's house and a search party was sent out. The road was empty. No one had seen anything. Then a famous shaman said that the girl had been swallowed by a stone. Some people said they had never seen a stone lying on that road. Others swore that they had seen a big stone. They went to look. The stone, if there had ever been one, had rolled away. The young bride was never seen again. It was a story Gimur had heard in her childhood. It had happened a long time ago but everyone still believed it. But why did this story come to her now, she wondered, what did it mean? The shaman said that once upon a time rocks were living, malleable beings. They were soft like dough; they could change shape and migrate from one place to another. Sometimes they rolled right up to your doorstep and stayed there resting, waiting…

Some things were hard to understand, the signs difficult to read. For some days now a vague anxiety had wrapped itself around Gimur like a thin mist. Tonight, she thought, she could feel the weight of that stone as she listened to the wind and stared at the fire. Fire, flames, white light blazing! She knew something had happened. She had known it the moment she had seen Awesa coming back to the house late the other night. Why was Kajinsha not back with him? What was keeping him in that village, and if he was delayed why had he not sent word with Awesa?

'Where is your father?' she had asked. And Awesa had stopped, startled. In a flash she had guessed that the boy knew something. But Awesa would never tell her. Instead he had mumbled something about a priest and rushed away from her. Miserable idiot! She had shouted at him.

Her heart was beating very fast. Curiously her thoughts were slowing down—thump, thump. Everything was slowing down, all the memories, all the words, slowing down into a single thought goaded by her intuition that Kajinsha was with Awesa's mother and that everyone knew he was still bound to her and not to her, Gimur, the outsider.

It was a thought that had been eating into her ever since the birth of Siengbow and the death of her other son. She was still a stranger here and she knew the only way to seal her marital status with Kajinsha was to bear his child again—a healthy child, a boy. In such matters society was implacable. No child, no acceptance. This was the pulse of destiny, the ceaseless agitation of birth and death that rested on one thing—the birth of a son. Her surviving son was born with a birth defect that made him unable to walk. It was a fit case for a man to marry again. If a man had no son his life was doomed. He was an object of pity since his bloodline was already ended with no one to keep his memory alive by performing rituals that only a son could do for his father. So far, Gimur thought, her husband had never given her cause for doubt. Kajinsha was an aloof, serious man. Sometimes he was reserved and undemonstrative, even with her. He did not talk of women like the other men who took many wives and bragged about it. But then, who was to know for certain? In her present mood Gimur doubted everything.

Her thoughts went back to her first visit to Sommeu… Kajinsha might have bonds and relationships that she knew nothing about. Men were cunning that way. She recalled the face of Auli as she had lain on the bed… No, the woman was too ill and angry. She could not be a threat. Kajinsha had told her Marpa had made the alliance… And now her thoughts flew to Marpa, she had but glimpsed him briefly—the man with the fur hat and Tibetan boots. What kind of man was he? 'He is cunning,' Kajinsha had told her. But Kajinsha still seemed to be under his sway. She remembered the darkness of the house, its oppressive air—and suddenly the face of Chhomu standing aside for her at the foot of the stairs flashed into her head. Auli's younger sister!

A slow heat suffused Gimur as she remembered the girl's braided hair and her fresh complexion. Why had Kajinsha not introduced them properly at the time? Was he hiding something? A terrible agitation seized her as she paced up and down the house, her thoughts in turmoil. She imagined Marpa, Auli, the girl, Kajinsha, all together in that house while she waited here! The feeling grew and grew that Kajinsha was moving away from her. Yes—he was having a liaison with his first wife's sister. Marpa's niece! Marpa must have arranged it, she thought wildly. Didn't the man trap Kajinsha once before? He could do it again and Kajinsha, stupid man, would be unable to resist! Angry thoughts welled up like bitter bile. Why was Kajinsha not back? What was keeping him in that village? The question turned over and over in her head. She clenched her fists and peeped out. There was no sign of anyone approaching. She was all alone with the bitter darkness and the cold mountains.

She heard her baby cry and went to pick him up. The bright, smokeless fire illuminated the room and she bounced him up and down on her lap. Hush, hush, she said, bouncing him up and down up and down, higher and higher. The boy made no sound, his weak legs dangling as Gimur bounced him harder and harder while her mind wandered back to that accursed village of Sommeu. 'Jump, jump!' she cried, almost beside herself now, shaking the child till his face turned red and he began crying and coughing breathlessly. She stopped at once and hugged him tightly. 'Oh my poor baby, what has happened to you? Hush, hush, forgive me, forgive me.'

When Kajinsha entered the house Gimur and the baby were curled up by the fire. It was the hour before dawn and the world was still dark. He stood motionless by the door, taking in everything. Gimur sensed his presence before she saw him, but did not open her eyes. There was a deep silence, as if the house, the baby and she had all stopped breathing, and suddenly he was there, coming in quietly through the door. He removed his bag and she saw him place his spear high up on the ledge, above the trophies at the entrance. He approached them softly.

'You are awake,' he whispered.

'Yes,' she said, lying very still.

'How is he?' He sat down and touched the baby's feet. Ah, so warm! How peaceful it is to be back in one's own home, he thought. 'Is Awesa back?'

She nodded.

Kajinsha sighed and stretched out on his back next to her. Quietly, slowly, he began to tell her about the priest and all the things that he had seen, the visit of the governor of Rima, and everything else that had happened while he was in Sommeu. He left out nothing—except that half-remembered night when he thought his senses had been stolen, and the one thing he had saved in his heart—that he was so happy to be back home with her again. He felt that she would hear his unspoken words and understand that he loved her and she need never fear anything like that one unutterable night. It was a dream, a magic spell, but he had survived the snare and had come back. He was home! This was what he wanted to express, but Gimur and the baby were so silent, as if asleep in a faraway place. He tried to touch her hand, seeking refuge, but she lay unmoving with her back turned to him, and he felt alone and outcast. Something had happened to her too, he thought. What evil, unhappy wind was stalking them?

I will tell you, thought Gimur, watching the fire through half closed eyes. Yes, something has happened. We thought we had climbed over the hill. All this time, what were we doing but climbing, moving up hill? Now I see it is but a little distance, maybe only less than half way... How painstakingly slow and circuitous the route has been. We made plans and drew a secret route wanting what we had done to be worthwhile, but in the struggle we are now trapped, ensnared, pushed forward, and held back. Now I know only one thing.

There is a wind that sows poison. I know something happened in that village. I know. I can feel it here... Her heart was pounding. She bit her lip and hardly dared to breathe. A big stone was pressing down on her. She tried to sleep, shutting her eyes tight. But it was no use. Her eyes snapped open. Even now, she thought, even now she could ask Kajinsha. She felt ready with her words and almost jumped up but the words would not leave her lips. The baby twitched and gave a muffled cry. Tomorrow, I'll find out tomorrow, she told herself. Tomorrow if I look on his face I'll know.

It was a cold, bleak winter. The fields of corn had turned brown and lay bent and torn by the force of the wind. One night Gimur had a dream. She saw a river and its surface was covered with a flock of white birds. They were a heaving white mass that suddenly rose up, all together, with their beaks open, and flew straight past her in a dense stream. Their bellies skimmed the water and she saw their bodies straining forward with a frightening determination. They were shrieking, but there was no sound. She woke up and knew without a doubt that someone dear to her had died in her village. Visitors passed through their house regularly but no one came from Mebo. Who would travel here to find her and bring her news of her dear village! She rushed out of the house every time she heard someone cough or footsteps approaching, but they were people from the nearby villages who said food was short this year, they were living on last year's harvest. Everyone was travelling into Tibet or Burma to trade aconite and musk pods, madder dye, rubber sap and beeswax, for salt and grain. Gimur also wandered farther and farther away from the house. Screened by the glistening pine trees she searched for fern and roots but she also walked to be alone and gather her thoughts. The slopes were littered with enormous granite boulders, some of them bigger than a house and here she liked to bask in the sun like a lizard watching the valley below. Sometimes she saw black dots that were herds of yak, barely moving, until she shifted her gaze for a minute and suddenly they were gone, swallowed up by a thin, drifting mist. It was a landscape of shifting images. The river sparkled and then disappeared, the light dwindled and the shining trees and the mountains turned into dark, brooding silhouettes where nothing lived. Only the tireless birds circled high above, piercing the sky with their fierce gaze.

Every day Gimur returned to this place and pressed her face

down against the rock. Like the birds above her thoughts circled round and round in her head.

Since Kajinsha's return from Sommeu she had not exchanged many words with him. She was still seething with doubt and anger. Every day she vowed to ask him outright if he had been with a woman in that terrible village but the words would not come. She had fallen into a dark place. What was there to do? Sometimes it was difficult to breathe. Her heart was being crushed. She thought she would break into small, jagged splinters… until one day something happened. She heard music! It was a clear, pure melody floating through the air, like someone urging the hills and trees to listen, and praying, waiting to hear if someone would answer. Gimur thought she was dreaming. Something was tugging at her heart. Her hands stroked the soft moss and the music rose again, moving through the darkness as if looking for a friend and asking, 'Do you also feel like this sometimes? Is something wrong? Are you sad?'

This was the question most difficult to answer. *Is something wrong*? No, there was nothing wrong. She was a woman, healthy; a wife and mother. She was unhappy, that was all. Who could explain this? She rose to a crouch and examined the slopes around her. Where was the music coming from? Her eyes focussed on the hill to her left where the trees thinned out into grassy knoll that jutted over the river. A man was there, sitting bent like a black boulder. She recognised him with a start. It was the priest! The music was coming from there—he was holding a tapung, he was playing the flute! She held her breath, staring at him with her mouth open. As if he felt her piercing gaze the priest stopped and turned a little towards her, looking to see if anyone was near him. Gimur ducked down and slid backwards off the rock as silent as a cat. When her feet touched the ground she ran swiftly back to the house.

Everyone knew of the presence of the priest near their village. Kajinsha told her, yes, Marpa had sent word that the Tibetan authorities had asked the man to leave Sommeu village. The mention of Marpa's name and his village made Gimur's heart jump. She hated that name!

'Why have they sent him back here to us?' she asked.

'He will not stay here. He will go back to Assam,' said Kajinsha.

'Why,' said Gimur archly, 'does *your* Marpa think he is a spy?'

There was silence. Kajinsha looked at her with the beginning of a smile but stopped when he saw her set face.

'I don't know what Marpa thinks,' he replied. 'And I don't know why he has come here and if he is a spy—to spy on what? But we can find out.'

The days passed. For Krick these were days of rest when he was camped on the hillside a few miles from the border of the Zayul valley. He had been in Sommeu less than a month when his host Norbu had returned with the tall Tibetan envoy of the Rima governor.

'You must leave at once.' The envoy had said.

When Krick protested Norbu told him it was best to obey. If he protested too much the envoy might throw him out with orders never to return. If he complied there might still be a way—it was a temporary absence. Krick looked at the face of the envoy. There was no other way. When the time was right, said the envoy, there would be no obstacle for him to return to Sommeu.

'In the meanwhile,' said Norbu, 'carry this.' He had returned Krick's Tibetan grammar book and held out a letter encrusted with seven red seals. 'This is for safe passage through Mishmee territory. We will provide you enough food and porters for your journey.' There was nothing more to say. Krick knew that this might be a polite way to get rid of him, but he could not argue.

He had to rely on the word of the envoy and his friend Norbu that the door would be open for re-entry into Tibet.

'Do not worry, priest, we will not forget you,' Norbu had said, but it was with a heavy heart that Krick had left Sommeu on the second day of February 1852. The villagers had poured out of their houses to bid farewell and as he walked through that narrow street he had thought—one day, yes, one day I will return and everything will be changed. Now you do not know how I came to proclaim the good news of eternal light and life, but one day these hills will echo with proclamation and song. Blessed is he who comes in the name of the Lord! I prayed for a way to reach Tibet and it was granted. Now I have to leave, but everything is in the hands of the Lord. One day you will recognise the blessed saviour and all will proclaim his name and sing praises for the son of heaven!

It was not long before Krick's porters deserted him. He felt his heart sink at the thought of entering the forests that lay between him and the plains of Assam and to pass through the Mishmee territory again. They would want gifts, and if he offered none they would hound him all the way until he could produce something. What could he give them? He had no money except for a few Tibetan coins. The clothes on his back and a blanket were all that he now possessed. How could he reclaim their friendship? He decided to camp on the hillside for a few days. Here the land was beautiful and after his anxiety and deprivation in the smoke filled Tibetan house he felt restored in the open space of enormous granite rocks and trees.

There had been days in Sommeu when he thought he would die of starvation. In the absence of Norbu his Tibetan host Marpa had barely acknowledged his presence. Krick had been given black, dirty rice and when he had once asked for some food, the man had shouted, 'So you don't like what you are given? Then you shall have nothing!'

Remembering that scene Krick could still feel his face burning with humiliation. It had hurt him deeply, but he had clung on with missionary faith, prepared to waste away and die in Tibet if need be. Some travellers who took pity on him sometimes shared a morsel of meat with him but most of the time Krick had been reduced to scrounging for crumbs and grains of rice that had fallen on the floor.

Now he had his baskets of food with him, and with Lorrain by his side it was enough to make him feel contented. The fresh air whetted his appetite and he rummaged in the basket for a piece of meat. He thought of a hearty broth but the meat was smoked and dry and too hard to chop. He stoked up a bright fire and placed a chunk on two strips of bamboo over the coals. A delicious smell wafted up and desire like a physical blow made the breath stop in his throat. He felt hunger. For so long Krick had been scrounging for scraps of food that he thought his stomach had shrivelled and the will to eat had gone away forever. Now there was food to be eaten. After all was said and done, this was all that mattered. He stared at the sizzling, spitting roasting meat and felt the tremor of anticipation that made Lorrain sit bolt upright. A strange thing was happening. His mouth was filling with saliva. His eyes, teeth, hands, all were working together, concentrated on food, its texture, taste, its weight on his tongue. It was a strong, chemical reaction. More saliva flooded his mouth, enzymes rushed to work, his teeth chewed and digestive juices exploded over some miniscule organism that lived and procreated like a feeding machine, a survival mechanism. Food! He was going mad with the desire to eat. The dog was better, he was eating steadily, solemnly, equally concentrated, but that was the way he always ate. The thought crossed Krick's mind that if anyone tried to stop them eating now it would be he, and not Lorrain, who would growl.

He ate silently, ravenously. Ah, he almost wept at the sweetness of the food. How good it was to dine like this. It was better than dining at any well-laden table. Here was a chunk of meat encrusted with charcoal and ash and how the juices flowed into his mouth! Who would want to spoil this moment with a spoon, his hands were better, he could lick the fat off his fingers. Hah! He munched happily, gazing at the hillside. The mist had lifted and he could see the river now. Everything was bathed in sunlight. Here a man could find his place and have the hillside for his home.

Solitude tests a man like nothing else, he thought. Now I know what I need. I have no cloth, no other raiment than this, no money and no defence, but here a man could sleep in the shelter of rocks and fear nothing because he sought to take nothing. 'Behold…the lilies of the field!' he cried, and laughed when Lorrain cocked an ear and thumped his tail once. All desire was gone except to breathe deeply and enjoy the winter sun shining on the trees and falling so warmly on his back. The air was pure and nothing like the sewage from the squalid Paris streets spilled into the river. Mysterious are the ways of the Lord, indeed! he thought. No one told me it would be like this, living in exile from a world I once knew, but I am happy. If there is meat and yam to roast on a fire a man can be content with no mark of Cain among brothers who share and share alike. He lay down humming a tune and smiling at Lorrain lying stretched out in the sun. He dozed, dreaming of green fields, bringing desire back from beyond the mountains with the scent of crushed herbs from sea cliffs and summer gardens. A few hours later his thoughts turned to the meat in the basket. He was hungry again!

It is the proximity of food, he thought. It is sheer greed! I know there is meat and rice and that is why I want to light the fire again and cook more meat. Double rations, just this once, eh? As if guessing his thoughts Lorrain bounced upright and waited expectantly. 'Why not, why not; just this once? Double rations, Lorrain, for you and for me. Bien! What say you? You say yes, yes!' He began to blow on the fire and took his time examining the pieces of dried meat. He had five strips and they were all hard and black. He picked one and placed it on a flat stone that served him as a table. No point in rushing, he thought, waiting for the fire to catch properly. A light footstep made him turn his head quickly towards the line of trees. A man was approaching. The priest raised his hand in greeting. Lorrain picked up his ears but did not bark. In a few seconds the stranger, carrying a spear, was standing before him.

His head was covered with a black head cloth. Krick recognised him. He was the man in Sommeu who had been pressed against him in the pandemonium of Norbu's house when the Tibetan priest had arrived.

'Hallo!' he cried, smiling a full smile.

Kajinsha nodded. 'Will you join us? The priest was holding out a strip of meat. Kajinsha understood, and sat down. It was with mixed emotions that he faced the priest again. The sight of his white face with the overgrown beard and his eager, shining eyes reminded him of the strange night of passion in Marpa's house. A soft shudder ran through his body. The priest was saying something. Kajinsha half understood, half guessed that he was asking about his village. He pointed towards the ridge. Then he picked up the piece of meat and both Lorrain and the priest started up a little. He put a bamboo skewer through the meat, pressing hard, and they watched him, entranced, as he laid it on the glowing coals. It was the start of something. There was fire and food, and for those brief days in February the two men continued to meet on the hillside.

From her perch on the rock Gimur watched them slyly. They were always standing under the trees, Kajinsha in his heavy Tibetan coat and the priest in a long black robe, standing together like two herdsmen exchanging news. What could they be talking about? Gimur saw that the priest would be doing most of the talking. She saw his movements, pointing and asking something. They said he was a man of God. Bah! Sometimes she thought she could hear them. They spoke in a mixture of Assamese and Tibetan words.

'Sommeu,' said the priest, trying to establish a link. Kajinsha pointed to the food baskets and tapped his woollen coat. He travelled there for trade, he said. Why did the priest travel there? The priest held up his cross, just like the hunter's talisman that Kajinsha wore around his neck. His reply was: 'Religion.' And with every word and sentence exchanged, they understood each other better.

'Does everyone in your country wear the same clothes as you?' Kajinsha pointed with his knife.

The priest made a sign of prayer, clasping his cross. 'It is our custom to wear these clothes.'

'So you have your customs,' said Kajinsha. He had brought dried meat and he shaved off pieces and held them out to the priest. They munched silently. ' It is my custom,' said Kajinsha, 'to sit like this and ask you why you have come here to tell us of a God you say is more powerful than any other god.'

'I did not say that. I am only telling you about my God. It is my duty.'

Duty. Custom. Words. The wind was moving over the mountain and creeping up over the grass. Soon darkness would fall and the valley would be a different place with strange shadows rimmed by the looming silhouette of mountains.

'Who do you believe in?' The priest asked.

Kajinsha threw a piece of meat for Lorrain and let his hands rest on his knees. It was the way he sat when he was thinking about something.

'I believe in life,' he said. 'There may be a chief God, yes, but it is better to be friends with all the gods. I do not pray like you, everyday. But we honour our gods when the kambring tells us. At other times we live. We have a life and our lives are also ruled by gods.'

'What gods? Tell me the names of your gods.'

Kajinsha pronounced the names—Matai, Amik, Broh, Khroney...and then stopped abruptly. 'Look at you,' he said. 'You have no land, no wife, no house. How can you think of trying to change my life telling me my life means nothing?'

Krick laughed. 'No, I don't have anything,' he said. 'Nothing to eat too, hah hah!'

Kajinsha looked at him. Yes, the man looked ill fed and hungry. He could understand that. A man needed food. 'I will teach you to fish,' he said.

'Oh no! I have food in the basket. I will soon be on my way to Assam. It is enough.' The priest laughed again, but Kajinsha knew that the man did not like their food. In Sommeu he had seen him looking at the meat he had been given and leaving it aside.

Kajinsha said, 'The Tibetan lamas have books and you read your book for knowledge of God. We read the land. The land is our book. Everything here on this hill, the grass and rocks and stones is saying something. And what falls from the sky—rain, thunder and lightning—are also the voices of spirits telling us something. It is how we have learnt what is good and what is sweet or bitter, by living here and remembering what happens during the day and the night, every day, for hundreds of years.' Kajinsha's arms swept the landscape. 'The time we have is what we call our life. It is how I stand, hunt, sleep, breathe. Who knows when life will end, and how death will come—by fire, water, a falling tree, illness, or from the hand of an enemy? But whether one will live a long life, a successful life, these are not considerations. The desire is to live!'

The priest listened. He was in a wilderness where there was no sign of an established religion, no Christians, Muslims and not even Buddhists, even though Kajinsha and his people were so close to Tibet. Here it was only great domes of rocks, a hard, physical world that demanded only the stamina to survive. Everything is in the hands of God, he thought. Everything is already written. Build me a temple and I will dwell amongst you… He thought about the innocence of the human heart given by God. How did knowing and not knowing help anyone to live better?

'The kambring sings songs. I can also sing,' Kajinsha said,

'songs of magic, blood and dreams. It is there from the time of our forefathers. I only have to recall and it is there, here...' he tapped his forehead. 'My father also told me that everything on earth and sky is connected since we are born of the same mother. It is very simple. We belong to the land. The land is a good mother. I take only what I need. Animals and trees offer themselves. We help each other survive. Tell me, priest, what do you think of our land?'

It was a question Father Krick had asked himself many times. He was in a pristine, empty world where he was alone. It was now up to him to respond. What could he say? What did he think? He tried to focus his thoughts. There were those summer days when he walked in the garden of the seminary in Paris. Life was gentle, obedient; his days and nights spent in prayer. But here? The thought hung in the air. He opened his breviary and knelt by the rocks thinking—Yes, there is a world where I come from, and another kingdom that lies beyond. And there is a world here that is drawing me in step by step into the life of water, stone, and the language of thunder, birdsong, and the shriek of the mountain sliding down. Kajinsha's words still seemed to float around him. 'The land is our book,' he had been told. He fixed his gaze on the sky. It was awash with the afterglow of sunset. Nothing there—no stars yet, just a pale orange sheet with a red pulse-beat at the point in between the two peaks where the sun had sunk. All around him a silence had descended that was steep, deep, high, and vivid as the green growth perfect in its beauty covering the hillside. I will walk, he thought, step by step, and keep my heart and mind open. Yes, an open mind. That was what mattered most. Once he had preached sermons about the language of a heart which knows what it is to love. It was what he needed now. If only I could learn the language of the people here well, and quickly, he thought. If I could speak to them from my heart, I would convince them of the words of the saviour, blessed, eternal. How wonderful, how glorious that would be

Every evening he took out his book and pored over his notes. And every evening, high on her hilltop perch, Gimur would sit and watch the priest. Sometimes she sat very upright with her legs crossed in front of her. Sometimes she crouched and stared straight ahead at the dark hill. Like this she could be a piece of stone. But the priest was not fooled. He was aware of her presence and even though he could not distinguish her exact features he sensed it was a woman. Once he had heard a baby's cry. It is a woman and her child, he had thought, suddenly remembering the face of the woman he had seen; it was somewhere here, he recalled. Who was she? He knew there were villages around but felt it was prudent to stay where he was and not provoke the anger of the chiefs by exploring the countryside. It was enough that he could meet someone like Kajinsha with whom he could exchange a few simple words, and yet understand so much more than the words and phrases they spoke. As for the woman on the hill, whoever she was, there was no sign that she wanted to communicate. In fact, he thought, she was stealthy as a lizard in the sun who wanted to be left undisturbed.

He turned to his writing with renewed attention. He had kept a record of Mishmee dress, food, and customs. In Sommeu he had made sketches of a prayer wheel, a woman's necklace, implements, and practiced writing the Tibetan script. It was an exercise in hope, as if something would change or he could make it change if he gave voice to his feelings. Will someone read my words? Today I saw some flowers that looked like the fleur-de-lis... These simple lines brought back a rush of other thoughts. Ah, the forests of Lorraine... how far away they were! And what had happened to the letters he had sent to his Directors in the Paris Foreign Missions? So far nothing had been easy for him. He was still struggling with hunger, fatigue and solitude. Who would ever know what he was going through? How would anyone in Europe ever be able to imagine what kind of world he had entered here? He stopped writing and listened to the wind passing through the valley, so soft, so stealthy and so determined. He wondered what news it carried to the outside world. Would they hear it beyond this valley, in Assam? Would it move around the world to distant homes and enter, soft as a dream, whispering tender words? He sighed heavily. Words… a breath of air shaped with the desire of hope. He lifted his flute and played a note. The wind was blowing harder now. What news? What news? He wanted to shout. Show me the cathedral again, that distant world, patches of sunlight, green trees and the light pouring in through the stained glass of old chapels!

The wind, only the wind could see him here and there was no shame in stopping for a moment, feeling its movement within him, making him want to weep. He breathed in deeply and the notes grew louder, stronger, reverberating against the rocks and trees. It is not I, he thought. Not him. It was the music that played him. He was nothing more than a note floating in the air. A stream of sunlight might capture him. He saw green trees, a drenching green entering his veins and humming melodies that soothed his soul. His soul was free then, rising above the lonely mountain and tracing its black silhouette with a burst of love. 'Save me, save me, oh music of heaven and earth!' he cried. 'Carry me with the song, with the wave that rises and does not fall, with the silver light that clings to the moon and with a love so bountiful that breaks open the darkness and floods the dark plain with the glowing light of eternal life!'

At night thunder rumbled across the sky. In his dreams Krick thought he heard the sound of running feet and voices. Someone was calling him. He woke up with a start and felt the first heavy drops of rain on his face. It was amazing! The sky that had been so clear was dark with clouds and his fire was going out. He jumped up aiming to shelter under the huge rock when he saw a young boy signalling for him to follow. Where had he come from? He looked familiar, with his white woollen cap, but where could he have seen him before?

It was Awesa. 'Go and fetch the white gelong and bring him here,' Kajinsha had told him, and Awesa had run all the way to do just that. He grabbed at the baskets and the priest lunged at him. 'Don't touch them!' he shouted. Awesa dropped the basket and stood, waiting. It was raining harder. Where was Lorrain? The priest looked around desperately. Awesa whistled and suddenly the dog was there, loping out from among the rocks. That was it. The boy meant no harm, thought Krick, feeling ashamed of his outburst. And that whistle, he had heard it before too, but where, where? He wondered, while he hurriedly put on his cardigan and grabbed his blanket. How strange. Where were these memories coming from? There was no time to ponder these things. I must have faith, he told himself. People are kind. Trust! I must trust this boy! He tipped his head and Awesa immediately picked up the basket and began walking. A cold wind was whipping the trees but perhaps it was blowing away the clouds too, he thought, as he followed Awesa's rapid pace. Ah, but it was bitterly cold! His teeth were chattering when he arrived crouched and shivering at Kajinsha's doorstep.

When Gimur caught a glimpse of the priest's white face she sprang back into the house. But it was too late. The priest had seen her and his eyes opened wide with a look of recognition. It was the face of the woman in the forest that he had seen when he was on his way to Tibet. Now he knew why Awesa's whistle had been so familiar. He had heard it at the time when the boy and all of them had watched him pass this way! Kajinsha stepped forward and signalled for him to enter. Krick stepped into the first room of the house lined with the trophies of animal skulls and taking his cue from Kajinsha he sat down gratefully by the bright fire. The woman had disappeared but again he heard the cry of a child. She is the woman of the house, he thought. She is Madame Kajinsha! He was wonderstruck. For no accountable reason he felt a great sense of joy and gratitude that he was able to enter this house. Peace be in this house. God bless them, God bless this house! He cried in his heart.

All the things that passed before the priest that night, or in that the grey dawn, because he heard the roosters crowing, were like a rich and unexpected dream. If Krick could think of himself as a shepherd with his flock he knew that this house and she, the woman of the house, would be the one whom he would watch over. He did not know why, except that he felt she needed watching over. Did he want to convert her? Did he sense something about this woman's heart knocking against her breast that found an echo in his own? He could not say. His mind was full of thoughts that came and went like a flashing glimpse of something lost and inexpressibly important, if only he could uncover its meaning. Was this not the history of man, he thought, always wavering between knowing and not knowing, always on the edge between darkness and light?

In any case, everything for him had changed and he was not the same man that he was. The ground beneath his feet had shifted and alone in the wilderness he wanted to know her and her house and these people before he could utter the message of God that he had once longed to carry to the ends of the earth. *Know* them! He had started, and knowing had changed him. That was all. He did not see as much as hear the sounds that came from beyond the room where he was sitting, and he saw Gimur only when she came in once to place a piece of yam before him, but it was enough. She was different. She was not from these villages, he knew, because he saw the tattoo like a cross in the hollow of her upper lip and another on her chin. He had seen it only among the Abor tribe when he had met them with Captain Vetch. Maybe she was an Abor. But he dared not ask. And now Kajinsha was telling him that he must leave immediately.

'Why?' he cried. Kajinsha said something. He was speaking emphatically but Krick could not understand. He looked around for help. How important it was to communicate! But all he saw was the young boy in the corner and Kajinsha with his head tilted back, looking at him with narrowed eyes. After a while Gimur came into the room with two other women. A discussion ensued and Krick heard the words Tibet, Oualoung, Assam, and Zumsha. Kajinsha was telling him to go to Zumsha's village! That was the name of the Mishmee chief who would not let strangers pass through his territory.

'The women will show you the way,' he said.

'Why?' cried Krick again. He would leave the valley but was there no other route? Why were they chasing him away in the middle of the night? What was happening? In his desperation he even turned to Gimur thinking somehow that she might understand him but her face was cold and haughty and he saw that her eyes were focussed not on him, but on Kajinsha. Dimly he understood that Kajinsha was telling him his best passport to reach Assam was to seek Zumsha's protection for safe passage through the Mishmee hills. And Kajinsha seemed to have enlisted the man's help. Perhaps they were related. He tried very hard to understand what was going on but it was beyond him. He felt cold and helpless and when the women hoisted his baskets on their backs he did not protest. Everyone stood up. Kajinsha's face was expressionless. Gimur was there holding the baby and when the priest, in a last minute gesture of farewell, turned to wave to the child and bumped his head against a low beam she did not smile as he might have expected a mother would. Instead she appeared to move back with a sigh. It was Awesa who smiled and pointed ahead. The two women carrying his belongings were already moving forward straight into the mist. Krick waved once more and soon he too was gone from view.

Kajinsha and Gimur moved back into the house cupping their hands over their mouths against the icy wind. A door was closing. At last the man is gone and now we can attend to other things, thought

Gimur. With the priest's departure her small window into another world had shut. Life in the valley could resume its silent momentum with no distraction. But she could not have misjudged anything more. Life and its small windows—a breath of something new blowing in through the smallest chink—offers a greater enticement than the large vista. Yes, they moved back into the house blowing warm breath into their cupped hands but a cold mist drifted in with them and with it, drifted in the music of the flute. From now on everything that happened in their lives would unfold before her as if from the realm of a dream world.

The reason for the priest's hasty departure was that Kajinsha had received word from Chowsa in Chunpura that the British authorities had negotiated a meeting with a Tibetan grand lama. They had asked Chowsa to select a suitable escort to bring the Tibetan regent from the Tibeto-Mishmee border into Assam. Chowsa had thought of Kajinsha. He would be paid for this service. What did Kajinsha think of this proposition? His first reaction was, No! We will never help the British enter our territory. Let them find another way. On the other hand, he had thought, if he could bring the Tibetan lama to the British it might provide a bargaining point to let them leave his land alone. The British and the Tibetans could do whatever they wanted, but in their own lands. The trouble was the route. He knew that once the British met the lama they would volunteer to escort him back with their own men who would stay in their villages and even establish posts along the way. He wondered if Marpa might be able to come up with a way of bringing the lama through another route that would skirt Kajinsha's territory altogether, maybe through the passes further west along the watershed. It was worth a try.

At the back of his mind he had an idea that a British presence in Tibet could perhaps be all for the better. If they could enforce their laws in Tibet it might check Tibetan inroads into Mishmee territory. His thoughts were a whirl with sudden possibilities. It had been imperative to get rid of the priest because his presence near their house could provoke distrust from the Tibetans and British alike, with the possibility of an incident breaking out from either quarter. He had seen the reaction of the Rima governor to the presence of the French priest in Sommeu. As for the British, they were always looking for a way to reach Tibet through Mishmee land. There might even be friction with the other Mishmee clans. Chief Zumsha had already declared that all outsiders were an ill omen.

It was a winter of secrets, thorns, unrest. Kajinsha prowled the countryside and went away on secret meetings with his uncles and brothers. He was the master strategist whose mind was full of plans to rally his people together. Sometimes they flocked to the house and their low voices were like the murmur of bees through the night. Gimur waited. Something would happen, she knew that, just as she knew from her dream of white birds that someone had died. She watched her baby changing every day. Little Siengbow loved to be carried outside as if he too craved the open sky and the light, but she was afraid he might fall ill if he was exposed to the wind. She bundled him up in blankets and watched over him like a hawk. One day she was in the house cooking when Kajinsha came in and said, 'I have to go to Sommeu.'

The mention of the place stung her, the words falling like poison. Without a word she threw the ladle down and walked away into her room. Kajinsha followed. 'Did you hear what I said?' he demanded. Gimur turned around and stood there, silent, unmoving. The baby was asleep in the corner and Kajinsha signalled for her to step outside.

'What is it?' she said.

'The baby is too hot. Why are you putting more warm clothes on him?'

'I think he's cold.'

'No! He wants to put his feet out. You'll wake him up, keeping him so hot!'

'Never mind if he wakes up. He'll sleep better at night.'

'I think he should sleep well even now.'

'If you are going to argue so much, baby and I ...' she made as if to snatch up the sleeping child.

'No no! Let him sleep here!' Kajinsha tried to hold her outstretched arm. Gimur slapped his hand away and making a loud, stomping sound stepped outside.

'What are you suggesting? Are you asking me to make you some beer?' She sneered at him. 'Do you want something to eat? What do you want?'

'I said I have to go to Sommeu.'

'Go then!' she shouted. All the angry words that she had kept hidden welled up and flew out of her mouth. 'You want to go there to be with that woman!'

'What woman?' said Kajinsha shocked.

'People are talking about you and Marpa's niece in Sommeu!'

Kajinsha looked at her hard. His presence was overwhelming and for a moment she felt ashamed of her jealous doubts. She heard him say: 'What are people talking about? And if people are talking, let them. You know how it is.'

But I don't, she wanted to scream. I don't know anything. I only know fire and smoke and this nagging voice that torments me night and day. 'Tell me,' she said. 'Tell me, is it true?'

'What is true?'

'That you lay with that woman!'

Kajinsha's voice was very quiet. 'Who have you been talking to?'

'It doesn't matter,' she said. 'Tell me, is it true?' She held his gaze and felt a wail rising up from the pit of her stomach. God, god, give me strength. Give me faith!

'Let us not fight,' said Kajinsha. 'Why are you like this? Why do you ask me these questions?'

Because I want to know, something inside her was screaming, because everything matters to me, that is why! It is only my heart that has let me down every time I wanted to ask you this. How have I failed you? Why have you failed me? But her tongue would not speak the words. She only laughed wildly and shouted, 'Just tell me!'

'If you have nothing else to talk about then, be silent!' Kajinsha shouted in return. 'There's no need for me to stay!' He banged down the empty cup in his hand and turned to leave.

Gimur stood up and pushed him back. 'You finish what you started,' she said. 'Why are you so afraid? Why can't you answer?'

Kajinsha pushed her aside. 'Let me alone. Enough is enough!'

Gimur leapt at him and tried to claw his face. He grabbed her by the wrists but she flung her arms out and clasping him around the shoulders tried to push him away. He was taken aback by her strength. She's mad, he thought. Her head was butting against his chest and to stop from falling he lifted her and tried to throw her off him. She hung on and swung on his body like a cat. She was livid. Her face was red with the physical effort of trying to defeat him and her eyes were black and merciless as if she wanted to kill him.

'Bah!' he shouted at the top of his voice. 'Get off me, you mad woman!' The words echoed around the small space like a thunderclap. She spat on his face and dropped her arms. 'Don't you dare touch me, you evil creature,' she hissed. 'Don't touch me with your dirt!' The baby started crying and she turned around and snatched him up from the cot. 'Hush,' she panted, bending low and clasping the tiny head against her cheek. 'Hush. Hush…I'm here.'

Kajinsha stared at her back. 'My God,' he thought. 'Look at her. She is mad!' One minute she was fighting him like a tigress and the next she was rocking back and forth crooning a pathetic song to a sick child. Marpa was right. A woman like her was bad luck. He could not understand love like this. He caught a glimpse of his son's white face and that frightened him more than his mother's anger.

It looked like the child had stopped breathing. 'Oh,' he groaned, feeling a deep remorse but Gimur had turned around. 'Yes! I am mad,' she cried. 'What do you think of this?' She snatched up the dao from under the bed and struck the loom with it, cutting the thread in two. 'There! One door is closed but I am going away. You live with this!' She saw the look of rage twisting Kajinsha's face. His eyes were wild. She held the baby tight and stood away from him. He might kill them both, she thought. The wind was rushing in through the open door and everything was swinging wildly in that little space. Kajinsha came forward one step, and then stopped. She saw his clenched fist and his hard mouth but she did not move. 'I'll attack you,' her eyes taunted him until she saw him clutch his head and whirl around to rush out into the night.

'Do what you want,' he shouted. 'I'll not stop you!'

Long after all the words were spoken Gimur sat alone. People seeing us together once must have wondered at our joy, she thought, how we crept into each other's bodies, how our souls clasped one another, how we searched and saw the light reflected in each other's eyes. Was it only a dream that the gods had spun out for their sport? If it was so, then she would spin it out even further, she thought, and let the gods be damned! She would give it shape and form with words that were raking her heart. Iron words, the taste of sword blade. Hot, burning words, plucked from the sun's blazing core and sorrow, like a long howl out of the black belly of the universe. Let everything gather force and carry her away like a terrible wind. She saw no reason to change or erase any part of it.

She looked at the broken loom. It was a sign that a relationship was over. Put out the fire, cut the cloth on the loom. It was time to leave. She had invested everything in this love. She had run away from her village. What would they say now? There was a way, she knew, how she and Kajinsha could get around the problem. She had to consent to live here and obey the laws of the land. It was a simple matter of saying, yes, I believe you. I believe you love me more than all other women. A man could father many sons and no one would question him. He could keep many women but no one would take her place as long as she said yes, I can live by the laws of the land. Who would ask? Who will know anything? But *I* will know, she thought. That was the unavoidable obstacle. I cannot say yes. It is too late for forgiveness and I will never forget.

Gimur waited in the house for many days. Sometimes she thought she heard Kajinsha calling her, but no one came with news of anything. She did not light the fire but gazed at the grey mist and suddenly remembered the priest. How strange! That man had gone away too. Everything was dwindling. Her own life was breaking. But I like the darkness, she thought, sitting patiently in the dark, empty house. 'I have no need of priests, of him—Kajinsha. No one. What help can they offer me in my life. *My* life? I have strength too,' she said, talking to her little boy. 'We will go back to Mebo. You see, I also believe someone will protect me even though I travel alone. I can walk across these hills. I am not afraid.'

1853

Flight to Mebo Zumsha. The Menace. A Miracle.
The Parting of Ways

She prepared to set out. There was nothing she wanted to take with her. Her pathetic belongings were not worth carrying. Her knife was securely tied around her waist and whatever she needed she would get from the land. She wrapped the baby in her old green ga-le and stepped out. A blast of wind almost forced her back into the house. She bent her head and walked out feeling the wind whistling in her ears. A figure stepped out in front of her. Kajinsha! He's back, she thought, but it was Awesa. Where had he sprung from? She hadn't seen anyone since the day Kajinsha had left. 'Go way!' she hissed at him. He stepped to one side murmuring words and smiling idiotically. Go away! She pressed against the wind clutching Siengbow. The wind was tearing the ga-le off him, flapping the cloth like a piece of paper. 'How will I travel like this?' she wondered. Awesa stood in front of her again and reaching his hand over his shoulder, tapped his back. When he saw Gimur stop he bent down and tapped his back harder in a gesture of carrying the baby. It's not a bad idea, she thought. I cannot carry him all the way. I might slip. I have to cross rivers. I might lose my way. I will need some help. Already a heavy mist was descending like a white blanket.

She nodded and walked up close to Awesa. He opened his eyes wide and began to blink rapidly. She gripped him by the shoulders and turned him around. He understood and bent his back, standing like a mule. She tied the baby firmly onto his back and he took the eppon, the carrying strap expertly and tied it fast across his chest. He smiled at her. She sighed. The baby was secure. That was all that mattered. She signalled for him to start walking.

It would be many years later that Gimur, remembering her flight from the Dau valley, would realize that without Awesa's help she would have never found her way out of that accursed place. The mist was so thick. She walked as if in a trance. Sometimes Awesa, a few paces ahead of her, disappeared from view. This made her panic and shout for him. Then Awesa would stand still and wait until she collided into him. She recoiled at this contact. He bent his head and plodded on. Gimur stared at his bent figure and wondered if he knew where she was going. She had no idea of the route and thought Awesa might be leading her into a trap. If he looks at my face he will know everything, she thought, but Awesa, even when she had narrowed her eyes and stared at him, had simply responded with a smile that stretched his mouth wide across his face, showing his big teeth. What happened to him? She wondered. Was he born like this? Kajinsha should be ashamed. He has done nothing to help his firstborn. Maybe he thinks there's a curse on the boy, and he is afraid. That's it. And he *should* be afraid! Curses on him and curses on the Tibetans and lamas and priests!, she thought angrily. Look at Awesa, so big and sloppy with his dirty white cap and his dirty, unwashed body. But he was lumbering along and carrying her baby. It was more than anyone would offer to do. Not that she would ask anyone in that shameful village for help. Curses on the village and curses on Kajinsha! Liar, coward! And that woman, may the spirits eat her up and destroy her! Curses on them all! She travelled swiftly with rage goading her on, stomping on the slushy path, tearing leaves, fending off branches and snapping twigs that got in her way.

One day they reached the edge of a high mountain. They were at the summit of the last chain of hills that marked the limits of Kajinsha's territory. Looking back she could see the northern circle of snow peaks. How peaceful they looked, shining in the afternoon sunlight. What had her life been worth in that immense landscape—a tiny speck moving in and out of a house, bending down to plant rice and scratch for food like an ant on the steep hill? Yet, there had been days when she had laughed and sung songs, weaving cloth in the peace of afternoon with her child asleep on her lap. She turned round and faced south. Rows of hills still lay before them but beyond, she knew, was the big river and the route that would lead her back to her village. There! She pointed her hand straight out. But first they would have to cross a deep gorge and climb over to the other side. This would be the most gruelling part of the journey. A shower of loose earth skittered down like hail stones as Awesa began the descent. Gimur gripped the roots of trees and clung to twisted creepers to slow her progress down the vertiginous incline. A slip would plunge her straight down into the wild jumble of rocks below. If they fell and died here would anyone find their bodies? No one would know where to look.

There was no time to think. All her thoughts were concentrated on escape and survival. She did not know for how long or how far they had travelled. Awesa carried strips of meat and dried fish in his pouch. She carried powdered corn and which she mixed with stream water to feed her baby. She began to trust Awesa and followed him blindly. She believed he carried a map in his head, or perhaps he could sniff the air and know which direction to take. Sometimes, when he was too far ahead for her to see him he left clues—a crushed leaf, a bent fern, a slanted stick. And she knew she would find him waiting by a tree or sitting on a stone, rocking back and forth and making deep, chuckling sounds to the baby.

On the fifth day they had squeezed their way through the crevasse in between the steep mountain wall. They were in a high valley strewn with enormous boulders. The snow peaks were no longer visible. Gimur wondered if they should rest for a while, but she was worried about the weather. A thundershower could cause landslides and turn the thinnest trickle of water into a brown flood in the space of an hour. She knew clouds were always creeping up over the hills they had left behind, following them, and there were clouds pushing up from the plains. When the clouds joined together above them, the sky could burst open. They had to cross the Tidding River before that happened otherwise they would be stranded. At four in the afternoon a cloudburst hit them. They were running and slipping, carrying plantain leaves over their heads when Awesa stopped dead in his tracks with his hand lifted to his ear. Gimur listened. At first it was only the sound of the rain. Then she heard voices. There were men approaching! Quick! She pushed Awesa and the baby behind a rock and crouched down. She saw Krick and two Mishmee men running, bent under the rain. The priest was following her like a ghost! What was he doing here? Kajinsha had sent him away to Assam. She wondered if he was staying with one of the Mishmee chiefs. How determined he was! Like a forest spirit, who had gone mad. She looked around. There were rocks perched on one another like houses and she decided to take shelter here for the night. She did not want to be seen nor follow in the footsteps of the priest. Let him find his own way if he can, she thought. He might look big, but here he was nothing. A mere speck, another creature who could fall, break his bones, or die of hunger.

The next morning the rain had stopped but the sky was grey and cloudy. They were hurrying on when they met a family who were also creeping out from one of the rocky caves. They had been digging the ground for yam but had found nothing. Awesa looked at Gimur but she made a face. They had no yams either, she said coldly. She had no wish to be friendly with anyone here and without any more exchange of words she walked on past them.

They reached the river and Awesa said she should cross first. No, she said. She wanted to see her baby safely across. She peered at his face and kissed his tiny face. He was so good! Who would not love him? His black eyes were shining and seeing his mother he tried to kick his legs, making Awesa laugh.

'Ssshh…' she said, ever cautious. It was unlucky to laugh loudly. Evil spirits might hear and become jealous. Who knew what spirit was passing by at that moment? She stared at the swirling water below. It had risen, but they could still make it. She twisted the eppo from around Awesa's back so that the baby was on his chest now and tightened the knot. Awesa grabbed the hoop of cane on the long bridge of cane and lifted his legs tightly around the cane ring as if he were resting in a hammock, his knees folded up. 'Go!' Gimur pushed him gently. With a whoosh the cane ring slipped down the length of cane like a swing and in a second Awesa and the baby were hanging over the middle of the river. Awesa now had to manoeuvre with hands and feet, pushing the ring forward, hanging upside down with the baby on his chest, inch by inch, until they reached the slag beyond which the cane ring zipped down easily to the other bank.

Gimur breathed a sigh of relief. She lit her pipe and inhaled deeply. She had taken a few puffs when suddenly out of nowhere she saw the priest accompanied by two Mishmee men. He was coming towards her. He had not seen her yet, as he was looking at the water. She jammed the pipe into her mouth and without looking back she grabbed the ring and kicked herself over the edge, lifting her legs high, as she got clear. Just at that instant in a flash she saw that the priest, who was closer now, had seen her. Their eyes met but she did not think he would recognise her. She was flying though the air and in a few seconds she was on the other side. Awesa was waiting behind a tree. 'Quick, let's walk!' she said.

But the priest had seen her. It is a dream, he thought, watching Gimur flying across the river like an insect on that strip of cane. One moment he knew it was her and the next she had vanished from view. Everything in the jungle and all that had happened seemed illusory. He had been approaching a village, he remembered, when an old man had appeared suddenly out of nowhere. 'Beware!' he had said, 'you are in a bad place. They will attack you!' Krick could not get anything more out of the man but his porters had dumped him and fled. There was nothing to do except approach the house that he had been heading towards. He went up and shouted loudly. 'Hallo! Hallo!' A woman peeped out. It was chief Zumsha's house! She signalled for him to enter. Chief Zumsha was away but he would be back soon, she said. Krick was constrained to enter the dreaded place. He saw many people sitting around the fire and heard someone groaning in pain. A man was lying on a mat in a corner. A fortnight ago a tree had fallen and hit him on the foot, shredding the flesh. The wound was deep and festering now. His hostess wondered if Krick could do something to help the man. Just at this moment Zumsha had entered. He looked tense and angry.

'Ho! There you are! I missed you the last time. Now speak! What are you doing in my territory?' he had shouted. 'If you come into my land you cannot go out again! You should know this. I will cut off your neck, no, not in my house, for it would defile my place, but you'll die and I will throw your body into the jungle!'

Krick had replied as he always did, that the purpose of his journey was religious. He was a priest. He was only passing through Mishmee territory on his way to Tibet. He showed Zumsha the letters of safe conduct that the Tibetans had handed him but this had only redoubled the chief's fury. 'Bah! Who is the Tibetan chief? You are his slave, but he is nothing here. Give me the writing. I will throw it into the fire! I can kill you just now. In my house I am the ruler!'

'I am helpless and I am in your hands,' Krick began, when the woman whispered something to Zumsha. Krick stopped, and waited. Zumsha looked impatient but then he turned to Krick and said, 'There is a sick man, there!' he pointed towards the corner. 'I give you three days to cure him. Listen well—three days!'

It had been a long, fearful night. The entire household stayed awake listening to the cries of the sick man. Krick looked at the rotten foot trying to imagine what Dr Lenoir of the Necker hospital in Paris might have done. Three days to live! How could he heal this wound? He pulled out his medicine box and applied a simple dressing. Like so many times before he would have to trust divine mercy. He watched over the patient who had fallen into a deep slumber after his ministrations. Miraculously, when he untied the bandage the next day the swelling had reduced and the deep gash looked clean and dry. Zumsha was overjoyed. He put his face close up against Krick and for the first time Krick saw him smile. He patted Krick on the shoulder and offered him two eggs. Zumsha's entire manner had changed. His eyes gleamed like those of an old fox. He pointed to Krick, to his mouth and then to his ear and enacted a pantomime that seemed to say, 'your ears do not understand what comes out of my mouth and your mouth does not utter words that I understand. But never mind. You are a brave man. Fear nothing. You are my friend!'

How could Krick describe this meeting with Zumsha—all his experiences—to anyone who had not been through what he had? If he said, 'It was like this—I saw this, I tasted that, we walked, I fell, I was afraid, I wanted to steal, I ate like a pig...' who would believe him? He had been allowed to leave Zumsha's house when a group of Tibetans arrived to visit the chief. Krick's porters had also returned along with two Mishmees, Khroussa, and Lamet who had left him at the entrance to Oualong. Had the man been waiting for him all this time? 'Sabe, we will take you back to Assam,' said Lamet. Krick felt unsure. He did not trust Lamet but there was no choice.

It was a journey Krick knew he would never forget for as long as he lived. The same rainstorm that had caught Gimur and Awesa had hit them soon after they left Zumsha's house. Krick had seen Gimur crossing the river and he would have followed her but he had been taken to another chief's house to shelter for the night. 'Sabe,' his guides had cried. 'It is a bad day. We cannot go forward.' The rain was falling in torrents and Krick, looking at Lamet whose lips were pursed in a sly half smile, wondered if they were planning to kill him. 'Sabe, boxis…boxis,' Lamet said. Krick understood, but he had no presents. He cut up his blanket to give one half to the man. He wanted to be out of this accursed place, but they had seen his rice and now threatened to keep him prisoner if he did not give them rice. 'Then keep me prisoner,' shouted Krick, incensed by their deception. What was real in this fearful forest? He saw leaves that looked like waving figures and then vanished. Trees crouched over him with dangling arms and limbs. He heard voices crying in the wind and saw men and women with bent heads, mud streaked and rain soaked, stumbling in that treacherous path staying close to him and crying, 'Oh sabe, boxis… the next time you return bring me money…bring me blue cloth…'

He was being stripped of everything in that jungle. The thunderous rain and the mist rising up before his eyes were sweeping into his soul. They were on their way again after the night of the storm. Many times he stumbled and fell on his knees and prayed. Here am I, he thought, the itinerant preacher with folded hands crying for deliverance. Where is the path? Show me the way! Lift me up with your mercy. But there was no response. The soaking forest rose higher and higher driving the sun away forever. His mind played tricks on him. He wanted to laugh and cry at the same time. He thought he heard church bells and saw green fields and the tender flowers of a peaceful valley drenched in the soft light of the Loire valley. Where was he? The distance shocked him. How far he was from his calm parish! Now he had to raise himself and clear his mind. That was the challenge, to clear his mind. But every day, bit by bit, everything was changing. There was another world where he knew the light of love would heal every wound and he would never walk alone. But here, day after day he faced hunger, injury and the temptation to lash out at his guides for their taunting threats and the obstacles they put in his way. He had suffered a severe fall and had been knocked unconscious trying to jump across a small ravine carved by a stream and landing on a granite slab. His body was badly bruised and swollen, his nails were broken and his fingers were bleeding. His body felt as cold as marble. His clothes were in tatters and rotting off his back. He was as naked as the guides who made him a bed of plantain leaves. He fell into it without resistance, trying to hide the tears burning in his eyes. 'Take this cup away from me, away, away,' he mumbled in feverish dreams. 'Not mine, but thy will be done, Oh Lord,' he groaned, rising up suddenly and looking around. Where was the house of prayer?

One day, dragging his tired body over the last ridge and following the slope of the mountain Krick reached the enclave of Chunpura. He was lucky. He found good people to take him across the river to Saikwa Ghat. He was saved!

When Krick entered the house of Captain Smith, the captain saw him and cried, 'Oh, l'abbé! You are back!' He came forward and then stopped. 'Good God, look at you!' His eyes were full of compassion. He rapped out instructions to a servant boy, 'Quick! Prepare hot water and soap and linen,' and then turning to Krick he said, 'let's get you washed and bathed. You will need at least eight days' laundry!'

'Do not come near me,' replied Krick, 'for I am covered in

vermin and misery.' It hit Krick then that for him everything had changed. In the interior of the house everything was calm and orderly. He had bathed and put on a clean white robe and anyone would have said, 'But you are back safe! You are lucky!' But Krick had walked the unknown landscape of the soul, and looking at the books, the walls, the bed linen and inhaling the fumes of hot water mingled with the scent of soap he knew he was a changed man.

On the other side of the river Gimur and Awesa were facing more streams flowing down into the Burhampooter that Father Krick had crossed. They pushed on steadily, clinging to boulders and turning their bodies against the current. Sometimes Awesa gripped her hand, but most of the time it was Gimur who went ahead, feeling the stones under her feet, testing them, avoiding the slippery ones and warning Awesa about them. One day when they were wading across like this she heard a soft plop. She turned around to see Awesa diving into the water. The baby had fallen in! She plunged back, almost drowning in the current and saw Awesa holding the baby, but the eppon was floating away. She lunged at it but the strap twisted and bobbed in the water for an instant, then it was gone. They climbed out of the water, shuddering. Awesa was clasping the baby tightly. Gimur faced him and slapped him hard on his face. He bent his head and did not look at her. She grabbed Siengbow out of his arms and shouted at him to go away. Awesa began to kneel down, still keeping his face turned away from her, panting and mumbling with his eyes shut tight. She sat down, breathing hard. The baby was not hurt, but his face was wet with tears and he was wailing. Gimur was afraid he would choke and stop breathing. She rubbed him hard to keep him warm. They made a fire of reeds and twigs to dry their wet clothes and Awesa stretched out his waistcloth close to the fire to use as the new eppon.

They walked on for two days and Gimur began to recognise the route. Somewhere here, hidden among the reeds, was a small boat that Kajinsha had shown her. A memory of his smile at that moment flashed through her mind. How surprised she had been! Slowly she looked all around her but she knew without Kajinsha she would never find it. Not that it mattered now. Nothing mattered now except to reach Mebo and forget Kajinsha and his accursed people. She thought about Awesa and when he would leave her. She knew he would not enter her village. How would he go back? He could be robbed or killed on the way. But he was a surprising fellow! Maybe he would run away. He could cross the river and go to that place called Suddya, who could tell? He saw her looking at him and smiled. She smiled back. His smile brightened. They were not very far from Mebo, maybe another three days, and Gimur was happy. She did not think about who would receive her. No one knew her whereabouts and she had no one to return to, except Lendem. Maybe he could sense her return. Let him know I am on my way back, she prayed. She needed succour. She had survived, but when she thought the worst was over there was one more blow, that was like no other.

In a barren land of white sand everything was still as if the world had ended and Gimur was the only living thing on the planet, who opened her eyes and peered into the darkest hour before dawn. Something has happened, she thought. She sensed Awesa was still asleep. She could see his legs out of the corner of her eye. Siengbow was asleep too. His tiny body was a warm presence bundled up in her ga-le. She turned her head to look at him, inch by inch, at his closed lids, his cheeks, his mouth. She put her hand on his chest and stopped. 'Baby,' she whispered, 'baby!' A terrible fear was creeping up inside her body and with a start she began tugging at his body, gently at first, than harder, grabbing his hands, and then pulling him up and shaking him, shouting his name. 'S-I-ENG BOW!

Wake up! Wake up! Baby, what is wrong with you?' She screamed into his ear and covered him with kisses.

Awesa now crouched beside her. He tried to touch Siengbow but she hit out at his hands panting and staring at him with wild eyes until Awesa jumped up and ran away from her, tearing his hair and uttering rasping cries punctuated by long wails. Now they were two figures robbed of every ounce of control, weeping and howling in the wilderness. Little Siengbow was dead in her arms and she was dying with him, begging the sky and the wind and the breaking day to take her away from this sad earth. What had killed him, she did not know. Why did he die? When she had left the house she had thought, who needs this world, who needs God? I have my son! She thought about the words of the priest. Kajinsha had told her that he had spoken about a God who could make the dead live again. Where was this God? She wanted to believe. She kissed Siengbow's hands, buried her head against his chest and rubbed his feet. 'My darling beloved child!'

The sun was high in the sky when Gimur collapsed over her dead child. Her head drooped and Awesa crept up and held mother and child in a close embrace, stroking Gimur's head and pressing his cheek against her tear-stained face.

The stars came out and still Gimur and Awesa did not stir, as if they were still waiting for Siengbow to wake up. A small fire burned silently and they heard a herd of elephants moving in the dark trees. Perhaps they will come here and find us, thought Gimur. She could not bring her mind back from where it had gone, into a bitter, endless space. She rocked back and forth all night listening to the elephants trampling trees in the forest and she wanted to be with them, to huddle together and remain forever with that big, strong herd on their ancient route patiently, tenderly, loving the bones of the dead. At dawn the next day Gimur decided to move into the jungle. She carried her baby, looking for a place that would be safe from floodwaters and sand. Awesa dug a small grave and they buried Siengbow beneath a small mound of earth indistinguishable from the heaps of forest debris. A patch of sunlight marked it and Awesa staked it with bamboo sticks but that too, Gimur knew, would soon rot away and no one would know what had happened and who was buried here, except for her. In the hundreds of miles of forest stretching from here to her village and wherever else the river flowed and trees grew, she would never forget this place. Awesa stood aside and they looked at each other. Without their planning anything they both knew that the time had come to part ways. Gimur came up close and looked into his face. She saw all the sorrow of the world deep in those eyes. She hugged him. He cringed and made a choking sound. She sighed and motioned that this was it. He should leave. Awesa started shuffling back away from her. She turned away and began walking straight on in the opposite direction.

◆

Mebo. The Curious Case of Nago. The Priest finds a Vocation. Gimur discovers a Banner of Love

It was past midnight when Gimur reached the outskirts of Mebo. How many times had she clambered up the steep incline thinking nothing of the sharp stones that littered the path? Now her footsteps were slow. Everything was reappearing before her with breathtaking familiarity. She was entering the landscape of her childhood but she was a grown woman now, twenty years old, and she was returning alone. She heard the soft gurgle of the stream and stopped by the bamboo arch that marked the final barricade into the village. Mebo! Her home! Her village! She crossed the threshold and walked swiftly, silently, finding her way like a cat towards a familiar house at the far right end of sloping path. Two dogs rushed at her growling but when she called out they yelped and started jumping up and down.

'Hush,' she said, stroking them briefly. 'It's only me. Hush. Hush.' She remembered her dream of white birds and felt her heart beating like a fluttering bird. Her mother's house loomed up in front of her. A hen squawked and she heard the snuffling of the pigs, but they were muted as if they too did not want to wake anyone. Everything was steeped in darkness. It was at this moment that Gimur felt the full impact of all that had happened in the short time that she had abandoned this village with such joy and her return in the middle of the night like a squirming prodigal who wanted to pretend that she had never left. Perhaps she had made a mistake. It was unlucky to return like this to the exact place that one had left. She thought of turning around and going away but something pushed her forward. Perhaps there was hope yet, she thought, even though I am certain no one will be there. But she was mistaken. Someone was already standing on the veranda and saying, 'Who is there?'

Gimur stopped in her tracks, recognising that voice. It was Lendem! She saw his frame standing still as a statue by the doorway.

'Gimur!' he cried suddenly. She bent her head. He came forward and grasped her by the shoulders. 'What... how?' He looked at her face and stopped. 'Come inside,' he said softly. 'Thank almighty Donyi Polo that you are back.'

Inside the house a low fire was burning. Slowly, gently, Lendem told her about the death of her mother. It had happened almost a month ago, but news did not travel so fast, not to where she had been, so far away in another tribe's village. Lendem had been contemplating coming to find her to tell her the news. It had been a bad harvest here in Mebo too. Gimur's mother had taken to staying out in the tiny ippo, the same shack where Gimur and Kajinsha had first met. Food was scarce and the old woman had been digging the ground for yam when she fell and rolled down to the bottom of the hill. Maybe working in the hot sun day after day had weakened her. She was lying there dead when they found her. Lendem had performed the burial rites and kept vigil in the house like a son of the family, waiting for the right time to set out and find her. Gimur wept. She felt blind, crippled. There are no more words now to say anything, she thought, but words were being wrenched from her heart as she began her story from the night of her departure from the Dau valley to the point where she crossed the last stream and collapsed on the white sands with her dead baby. One by one the words of sorrow and pain fell like drops of blood leaving Lendem stunned and distressed. He had condemned Gimur's actions. Sitting alone in this house he had cursed her for the death of her mother, but now his heart was full of pity. 'We must pray to earth and sky for bringing you home safely,' he said. 'Don't speak anymore. Now we must only say the words we give to the living. Pray: Do not let death enter this house.'

It was a long, warm night. In the middle of the sleeping village Lendem and Gimur were two shadows bent close to the fire. The pages of life were turning. They were reading its letters, feeling every jolt and cry falling into their hearts. At last the first cockcrow startled them. And then birds began to twitter. It is morning, but it is the end of everything for me, thought Gimur. Her eyes were drooping with sleep. I will never awaken. I will sleep and forget everything as if it never happened. It is all a dream. It is the end of life. But a gust of wind was blowing in from the east, opening doors. All the lines that had been drawn from the time of her birth were drawing closer into a diagram that only invisible gods flying high above in the sky could design, and no matter how tightly Gimur shut her eyes and tried to embrace the darkness, a field of white light hovered over her trembling lids. This was not the end of the story.

From her perch on a high rock Gimur could see the land spread out like a map. She saw the confluence of rivers and streams rippling with golden brown water moss, and she saw solitary old men walk up and down checking their fish traps. What labour, what patience. In the green jungle men stand on the side of the narrow path and look around shielding their eyes against the sun. They have nothing to say. The land is behind them. Maybe they are talking to the trees. The ground is covered with fern. They know those creepers, what lies under the fern and who lives in the tall trees. Despite the apparent stillness of days there is an unwavering quality to village life. Food is a preoccupation, everyone works from dawn to dusk, and right from the start Gimur knew that her sudden reappearance would cause less stir than the scandal of her departure. There were so many things to talk about—the weather, plant life, someone's dog, fields, hunting and who had caught a squirrel or a fish. When they saw her the good people of Mebo responded with the old affection they had borne in their hearts for her and her dead parents.

'Hai! You are back! What happened to you? You look old!'

'Here, I have brought some rice. You must eat!'

Like a kind messenger Lendem had already spread the news of her return and told them a little of what had happened. He wanted to shield Gimur from indiscreet curiosity and as one of the respected men of the village his words carried weight. 'It is the will of Donyi Polo,' everyone agreed. 'Sometimes we lose our way, but in the end everyone comes back to the place of their birth.'

Lendem also said, 'It is better like this. The innocent are in God's hands.' He had brought the miri to the house who said he would perform rituals for her, so that she did not lose her soul in the land of sorrow. But for Gimur the days were bitter. Every day she sat on the rock gazing about her like someone in trance. If she stood up she could see the tips of trees where the river turned, cutting into the forest through which she had travelled and where her child lay buried. She deeply mourned him. She wanted him back from God. She wanted him in her arms. She would heal him with her love. It was something only a mother could do, not an invisible, faceless god, she silently hissed at the shaman. She thought she would never recover. But a distraction offered itself. It was the strange case of her friend, Nago.

'Hai ! What happened to you?' she had cried, rushing into the house to embrace Gimur. 'How sad I was when you left. I have been alone all this time! Here, let me look at you.' She pushed Gimur away from her and stared into her eyes. Gimur saw her friend's round face smiling in sheer joy suddenly crease into an expression of pain. 'Oh,' she said sharply, 'what will happen to you?'

Gimur had to smile. 'Nothing will happen to me,' she said. 'I will live and I will die and that is what will happen to everyone.'

'Hai… but there is more,' continued Nago. 'I see a town and I see water…' She stopped abruptly when Lendem sat down by her side and touched her gently. Then she laughed in her old carefree way and they talked about other things. While Gimur was away Nago had been wed to a young man of a nearby village. It had been a welcome relationship and the man had come to live in Mebo and started working in his in-laws' fields as was customary for a young groom to do. This was the traditional period of probation before he could build his own house and take the bride away from her parents' home. Everything had been all right until about six months ago when Nago had sat up bolt upright one night and recounted a dream. She had been carrying bamboo shoot in the deep jungle and had stopped by a stream to rest. She thought she heard whispering and she had begun walking upstream, higher and higher through the overhanging trees until all she could see were her white feet, ankle deep in the water moving up and up like floating fish. Suddenly there was a violent rumble. The banks around her crumbled and she saw the trees turning and the stream rising up like a rainbow. She screamed as she felt herself falling. Then she saw a woman waving to her. Nago stretched out her hand and the woman had pulled her up and placed a stone in her hand. It was the burning weight of the stone that had awakened her. 'The moment I held it the stone burned my hand,' Nago said. 'It was like a living thing. It was full of fire and flames.'

It was a dream and could be interpreted as something that had been on Nago's mind but the matter had not ended there. When Nago woke up that night she had spoken words in a language unintelligible to the villagers. It was the old miri who recognised them as the sacred songs of the past. Where had Nago, the lively village girl who had never uttered a word of the archaic chanting, suddenly picked up this fluency in the language of a powerful miri?

'It is a sign,' said everyone. 'Nago is turning into a miri!'

'Don't be foolish,' cried Lendem. 'Nago was remembering something from her childhood that is coming back now. It can happen to anyone, when you are exhausted or thinking of too many things. Let her rest. She will be all right.'

Nago would be normal until without warning she would become possessed of a terrific strength that sent her running over the stones into the forest or into someone's house. Her young husband stood aside, unable to comprehend what was happening. He was frightened and dejected and it was not long before he decided to return to his home village.

'Let it be,' said Lendem. 'Everything will be all right when Nago recovers.' But the spells continued. Nago would suddenly start chanting and recount past events and sometimes, looking at someone's face, she would pounce on an ailment that the person was suffering from, or tell of some hidden sorrow so vividly that her words had the nature of prediction and her insight the powers of a visionary.

'Why are you like this?' Gimur asked her friend. 'What happens to you when you go into a fit? Do you remember anything?'

'No,' said Nago. 'I don't remember what I said or did. The

thing I remember is that I am at the centre of a bright field of light. I feel someone is talking to me. I repeat the words that I hear and suddenly everything is very clear and simple. I can feel the icy wind before that sun peeps over the mountains. It is a feeling that falls on me like a rushing wind as if my body is being lifted like a bird. After that I don't know what happens. Perhaps I step into another world but at that moment I am filled with happiness as if my heart would burst.'

These fits or spells reminded Gimur of Awesa's mother in that distant village of Sommeu. They said she had the falling sickness but Gimur knew that in her lucid moments Auli too said she could 'see' things that no one had interpreted yet. Do these things happen everywhere, wondered Gimur. Or were they following her wherever she went?

The village miri performed rituals. He was busy all the time for there were many people who fell ill or said they had encountered uyus—evil spirits. No house was safe and every day some ritual was performed by a household to ward off disease and death. People gathered together and women bent their heads and chanted with the miri. But for Gimur there was no one in the house to ask for rituals. She mourned her dead mother and wondered what she would have said to see her daughter like this, sitting alone in the empty house. What had happened to Awesa, she wondered. Had he reached home? Had he told Kajinsha about their son's death? How would Kajinsha react? He had not sent anyone to bring her back. A slight shudder ran through her when she thought that maybe their love has ended forever. She listened to the chanting echoing all around her and watched the women of the village joined together in prayer.

'Don't you see how wonderful it is?' whispered Nago. 'Like this we can talk to the gods.'

'No,' thought Gimur. 'I know about prayer. I have prayed all my life. Since the day I was born I have been moving from ritual to ritual. The miri says we came from a land beyond the skies. It is there we will return when we die. So be it. Every prayer, every ritual is a knot. This is the way we measure time. But all the prayers and rituals will not erase what has happened. This is fixed forever as another knot in my life.'

In February the tagat trees began to bloom again. Everyone was busy building new houses or replacing old thatch roofing, going hunting or simply going in search of their mithun into the forests where they would roam around for days. It was also the start of the sowing season and Gimur returned to her fields with an iron will. I will stake my claim on this hill and live my life here, she thought. A year had come around full cycle and she was back in her small hut on the hill. One day she saw a small figure approaching her. It was Moi! This time Gimur did not run away. Instead she ran out to greet the old woman who looked red and bloated from her exertions. Moi had not been well, sometimes her limbs and hands became stiff as claws and she said she could not move. She used a cane stick to hobble around but this did not stop her from going from house to house and chatting with everyone.

She said, 'A miglun is coming. Have you heard?

'Who?' cried Gimur.

'Aah, who, I don't know, but Lendem has met him before.'

Gimur pondered this. Lendem had not mentioned anything to her. When she asked him he said, 'Yes… He was here with the miglun captain. It was after you had left. He asked me if I knew of a way to reach Tibet.'

Tibet! That was a name rising up out of her recent past. Ah! So that was why Lendem had not mentioned anything to her. Maybe he wanted her to forget her association with that place.

'Who is he? What does he look like?'

Lendem shrugged. 'He is big just like the other migluns. But he carries a tapung, and when I saw him he said he was a padari.'

Gimur started. How many priests could there be, she wondered, and how many who carried a flute? It had to be the same padari who had been wandering around in the Dau valley. He had come to their house. Why was he coming to Mebo?

'How should I know? It was Chowsa who sent me news that a priest was on his way to our village. We will know more once the man is here.'

Chowsa, another name out of the past. Chowsa was Kajinsha's friend. How did Lendem know him? Gimur was surprised. She looked at him slyly. He looked back at her and she suddenly realised that all this time Lendem had tracked her route from the time she had left the village and taken all the news of her and Kajinsha from people he knew stationed along the way, people she had had no idea about. He was a brave, honest man. Once he had tried to give her advice and help but she had spurned it. When she had left Mebo he had prevented a chase that might have ended in bloodshed by saying, 'Let her go. It is of her own will. I know Kajinsha. He will honour his commitment. One day we will see them here again when the time is right. Let her go.' Oh, how foolish she had been! Now looking into his eyes she hoped with all her heart that Lendem would be her friend forever and become a great chief and leader of men.

A few days after this meeting with Lendem, the arrival of Father Krick into Mebo was heralded by a great shout from the foot of the hill where Lendem had gone with eighteen young men to meet him. Gimur heard dogs barking and peered out to see a shaggy dog with his tongue hanging out turning and twisting in excitement. It was the dog, called Lo-rr-an! She recognised his tail waving like a plume and wanted to laugh. The name was on the tip of her tongue but she stopped herself in time from calling out. It would lead the party straight to her door. She darted back into the house and watched the strange procession through the cracks in the bamboo.

'Hoi! Hoi!' A shout went up and as if by magic a throng of people surged out of nowhere to join the young men escorting the priest to the village moshup. Men leapt over the stones. Women screamed and covered their faces with their hands. Children climbed up trees and clung to branches like monkeys. As if not to be left out the entire canine brood of the village followed hot on Lorrain's tail adding to the pandemonium with their wild yelps as if they, too, wanted answers to questions like where had he come from, and what was life like elsewhere? Everything was movement and noise and shouting and laughing as the people of Mebo jostled and jumped up and down to get a look at the stranger. Gimur caught a glimpse of Moi trying to touch the priest with her walking stick. Moi was so small Gimur knew she could only see the bulk of the man's shoulder. She looked across and saw Nago sitting upright in her veranda with no expression on her face. Lendem walked past. She saw the priest wiping the sweat off his face and smiling. She recognised him so clearly. He was always smiling. I hope he leaves soon. What will he do here? she thought.

For the priest his entry into Mebo was the culmination of a plan that he had secretly harboured since the time he had first set eyes on the Abor a year ago. So many things had happened since then. His colleague Louis Bernard was now confirmed in his duty of procurator but the missionaries had given up their residence in Gowhattee and Krick had spent the whole summer in Dacca writing a batch of reports for his professor of Tibetan in Paris. Now he did not want to waste the dry season. The future of the Tibet mission might be uncertain but Krick was not one to give up easily. He had been to Tibet and back. The expedition had tested him to the limit but he had not given up the idea of a return, if only he could find another route to avoid passing through Mishmee territory. A letter from the Directors in Paris also urged him to continue his exploration for a route into Tibet from the east and announced the impending arrival of a young colleague to assist him in his endeavours. But Krick knew from experience that his colleague's arrival in Assam would not be before the spring and that there was still time for him to visit the Abor. Just before his departure for Mebo he received another letter from the Directors informing him of the resignation of Jules Rabin, his former superior, and his appointment now to the post of superior of the mission of south Tibet with the title of Prefect Apostolic.

The south Tibet mission… Perhaps that was what Krick was smiling about. Despite all his brave attempts in the past, he was still looking for a route to reach Tibet. It was what had brought him into Mebo, and he was smiling because he knew that this was perhaps his last solitary expedition. From now on his appointment as the mission's superior would limit him to a supervisory role but until then he had this time to be on his own, though now he was being crushed and deafened by the cheers and roars of the Abor as they wended their way up a steep path. Krick was aware that ever since the British had occupied Assam the Abor had viewed every man with white skin and a protruding nose with suspicion. It was a case of timeo danaos et dona ferentes… beware of Greeks bearing gifts, because experience had taught them that whether he came as an explorer, friend or trader, following on the heels of every white man came the army. They brought war and captivity. Yet here he was, a white foreigner who only carried his cross, a medicine box and possessions more modest than their own. He was a priest, a man of God, not a soldier carrying a gun. At the village gate two young warriors had brushed him down with enormous leafy branches. Krick thought he was being thrashed. 'What is this?' He laughed when he understood that it was a ritual to expel any evil spirit that might be stalking him. His feet scraped against the stones. He saw trees and a clear sky beyond. At last! He was among the tribe with the tattooed cross and the explorer's heart in him was full of curiosity and excitement.

When they reached the moshup a mighty roar went up as if to dispel the last of the demons that he might have brought with him and he was led into a spacious interior illuminated by several fires. It was a very long building with some twenty hearths that Krick could count before his eager hosts circled him and blocked out everything from view. They called him 'Padari' and placed an enormous helmet on his head that was decorated with a red tuft of dyed goat's and bear's fur with the tusks of wild boar crossed in front over his forehead. With this ceremony the meeting was declared open. He saw their staring eyes, felt their hands touch his robes, hair, everything, and heard their laughter and their shouts. Some food was placed before him. 'Eat,' they cried. 'If we eat together we are friends till the sun sets!'

It was a long night. The village chiefs surrounded him, asking him questions. He had been learning Abor for some months thinking it was a very pretty language, but now he found the words stuck in his mouth and wondered if anyone would understand his garbled speech. Nevertheless they cried, 'We believe you! We believe your intentions are pure!'

A young man who seemed to command respect said, 'We will allow you to pass through our territory to Tibet.' His name was Lendem.

'A colleague is coming from my country to join me in this mission. I request permission to wait for him here,' said Krick, addressing Lendem.

'Yes! You will stay here,' the crowd answered in one voice. The fires burned steadily, everyone seemed wide-awake, overjoyed, including the village cattle, pigs and fowl and especially the fleas that he could feel jumping on his body. Many times Krick had to step out to appease the curiosity of the crowd who had gathered outside the house. The scene reminded him of the reception in that far village of Sommeu. A vivid memory of a woman with a tattoo on her chin flashed before his eyes but in the sea of upturned faces he saw no one who resembled that unforgettable apparition. At last the man called Lendem announced that the miglun padari would sleep in the guardhouse adjacent to the moshup and slowly the crowd of onlookers began to disperse.

It was after this that Lendem came to Gimur's house. 'Do you recognise him?' He asked.

'Yes,' she said. 'He is the same man who was travelling in the Dau valley. He came to our house. Kajinsha had asked him to leave and I saw him travelling back to Assam when I was returning here.'

'Is he really a priest?'

Gimur thought about this. She had never exchanged a word with the man. She had only watched him from a distance talking to Kajinsha during those days they spent on the hill, and everything that she had seen about the man had puzzled her, but she was sure he would not strike fear into anyone's heart. She thought he was a stupid man who acted as if he was out on a walk ready to go on and on wherever he could find a path and shelter for the night.

'I don't know,' she replied.

They sat together in silence for a while, then Lendem said, 'Tomorrow we will know. If he is a man of God, he will heal the sick.'

Early the next morning Gimur went to sit on the rock overlooking the valley. It was the time that she loved best. Everything was wiped out by a mist as if the sky was still pressed to the earth's bosom and the intoxication of the night had drained it of colour. It was the hour of hushed expectancy when all creatures held their breath until the morning breeze whispered something and earth and sky began to draw apart to make way for the sun. Nothing would awaken until the sun, almighty Donyi Polo, the eye of the universe, opened over the rim of the mountain blazing with light and warmth.

Gimur waited. Soon she heard the sounds she had been listening for. A piercing shout echoed round the village. 'All you in your houses listen! Listen! The stranger sahib, PADARI migom, in our village is coming to visit the sick! Everyone, everyone! The padari migom is going to heal the sick!' The announcement was repeated several times and in the council house Krick was up immediately.

'Yes,' he cried. 'Let us go!' Invitations were already pouring in from everywhere to go and look after the sick. He met Lendem and told him, 'I am a priest. I am not a doctor, but I will visit all the houses as you desire. If the simple ointments I carry can be of help I will be happy to administer these in the name of the Lord.'

'It will be fine,' said Lendem.

Krick soon discovered that there was someone ill or bedridden in every house. His notes of the time spent in Mebo testify to the number of patients who willingly submitted to his ministrations. Here is a young woman, he wrote, whose arm is covered with a horrible ulcer… When he asked when she had got that the woman replied that three years ago she had killed a rat and the disease had started then. Another patient exposed a stomach swollen to awful dimensions and a young man lay like a corpse eaten up with scrofula. His legs were swollen and his body was covered with ulcers. How long have you been ill? The man replied that he had been a stout, brave warrior until the evil spirits had got hold of him. Krick realised that the people here had no faith in drugs and medical diagnosis. Everything that befell a man came from the spirit world and the only physician was the shaman who could intercede with the spirits that caused human beings to fall ill and die.

He was in the midst of a sea of suffering. He opened his medicine chest and began to treat the sick. All he had were simple remedies, the bare minimum of liniments, poultice, sometimes it was just a sip of water he held out to a man. 'I am not a doctor!' he exclaimed many times, feeling helpless, but the sick everywhere are willing believers. They turned their faces to him. 'Give us hope!'

they beseeched him. Krick worked all day. He applied ointments with his hands and bandaged the worst festering sores. He felt the breath of the poor, suffering men and women on his face and prayed that his ministrations would bring them some relief. If the power of the shaman was based on exorcism and unshakeable faith in the unseen, he too had turned into a foreigner shaman, the man who created belief that his touch would cure them. In some houses the old and infirm sat up and said they were already feeling better. It was a strange alchemy. It is through faith that we are healed, he thought, smiling at their loud proclamations and the way he was working like a French Hippocrates when he had no knowledge of medicine. All he had was compassion and a feeling for friendship for Lendem and the excited villagers who now cried, 'You are a great man.' He learnt a new phrase then—kusereng migom—a great healer, a medicine man.

Gimur heard their voices rising and falling. The sun was drooping over the hill when she decided that it was safe to return to the village and hear all the news about the priest from Lendem. She jumped down from the rock. The light was fading and her movements were swift and silent when suddenly she stopped. A strange, slow melody was breaking over the treetops. She recognised it. It was the music of the flute. Quick! She wanted to turn around and run but it was too late. There was a break in the music, Gimur heard a soft footfall, a murmur of voices, and the priest was standing right before her with a look of utter astonishment on his face. The woman with the tattooed cross! He recognised her immediately.

'Ho!' he cried, 'Hallo!'

Gimur stared back at him. It is my village. Why should I run away, she thought, standing unmoving and blocking the narrow path. Just then Lendem came up. He was smiling. He held the priest's flute in his hand and was admiring it. 'Did you hear him playing this just now?' he asked Gimur as if they had all been strolling together. She nodded. Who would not hear and remember that sad music? It had wrapped itself around her soul a long time ago in those mountains where she had lost a part of her life. Now she did not want any more of it. But Lendem was telling her about the healing powers of the priest and how everyone now wanted him to stay with them forever, and Krick, observing their interaction and hearing Gimur speak now understood that this was her native village. For the remainder of his stay in Mebo he would see her every day, and Gimur, on her part, would watch him closely and feel her hard heart stirring, as if she was waking from a deep sleep.

Something had been returned to her with the music of the flute. While life in the village swirled around her Gimur sat on the hillside barely heeding the shouts of men and women who were crowding into the priest's shabby hut and turning it into a hospital. Her thoughts were far away.

She saw a slanting house high on a ridge in the mountains of the Dau valley. How unfortunate I am! She thought. But I was looking for love; that was the reason I ran so far. Even now when she knew deep in heart that she had lost the battle it was impossible to say she was defeated. Perhaps I am being punished. Did I forget the taboos? Yet, as long as there is breath in my body I will never bow down to any god and beg for mercy, she told herself. We are all created, all the offspring of Donyi Polo, from the bat and the worm struggling to mate and breed, to man and woman, for this one purpose—to love. I am unfortunate, but I did nothing wrong!

In those final March days Gimur was entering a realm from which there was no turning back. The arrival of the priest had changed the landscape. How could he have climbed these mountains? He had legs the colour of ivory, she had seen them once when he was crossing a stream and he had pulled up his robe, and his trousers underneath, a little. The man was always dressed in a black robe except for the time on the hill when Kajinsha had befriended him and they had shared food, water, salt. Then she had seen him wrapped in a long, grey coat as if to hide his hunger and weakness. In Mebo, now, she watched him slyly. He was surrounded by her people and he was washing their sores, wiping away blood and pus and dressing their injured flesh with cloth. His eyes were downcast and his face was white and pointed at the chin where it was covered by a full beard. Something was tapping in a corner of her heart. Look! See those hands? His fingers were long and bony. Look, look at his face. He was so thin. His eyes had changed. They were darker, sadder. What had saddened him? A broken love? A child buried by a river? His sorrow could not be greater than hers. But there it was, in his eyes, like the shadow of a ghost. And yet, this priest was still struggling with his mission when she thought he had been defeated. What kind of love did he carry in his heart? He did not smile at her anymore, but he came to the ledge on the hill and stared down at the valley.

Krick followed the path that Lendem had shown him. It led to a small clearing where Gimur went and he watched her as she walked before him. She had a very straight back and walked with a peculiar tilt holding her arms still by her side as if she was guarding something. Her narrow eyes were stretched back so tightly in her pale, taut face that they looked like black streaks painted on a mask, but it was an animated mask of changing expressions and vitality. Every time he saw her he thought of Bellona, the Roman goddess of war. Her aloof manner and posture intrigued him. He knew by now that Abor women possessed great spirit and vigour. When he had come into the village they had shown no fear of him. Instead they had unabashedly examined his arms and legs and face and some were even saucy enough to poke their heads into his hut and then run away laughing raucously, no doubt at his expense, he thought. Now he knew a little bit more about Gimur from Lendem. She had done the unthinkable. She was the female warrior who had crossed rivers and mountains carrying a bright banner of love with the man called Kajinsha. He did not know everything but from what he had learned from Lendem he knew about the death of her child and understood her grief and suffering. He remembered the way he had seen her in the Mishmee hills on the way down to Assam. She had been returning home, Lendem said. He had also seen her puffing a pipe near the bridge and all her movements then had indicated to him but one thing—flight. What else was there? He wondered. What was she running away from? He wanted to talk to her, offer some words of friendship, because of the time he had spent on that hillside when Kajinsha had brought him strips of meat and fish from their house.

'The hands of God are always stretched out to help you. His arms are open to receive you. Don't run away!' he wanted to tell her. But she did not turn to look his way. Her thoughts were hidden from him. They sat in silence, only a few feet separating them. On the black hill they were far away from people and though she did not speak to him, he felt he could hear her thoughts—so clear and so fiercely concentrated was his mind on her.

'I am pining,' he heard her say. 'The days move, one day after another. The flow of time is a stream. I will save myself, but I need some time. This is the reason why I am hiding my thoughts. If I speak it will mean I am seeking help and that will be the end of my strength. Do you understand?'

She puffed on her long Mishmee pipe. Krick waited. If she turned her gaze away from the mountains she would see his eyes looking at her before he quickly turned them away. People said he was a good medicine man. She had seen him stooping over the sick woman in the shabby, smelly hut. What does he think I will do? She wondered. Does he know there is nothing that I can do? My heart is dead. And there is nothing that I want to do except remain unmoveable as this rock. Only the soul of a child can reach my heart.

The priest stirred when she bent her head. He could not see her face but he leaned forward a little, shifting his arm because he thought a sob had escaped her lips. He longed to lay his hand on her head. She sensed his movement and in a minute her face was distant and set. She stared at him fiercely with bright eyes and then turned away staring intently into the distance. The words he thought he heard her speak gave utterance to his own tortured questions.

'You tell me about love. The love of a God whose name we have never heard. Where does he live?'

This was a question Krick could not answer. What answer could he give this woman who held his gaze with such unflinching ferocity? Sunlight flooded the hills. A pool of light rose up from the valley below and the broad river shone through cracks in the tree cover like molten gold. 'There is a God who dwells in heaven.' He could have said this to the initiated, but how could he explain where heaven was? He could not describe the physical features of such a place to her. A place beyond the clouds surrounded by the saved souls of all the good men and women would be an alien and hateful place for this woman. The shaman had also scorned his explanations, but the shaman knew about souls so he had a connection there.

'Do you believe in the words of your miri?' he asked. There was no response. He sank back with a sigh when he suddenly thought he heard her say, 'The miri says we came from a land beyond the skies. It is there we will return when we die. You, priest, you tell us we will be born again the same way. Everyone wants to believe this—life after death. It is a beautiful dream. It is not for me. I have entered darkness. It is only in this darkness that I can now see the light. It is not the light of God that you tell me about. It is not the spirit of my ancestors. It is something I have given birth to. It is all I have and all that I know. But I will never give up. Perhaps there will be a second chance.'

A soft breeze was blowing in bringing another invasion of clouds creeping up over the mountains to the north and west. The priest began to pray silently. He felt he was standing on the dome of the rock. This was a holy place. There was no deception here. Everything he beheld was true to its original nature. This included the tribes he had met and the people of Mebo who, in the estimation of many like him, were considered uncivilised and debased natives. They had treated him well. He knew many of his countrymen and the British captains would not survive in these jungles without the help of the natives. Had not Kajinsha the Mishmee told him the land was their book? The memory of Kajinsha brought back thoughts of his south Tibet mission. Soon he would have to leave this place and travel northward again across the mountains. Far below him the Siang River seemed to stand still against the curving flank of the mountain before it cut loose and spread into a thousand silver strands that swept into the distance reflecting the rays of the sun. And in that moment he knew, without a doubt, that the end, whichever way it came or form it took, either cruel death or resurrection, would come from these hills.

'Help me Lord,' he prayed, 'to be patient in suffering and to persevere in prayer!'

That evening Father Krick was seated in front of a throng of people in Nago's house. A great shaman had arrived in the village. He had come to see Nago but tonight he was going to perform a ritual ipak for the sick young man whom Krick had already met.

'Come padari, sit near the fireplace,' Lendem called him. From here Krick could see the sick man lying on a mat in the corner with Nago seated beside him and next to her, Gimur. A man stood up from the shadows behind them, and a hush fell over the crowd. He was stocky, dressed in a red woven cloth knotted around his waist and a heavy necklace of blue beads covered his bare chest. In his hand he carried a long sword, and as he began to move around the room, swaying on his feet as if about to leap into the air, he brandished the sword, making the metal discs on its handle sing. 'His name is Mutsang. He is a very powerful miri,' Lendem whispered to Krick. The miri was chanting. Lendem explained, 'The ghost of a dead warrior rises up and searches the land looking for a victim. If a person is weak the spirit alights and sits on his mouth, on his eyes and on his head. It requires a very powerful shaman to drive him away…'

What is that curious light hidden in the eyes of the miri? Krick wondered. It was a light that was both alive and passive. It was impossible to describe. As the miri entered a trance his pupils dilated and he looked like a wild cat caught in a ferocious battle with a shadowy predator. Everyone stopped breathing. The miri was jumping from side to side. He had cut a chicken with his sword, and now his rasping voice was ordering the spirits to move out of the house. The spirits were moving at his command, emerging out of the darkness. 'Begone! Out, evil one!' Father Krick stared, entranced. He felt drawn to the miri as if they were allies, kindred souls. The miri held the slaughtered bird over the sick man, laid his beads on the man's head and slashed the air with his sword. In another world, thought Father Krick, a priest might have done the same, holding a cross aloft and lighting a candle to dispel the darkness. Darkness and fear that steal into the labyrinths of a man's mind which is always tilting towards darkness and dreams, causing pain and sickness… Sursum Corda! Lift up our hearts! Let us stand well. Let us stand in awe. Let us be attentive so that we may present the holy offering in peace…

The ritual ended, and Krick emerged from his own trance. The dead chicken would be offered as appeasement to the spirits who had been driven out. Everyone was talking animatedly now as if each one had been given a new lease on life. Out of the corner of his eye Krick saw Gimur rising up and he thought she was smiling at him. If only he could follow her. The house, the fire, the children and everyone within seemed to be rising up and coming towards him like old friends and he felt frightened by the state of altered consciousness that had seized him. It was the same way he had felt when he had watched in admiration one morning as the people of Mebo made a bridge across the river using only twisted cane rope and rattan. This swift, miraculous construction had been preceded by the sacrifice of a dog.

'We have to keep the jealous spirits busy,' Lendem had told him. 'Otherwise a man may fall to his death, a knot may slip. Anything can happen.'

Krick had looked into Lendem's black, serious eyes and begun to believe him. Now he felt convinced again of the power and rightness of what he had just witnessed. Was it not the same elsewhere, he thought—all rituals have their roots in tradition. This was the tradition of the Abor who believed that everything that happened to a man was controlled by good and evil spirits. It was man's obligation to pay heed to and respect the unknown and unseen. It was a tradition rooted in faith. Where, then, was reason? Perhaps there was a place here, Krick thought, where reason and faith were not in opposition but seemed to combine. It was the way a dying man could believe in the return of his soul and be cured by faith in the miri who could divine cause and reason after communicating with the spirit world. Was it not the same with the holy sacrament and prayer? Mercy and peace, a sacrifice of praise… When we close our eyes to pray we become believers. When the shaman chants and the women sing they forget everything. They are singing love, singing hope. Do not be sad. I will return to take you home with me. There is happiness in store for you. The faithful will be rewarded. What do you want? Deliverance! Then open your heart and let the Holy Spirit enter. The Holy Spirit of happiness, of joy, of courage, war, and triumph!

Alone in his shack Krick pondered over all that he had witnessed.

It was March, the day was Good Friday, and he wanted to pray and gather his thoughts but his mind was restless. I am here, a Catholic priest, he thought, but my stay here is permitted only because I am regarded as a healer, a doctor priest. Medicine, it was medicine that had saved him with the Mishmee and it was the same here. What power lies in the hand that cures! If I had had the chance to use this art in Tibet no doubt I would have been allowed to stay on in Sommeu too, he thought. He pulled out his papers and wrote to the Directors in Paris asking for some forty kilos worth of medicine packed into a box that he could carry on his back. It would be his vade mecum, he said, with which he hoped to make his way into Tibet again. It was the sick in body that had followed Jesus and the apostles. May God grant that by these bodily ministrations I can reach their souls!

He took out his flute and tried to play a tune. Without moving Lorrain opened his eyes for a moment and the spots above his brow moved a fraction then drooped again. The priest thought he heard a movement outside. Maybe it was Gimur? Sometimes he felt she was shadowing him, spying on him. He wished he could waylay her by turning around a corner with words of greeting in her language. 'Hello! Kapeii, no aidung? How are you? Are you following me?' he would ask. He stopped playing and smiled to himself, tapping on his basket with his fingers. 'Come, I will give you some tea. Sugar?' He wondered what she would say to that! It was a passing thought to make him feel light-hearted. Her black eyes might meet his and perhaps, perhaps, she would part her lips and smile.

He must have dozed off, for the next thing he knew Lorrain was barking furiously and someone was shouting. 'Quick padari! Fire! Fire!' The shouting grew louder. 'Quick!' A blast of hot air hit him when he ran out. The priest thought his shack was on fire but it was a house a few metres above from where a cloud of ash and smoke was blowing downwind. Father Krick was stunned to see a group of men armed with long spears leaping up and down around the flaming house. 'What are they doing?' he shouted. 'They are chasing away the fire demon!' someone shouted. 'No, no, fetch water,' he cried. He grabbed his water bottle and ran towards the fire. 'Stay back! Stay back!' shouted Lendem. Some young men were in fact trying to turn the long bamboo water pipe that ran through the village towards the burning house.

'No!' Father Krick could not wait. He threw his bottle into the fire and watched it sink into the flames with a small hiss. 'More water! Asi! Asi!' he shouted. Lendem shouted again and the crowd began to run to the water point shouting for everyone to come out of their houses with water.

It was pandemonium. The fire was indeed a demon with grotesque arms and legs twisting higher and higher in the wind and shooting bright sparks into the trees as if determined to burn the village to the ground. It was a battle with a mighty enemy. Everyone was involved and everyone cursed the fire with screams and threats as they ran back and forth carrying water until at last a shout of triumph went up as the flames spluttered and died down into a black mound of charcoal. The fire demon had been slain but something else had been ignited. There was fear in the eyes of women as they went back to their houses and a silence among the men as they stood there panting after their exertions.

In the middle of the afternoon Lendem came to him. 'Padari,' he said, 'you are my friend. I have enjoyed your stay with us. You are a good man, but now…'

'Now, yes?'

'The fire… It is not a good sign. The kebang has decided that you must leave.'

Father Krick sighed. This order did not surprise him. A few days ago a rumour had reached the village that the priest was a spy for the migluns. The village council had decided then to expel him but Lendem had quelled their fears; more than that it was the sick villagers he had treated and their families who had come out in protest. 'Stay with us! You are our father and our children will bless your memory,' they had cried. He knew Lendem had defended him again but this time his had been a lone voice. Superstition still ruled the people here and the fire had frightened everyone.

'It is all right, I will leave,' he said.

Lendem stayed silent. When he saw Father Krick preparing his baskets he lurched forward as if stop him. 'You can stay a few more days!' he said. But Father Krick knew that it was prudent to submit to the popular wish of the village. It was a way to safeguard the future of the mission, for if anything happened, if someone died or some cattle went missing, it would reawaken suspicion and that would mean the end of the mission. 'Fiat voluntas tua... they are chasing me away but one day I will return.' He wanted to keep a line open and leave while he still had Lendem's friendship. For now he was happy in the knowledge that he had made himself everything for everyone in Mebo and he was going away with a first-hand account of the Abor that it was not given to many to know. One day, he hoped, they would be happy to see a Catholic missionary in their midst again.

Krick left Mebo on Holy Saturday of March 1853. He visited his patients and treated them one last time before he stepped out through the gate bristling with totems that had so shocked him when he had clambered up these stones and entered the village. He was accompanied by Lendem and two young men to escort him to the outskirts of Mebo territory. From there on he would be alone. Another chapter had closed. On Easter Sunday a violent storm broke over the hills as if to tear open the earth and bury all traces of Krick's presence in Mebo. And it happened that way. As he stumbled through the labyrinth of bamboo, rocks and trees Krick felt a terrible illness creeping up on him. He had treated the sick and now a fever was gnawing at his bones. It struck him down with overwhelming force as if to slay him and indeed the records are silent about the journey of the priest during the intervening period from the time he left Mebo till autumn of the same year.

◆

The Days in our Hands. The Truth about Love. Lendem's Wisdom

In July clouds hung over the mountains surrounding Mebo and slipped down the valley like floating ribbons. Everyone was talking about a strange thing that had happened. Nago had a dream about a tree standing by a small path that suddenly splintered into pieces. She woke up shouting, 'Moi is dead! Moi is dead!' Everyone in the house cried 'Hai! It's a dream. It's a dream.' Moi was alive and well in the next village. Nago went back to sleep but in the morning a runner arrived from Moi's village shouting that Moi had been crushed to death in her hut by a falling tree.

Everything in that dream had happened! The villagers were aghast.

'It was an accident. Didn't you see the storm, how hard it rained? How hard the wind was blowing that night?' cried Lendem. But no one listened. With the death of Moi a thread seemed to have snapped. Gimur felt another door close. Beloved Moi! In this small superstitious village she had been a beacon of light for Gimur. Had she not given her a book and a pencil? With what thoughts had the old lady bestowed these things on her? 'Don't go,' she wanted to cry out. 'Moi! I have come back! I want to hear what you have to say to me. I thought you would be here forever. Don't go!' But a thin trickle of blood staining her mouth was all that Moi showed her now. Moi had died with all her secrets of another life in a long forgotten past. Gimur saw Lendem mopping his face and felt the first prickle of tears behind her dry eyelids. No, no, she did not want to weep. All her tears had been shed for her dead child. But her heart was thudding. She struggled to focus on other things. Nago was telling everyone that after she went back to sleep she had returned to the exact point of her dream before she had woken up shouting that Moi was dead. 'I was standing on this road,' she said, 'and I was picking up every leaf and twig. After a while I created a tree.'

People exclaimed that Nago had received a special gift from Donyi Polo. She had been granted the power of healing. It was at this point that a rite called taagil panam was announced to secure Nago's status as a true shaman.

'Don't be stupid. Nago has fits. It is due to her emotional nature that she is having dreams and seeing these things!' cried Lendem.

The miri looked at him angrily. 'I know where the taagil grows,' he said. 'The time has come for us to perform this rite. Don't tell me it is not necessary. It will be done.'

One day Gimur was sitting in Nago's house where people gathered every day when she heard the miri saying, 'The uyus are taking Lendem away from us.'

The uyu, the ghost, was the French priest and Lendem's friendship with him when he was in the village had offended a group of village elders.

'Hai... ever since the arrival of these people our lives are changing,' they said.

'We will put an end to it,' said the shaman. There was a moment's silence, then Gimur heard his voice again. 'We have sent out word for everyone to assemble here to talk about these things. It is not good to take no action. The minds of our people are easily stolen. I am worried.'

What a place, she thought. No sooner is a man's back turned than they begin to talk about him. How suspicious they are! This was what she hated about the village. It was so small, with all the families huddled together. There was no space for anyone to escape. The collective superstition and fear suffocated their lives. And yet, weren't the elders justified in their suspicion and anger? History had shown them that no matter how friendly they were, in the end the migluns brought only death and destruction. When she asked Lendem he said, 'The priest is a man just like us. If he wants to know something about us why should we be afraid? We are honest people. If we speak the truth Donyi Polo will protect us.'

Lendem had changed. He had once opposed the entry of strangers into the village, and Gimur recalled his reaction when he had found out about her relationship with Kajinsha. Lendem's speech and manner had been contemptuous and challenging. Anyone leaving the village with an outsider would be an outcast. But she had returned and he had helped in her rehabilitation. And he had let the priest in. Now with Moi's death it seemed to Gimur that he had taken on another mantle. Lendem was asking questions. 'If a stranger asks us about our beliefs, why should we suspect his reason for asking?' he said. 'A question deserves attention and an honest answer.'

'The miri thinks you are trying to follow the ways of the miglun,' Gimur said.

'Hai, I am but an intermediary and interpreter. I gave my word to protect the priest. Poor man! He was only looking for a way to reach Tibet. Now he is gone, why should anyone worry about him anymore?'

But they were worried. The priest had gone but his visit had created something. Surely someone had been touched, someone would remember his face, someone would feel drawn to his words or his clothes or anything at all, and it would mean the beginning of change in someone's heart. Even Gimur found herself seeking answers. Kajinsha and Lendem—people like them, and maybe even Moi, who had told her about the ways of the migluns…they were the ones who wanted to know more. They wanted to be ready for everything. Maybe, she thought, they were braver than the others because they were willing to try. Try to see if change would bring a better life, bring peace, and most important of all, in these dark hills, banish fear from the lives of men and women.

'We can sing new songs,' said Lendem. 'Our miri, padari and his cross, the miglun gods, there is no contest here. All gods are equally powerful. And if there is a contest among gods than let it be their contest,' he said.

'What about our rituals? Are you giving up our beliefs?' she asked him.

Lendem was genuinely shocked. 'Hai! What do you mean? I might as well let the blood drain from my body than say I give up our beliefs. How can I be anyone but the way I was born? I believe in our gods as much as the miglun does in his. I am only examining some things in order to know more. One day our children will ask us, what is this belief, who created it?'

She looked at him and smiled. Lendem, her warm hearted brother! Friend and companion! She had never heard him talking so much before. It seemed to Gimur that they had exchanged places. If he was full of eager curiosity to know about men and strangers and the new migluns settlements creeping up along the banks of the river, she was full of doubt and unwilling to venture out anywhere. When evening fell she retreated to the veranda at the back of the house and sat like an old woman who wanted to be left alone. Sometimes she took out the book Moi had given her and stared at the letters as if they would suddenly begin speaking to her. She thought about the priest. She could not say his name. She had no image of the land he came from. It was a blank space. But here, in their midst she had seen him as another ami—man. Everything about him, from his eyes and nose, skin and clothes and the words he spoke were different; but when she spied on him, she had found what was invisible; that his heart, thoughts and needs were just like theirs. Food, water, shelter. This was what everyone needed in order to live. Beyond this there was hope and fear, and longing that he expressed by his attention to the sick and even to her...and beyond this, beyond them all a vision that she too was striving for—courage! How to face adversity? Be patient, she told herself. Wait. Something will emerge out of this broken landscape.

From Lendem and Moi, and Nago and the words of the shaman she had learned a new respect for the things that were theirs. With respect came a new humility equal to an all-encompassing love and forgiveness for all that had happened. It was a mysterious state of being where all rage and sorrow had fallen away, leaving only the passion.

She did not dream anymore but she stayed awake listening to the dogs barking all night. Were they dogs from the nearby villages or was the sound of barking carried by the wind from across the river? Everything was close and far. She thought time had stopped. Then a breeze touched her face and she recalled it was planting time again. There was no rest. Heavy, torrential summer rain flooded the village and fields and wiped out the mountains from view. What occurred during this time? Everything fell into silence beneath the blanket of cloud and rain. All the stories were drowned. Someone was spinning on a loom spreading pillars of clouds into a black mantle that would fall on these trees, this path, and sweep everything away. No one would remember what lay buried beneath this avalanche of time.

But a clear, strong wind was blowing day and night as if in search of something beneath the silence, to pull out a long lost story. A man was approaching from the east. Kajinsha was following a hidden path in the labyrinth of trees and rocks. His shoulders gleamed. His eyes shone with a fierce, compelling light as he raced against the wind while high above him big clouds gathered, towering higher and higher into dark wings ready to cover the world. A storm was approaching.

One day Gimur stood knee-deep in mud on a narrow ledge cut into the mountainside. The sound of water thundered in her ears. The rain had stopped but the small stream that ran past her field had turned into a gushing torrent swollen with silt and debris from upstream. She was bending, planting paddy, feeling the warmth of the sun on her back when someone hailed her softly. She froze. It was a voice she recognised. The bunch of paddy shoots slipped from her hands. Without straightening up she turned her head slowly and looked over her shoulder. She saw the figure of a man silhouetted against the sun craning towards her. He was twisting a white woollen cap round and round in his hand. Awesa!

'You!' she cried, and stopped, not knowing what else to say.

A broad smile stretched across Awesa's face. Then he gulped and his eyes began flickering here and there as if he was shy or afraid to meet her gaze.

'How are you Awesa?' she said.

His face broke into a wide smile again, showing all his teeth. Gulping with excitement he told her that Kajinsha had sent him to find her. 'Tell her I am in Chunpura,' he had instructed Awesa. 'Tell her I am waiting here for her to come back with you.'

No, no, I cannot leave now… was Gimur's first thought. Why have you come now? But she saw Awesa's eager face and stopped. She wiped her hands on the wet leaves and took Awesa to the hut. 'Tell me everything,' she said.

It had taken Awesa a very long time to reach his village. After he had left her he had wandered like a lost soul eating leaves and shoots in the forest. Gimur suspected that Awesa had deliberately avoided returning home because he was afraid of facing Kajinsha and telling him that his son was dead. Awesa might have continued living like a forest animal without anyone finding him but one day he fell ill. He was starving, and suffering from a sadness that made him weep uncontrollably as he lay burning with fever on the forest floor. Somehow he had made his way to Chunpura where Chowsa had found him and helped him. It had taken him two months to make his way back to the Dau valley. All this time Kajinsha had been alone. He did not know about the death of Siengbow until Awesa returned and told him everything. A terrible silence had descended between father and son. Then one day Marpa had appeared at their doorstep.

'Greetings, my friend!' he had cried. 'How is everybody? May the blessings of ten thousand Buddhas be upon you!' Marpa had brought maize and a thick slab of yak cheese. As they ate together Marpa said, 'I have come to propose an idea. The British have sent word that they are willing to meet a regent of Tibet. However we do not want them to come to us. Heh heh, you understand, don't you? And you, I know, will never allow them to pass through your territory. So what have we here?' Marpa stopped and, chewing, looked around. He lowered his voice. 'A plan…' he whispered. 'We have a plan for the regent to meet the British without them coming into the Zayul valley. A lama will carry this message and I have convinced the dzongpon that you, Kajinsha, will be the best escort for our emissary to meet the British in Saikwa Ghat. What do you say to that?'

'Why don't you be the escort?' said Kajinsha.

'I would, I would. But the summer is too hot for me. I cannot tolerate heat! And, ahem! I am tied up with some business, you know,' he continued, looking pointedly at Kajinsha all the while. Chhomu, his niece, the girl with the red cheeks, was ill with a strange ailment that kept her in bed weeping that a devil was taking possession of her. 'Ah, poor girl! She is so young, but I know it is a passing phase. Too much imagination,' he said. 'Awesa's mother is too sick to look after her so you see, I have to be there. We cannot leave her alone. Ah… well, everything is in God's hands, is it not?' he finished.

Kajinsha was silent, like a trapped animal.

'I will go to meet the white men,' he said finally. 'Tell me what message you have for them.'

'Oh thank you, thank you! You are a good friend! Everything is here,' cried Marpa, opening a parchment and quickly rolling it up again. He stuffed it into a bag and began eating again with great gusto. 'The lama will join you and he will be supplied with provisions. I would go with you, my friend,' he repeated, 'but as I said, it is too hot for me, hah! Hah!'

Kajinsha made this promise to Marpa so that he could get away from the man and the insidious reach of his Zayul valley connection. He felt hemmed in, poisoned by the presence of Marpa. At the same time he knew that as escort to the emissary he would have official status to enter the British camp. It was time to meet the strangers face to face. He thought of the priest. The man had not been as threatening as he had imagined all white people to be, but in a corner of his heart he kept his distrust alive. There was another reason why Kajinsha agreed to Marpa's proposal. It was something that he would never acknowledge or speak about. He was in search of Gimur. He buried his face in his hands. He did not want to travel through Abor territory just yet. Chowsa had told him about the visit of the priest to Mebo there and he did not want to enter Gimur's village as if following in the footsteps of a miglun priest. So he had decided to send Awesa.

'But I cannot come now,' cried Gimur. 'Later, later, I will come later, I will send news,' she repeated as she hastily sent Awesa off on the path leading out of the village.

When she told Lendem about this meeting with Awesa, Lendem said: 'Yes, I thought Kajinsha might be close by. If he came here I would give a feast for both of you. It is time to settle these things.

Tell me, what do you want to do?'

When she did not answer and Lendem asked 'Is something wrong?' Gimur bent her head. That same question again… No, there was nothing wrong. Everything was in place. She was a woman, Kajinsha's wife; young, in good health and still capable of bearing children, but—what was this hollow feeling, this cry of frustration? Who could explain? She felt time was moving and she didn't know if she had lived enough or if something else was possible.

'I will go when the weather is better,' she replied at last.

'Good! I will send word,' cried Lendem. 'It is the right thing to do. I will take you to Kajinsha.'

It was November when Gimur and Lendem finally set out from Mebo. Gimur had the impression of leaves swirling down on her head…a shower of leaves brought by an invisible wind—then it was gone. Lendem was leading the way and saying, 'Kajinsha is a good man. I know of his courage and strength. I hope he's still there in Chunpura.'

I know he will be there, thought Gimur, but she did not say this aloud. What she knew about Kajinsha was her secret. He would be there if he had told Awesa that he would wait until she returned to him. Otherwise he would come to Mebo to find her. There was another secret. She knew Lendem was sad to see her go away but he hid his feelings behind a cheerful face. Sometimes I have played with you, she wanted to tell him. I wanted to make you jealous and I wanted you to think of me as unpredictable and wild so that you would be forever bound to me if I kept you in suspense. But here is the truth. I have needed you but I do not love you. I need your friendship. In a way, yes, I need you to let me use you. Is this fair? Can we be friends like this? She looked at Lendem carrying all their provisions and even as she thought this she knew she was using him again because she knew he would say, 'Yes!'

Mamang Dai

When they passed the patch of forest along the river bank Gimur thought she would see the spot where she had knelt over the small grave of her son. She had sworn never to forget but everywhere she looked she saw new growth of giant fern and bamboo. The jungle had reclaimed everything. She felt a sudden spurt of anger at Kajinsha who she felt had started all this. It was his stubborn will and insistence that had drawn her out of Mebo, she thought, that had caused so much pain. What have you given me? She recalled shouting at him—and his answer: I have given you love! Hah! A broken, thwarted love, she had thought.

But it was love, yes, she told herself now. She had loved and tasted a passion that was equal in grandeur to a state of being alone and complete. Every step of the way had been a quest for this. Sometimes it was full of joy, sometimes it had been hard and bitter, but no matter what, one could no more give up this quest than give up breath and life. Otherwise why would she be undertaking this journey again? Sometimes she saw Lendem who was walking ahead also stop and look around as if he was seized with doubt, wondering what they were doing here in the middle of the forest. Were they really moving on the path towards Kajinsha? She remembered the small boat hidden in the reeds—where was it? Everything looked different. All she could see were trees, a glint of water shining like glass, and now and then a full view of mountains stretched across the horizon. They spoke little to conserve energy and the speed and silence of their travel was like that of the bat and bear, and leopards hunting at night covering hundreds of miles of territory.

It was an unbelievable moment when late one evening Gimur heard Lendem say, 'We are near Chunpura. Here is the path to Chowsa's house.'

Gimur felt she was looking at herself in a dream. She was approaching a hut in a small clearing under a deep, inky blue sky. A fire was burning outside and a man was sitting hunched up close to it with his back to them. Chowsa sat on the other side facing them. Lendem raised a hand in greeting and Chowsa's eyes flicked towards the other man. Everything was silent. They were drawing closer. Kajinsha did not move but now Gimur saw the outline of his cheek puff out in a broad, self conscious smile. Her heart leaped.

'Hai, Lendem!' cried Chowsa. 'Hai, capmi! Brother!' Both men were standing now and for a moment Gimur thought she had lost her sight. She could not see nor hear anything, so loud was the beating of her heart when Kajinsha turned and his eyes met hers in a fierce, concentrated gaze.

Every day the sun travels across the sky. Even when clouds block out everything her orange glow can be seen moving behind the clouds. Sun mother! Gimur had heard a story about her. She had a beautiful baby whose nursemaid was a dove. Every time she went away on her great journey it was the dove that carried the child on her back and sang songs till the day ended and the sun returned home. In Chunpura, as night fell and Kajinsha lay down next to Gimur, she told him the story: 'One day, the cane strap used for carrying the baby on her back broke and fell to earth. "I will fetch it!" cried the dove and flew down. She retrieved the strap but could not make her way back to the house of the sun. Now the dove sees the sun moving across the sky throwing its light over fields of paddy, river and grass, and weeps.'

What are the words of love? What is their sound? Desire grows out of small gestures and pure thoughts. Sometimes it is simply the silence of loving. In the first days after Gimur returned, she and Kajinsha talked to each other in soft words to overcome their grief for the death of their child. Their relationship was still fraught with danger. Kajinsha could blow up and blame her for everything. She, on the other hand, was poised, ready to turn around and return to Mebo if he so much as whispered one wrong word. She would never be subdued, but step by step they were returning to a remembered place from where they had started when everything was new and shining with promise. Sometimes Gimur saw Kajinsha looking at her obliquely with the languorous eyes of a young boy. 'You are mine,' he would say and she would reply, 'Just because I have come here doesn't mean everything is all right.' But everything was all right. He nodded. She smiled at him. They occupied the hut while Chowsa slept out in the open with Lendem and Awesa and for the first time Gimur understood the sweet companionship of friends. She slept peacefully and woke at first light to the sound of birds and a breeze stirring the leaves. Kajinsha would be asleep, as if he too had dropped his guard in this peaceful place. Soon Lendem would be up and they would hail each other as she stoked the fire in the semi darkness. Every day they ate fish and rice. Chowsa liked to fish and he took Awesa to the best spots. They would be gone all day and return late in the evening, Awesa carrying a prize catch strung by the gills. Every day Lendem said he was off, going back to Mebo, but continued to stay because Kajinsha would cry out, 'No! Stay, stay one more day!' It was a happy time.

Kajinsha had finished his work with the white men, he had escorted a young lama from Marpa's country and he had seen the British trying to understand what the holy man was saying. 'I did not say anything,' he told them. He had been disgusted to see the Assamese and Singpho slaves working for the British and had simply handed Marpa's letter to the white man who had looked him up and down once and then told him that he could leave. 'They are scared of us seeing too much. The man who took the letter from me was surrounded by guards.' The lama had already left for Tibet but Kajinsha had stayed back, waiting for Gimur.

Gimur had thought Chunpura was an isolated place but Kajinsha told her that they were, in fact, very close to the British settlements. It was the dense forest and the swampy strip of reed grass—the haunt of herds of wild buffalo—that screened Chowsa's hut like an oasis.

No one could venture here unless they could navigate the network of watercourses and know the exact spot to come ashore.

'The place called Suddya is not far from here,' Kajinsha told her. 'And there are many families living in the villages around here that have carried on trade with the hill people since the time of the Ahom rulers. In my father's time, our people used to trade gold dust, amber, musk, daos and Burmese cotton cloth. Sometimes we used to come here and carry off not only food and cattle but even members of a family to work as labourers in our fields. Today Suddya is the place where the white men keep their gunboats and soldiers.' Then he pointed into the distance across the river and said there was another important post there called Dibru. 'It is even bigger than Suddya and the white men have offices and houses there. Look,' he said, 'remember it. These are the places from where the white men come into our hills. Don't forget this route.' Gimur looked but all she could see was dark, flowing water.

Soon the day came when Lendem said he was ready to go back to Mebo. 'I have rested long enough,' he said, laughing.

Gimur felt a twinge of fear. The first time she had left Mebo she had been less afraid. Now she had Lendem's blessings but this leave-taking was harder. Kajinsha stood with his arms folded across his chest and Chowsa handed Lendem his bag.

'I will send news,' said Lendem. 'Or I may come to visit you.'

'Yes, let us meet again', said Kajinsha. 'We will welcome you.' They stood together for a while, a little to the edge of the path in the green forest with nothing more to say. It was a moment when two men look into each other's eyes and realise they are holding the same belief, that the other knows what each is feeling and respects it. No words were needed. Lendem waved and Gimur flapped her hands madly feeling sudden tears pricking her eyes.

'We will also be taking your leave. We must go back to the Dau soon,' Kajinsha told Chowsa the same evening.

'Oh no, stay!' cried Chowsa. 'There is enough time. The weather is good and Awesa is learning to fish.'

But Kajinsha was restless. They had heard strange news— another white priest had arrived in Saikwa Ghat.

'How many priests are they sending, why are they all coming here?' Kajinsha wanted to know. 'And where is the other one?'

Chowsa looked at Gimur. 'I heard Krick was very sick after he left your village,' he said. 'Someone who saw him thought he was going to die. They sent him on a boat to a place in Assam for treatment. And now, can you believe it—he's back in Saikwa Ghat looking for guides to escort him north!' He asked Kajinsha, 'Will you let them pass?'

'They know the way. They can go to Tibet if they want but they cannot stay in our villages,' said Kajinsha. 'I don't know about Lamet and Khroussa and Limsa, they are friendly with the plains people, but I will never allow it in my territory.'

What is this man, thought Gimur, remembering padari Krick. He seemed to be dogging their footsteps! 'Why does he not go home?'

'The new priest has been sent from his country to help him,' said Chowsa. 'Their rulers are determined to send these poor men to Tibet! I wonder why.'

It was a question only the Directors of the Missions Étrangères de Paris could have answered, but at this point they were facing a dilemma of their own. Taking their cue from a letter Krick had sent the previous year telling them of his Tibetan journey to Sommeu and how he hoped to return there with bag and baggage after he had completed his journey to the Abor region, they had assumed that everything was going well with the south Tibet mission. This was before they had access to the other report Krick had sent to his teacher of Tibetan, Phillip-Edouard Foucaux, about his nightmarish return journey to Assam through Mishmee territory and his letter to Dr Bousquet at the Necker hospital in Paris informing him of his recent expulsion from Mebo. They were looking at two versions of Krick's journeys now. The Directors were confused. What kind of place were they dealing with here, where no known language was spoken, where savage tribes attacked and killed any stranger who dared to enter their terrible land? No one in Paris or Rome or anywhere in Europe could imagine the physical features of a land so remote, so densely covered in forest and dissected by mountains and rivers and battered by rain and crumbling earth, where a man could go mad wrestling with the elements in order to survive. All they knew was that a map of bewildering images was unfolding.

In anticipation of the establishment of a Tibet mission the Directors had already sent a young priest as reinforcement to help Krick in his work. His name was Augustin Etienne Bourry, from the diocese of Poitiers who had joined the Paris Foreign Missions in July 1851. They had first planned to send young Bourry to the mission in Korea, but now he would never reach those shores as he had already set sail for India on the *Vallée de Luz* several months ago. In Paris confusion turned to alarm. The dream of a south Tibet mission was turning into a nightmare but Krick and Bourry could not be recalled at a moment's notice. It was evident that they were pursuing an impossible task, perhaps at the risk of their lives, but from the rue du Bac there was no action possible other than that of despatching a letter urging Krick not to venture up the dangerous route through Mishmee territory a second time, but to travel with his colleague and draw up his future itinerary guided by experience and any information that he could gather. Father Krick's most recent mail had been an enthusiastic account of the Abor and in this case perhaps the Directors too were hoping for a new route into Tibet through the tribe of the tattooed cross.

1854

A Cherished Goal. Return to Sommeu. The Last Communication

The letter from the Directors lay in front of Krick. What information could he give them? What? First there was water. Then light, sunlight, then green…and always, hills—blue, pale, misty, inky blue, black. A black hill… he had been moving in a shifting world of water and sand and mountains. This was all Father Krick could fathom. What would the Directors make of this? It was no use, no use. He sat with his head clasped in his hands. Since the thunderstorm of Easter Sunday when he had left Mebo, the fever that had been gnawing at him for weeks had finally taken violent possession of his body. One morning he had woken up and felt his head was going to split open. He could not open his eyes which were on fire, and he was shivering. His legs buckled under him and it was only through sheer force of will that he had managed to drag his body towards the dim lights of Saikwa Ghat. A six-month nightmare had followed. He felt he had died and his soul had gone somewhere else; but even if he was dead, floating above the earth or sinking into a giddy emptiness with his eyes shut, he could still see water, and light, and green, and the inky blackness of the hills—only this, as if a rising mist had wiped away the memory of everything else in the world, leaving only these images thumping under his swollen eyelids.

'There is no way of saving him,' he had heard Dr Pingault say when they had carried him to Nowgong. It was a fever unknown in Europe and it killed in less than twenty-four hours. But he had survived. Perhaps it was his great will power that saved him, but he was returning from death's door a mere shadow of the man he was. His cheeks were dry and wrinkled and the slightest effort left him exhausted. He knew there was a route to Tibet but who would guide them now? The worst effect of the illness was the depression, a terrible ennui that frightened him more than anything else. The green gardens of the seminary in Paris—the striped sunlight and the shade under the big trees—were distant memories. Names floated out of a world he had left behind—names that were smoke when he tried to hold them, to remember. One name stayed: Charles Renou, his colleague in southeastern China. Krick had heard that Renou had received the title of Prefect Apostolic from Rome and spent a year incognito in a Buddhist monastery with a lama who had taught him Tibetan. Tibet! Even depleted and disoriented by illness and exhaustion, Krick's mind was focussed on that forbidden land.

Perhaps, Krick thought, if he kept pushing north he could link up with Renou in China via Tibet. But he would not travel incognito like his friend. He would travel as he always did, in broad daylight carrying his sextant and cross and to anyone who asked him he would say the same words that he had said so many times before: 'I am a priest.' There was no fear in his heart, neither of wild beasts nor of men, but after the hardships he had endured, he harboured a small doubt about travelling through Mishmee territory again and still hoped that a passage into Tibet through the Abor hills would be opened to him. Where was Lendem? He had requested that a message be sent to him from the office of Captain Smith but so far there had been no response. His other hope was Kajinsha. But the few people he could talk to were sullen and uncommunicative when he mentioned the name.

December passed and January had almost ended and still Krick was nowhere near reaching his destination. There was no word from any of his contacts. In February he gave up the dream of crossing into Tibet through Abor territory and decided to push towards the Mishmee hills. They crossed the river in a small boat struggling up against the current and reached the vicinity of Chunpura where they set up camp by a stream at the base of the mountains. It was a time of waiting. In this dry season several forest fires broke out, setting the grass and reed beds ablaze. Flocks of birds rose up into the air and herds of wild buffalo moved through the landscape, sometimes breaking into a stampede in the middle of the night. It was a sad, lonely time.

At daybreak Krick stared at the thin band of yellow light breaking through the pall of smoke. Then he would look up at the towering mountains and think, 'What kind of man would want to go there?' In another time, he knew, he would have answered, 'It is I—*I* want to go there! I want to know. I want to be there, to love and to serve!' But now he was tired. Words and thoughts were a burden. His face was swelling up again and he felt a deep bitterness threatening to explode at any moment into fierce rage and reproach. 'I do not know if what I feel is what I should feel in the way that I have been taught. Dear Lord, help me!' He muttered these words and was shocked to see the fresh face of Augustin bending close to him.

'Father, are you all right?'

Yes. He laughed. He was returning from death's door. It was like learning to walk again, but walk again he would. He clasped his hands together as if to give himself strength and grasp the meaning of salvation as deeply as he could. The salvation of souls, of *his* soul. He remembered the start of this journey. How determinedly he had walked this road. What secret messenger had come in the middle of the night whispering: 'This is the path you will follow. Take it. It is the right decision.' His heart had nurtured this unknown road. His love had nourished it. But now, oh secret messenger, he thought, you did not tell me, as I rushed headlong, that finding the path was but a small step in a long journey. We started walking and found the path is a testing ground; a thin, wavering line drawn with blood, death and dreams... He had been brave and untiring but the supreme test still awaited him. 'Compassion, fill my heart with compassion,' he prayed. He knew it was with compassion alone that he would be able to survive the trial set before him.

A man needed a big heart to laugh in the face of sorrow, a big heart to win friends and keep them and return to life when all strength and will had been taken away and a terrible illness had disfigured your body and mind. He looked at his fellow priest. Augustin Bourry was just twenty-six years old. He was young and pious and Krick knew he was physically fit to climb mountains and walk for days on an empty stomach, clinging to bare rock along treacherous paths—but what about the treachery of men, and the dark thoughts that grew out of solitude in this cruel and bewitching landscape? Here it was relationships that mattered—the kinship of man and animal, of fields and stone, river and rain—and above all, the will to survive in the endless battle of species where everything was stripped bare of extraneous cover and protection. This is the test, thought Krick. Victory was for those who were brave and true to their original nature.

One day a tribesman appeared before him. 'Sabe, sabe, do you remember me?'

It was Lamet! An involuntary frown creased Krick's face. How long ago was it that he had cursed this man for a thief and a blackguard who had demanded his shirt and his last rations? Now he was here—the butt of a bidi was hanging from his mouth and his head craned forward as if in supplication. What did he want?

Lamet removed the burnt out bidi, made a deep sucking sound and said, 'I will take you through the mountains.'

A guide, at last! It was an unexpected offer and Krick should have been overjoyed, but this was the wrong man. He had no confidence in Lamet and wished someone else was standing before him. To gain some time he said that he would have to talk to his colleague. 'You know there are two of us,' he said. Lamet smiled. Yes, he said, he knew. How would he not know about the arrival of another holy man? Everyone knew, but he, only he, Lamet, was offering to escort them to Tibet. He was their friend, was he not? And he was a friend of the British sabes too. A strange light shone in his eyes. Was it anticipation, greed? Or fear that he would be refused? It was impossible to read the man's mind.

'Yes, yes,' Krick nodded. How happy he would have been to see Kajinsha instead of this man! If they had to pass through Mishmee territory, Kajinsha's help would be the only thing he needed. But would Kajinsha offer it? No one knew his whereabouts. He still hoped he would be able to contact his Khampti guide, Chowsa and send a message, but time was running out.

'You can begin looking for porters among your friends here,' he told Lamet who was still standing there watching him.

'Sabe, I will get everything ready,' cried Lamet, bowing and clapping his hands before he scampered off. Krick felt a wave of bitterness. There was no guarantee that Lamet would keep his word, but now he felt a great determination to press on towards the final goal. If all else failed and even if Lamet failed to return, he decided that he and Augustin would begin their journey carrying their bags and boxes on their backs. It was time to conquer or die.

When the world was new a god prowling the universe created something called Time. It was a mysterious thing, as mysterious as the invisible god tilting the sky to create night and day, a past as irrevocable as the future, and the fleeting moments before us of which none can say with certainty if their meaning is bound by fate, or simply a game of someone rolling dice.

The way things happened was that one fateful day while Krick wondered about Kajinsha's whereabouts, Kajinsha and Gimur were within walking distance, if only he had known. They were in Chowsa's hut and they were also making preparations to leave. Kajinsha said if they did not take advantage of the fine dry weather they could be held up again by unpredictable thundershowers that broke over the hills in March. Gimur thought she was ready but as the days passed she was seized with a sudden dread. In her dreams she seemed to hear her friend Nago's voice: 'I see water... and men and boats...' She did not say anything to Kajinsha but sometimes she stared at the mountains, expecting great misfortune to fall upon them like a black shadow.

One evening she was packing several bundles of smoked fish, salt and tobacco when she heard a commotion outside the hut that made her blood freeze. A man had come running, shouting at the top of his voice, 'Chowsa! Chowsa!' His hands were bloody and he was saying something rapidly, and in an instant he was running back again, into the forest, with Chowsa and Kajinsha following him. Something had happened! She called after them and the wind carried their cries back to her. Awesa had been attacked by a buffalo. He was dead! Gimur felt her breath stop.

Out of the darkness men and women suddenly appeared carrying bamboo torches. Gimur had not been aware of so many people living nearby. They held the burning torches aloft and circled the compound as if awaiting something. Kajinsha and Chowsa returned carrying Awesa wrapped in a red cloth.

He was alive. An elderly man had stepped forward and they laid Awesa down on the ground. Gimur realised the cloth was red with blood. There was a deep gash on the back of his right thigh just above the knee where the flesh had been ripped open. 'Move aside, move aside,' said the elderly man. His face was brown and calm like a piece of carved wood. He was a healer whose knowledge of plants and their medicinal powers was legendary. 'I will see what I can do,' he said. Some of the onlookers said they had seen Awesa chasing egrets and perhaps this had disturbed a herd of buffaloes hidden in the reeds. Others said he was hailing someone. Awesa had seen a boat being hauled up the creek and was waving when he felt the ground shaking under him. An enormous buffalo had suddenly risen up and thudded across the flattened grass to crash into him, his massive head bowed in rage. Those who were there had shouted at the top of their voices and pelted the brute with stones. Someone had fired an old rifle. It was their intervention that had finally driven the beast away.

The first thing the healer did was to stem the flow of blood using a flat strip of twine that his daughter, handed him. He put some leaves in his mouth and rapidly chewed up green mulch that he then placed over the wound. Awesa screamed. Gimur stepped back, covering her mouth. The air was foul with the stench of sweat and blood. Awesa seemed to be bleeding from everywhere. At a little distance Kajinsha and some other men were cutting long boughs off the trees and building a makeshift hut. Awesa was carried into this hut. The healer followed, making a sign for everyone to stay back.

'He's not a shaman,' whispered Chowsa, 'but he has great powers of healing. Pray that he will save Awesa.'

Gimur wondered how he would save Awesa. If the healer did not use spiritual powers and call on the gods, how could he save poor boy? In Mebo shamans chanted and went into a trance to call on the gods for help. Here everything was silent. All eyes were turned towards the hut. Slowly, a thin plume of smoke curled up through the roof of green boughs. A fire had been lit. It was a signal for the crowd to disperse. From now on, no one would enter the hut except for the young girl who brought bundles of plants, packets of herbs and stayed nearby to fetch whatever the healer demanded. No one else was allowed to touch the plants. The fire was of a special wood and creepers, and day and night the healer lived in the hut placing leaf packets on the embers, turning them over and over and pressing them down on Awesa's body patch by patch, from shoulder to thigh to knee and along the calves down towards the ankles and toes. Sometimes the hut seemed to disappear as a cloud of smoke mushroomed out over it before floating away into the trees. Sometimes Gimur thought she heard a wail, a shout of pain that set her teeth on edge. The smoky hut became a permanent image fixed in that shadowy corner until she had almost forgotten about it when one day the healer emerged and said, 'You can come in now. He will have a limp, but he will live if god has mercy. There is no more to be done.'

When they entered the hut Awesa was asleep. Looking deep into his face Gimur saw that the large, rough face that she had once considered ugly had thinned and become pale and ascetic. How could I have thought of Awesa as anything other than a saint? She wondered. All the images of his silent loyalty to her and his patience and strength came rushing back. She bent over him and prayed. 'Awesa, wake up! Be strong again. It is I, Gimur, calling you.'

Kajinsha watched everything without a word. One day he slipped away and returned late at night when the fire that Gimur kept burning in the compound had almost died out. He took his place by the fire, next to Chowsa. His eyes were black, like a panther's. 'I saw a white priest,' he said.

Chowsa picked up a log and tapped chunks of coal off it. 'Who was it?' he asked. 'Was it the priest who was here before?'

'No, another one…younger than that padari, Krick,' said Kajinsha. 'He was sitting by the stream. I know he is travelling with Krick and it was them that Awesa saw when he started waving… I told the man they should turn back. Now it is war to death between them and me and they should not enter my territory. If my son dies I will kill them.'

Gimur stared at the fire. Chowsa prodded another log and a shower of sparks flew up. No one said anything. What words were there to say now? Nothing that they could think now or imagine would change what had been set in motion and was waiting to happen.

When Kajinsha had seen Bourry, the young priest had been sitting alone on a stony strip of beach by the river. He was writing a letter to Paris describing the fury of the Burhampooter River and how their boatmen had refused to advance any further fearing the currents and the risk of being trapped in the wild jungle that surrounded them. It was but a few days ago that they had left the relative safety of Saikwa Ghat, bidding goodbye to their colleague, Father Bernard who was returning to the mission in Gowhattee. Krick and Bourry had crossed the river in the first leg of their journey north towards Tibet again. Krick had gone in search of the porters that Lamet had promised would be waiting for them and Bourry was looking after their bags when Kajinsha appeared before him. What! He jumped up in surprise. Where had the man come from? He looked around quickly. There was not another soul in sight. The man was alone. He was saying something in a cold, calm voice with his hand on his sword hilt. 'He must be Mishmee,' he thought, looking at Kajinsha's black turban and his sword. Maybe he had been sent by Lamet? But his voice and demeanour were menacing. 'Do you want something?' He asked. 'Can you help us to cross these mountains? We will give you a piece of cloth and money....' he offered tentatively.

The man crossed his hands and pointed towards the mountains as if to say that Bourry should go no farther. Bourry listened, concentrating very hard to make sense of the harsh, bitter language. Bourry had taken great pains to learn Tibetan and Hindustani, and since his arrival in Gowhattee he had laboured over Assamese and the rudiments of several tribal languages and slowly he understood that something had occurred that had made this man very angry. He was talking about a son... an accident, or he had drowned in the river, he could not make out, but the man was pointing at him as if he was responsible for whatever it was that had happened to his son who was dead or dying!

Oh! If only his dear colleague had been here, he would know how to deal with this man. At this moment all Bourry could say was, 'Wait, please wait. My colleague Father Krick will be back...' but Kajinsha had already disappeared into the tall grass as swiftly as he had come.

By the time Krick returned, Bourry had recovered from the strange encounter and gave him a quick account of it, and then the incident was forgotten in the rush of packing and loading their boxes so that they could begin their journey immediately before the porters changed their minds. There were only two porters, one a dark, surly Singpho and the other an Assamese servant who had probably been captured or sold to Lamet as spoils of war.

'They will bring you to my village,' Lamet had told Krick. 'I will make a feast and show you the way to Tibet.'

This time the route they took was different from the one Krick had travelled along in the winter of 1852, but to Krick everything seemed the same as they left the riverbank and followed their guides into the jungle. There was hope and there was fear, and there were the same mountains and cliffs ready to engulf them if they were not killed by the inhabitants or devoured by wild animals. They were like little ants creeping along treacherous precipices and running back and forth on rocks and thorns. The guides lost their way and they all travelled in circles trying several different directions following rivers and streams. Sudden thunderstorms

Mamang Dai

drenched them to the bone. Soon they were reduced to walking barefoot. Bourry kept his last good pair of shoes to use for Holy Mass even though their boxes and books, their breviary, the Imitation and everything else were ruined by rain. 'Sabe, sabe,' cried the Assamese servant. 'It is a bad start! It is a mistake.' He recited this like a litany. 'The first person we meet will rob us. They will kill us! We must turn back. We have no food. Sabe, sabe!'

'We will not stop until we reach Tibet,' said Krick in reply. 'Quick! We must keep walking. We cannot stop.' He seemed beside himself with impatience. Both the white men were covered with sores, insect bites, and suffering from fever and dysentery, but neither would give up.

At last one of the guides said they were approaching a village. He pointed. Father Krick recognised the place. It was Khroussa's village where he had stopped on the way back from Tibet. He had received food and shelter in this village but now the place looked deserted. If Khroussa was there he would surely have known of their arrival and come out to meet them. Krick decided to move on. He had to stay on course and find Lamet who had promised to be their guide. He remembered that from here it was only a two-hour hard trek to Lamet's house. The height of the mountains obliterated the sun and they were climbing up over bare rocks. Lamet's house was dark and hidden. As they approached Krick had a premonition that they were once again on the border of Mizhou territory and that their route might be cut off by chief Zumsha and his men.

'Welcome! Welcome!' cried Lamet when they reached his house. A brood of children rushed out, followed by Lamet's family members. A woman said something and everyone laughed. Father Krick recognised the voice. It was Yenjee, the Burmese slave girl who they said belonged to Lamet. And this, too, was a meeting awaiting its moment. From now on, step by step, the coming days would unfold what was already written, but for now, hidden behind the bright light in Yenjee's eyes.

Krick and Bourry entered the house. It was dark and narrow. The air was foul.

'We will not linger. We will leave as soon as you are ready,' said Krick.

Lamet waved his hands. 'Sabe, stay! There is no hurry, and I have to go to Assam before taking you to Tibet,' he said.

'But you promised to take us to Tibet!' cried Father Krick.

'I will take you, sabe. I just need to get some potika! Hah, ha!' Lamet made a gulping motion of drinking out of a bottle.

Krick considered the situation. He felt trapped by this man who he felt was using them to drive a hard bargain and was testing them now. He tried a tactic. 'I know we are near Zumsha's territory. Will he not be angry if we stay here?'

Lamet laughed. 'Zumsha is in Tibet and Kajinsha is in Assam. No one is here, sabe. I will take care of you!'

This piece of news jolted Krick as if a hidden voice had suddenly come alive in his head. He thought about the man who had appeared before Bourry by the stream. If only he had paid attention to Bourry's account of the meeting! Could it have been Kajinsha? The man was angry and had threatened him. But why? Oh, if only he had been there at the time! Now there was no way of finding out except to return to Assam. And perhaps that could be done. They had no medicines and Bourry, who despite his robust physical condition was also suffering, said he could accompany Lamet to make the necessary purchases. 'I can keep an eye on Lamet, and make sure we return quickly,' offered Bourry. Krick agreed. He needed a few days' rest, even though he dared not admit it.

'Try to find the Mishmee who threatened you,' he said.

When they were gone, Krick retired to a corner and stayed there with his eyes closed. He felt tired beyond words. He wondered why Lamet's guides had brought them by this tortuous route. Everything suddenly appeared devious. He wished he could contact Kajinsha but he knew Lamet would never agree to carry any message to Kajinsha or the powerful Zumsha. Here each man was independent and master of his house. There was no love lost between rival clans and he knew by now that there was no trust, not even among brothers, in this wilderness. He dozed and the sounds of the house echoed around him. Lamet had two wives, both stocky, maternal-looking women with skin burnt brown by their outdoor work in the fields. They had borne Lamet many sons and daughters and each kept to her place. Yenjee was also Lamet's wife but as an outsider and the youngest of the three her position was more that of a kept woman, a concubine who wielded great influence over Lamet. He was infatuated with her. In a society that Krick had observed to be serious and conservative and where women bore the greater load of work Yenjee enjoyed great freedom. She was not relegated to a wife's sphere of housekeeping and childbearing. She flitted about the house singing like a bird. If one of the older women said something Yenjee would smirk and stomp off, her eyes glittering like the cornelian beads around her neck. When Lamet and Bourry returned she was the first to run out. Lamet had brought her a piece of blue cloth. She grasped the material and showed her delight by tying the cloth around her waist and swinging her hips before she squatted down beside the fire.

'Ho!' Lamet called out for food. He was in a good mood and he smacked his lips in between sucking at his bidi. A cock had been killed but there was no fat or seasoning in the food and the result was a thin watery soup. For a while no one spoke as all the members of the household, young and old, ate together off the same vessel. Only Yenjee sat apart, stretching out her palms towards the fire. Now and then she turned her head sideways towards the corner where Krick and Bourry sat, and stared at them with keen interest. Krick could sense the young Bourry's discomfiture. We must leave this place quickly, he thought. During his trip to Assam, Bourry had not seen the Mishmee who had threatened him again. Lamet had hounded him every step of the way reminding him about the boxis, the money and gifts that he expected from the two missionaries.

'He will get nothing until we reach Tibet,' said Krick, determined to get away from the house as soon as possible and reminded Lamet of his promise. But the next day he was knocked out by an attack of nausea and agonising stomach convulsions that made him retch as if he had swallowed poison. He lay in a stupor sweating and panting like a stricken animal. The sound of voices grated on his ears and dizzying images passed before his eyes. He saw Lamet standing up like a giant with his mouth wide open. He was posturing and walking round the house saying something to Bourry in a grandiloquent manner. What could he be talking about? Everyone was laughing and jeering. The presentiment of some terrible danger that had troubled Krick ever since the beginning of this journey struck him again with full force. A shadow was creeping up and he saw Yenjee holding a long pipe blowing a plume of smoke into his face. The house was turning, the wind was blowing everything away and suddenly he was a weightless being spinning through the air reeking with the sharp fumes of opium.

When he came to his senses, everything was calm. His eyes were clammed shut but he could feel the warmth of sunlight and hear voices. Bourry was calling him.

'Yes,' he replied, 'I can hear you. I am all right.' The bout of sickness seemed to have left him. By mid-afternoon he was pressing the recalcitrant guides to follow Lamet up a steep path that led out of the clearing. Krick had exchanged hot words with Lamet who had pretended to be ill and unfit to walk. 'Sabe! We will leave day after tomorrow,' he had said. Krick had been adamant, they would leave immediately, they had wasted too much time already.

'I can keep you and your friend as my prisoners. What will you do without my help?' Lamet had retorted angrily.

'We will go without you and you will receive nothing from us,' Krick had replied, equally furious.

'Hah ha! You are angry with me. Sabe, don't be angry,' said Lamet, twisting his lips and pretending to smile. 'You are sick. I will help you.' He had cast a look around the house and said something to Yenjee who had rushed up to him. Then they had left.

Now he was walking quickly ahead as if he wanted to lead Krick and Bourry into the wildest jungle and abandon them to their fate as soon as possible.

It was the hardest ordeal that the two missionaries faced. Lamet's route was circuitous. He said they had to avoid Zumsha's territory but Krick felt he was lying to them. Sometimes he disappeared from view and did not answer when they called out. Then they would see him standing by a tree as if he had been waiting for them. 'Are you tired?' he would ask. When Krick shook his head Lamet would forge ahead again, slashing at the undergrowth in a mindless, provocative manner. All they had was rice and water. There were many days they walked miles on an empty stomach.

When after a particularly gruelling trek Lamet announced that he had to return to his village and asked for his money Krick's patience snapped.

'You are cheating us!' he cried out in anger. 'I will give you nothing!'

'Oh no sabe, we are almost there,' said Lamet. 'You can walk straight and you will be in Tibet. This man,' he pointed to the Singpho servant who was following like a dumb animal, 'he will take you there. It is not far... sabe, my family is alone. We are poor. Sabe, my money!'

They had reached a high, grassy field and Krick was sitting under a big tree. Lamet had taken his money and disappeared. He had argued vociferously pleading for more but in the end he had backed down saying he would expect more—'When we meet again, sabe!'

Bourry, looking about him, saw a line of pine trees and his heart leapt. There was a river, and in the distance he saw a valley with cultivated fields and unmistakable signs of habitation. What was this place, he wondered. Perhaps they had reached their destination? Krick, standing beside him, now suddenly broke into a smile and exclaimed it was true, what Lamet had told them! They were in the vicinity of the place called Oualoung, the hamlet of farmers and herdsmen that he had passed through two years ago! He recognised the rural countryside. It was what had haunted his waking hours and lodged in his dreams. The Zayul valley lay straight ahead.

All the hardship that they had faced, the foul days of rain and hunger, dirt, rage and frustration suddenly melted away. Krick felt as weak as a baby. His heart was pounding and something was thudding in his head. He sniffed the air and thought he caught the scent of lime trees. They marched on goaded by a desperate impatience to reach their long cherished destination, the Tibetan village of Sommeu hidden behind the trees. They were running, splashing across streams, crawling and falling down on the slippery stones, shouting and laughing, and all the time Krick's heart was beating thud, thud! The journey to the Zayul valley that he had earlier completed in ten days had taken them two months. But they were almost there, they had found a way, the mountains had not swallowed them, they had beaten the devil at his tricks and emerged alive and triumphant!

Father Krick and Augustin Bourry reached Sommeu on 29 July 1854. They had been in the village no longer than fifteen minutes when the guides wanted to leave them, but Krick persuaded the Singpho servant to stay, assuring him that they would go no further. They would stay in Sommeu or somewhere nearby so that they could correspond with Assam. In a message to the Directors in Paris Krick announced their entry into Tibet on the day of Saint James the apostle. Their arrival in Sommeu was a Saturday, the day dedicated to Mary, and Krick dedicated their mission to Tibet to her. He noted it was also the day of Saint Martha, whom Jesus loved, and lifted by a feeling of confidence he urged his colleagues to join his and Bourry's fervent prayers for the success of the mission. In a letter to his spiritual director Fr Ménard, Bourry also wrote that he was in good health again and promised to send their mail through the Mishmees doing trade with Tibet. They had found a place to stay, he wrote, expressing his feeling of joy 'at coming to the people who were to become his first flock, especially when they were still pagan.'

These letters were the last communication from Krick and Bourry about their journey and their arrival in Tibet. After this there was silence. In their last letters, they had asked for a long list of items: seeds for peas, carrots, limes, melon and celery; medicines like purgatives, essence of absinthe, peppermint, Rosseau's laudanum, emetic tartar, quinine, gum Arabic, linden blossom, jujube, liquorice root, olive oil, vinegar and orange blossom water; syringes and scales and a horn or ivory spoon to take the medicine. Perhaps the two missionaries were fully occupied with planting a vegetable garden and practicing medicine to heal the sick and befriend the simple people of Sommeu. Perhaps they were building a house in the isolated village and setting up a standard mission with a chapel and annexes, because they also asked for carpentry tools—a hand-saw, an axe, wire cutters, screws and screwdrivers—and tailor's scissors, sewing needles, thin white braids for the altar… And they asked that all this be wrapped in newspapers so that they could find out what was happening in Europe. It is likely that it was a happy, peaceful period for the two priests. But there is no proof that it was or was not. There is only conjecture based on a few reports floating out of the past like smudged, rain-wet images revealed in a dusty mirror.

The inhabitants of Sommeu remembered Krick from his earlier

visit of two years ago, and among them none more so than the sick woman who was Awesa's mother. 'So, she thought, 'the white gelong is back. A lingering dim hope burning in her breast flared up again. She remembered how some people had begun to believe that the priest had healing powers. His manner and voice had been gentle and consoling. She would see him, and offer him help and shelter, if he needed it. She began to stomp on the floorboards in a loud, deliberate way. This was her way of calling attention and she knew her sister would soon be coming up the stairs to find out what had happened. A thin smile creased her face. In the last year her seizures had grown in frequency and violence. Her body had curved a little lower after each attack and she resembled a bent bow ready to snap. But I will live yet. I will outlive them, she thought. Her sister Chhomu appeared at the door. She was nursing a baby girl held close to her breast and her face was red and puffy.

'Come inside,' said Auli. She is growing old, she thought, staring at her sister's face. So be it. Everything comes round full circle. It is the Buddha's way. A thrill of joy made her breathing loud and uneven. She tilted her head like a bird and looked at the child. 'How is she?'

Her sister crossed her arms over the child as if to shield it from her gaze. 'She is asleep,' she replied.

Auli nodded. 'Sleeping... Everyone was sleeping. Everything happens when everyone is sleeping.' She gave a harsh laugh. 'But I am awake. I stay awake and listen. And do you know what I hear? I hear your uncle Marpa's footsteps moving around this house. I hear his body sliding up and down these rooms like a snake. I stay awake. I hear his breathing and I hear the thoughts in his heart—like a snake, yes, in the middle of the night he is crawling over you like a snake, a big, terrible snake!' Auli stopped walking and suddenly clutched her head with clenched fists.

'Sister, what is it?' cried Chhomu.

'Nothing, nothing. I have not slept well, that is all. I hear that the priest is back. In fact there is another young man with him. If they are looking for shelter I want to offer them the use of this house. There is no one here except the two of us. What do you think?'

Chhomu said nothing. Auli looked at the younger woman with scorn. 'Go and tell the priests what I have said,' she commanded. 'I will inform Marpa,' she said. 'I am certain he will agree. They are holy men. May Buddha grant us compassion for all living beings.'

Chhomu hurried away to do her sister's bidding. Her life was not her own, she knew that. Since that night of passion, here, in this house, she had never seen Kajinsha again. Marpa had crept in to claim her, and her life was ruled by Marpa and his desires but she could overlook that. Her nature was soft, pliant. He provided for her and her child and that was all that mattered. Now she braided her hair quickly, packed three cupfuls of dried maize and carrying her baby on her back she began to walk towards the place where the priests had set up their temporary shelter.

Augustin Bourry saw her first. 'Hallo!' he greeted her. Chhomu extended the offering of maize. Bourry received it and thanked her but she could not understand a word. She quickly said what her sister had instructed her to say, bowed several times and left. Krick understood what had been said, but it was an offer he could not accept. If they were unable to stay here they would do everything to head towards Lassa or towards where their colleague Monsieur Renou was. But before that he would remind his friend Norbu, the tax collector, of the promise the Rima governor had made two years ago when he had ordered him to leave the Zayul valley. 'When times are better you may return and stay here with us,' he had said. He watched the girl walking away and thought her face and manner appeared familiar but was unable to recall where and under what circumstance he had seen her before. Maybe it had been at that terrible inn where he had begged for crumbs and nearly died of hunger? His illness had also impaired his memory, he thought dejectedly. Two years ago everything had been different. He had survived all manner of hardship and risks to his life and the will to conquer or die was a burning flame. It was the time when Kajinsha had told him, 'Your God is lucky to have believers like you.'

And now something stirred in his memory. Kajinsha lived somewhere nearby... 'Does he know I am here?' he wondered. 'Will we meet again?' A sense of amor fati pervaded all his thoughts. It seemed as if all his work, the effort, the desire for a Christian Tibet was leaving him. Europe, Paris, the rest of the world... all was being swept away by a soft, invisible wind. What next, what next? He would die in the attempt to establish a Tibet mission—this thought never left him. It was as if the universe itself had uttered these words in his heart. All he needed now was not learning but understanding.

Bourry, watching his friend out of the corner of his eye, felt worried. Although Krick did not say anything Bourry knew he was still suffering from the terrible strain of the journey. And their journey was not over yet. Alas, we are but two young missionaries, he thought. What would happen now? Krick always said, 'Providence will guide us,' but Bourry could not help but feel burdened by his inexperience and weakness. He felt a sudden longing to bring back love and grace in this strange, desolate landscape. There among his bags lay something that he had long been dreaming of touching once more. It was his accordion. He clasped it and turned his pious, young face towards the last rays of sunlight slanting away over the steep hills. He played the missionaries farewell songs hoping Krick would accompany him and play the flute, but his companion was silent. Everything was still. The pure music floated around them like a prayer.

◆

High above on the ridge Gimur and Kajinsha stopped to listen. Was it the wind rushing through the trees, or was it a song that they were hearing? Gimur listened hard. The sound grew louder, it was like the pounding of the earth, and soon she glimpsed two horsemen heading towards them.

'Go back into the house,' Kajinsha told her. 'It is Marpa. I will talk to him.'

Gimur saw Marpa ride up in a swirl of dust. His hair was flying loose under his tall hat. He alighted swiftly and signalled to the other man to take the horses.

'Ho! Greetings my friend!' he cried, and embraced Kajinsha.

The two men began walking back towards the house and Gimur quickly darted away from the front room into another cubicle. 'Ah,' said Marpa, 'it is good to be a guest in this house.' He put his hand inside his voluminous robe and brought out a wooden tablet containing a book and another bundle of papers loosely tied up with string. He untied the string and hunched over the pages like a bird of ill omen. 'This is the record of the white priest's movements,' he said.

Kajinsha kept his eyes on Marpa's face.

'It was an order to leave our territory. But now he's back. What do you make of that?' Marpa grinned at Kajinsha.

'Yes, I know he's back,' said Kajinsha.

'You know!' Marpa pretended to look around with a delighted smile. He lowered his voice. 'Did you meet him in Assam?'

'No, I did not. But I went to look for him,' replied Kajinsha.

'Ah, yes. I heard something about that. You were angry because of the accident. How is Awesa? Where is the boy?'

When Kajinsha did not respond Marpa continued, 'Is he better? Worse? Why's he avoiding me?'

'He's here, recovering,' said Kajinsha

'Ah...' Another delighted smile distorted Marpa's face. 'You know, ahem, Awesa's mother was quite taken with the priest. The first one, Krick, you know... She's even offering them her house—*your* house, to stay in Sommeu and do their work.'

'She can do what she wants,' said Kajinsha quietly. 'I make no claim on the house.'

'It is your wife's house, but never mind.' Marpa's rubbed his hands together and carried on, 'The priest... you were friendly with him here. It seems he's following you—and there are two of them! Hah ha!'

'What do you want me to say about this?'

'Oh nothing, nothing, Kajinsha, my friend, I have only come here to inform you about these things,' cried Marpa. 'You must know how we feel and how the dzongpon feels about these things.'

'Let him be. The white priest and his friend are not in my territory.'

'Ah—that is what I mean. They are in *ours*, in the Zayul, and everyone is asking why they have come back.'

Kajinsha shrugged. Marpa leaned forward and whispered, 'The lama you escorted to Assam said you did not want to come back with him. Were you waiting for the priest?'

Kajinsha became rigid. Then he pushed his face close to Marpa's and said in a slow, expressionless voice. 'I was waiting for my wife.'

'Oh ho! That I know. Your other wife, she's back. It is wonderful...these young girls, so impulsive, eh? I'm very happy for you that she's back. But—she may not know it, but maybe the priest followed her?'

Kajinsha stared at Marpa and then burst out laughing. 'Marpa my friend, you are mad!' he said. 'What are you up to now? Why all these questions and tricks? Who sent you here to come and disturb us for no good reason?'

'The priest visited her village,' replied Marpa. 'Why did the priest visit her village?'

'How should I know?' shouted Kajinsha. 'If you have so much information about everything how is it that you and your dzongpon don't know why the priest went to Mebo?'

'You were friendly with the priest. You gave him food. He came to your house. When he left you said goodbye like old friends. Do you remember?'

'Of course I remember. And you tried to starve him to death, do you remember?' Kajinsha was on his feet now. 'Don't come here and tell me what to remember and what to forget. And don't talk to me about the priest. He is not in my territory!'

'Oh, don't be angry, my friend. I'm only trying to help you,' replied Marpa pretending to look offended. Kajinsha knew, and so did Gimur peeping through the cracks from the next room, that nothing would offend Marpa except perhaps having all his money and belongings stolen, or being struck by a lethal sword blow. Even then, thought Kajinsha, the man might end up laughing. His grin stretched so wide you could see the glint of gold teeth at the back of his mouth. He had no shame. It was the result of having no conscience. Marpa, with his flashing eyes and teeth and his vigorous good health, was born without a soul.

After Marpa's visit the countryside was very quiet. The warm July days passed. No one came by their secluded ridge and Gimur worked hard in the fields thinking of the old days with her mother and all the women before them in her village. Whom did they consult when they were tired and afraid? They were calm. They had courage and stamina. I understand them now, she thought. I will do whatever is necessary to fill our granaries with meat and fish, and grain and corn and millet. Awesa helped her. After the hideous accident in Chunpura his shuffling gait was now marked by a limp, but the boy had changed. He still shied away from looking directly at Gimur, but his manner was less awkward and his speech more coherent. *He knows his father threatened to kill the white foreigners for his sake, and that has changed him,* she thought. In fact, Gimur noticed, Awesa now stuttered only when he was happy. It was a delight to have him working by her side. She struggled on the hillside every day, lost to everything else except the warmth of soil, the bright green of moss, the desperation of worms exposed to light. But rain—rain fell so hard, as if to wipe them off the face of the earth.

Thunder rolled across the sky and Kajinsha was restless. He knew there must be a cause for the absence of visitors. In the past such prolonged silence made men edgy and village elders sent warriors out to scour the hills and jungle paths for signs of an impending attack from an enemy clan.

He was surprised one day when he saw Zumsha walking swiftly to his house. He was unaccompanied and he did not waste time.

'Kajinsha,' he said, 'I have heard about everything from Marpa. No more strangers.'

'They are not in my territory,' said Kajinsha.

Zumsha raised a hand. 'Yes, I know that. But you know Marpa. He's feeding enough words to the dzongpon to make him angry and poison him against us. I do not care for the dzongpon's anger or even Marpa's words, but there is a risk Marpa will blame us and use this to start an attack on our lands. That is his plan.'

'So let him,' said Kajinsha. 'The worm! He can try but he has no followers.'

Zumsha laughed. 'Ah, that is so. But we cannot become enemies now. He's talking to Lamet. Lamet is our enemy and Marpa knows the best weapon against an enemy is another enemy. Hah! What men I have seen!' Zumsha shook his head. 'There will never be peace, not like the peace your father dreamed of, not like the peace the white priest talks about. There is only war. If not I, then someone else is going to kill that priest. He has to be removed before the Tibetans are provoked and Marpa is going to make sure they are provoked. I saw Lamet escorting the priests. He left them but he has slyly gone back again. He must be there with Marpa now, hidden somewhere. Think about it.'

After Marpa left, Kajinsha paced up and down the narrow gallery running round the house, trying to focus his mind on all that had been said about the priest and what hidden meaning lay in the words uttered by Marpa and Zumsha. A burst of sunshine flooded the valley. He looked across the river towards the furthest hills wondering about the priest. He saw big clouds riding up to cover the sky. What did it mean that Lamet was now visiting Marpa? His instinct told him to be watchful. He remembered Marpa folding up the papers that he said was the order for the priest to leave their territory. Then he had put them away in the box with his holy block prints and lovingly folded silken cloth over it before tying up the whole bundle and pushing it carefully to one side. 'These are precious,' he had said, and Kajinsha had taunted him, 'What is the purpose of folding away your thoughts and tying them up in a bundle?'

Marpa had laughed heartily. 'These are texts that are thousands of years old, written and passed down from generation to generation but it will not interest you because you do not know what religion is, what a script is. It is what makes us strong and invincible. It is what keeps us safe from strangers,' he had said.

And now, watching the sky meet the far bank of the river, Kajinsha thought, I too have known things. What have I not known? I know this land, I have been here for all time, part of all this through my forefathers—if I do not speak of what I know, it is because I know words can be stolen. And what is the need to say anything? Yes, he had words to give Gimur, but even with her he was reserved, because in this matter there was too much in his heart to say. It was good to live without too many words. If he spoke anything aloud his thoughts might lose their power or, worse, some jealous spirit might try to prevent him from doing what he was thinking. It was better to be silent and carry his words inside.

He thought he would cross the river to meet the priest and tell him to leave the valley. He had done it once before and no matter if the priest felt betrayed, he would do it again. He had thoughts of a peaceful life, of work and labour and love. No more bloodshed, he wanted to shout, but he knew from the example of his father that words created unrest and provoked wars. Words—Marpa spoke words to hide his heart and hide his fears. He, Kajinsha, had no need of words. His forefathers were quiet. They were resting, but he knew they were watching his every move. He felt his father's eyes on him and instinctively he knew that what he was planning was right. He would drive Lamet out of the territory and then accost the priests. Then we would see what happens. What did it matter if Marpa thought he had no religion and was a savage? What if all he had inherited was rocks and trees? None of it mattered as long as a man was unafraid knowing that everything would end in death. All that Kajinsha wanted now while he was alive was control over what happened in his life and his land, and for this words had no power. Only action counted.

In their small lodging Krick woke up every morning to the sound of rain. It was a wooden house surrounded by evergreen trees a short distance away from Sommeu, on the road to Rima. Every day a dense fog crept over the hills and suddenly there would be a downpour that would send Bourry, out in the tiny garden, running for cover. Krick wondered if his dream of reaching Lassa and building a church in Tibet would ever be fulfilled. No one troubled them. They were free to stay, or leave anytime and go back to Assam to establish a strong mission base there and then return when they were better equipped, perhaps even more in numbers. But the two priests stayed. In his wanderings around the countryside Krick met men and women who were gentle and humble. They bowed their heads and moved aside to let him pass. If he tried to greet them they averted their gaze. Only once he met a young man whom he recognised as a lama by his maroon robes and the prayer beads twined around his wrist. Krick stopped him for a moment, wishing to exchange news. The lama pointed to the crucifix Krick wore and Krick pointed to the man's prayer beads. The man laughed, his eyes alight in his hard, tanned face. It was the first time in weeks that anyone had returned his gaze so openly and in the lama's eyes he saw happiness and compassion.

Slowly more and more villagers began to approach their dwelling. As in Mebo Krick saw it was only by tending to the sick and needy that they could ever hope to gain the trust of the people. They came in the evening after work in the fields and the two priests provided ointments and simple remedies for stomach ailments, flu, skin allergies. Bourry was trained in nursing work from the seminary and it was evident that the patients could sense his medical ability when they submitted to his calm and dedicated ministrations. Sometimes Bourry sprang up in a burst of joy and played the accordion. He closed his eyes, the villagers clapped, Bourry's voice boomed out over their chatter until Krick felt the music tugging at his heart and was compelled to join in with the flute. Medicine and music. That was the secret of winning hearts and minds.

The woman who had found them the house sent them daily gifts of maize. She rarely visited, but one day Krick was out walking and saw someone he recognised walking with an elderly Tibetan woman. It was Awesa! 'Hallo!' he called out. The boy was limping. Krick remembered him clearly from the night of the thunderstorm. He was the boy who had led him to Kajinsha's house. 'Hallo!' Krick called out again, trying desperately to catch their attention.

He wanted to ask, 'Where is Kajinsha?' A tall man in a fur hat was walking ahead. He turned around and looked at the priest without moving. He said something to the woman and the boy looked over his shoulder quickly. When Krick waved the tall man spun away and both Awesa and the woman also moved away hurriedly before he could approach them.

If Krick had been in the house that day, he would in fact have met Kajinsha and all the stories might have been linked in a different way and turned off in another direction. But he was out, walking, lured away from what could have been by—who knows what, who can explain these things?

So it was Agustin Bourry's fate to meet Kajinsha that day. Bourry was sitting on his cot when the Assamese servant came in hurriedly and almost fell at his feet. When Bourry looked up Kajinsha was already there. Bourry recognised him with a start. He was the same man with the black turban and the set, angry face who had threatened him near the river when Father Krick had gone to look for porters.

'What do you want?'

Kajinsha seemed to understand Bourry's rudimentary Assamese, but he did not answer. He looked at the servant and began speaking. In between he looked at Bourry and pointing with his hands made gestures that could only be interpreted as an order that they should leave immediately. The frightened servant could barely translate what the man was saying. But Bourry grasped the gist of it. He jumped up. He was young and pious, and his temper was roused. After all that they had been through, after all the misery and perils—it was God's will that they had survived. Who could do anything to them *now*? He was incensed that this man should enter their dwelling so rudely with what he construed as dire threats.

'Be gone!' he shouted. 'How dare you come in like this? You cannot drive us out! We have authority to stay!'

At this point there was a commotion outside and Lamet made an unexpected appearance. 'Salam sabe, oh sabe!' he cried.

Bourry was confused. What did Lamet want? He looked from one to the other. Kajinsha stood unmoving. Lamet's eyes were darting around and he was grinning at Kajinsha. 'Oh ho, you are here! Of course, of course—you are good friends...' he said, indicating Bourry.

'I do not know this man,' said Kajinsha.

Lamet looked at him cunningly. 'Why are you here, then?' he asked.

'It is my business,' replied Kajinsha.

Lamet began rubbing his hands together. The servant who had run out suddenly returned with a bowl of maize. He appeared to be trembling. 'Give them some,' said Bourry.

Lamet's hand reached out and scooped up a handful from the bowl, spilling some. Kajinsha moved back. 'Go away!' he shouted again, facing Bourry. 'Otherwise there will be trouble!' The last thing he saw as he left the house was Bourry glaring at him and Lamet saying something in great excitement while the servant was picking up spilled maize from the floor.

Curse the man! thought Kajinsha as he made his way out of the place. He was thinking about Lamet but it was Bourry's eyes that he felt following him. The idiot! Again he felt the frustration of not being able to communicate what he wanted to say. Go away. It is not safe for you to stay here. Where is my friend, the other priest? This was what he wanted to say, but he did not want to say anything in front of Lamet. All his instincts were roused. Lamet's appearance had shocked him and he knew it boded ill. It is all Marpa's doing. They are plotting something, he thought. Marpa is using Lamet and Lamet is too stupid to realise that he is nothing in Marpa's hand. As for the priest with his stubborn face and useless words—he does not know anything. He is a fool and if he does not

The Black Hill   233

go away I will send my men to beat him! he thought.

Dusk was falling and Kajinsha walked swiftly, hardly looking where he was going, so deeply lost was he in his thoughts. He reached the stream. The water was high and swift but he splashed in with strong, angry strides. Soon he was crouching, stumbling on slippery boulders and pushing on against the current until he was finally across on the opposite bank. He was turning into a hidden path when he stopped dead in his tracks. He sensed, more than heard, the vibration of strained breathing. He stepped back slowly without turning around. There it was, that sound again. He moved his eyes towards the bushes to his left. On a bright green leaf he saw spots of blood. His hand was on his sword. He swept the thin branch aside. Two gleaming eyes gazed back at him. It was a chal—mithun lying on its side on the ground, its head twisted. Hai! It was an unnatural sight! Kajinsha had never seen a chal lying vulnerable like that. 'Here, here,' he said softly. The animal struggled to get up but its legs failed and it slumped down again, turning its eyes away. 'Ssh… sshh…' said Kajinsha, drawing near. The animal was quivering. There was no sign of blood on it. He touched the animal's ear. It was his uncle Zumsha's mithun. He could tell by the notched mark cut with a knife on its ear. What had happened? How had a strong, healthy male mithun come to be lying there? The animal was straining to breathe. He has been poisoned, thought Kajinsha. Someone has fed him poison or shot him with a poisoned arrow! He found a small puncture wound high on the animal's foreleg, under the shoulder blade. It was already congealed under the animal's hair. Kajinsha stood up slowly and looked around. There was nothing he could do now. It was better to hurry home and send news to Zumsha. Someone would pay dearly for this. He pressed his hand on the warm flank of the animal.

'Let the man who did this to you be punished with death,' he said.

When Kajinsha was a few yards from his house he saw a figure running into the compound. He stepped back and waited. He heard faint voices and then all was quiet. No one else appeared.

He waited a little more and then reached the house quickly. 'Hai!' He called out loudly. Gimur appeared.

'Who's there in the house?' he asked.

'It's Yenjee,' Gimur replied.

Ah—first Lamet, and now Yenjee. Something was afoot. Kajinsha could feel it in the thumping of his heart and the slow intake of breath that these words caused. The ticking seconds were telling him something. Beware. Be careful.

Yenjee was standing close to the door when he entered. She appeared to be frantic. 'I'm looking for Lamet,' she said. 'Where is he? Do you know where he is?' She threw back her head and flung out her arms as if to grab Kajinsha and cling to him.

'Quiet down!' said Gimur. 'Why are you looking for Lamet? Has he left you?'

Yenjee stopped and stared at Gimur. 'Everyone is looking for him. I came this way because I remembered your house.' Then she turned towards Kajinsha and said, 'He told me he was going to look for his chal. I've been waiting for him for one...two...' she counted on her fingers, 'five days! Where is he? Maybe he's dead. Aiii eee—', she started wailing.

The word 'chal' echoed like a bell in Kajinsha's head. It was a mithun she was talking about. Slowly he put away his spear and took off his jacket. He did not look at Yenjee. He was listening to her words, to her voice and its vibrations. He had seen her running towards his house. But that could be a ploy. She did not seem out of breath and her face and eyes showed no signs of fatigue for someone who had been in the jungle searching for someone. 'Have you had food?' he asked.

Yenjee's voice was shrill. 'Hai... I have been looking for him everywhere. No, no, no food. How could he leave me like this? He's lost. Maybe he's in Tibet, a prisoner!'

Kajinsha wanted to laugh. Lamet, lost? A prisoner in Tibet! He did not look like any prisoner. Lamet had been dictating terms and eating maize! But he, Kajinsha, would disclose nothing. 'I'm sure he's around here somewhere,' he said at last. 'I'm sure you will find him.'

No one said anything anymore. The fire was burning brightly. Yenjee sat down and remained seated like a statue staring at the flames in the hearth. Her face was the colour of gold. Her eyes were gleaming. At last she stood up and sweeping back her hair into a tight knot she said, 'I will go now. I must find him.' She looked at Gimur and gave a strange laugh. 'Who knows what he might be up to, eh?' she said.

Gimur stood watching from the door as Yenjee took the path down the ridge and disappeared from view. 'I don't trust her,' she said.

Kajinsha nodded. 'There's something going on but I don't know what.' He told her about his meeting with the priest and how Lamet had appeared suddenly, but he did not say anything about the mithun he had seen on the way back. It was what was worrying him most but he did not want to add to the air of alarm that he felt was threatening to overwhelm him. He needed to think quietly. He concentrated his gaze on the fire. He felt he was on the verge of uncovering a plot but his thoughts led him nowhere.

I must send word to Zumsha, he thought. At daybreak I will send Awesa, or go there myself to tell him about the mithun. He lay down by the fire, awake, thinking. The next thing he knew was that he was dreaming. Someone was shouting his name. He woke up with a start. He must have dozed off. Someone *was* outside! They were two men who had been sent by Zumsha.

'Someone has killed our chal,' they said. 'We are on our way to Sommeu.'

'You must come with us,' said the other man.

'Yes! Do you know who did it?' he asked.

The men shrugged. 'It must be the white strangers. We'll find out.'

Kajinsha stared at the men. 'No, it was not the white strangers,' he said.

'How do you know?'

'I know because I saw the chal. Who told you?'

'Marpa sent word.'

Aiih... Something was glimmering again at the back of his mind. *That* was the plot! Suddenly Kajinsha saw everything in a bright flash as if his head had been struck by a blow. Marpa was trying everything to get rid of the priests. What he could not understand was the presence of Lamet and Yenjee. If Marpa wanted to use Zumsha to get at the white men he could have done it openly and approached him. Zumsha had no love for the priests. In any case Marpa had cast his net wide. Lamet had already been called and perhaps Lamet had given Yenjee some instructions of his own. Everyone was involved. What still eluded him was the role of each man and woman in this complicated plot that was spinning around him. All he could grasp was that it was Marpa's way to sow confusion and bad blood, and in this he was succeeding.

Gimur sat by the fire with her eyes closed. It was not yet daylight but Kajinsha and the two men had already left. They must be near the river now, she thought. Like so many times before she was peeping through half-closed lids. She did not see the fire or the house post and the basket and wood lying before her. She saw white birds and snow. A storm was blowing. She saw a woman running towards her but she could not see her face. She felt it was someone she knew. As the woman ran the ground under her tilted down but the woman was still running with the sky poised over her like the sloping side of a giant bowl. It is I, thought Gimur, concentrating hard. My heart is running. All around her leaves were swirling down. She stretched out her hand to catch a floating leaf and felt a sharp pain shoot through her hand. She heard the words of her friend Nago rumbling in her ears. 'Water! Water, sorrow and death!' The whole world was spinning. Her mother was calling her. Lendem, her brother, was saying something. She did not know if she was running upside down or falling. Other shadowy figures were appearing in the background. There was a man but he was a black silhouette. A woman's face brushed close to hers. She saw gleaming eyes and the woman's hair streaming in the wind whipped against her face. In a flash Gimur saw it was Yenjee, laughing. She opened her eyes with a start. She had been in a dream. I must wake up now, she thought, taking deep breaths to slow her breathing.

All the words of her dead aunt Moi, and the premonitions and cryptic warnings of Nago returned to her in a rush of remembrance. What had her mother told her? 'Trust your instincts. It is the way to survive.' Yes. Gimur squeezed her eyes tighter. 'Hold fast. Believe that anything can happen.' Her limbs felt heavy. Her mind was still far away and her face was furrowed with thinking. But now she felt the fire. She saw the empty house and she wanted to shout: 'Come back! Kajinsha! It is a bad time for us. Be careful, be careful!' She wondered why Kajinsha had been unable to meet the priest every time he had gone looking for him. There must be some meaning in that, she thought. When Awesa had been injured it was padari Krick that Kajinsha had gone to meet. Instead he had met a strange new priest who had rudely told him to go away. In fact it was said that padari Krick was leading the other priest here but even now when Kajinsha had gone to meet him the padari was not there. If only I could meet him, she thought. She could appeal to him like Lendem had done. The padari had left Mebo when Lendem had told him about the superstitious fear of the villagers that the fire that burnt their homes was due to his presence. It was the same here. It was not safe for the priest to stay. And his staying would harm Kajinsha. Maybe he would listen to her and go away.

There was nothing else to do now but follow her instincts. She stood up slowly and looked around. She saw thin streaks of sunlight beginning to pierce through the cracks in the bamboo. She pulled the big logs out of the fire and doused the flames. Her mind was made up. She would go to Sommeu to meet the priest.

It was broad daylight when Gimur reached the river. There was no sign of Kajinsha and the two men, nor of the injured chal that she had heard the men talking about. She knew she was standing in the right spot from the strong odour and the crushed leaves where the animal had lain, but of the animal there was not a trace. How could it be? Everything had vanished. She lit her pipe and looked around carefully. The sun was pouring down its golden warmth on the land. The green leaves of the trees were transparent with light. She looked at the river and her heart sank to see the deep, swift-flowing water. There was a makeshift bridge lower down but to get there would mean a long walk. She tried to gauge her strength against the power of the current and decided to move upstream. There were places where the water was broken up by stretches of sand and gravel and she might find a way to negotiate her way by stepping on stones and clinging to boulders. She started walking with a sense of urgency. The banks of the river began to converge. She felt like an insect labouring over the boulders strewn around her in wild confusion as if to block her path. At last she reached a place where a big boulder jutted out of the green, rippling water and she saw a weir of stones where someone had once tried to dam the river to trap fish. She stepped in and gasped. The water was waist high and icy cold. Her dread of water returned with full force making her slip and stumble. She thought she would drown. Her mouth filled with water. Her arms stretched out and grasped the boulder. She clung to it and shouted curses with all her might. It was her way of drawing strength. She filled her lungs with air and plunged on, thrashing her legs wildly to reach the next boulder. Her feet were talons gripping the pebbles. To reach Kajinsha! She felt danger lurking all around her. The current hit her and swept her off her feet. Another wild plunge and she was submerged, but the worst was over. She was coughing up water. The water was receding, sinking lower than her knees, and suddenly she had forded the river.

She did not stop to rest. Her detour to find a fordable place had brought her north west to a point where the river made a wide loop skirting tall pine trees that screened the village of Sommeu. It would give way to the cultivated fields, she knew that. All was green and peaceful. A rustling breeze started up and touched her face like the flapping of a bird's wings. She looked up. There was something there… There, just beyond where the Dichu stream meandered down through the trees from the ridge above. She knew she was about to see something. For one moment Gimur paused to catch her breath, bent over a stone. Now she could hear murmuring sounds, human voices! She saw a stout stick. She picked it up. Then she was on her way, flying over the stones.

Unknown to her Kajinsha and the two men had reached the river and spent a long time looking for the dead chal. It was nowhere to be found. They looked at one another in surprise. Who could have removed an animal that did not belong to them? The white men must have taken it away, said the two men. Kajinsha frowned. Something was not right. But there was no time to ponder on what was happening. He had to lead the men, otherwise what control he had over them now would slip away and the outcome would be war. 'We'll find out,' he said. 'We'll go and ask the priests.'

They crossed the river boldly using their spears to steady themselves against the current. It was close to midday when they reached the lodging of the priests.

'Ho!' The Singpho servant was shocked to see Kajinsha again.

He ran forward and whispered, 'The sa'ab is sick!'

'We want to see him,' said Kajinsha.

'No, no, cried the servant, sa'ab is sleeping. He is sick!'

'Who is sick? We will meet the other one who is not sick,' replied Kajinsha. 'Who is NOT sick?'

'He is…the other one is not here. He is not sick,' blabbered the servant.

'Who is not here, you idiot! Get out of my way. Let me find out!' shouted Kajinsha.

At one end of the room Bourry was sitting up in bed. His face was red and his eyes were burning with rage. 'Get out of here,' he shouted. 'How dare you enter like this?'

His words spoken in French fell on deaf ears. The two men moved forward and stood towering over the priest. 'Stop!' cried Kajinsha, who was still standing by the doorway. 'Where is Krick?' he yelled at Bourry. Bourry stared at him and did not answer. Instead he began to get out of bed and when the two men did not move aside he pushed one of them and shouted at him. The man struck him a blow on the head. Bourry screamed. The servant rushed in and started shouting, 'Stop! Stop! The other priest is somewhere nearby. Stop, sa'abe!'

The other man leaped forward and pulled the servant in roughly. The servant became silent immediately but suddenly Bourry had sprung on the man and was pounding his back wildly and shouting at the top of his voice. Kajinsha yanked him back. 'Stop shouting, or else I will kill you!' he said. He looked up at the faces of the two men. Their eyes were hostile. Kajinsha could feel murder in the air. It would be difficult to stand in the way of their purpose but perhaps there was still a way to prevent bloodshed. He pressed his face close to Bourry's and pushed him back on the bed. 'Stay here!' he commanded. Then he turned to the two men. 'Wait,' he told them. 'Wait. If he moves, beat him!'

'Hai,' cried the servant again struggling to free himself from the grip of the men. 'The other sa'ab will come back. Sa'ab, oh sa'ab. I will go and find him. It is a bad day! Help! Help!'

Kajinsha pushed him aside. 'Be quiet, you dog!' he shouted. 'You will not go anywhere. I'll go and find Krick.'

It was a day when the whole world was quiet and peaceful. The inhabitants of Sommeu were out in their fields. Some of them waved as Father Krick passed by. The priest was a familiar figure now and everyone knew where he was headed—towards the spot where the river bifurcated into shallow channels curving against a high plateau intersected by rivulets and glens.

He carried his notebook and his flute but these days he wrote little. Just as he had noted in Mebo he felt he could not say anything more about the place until he had lived here for years like a native. Since there was no more communication with Paris he did not send letters any more. Instead he wrote: What is a good thing in life? A good place to get well.

Once he had asked blessings for his work and the words to write and give expression to hope and faith. But now he hesitated. How can we pray and ask blessings for our words? he thought. They are there, already sacred, if they spring from true feeling and if our thoughts are pure. He climbed higher up to an elevated spot overlooking the river. All around him mountains reared up like a line of ships. Sometimes, they looked to him like strange gods with unknown faces, eyes, shoulders. So silent. So mysterious. So powerful. From this height he could see the prayer flags of Sommeu flapping in the wind. Some of them were in tatters, beaten by wind and rain, but they still carried the remnants of prayers—mantras he had been told—that were answered or dispersed in silence, who was to know? He did not know what he wanted to pray for now. Peace? Consolation? Success of the Tibet mission? Ah, but here, on this little patch of earth in the Zayul valley, in a wedge in the mighty chain of mountains carved on the surface of the earth, Father Krick did not feel lost or disconsolate. He heard the sound of water, the breeze moving through the trees and he felt the land was drawing him in. The sky and hills were becoming familiar and entangled in his heart. Perhaps this was home now. When he first came to these parts, he had thought he had reached a place where everyone was engaged in a war of extermination, one clan against the other, but here he was again surrounded by the patient, dreamy beauty of undisturbed life around him. What belief did men and women cherish that kept them tilling these cold fields from dawn to dusk? Sometimes the music of cymbals and the chanting of lamas at prayer reached him like a medieval chant. This was life in the Zayul. Everywhere people clung to their beliefs, and why not, he mused. It was a person's claim to being someone on earth. It added up to a life. He knew it well now and he felt closer to the nature of the sacred. Every moment was complete and important. Now, here… under the cedar he thought, on this earth where no white man had ever set foot—here my footprint! See the light, hear the sound of water. Look at the small stream no other western eyes and few passersby have seen, a lonely stream, but the water is happy! No commerce, no ships, but how beautiful it is in its secret serenity. And I am blessed to see it! Indeed God's work is marvellous. It is beyond imagination and hope to feel like this, to be the recipient of this shower of love and feeling! Why, here in this very stream he had once tried to boil his clothes to kill the fleas trying to eat him alive. He laughed and was surprised to hear the sound of his laughter echoing back. So many things, so many things have happened and passed away, he thought. What awaits us now?

He thought he heard a sound and turned his head to look if someone was walking nearby.

He saw a woman. Who was it? He thought it was the Tibetan lady who sent gifts of food, then the thought flashed through his head that it was Gimur, who else could it be? A smile lit up his face and died as quickly when he recognised the figure of Yenjee.

'Sabe!' she called out. Her voice was unmistakable. But what was she doing here? Krick and Bourry had last seen her in Lamet's house. That was a long time ago and he could not imagine how she came to be in Sommeu, so far away from Lamet's territory. She seemed to be swaying towards him with outstretched arms. 'Hallo,' he greeted her tentatively.

Yenjee was laughing. 'Haiiee, oh sabe!' she exclaimed, splashing into the stream. She lifted her arms and threw back her head as if tasting the sweetest happiness. Then she turned her head and looked at the priest. 'Come in,' she signalled. 'Are you afraid of the water? Hah ha ha!' Father Krick was too taken aback to respond. He stood staring at her, dumbfounded. She splashed water on him. He leapt back. She came forward laughing, scooping up handfuls of water and throwing them at him.

'Stop, stop,' he cried. 'What are you doing?' He felt disturbed by this sudden overture. Yenjee ran out of the water. Her hair was wet and her cloth clung to her body. He watched her approaching him. He felt confused by her presence. He did not want her attention. He did not want any attention like this but he wished her no harm. She is a poor village woman, he thought. But Yenjee's eyes taunted him—what kind of man are you?

He's like a young boy, she thought, intrigued by him, and amused. He was so different, this padari, from Lamet and the way he behaved with her. In Lamet's house when the priest had been sick on his way down to Assam she had sat by his side all night watching over him. And no one had praised her or given her gifts for her work. Instead Lamet's wives had taken the cloth and the trousers of the priest. Was she not beautiful, more beautiful than any of Lamet's wives? And she was only doing Lamet's bidding. 'Go and find the big priest,' he had told her. 'I will come and join you.'

And she was waiting for Lamet, but he was not here yet, and she was happy singing and smiling at the priest and touching his shirt.

'Stay away from him!' Gimur had stepped out so silently, Yenjee stopped, startled, wondering where the voice was coming from.

'Don't turn around. Go away.'

Yenjee stood frozen, but only for a moment. Like a wild cat she lunged at the priest.

'Aiih, save me!' She shouted, wrapping her arms around him and pressing her head against his body.

'I said stay away! Don't touch him!' Gimur raised the stick and struck her hard across the body.

'Aiih! What is she doing? She has gone mad. Save me, holy man, save me!' Yenjee wailed.

'Stop, stop!' The priest was trying to push Yenjee away from him and trying to raise his hands to ward off Gimur, but Yenjee was pushing harder against him and they fell together on the stony bank of the stream. Gimur stared at them in disgust, at Yenjee's behaviour and the stupid priest who was struggling to disengage himself and shouting something in his language until suddenly, using all his strength he pushed Yenjee away from him and stood up.

'Move aside. I know your plan,' said Gimur. She had stepped out into full view now. 'Don't try anything.'

Yenjee had rolled into the stream. Gimur stood over her with the raised stick. Yenjee was laughing, lying in the water. 'Oh, look what you have done!' she raised her legs and splashed water on Gimur. 'Why are you so angry, my friend? Look at the sa'ab! Is he not funny?' Gimur knew Yenjee was playing for time, eyeing the priest slyly. Perhaps she was waiting for Lamet to arrive. The thought flashed through her mind and she turned to the priest. 'Go!' she shouted at him. 'Quickly, go back to the house. Quickly!' She stretched out her hand and opened and closed her mouth making mouth signals to emphasise her words. She glanced around quickly. She heard the crack of a twig. 'Go!' she shouted again pushing the priest.

'Aiii, oh…' Yenjee groaned loudly.

Lamet's sword was a streak of light. There was a loud scream as he leaped out from behind a huge rock. Lamet was striking the priest. One blow. Another… 'NO!' shouted Gimur. 'Stay away! Stay away!' She threw herself forward to knock Lamet off balance and raised her stick to catch the curving slash of the sword, but too late. Ah… too late. A sharp shot exploded in her ears and the whole world was ringing inside her head. A gun shot. Kajinsha's gun! He was there, standing beside her like a dark giant glistening with sweat.

'Don't move,' he told her, and then he was running away from her, away from the crumpled body of the priest and sprinting across the stream chasing Lamet and Yenjee who was still laughing and running in her wet clothes into the dark row of conifers.

'Don't move, stay there,' shouted Kajinsha again before he too disappeared into the trees. Gimur was left alone with the priest.

Krick lay face down pressed against a granite slab. Gimur thought he was dead. He groaned and she sprang to his side. The priest was alive! What was he saying? She struggled to turn him over but he was a big, heavy man. She bent down low. How pitiful he looked with his eyes closed. She stooped close to his face until her nose was touching his when he suddenly opened his eyes and stared at her. He was breathing hard as if remembering something painful, something that caused him sorrow. His hands fumbled around in his shirt and Gimur tried to help him, pulling at the layer of clothes. His clasped her hand and closed his eyes. She heard him whisper something that sounded like 'aenjal'. What did that mean?

Krick blinked, trying to open his eyes wider, in order to concentrate on what was happening around him. Where was Bourry? 'Brother!' he wanted to shout. He saw the trees whirling overhead like a dancing screen of green and through this green he saw Gimur bending over him. How happy he was that *she* had arrived! He tried to smile. Are those tears in her eyes? Is she speaking to me? What tender words was she giving him? He felt her place her hand under his head. Her other hand was stroking his hair. Ah! Mother, sister, friend! Lost in the forests of Lorraine… they were all returning to him now. His heart was knocking so hard… and she was touching his chest and though he could not move nor see anything clearly he knew her head was pressed over his heart and his hands that clasped the crucifix. 'Do not weep,' he wanted to whisper. There are more rewards in heaven… He wanted to sit up and talk to her. Now he felt he could reach her. They would understand each other through any language. See, this is how it is. The time we are given is not in our hands. It belongs to God. The words we did not say, the things we could not do… Even the suffering and shame we live through have their purpose. Not my will, oh Lord, but thine… He struggled to sit up, it was very important to speak to this woman, but his breath was escaping fast. Something was tugging at his heart and a terrible pain was shooting through his body. Summoning up his last ounce of strength Krick put his hand on her head. One day, he wanted to say, one day a greater light will shine on us. Do not be afraid. His eyes turned skywards and he could not pull his gaze away. He thought he was kneeling. What crime have I committed? he wondered. He was carrying a cross and falling on sharp stones. His mother was calling him, and he was struggling to get up and walk to the site of the crucifixion and the tomb of the Lord. He fell again. He heard church bells and canon fire. All around him the trees were turning into clear wooden crosses and through the leaves a cathedral window was shining with streams of light pouring in through the stained glass.

Gimur closed his eyes with her hands. There was no other sound now except the sound of the stream. The priest had stopped breathing. She thought she would sit like this forever, alone and unmoving, but she was aware of a shadow creeping up on the enormous rocks. The two men who had accompanied Kajinsha had arrived. They stared at her. 'Is he dead?' they asked. She nodded. 'The other one is dead too,' they told her. 'He killed our chal.'

She did not heed them. They were figures coming to life out of her dream. Their faces were sweaty and they were washing their swords in the stream. For no accountable reason she felt that the death of the priest was a great blow to her. Her heart was turning into a dark cave. Somewhere in the emptiness of that lonely countryside she had seen a small, glimmering flame. She was moving towards it when suddenly, as if by the blow of an angry God, it had been extinguished. What will happen now? Is every one dead? she wondered.

It was evening when she saw Kajinsha walking across the stream towards her. No one greeted each other. He looked at her and then turned to the two men. Once she heard him cry, 'What have you done!' when the men told him about what had happened in the priest's hut. 'The white man was unstoppable,' they said. 'He was shouting all the time. We pulled him out of the hut and tied him up. He kept shouting. So we hit him. Then we came to find you.'

'What about the chal? Did he say anything?'

'No. But the servant told us Lamet had met the priest just before we arrived. The servant heard him telling the priest that the chal was dead. He said they had carried the dead animal to a Tibetan lama's house. It is proof. We know the priest killed our chal.'

It was a confusing story. Kajinsha could focus only on the word 'lama'. Who else could it be but Marpa, he thought. Marpa must have paid Lamet to do it. Lamet would do anything for a price, even if it was only a bag of grain. He was a mean, greedy man with a grudge against Kajinsha and his clan. Marpa would then move evidence to prove the priests had something to do with it and instigate Zumsha's anger. The presence of Lamet would fuel suspicion and enmity between the clans. Marpa was sowing doubt.

If the ruse worked no one would know who was to blame and everyone would turn against one another and Marpa would sit back and watch them cut each other down.

And now, what is to be done now? he thought. For a long time he stood in silence looking at the priest and then he bent down and looked more closely at the inert body. There was no bullet wound. His old gun had missed its target, Lamet, but it had not claimed the priest instead, as Kajinsha had feared. The priest had been killed by Lamet's sword. Blood had soaked through the priest's vest and coagulated like rust on his pale hands. Kajinsha knew that this act would not go unpunished. The white men would hunt them down. He had seen their guns and boats. They had conquered Assam and burned the Abor villages. And he had looked into the eyes of the white sa'ab in Suddya and seen what any man would recognise—that the sa'ab believed he was more powerful than them. Maybe it was so. But now, more than all this Kajinsha felt his anger rising up against the priest. 'Why did you come back?' He wanted to shout. 'Now look what has happened, just because of your stupid God and your Tibet! Tibet! Now you are dead! Where is your God now? Ah...! Priest, you should have waited for me! What does it matter what a man believes, if it is the same or different from your beliefs, as long as he has a life that he knows and loves?'

He had chased Lamet through the jungle. At one point Yenjee had stumbled and fallen and Kajinsha had jumped forward thinking he had them then but Lamet, quick as a flash, had drawn his sword and slashed at him. The dao had swung against his hip and cut him in the calf as he had leapt sideways to avoid the blow. At the same time Yenjee had scrambled up and Kajinsha had seen her and Lamet running and disappearing into the thickets of bamboo before they suddenly rose up again and he saw them leaping off the edge of the precipice into the green undergrowth below. 'Die!' he had shouted, and hurled his spear after them. He had waited a long time to see if they would climb back up. He had mashed leaves in his mouth and plastered them over his wound. There was no possibility of giving chase and when the last streaks of light disappeared from the treetops and there was no sign of Lamet and the woman Kajinsha had decided to return to Gimur and the priest.

It was dark and cold now and a din of mosquitoes buzzed around them. The two men were edgy and restless. 'We must go back,' they said.

'No!' cried Kajinsha. 'We must move him.' He pointed to the priest.

The men moved back. They did not want to touch the dead man.

'We must move him,' repeated Kajinsha standing up close to them. The older of the two shrugged. 'Come, come,' said Kajinsha, kneeling down and putting his arm under the bloodstained body, 'help me carry him.' He did not know where to, but he knew something had to be done, perhaps some last rite... But he had never seen a dead white man before and he did not know what to do. Oh fathers! Why are we slaves to this earth? What must I do now? He wondered. It took all his strength to hoist up the body of the priest and with the help of the two men Kajinsha led the procession upstream. He feared Lamet might be waiting somewhere and he did not want to cross the water. They had not moved a few steps when the two men said, 'Stop! We will go no further.' They laid down the body of the priest. All of them were panting and unable to speak more than a few words. 'We have done what we had come to do,' the men said. 'We must go back.' They were in a high, lonely place where the trees thinned out and they could see the stars glimmering in a pale, clear sky. Kajinsha nodded. He could not force them to carry the body of a dead stranger. Who knew what god was flying high above them watching their actions. If they were not careful they could be cursed and their lives could end in violent death. 'Go then,' he said. 'Tell Zumsha everything. I do not know about the other man in Sommeu but I will take care of this priest.'

According to the records the bodies of the two priests were never found. The day and date of when and how they were killed is also not certain. It is a guess that it happened one day sometime in early September that a Mishmee tribesman stormed into the village with an armed gang and killed them with spears and swords. The first report of the killing reached Father Louis Bernard in mid-December 1854. Apparently the news was conveyed through the son of a Khampti chief. Who was this man? Some reports say he was the man who had accompanied Father Krick on his first journey into Mishmee territory. Could it have been Chowsa? Rumours were rife about the motive of the crime. At first it was thought that the priests had been killed simply out of greed. Then it was said that the motive was revenge. The priests had refused to give the Mishmee a piece of cloth when they passed through his territory. Another version said it was a case of mistaken identity. The ringleader had mistaken the priests for Englishmen and had killed them in retaliation for the death of his son who had drowned during a journey to Assam.

Stranger stories were to appear in the years following the murder. In 1862, far away to the north, Father Krick's colleague Renou and others of the Paris Foreign Mission who were posted in Tibet found objects which had belonged to Krick and Bourry in the hands of certain Tibetan officials. This led to a suspicion of complicity or encouragement by the authorities of the Zayul valley in the murder of the two priests. Many years after the incident another observation by a British officer recorded in the Assam Secretariat papers pointed fingers at a Mishmee as the perpetrator of the crime but the report claimed that the man had killed the French priests because his mithun had been killed at their protest, or instigation, for making too much noise.

Every breath of wind that blew across the hills whispered a new story. A cloud was moving across the land. And Gimur and Kajinsha trapped by the side of the stream with the dead priest could not know then that every ticking second on that day was moving them into a sad oblivion that would obliterate the terror and pain of their thoughts and bury their story in the darkness that was falling like a curtain over the stones and cliffs and the thin stream and its ephemeral waters.

Gimur was sitting bent and shivering when she heard a short, swift whistle. Someone was approaching! She listened intently. There was no other sound. Kajinsha, crouched beside the body of the priest, was staring towards the trees. He had lost his spear, but his hand was on his sword. A dark, round figure was creeping towards them and Gimur suddenly recognised Awesa. She jumped up in joy but Kajinsha pulled her back. 'Stay down,' he whispered. They were on a ridge and their standing figures might be visible to anyone looking out for them. Awesa was now running with his body bent low and he landed right beside Gimur with a sliding thud. A bundle of dried maize and two swords were hidden under his voluminous clothes. 'I was hiding in the jungle,' he said. He had seen everything in Sommeu and had followed Kajinsha and witnessed the tussle by the stream with Lamet, but after the death of Father Krick he had crept back into the line of trees and made his way back to Sommeu.

'Sommeu,' Awesa whispered. 'They are having a meeting in Sommeu.' He pressed his knuckles against his mouth. 'Everyone is saying you killed the priests.'

'Did you see Marpa?' Kajinsha asked.

'*He* called the meeting! Awesa stopped, catching his breath and struggling with a word. 'Marpa…! He blurted out the name. 'Marpa is taking some men to meet the governor in Rima.'

Kajinsha didn't say anything. A stiff wind was shaking the tussocks of grass and the stars in the sky were disappearing as daybreak crept closer. A sharp shout startled them. They heard the clatter of hooves, faint at first, and then suddenly loud and thundering below them.

'It is Marpa!' cried Awesa. 'We must run, fast!' The light of bamboo flares appeared everywhere. Kajinsha was familiar with this ridge. He knew they were close to a big cave in a place strewn with boulders. 'Quick, we must reach the top.' He tried to lift the priest and Awesa stooped down to help him but it was beyond his strength to lift the body. An eerie light was snaking its way up the hillside. There was nothing else to do but run for it. They left the priest where he lay covered by the tall grass and scrambled up towards the summit.

Kajinsha led the way towards a narrow cleft amid a pile of boulders. 'In here, quick!' he cried. They crawled in and found a huge cavern of crystalline limestone like the interior of a house. It was a place that Kajinsha's father had showed him once when they had hunted together. 'No one will find us here,' said Kajinsha. He sat down with a grunt. His leg wound was bleeding again with the exertion. 'It is nothing,' he said when he saw Awesa looking at it. He used his head cloth to wipe away the blood. 'In a while we can climb down and cut across the track just below and follow the Dau River,' he continued. 'It will lead us away from the Tibetan villages.'

Gimur heard him and thought—this is what it has come to. We are fugitives. They would never find rest anywhere. There was nothing to do but wait in this dim hole like trapped beasts. She was about to close her eyes when she caught Kajinsha staring at her with such passion in his eyes that she sat upright with a start. 'What is it?'

'You saw it,' he said, 'I did not kill the priest.'

'No, no! Never! You did not!' she cried, her heart responding to the desperation in his voice. And she wanted to say, 'It is a dream. I saw it all in a dream. When we reach home and wake up everything will be clear.' But her words were lost seeing Kajinsha sitting so still as if he had stopped breathing. His lips were blue and his face was as dark as night.

They crept out of the cave when the sound of men and horses had died away. It was still dark, but they dared not creep back down the mountain towards the place where they had left the priest.

'Marpa and his men will be waiting for us. We have to cut around to the other side,' said Kajinsha. What could they do? They were running away and leaving the dead priest. The history books would record the murder and death of the priest but their story would fall away into an unknown place buried beneath rocks and stones. No one will find him, thought Gimur. Only I and Kajinsha will know that we left a man lying here with his eyes closed. Why should he be found? The boulders and beds of grass can hide a hundred men. He can lie here in peace. She remembered the music of the priest's flute, his pale, ghostly skin and his thin, troubled face with eyes like glass beads that had once looked at her so intently. He was dead now. It was sad, but she knew she would forget him. Perhaps, one day, they would return to look again on this spot and dream that the priest had found his ancestors and that he had found new clothes and food and shelter in the other place. Now they were racing against the wind and the darkness. She turned around once and looked back. Black clouds were already rolling up over the mountain top and she thought she saw the figure of the priest standing up straight against the skyline, his shoulders touching the sky.

'Quick, quick, don't stop!' cried Kajinsha.

They were clawing their way down a ravine that was like a black hole in another universe. Gusts of wind blew sand into their eyes. They had very little time to make it to the cover of green vegetation far below them. If the wind gained in strength it could blow them off the narrow ledge and plunge them into the river.

Awesa led the way clinging to the rock wall breathing like an ox and Kajinsha moved step by step behind Gimur. 'Keep moving. Don't look down,' he commanded and goaded her on, grasping her by the forearm when her feet skidded trying to find purchase on the granite slabs that slanted down to the water's edge. The sun was not up yet over the mountains when they completed their descent and were at the level of the river again. Gimur felt she could not move another step. 'There is no need to walk anymore. We are trapped. We can sit down now…' the bitter words rose up in her mouth.

'It is not safe here,' said Kajinsha. He feared an ambush. They must move on into the dark vegetation of giant trees and prickly cane. 'The way out of the forest,' he remembered his father telling him, 'is to see it at close quarters and make your way slowly through it, studying the faint path that your hands and your feet makes on the silent earth. It is not the time to be afraid. If your heart is patient, the jungle will let you pass. The night creatures will move away from your path if you stay calm and walk with ease, because no matter how hard you try, no matter how furtively you slide through the foliage, no matter if you stand still and look around with frightened eyes, the creatures who live here will have seen you already, and they will see you all the time before you see them, if you ever see them.'

They were moving through a space where no villagers ventured and trees stood close together with their branches interlaced in a net of green through which the fractured sunlight glinted and played tricks with their eyes. Perhaps the trees were whispering something. 'Look out! That way is covered with sharp cane and here the path is sticky with the tears of trees and mashed leaves dissolving beneath your feet to form new life.' Giant creepers twisted skywards to reach the sun. To live! To survive! That was all that counted. Kajinsha slashed at the undergrowth to clear a path. He turned to Gimur and Awesa.

'Follow me,' he said, and they entered the cavernous forest that stretched all the way between the lama villages of the border and their destination to the house on the ridge overlooking the Dau River.

1855

An Ambush in the Wilderness. The End of Solitude

According to accounts of travellers in the early nineteenth century the eastern frontier of India was a region that attracted few visitors and remained cut off from any outside influence. This was especially true of the Mishmee region in the extreme northeast corner of the country where the events of this narrative took place. Imagine a vast landscape nurturing villages of only one or two houses. The fast rivers are impossible to cross and any traveller coming this way must wait for the dry winter months to be able to lay a single log across in order to ford them. The mountains are steep, offering no foothold. They shoot straight up as if to pierce the heavens. No one comes here. Perhaps a man and his brother are happy living here. They have inhabited these mountains since the time of their fathers. They have their women with them and the family is safe in this valley. High above in their mountain home perhaps Kajinsha and Gimur were happy too, believing that time was on their side and that they could start life anew. They had built a small hut beyond the granary away from the old house that was now occupied by Awesa and many clan relatives as a decoy in case any one came looking for them. But no one came, except Zumsha.

'Everything has happened as I had predicted,' he said. 'The white men are dead. No one will enter this territory now.'

Kajinsha knew Marpa and the Tibetans would not come after him. Marpa had got what he wanted—the elimination of the priests. But surely the priest would have his clansmen, too, however far away, and they would come in search of him.

'No one came to look for the other priest,' said Zumsha, reminding Kajinsha of the man who had been killed six years ago.

'What happened to Lamet?' asked Kajinsha.

'He lives. I have word that he is back in his village. But it is of no consequence. He will not dare to come here.'

Kajinsha looked at the mountains. He had seen his father in a dream. The old man was saying something but he could not hear his words because of the loud chirruping of birds. He had woken up wondering if the birds were real or a part of his dream. The sound of birds could be a bad omen. Sometimes he thought he heard the hills echoing: revenge, revenge! Two men had been killed and he felt the need to perform rituals to cleanse his household of all that had happened. Their hands had touched blood and the flesh of the dead. If his father were alive he would have called the kambring and invoked gods to protect them from bad spirits and the revenge of the priests who had been killed. Benevolent spirits, loving mother, sky father, hear the words of the living: We offer sacrifice! Do not let death enter this house! But for such a ritual they would require preparation and food—rice, maize, sacrifice of chal and baskets of meat and fish. Gimur had looked in the rice bin and said that there was rice, but not enough. Their fields lay untended and they dared not leave their hiding place, not yet...

Now and then Awesa's sharp whistle startled them but it would be a false alarm. Kajinsha's clansmen would appear out of nowhere with information. They said no one talked about the priests anymore and no one among them knew what had happened to their corpses. They had not seen any activity of burial or removal of the bodies. Everything had vanished. This is what death means, thought Kajinsha. One moment a man was worrying about the weather, wondering whether the hunting would be good and whom you would call to a feast, and in a moment everything was changed, everything ended. Their lives too would slip away, he thought, but while he lived the death cry that he had heard rattling in the throats of the victims told him no matter what he did or where he went his life had been irrevocably changed with the coming of death. Everything in his life now was between him and the dead priest.

Two moons passed. Villagers on the lookout said there was no sign of activity from the Assam plains to the south. Everyone was warned that this was the direction from where danger could come. But all appeared peaceful. Their worst enemy was the weather. A freezing wind swept down from the north and their meagre crops were flattened by pelting rain. Gimur worked like a mule to pull in the remnants of the harvest but rodents and birds had already devoured most of the crops even before the rain destroyed what was left standing. She piled everything into the granary wondering how they would pull through the winter. An open gallery ran around the house jutting out from the mountain slope and she saw Kajinsha standing there silently, smoking his pipe. His shoulders were stooped and he was looking down towards the valley below. He looked like another person. She stared at him, suddenly aware of his weakened frame and his thin, serious face. If there is no food we will starve, she thought.

Day and night she thought about food. Every night when the wind blew hard and she closed her eyes she heard footsteps and voices and knew they were the ghosts of men and women prowling the earth in search of food. Every house and village was reeling under a famine. Kajinsha had forbidden her to go out too far from the house but hunger kept her awake. One night she sat up, famished and shivering. Quietly, she crept outside. She walked quickly to a spot far below the house that she had kept her eyes on for many days. She bent down and searched for thin cracks on the hard ground. She was digging for food in the dark. She knew tubers were buried deep in the earth but she only had a pointed stick and her knife. She was crouched under the ferns and leaves. Ah! Something! She had found a yam shoot. She clutched at it but it was mud that crumbled in her hands. She stretched back, staring at the specks of moonlight scattered everywhere. A waxing crescent moon had risen over the hill. She exhaled a long sigh. Moonlight was filtering down through the chinks in the tall fern bushes. She remained motionless for a long time. Once she had talked to the moon. Was that not what she had told Kajinsha when he had first appeared before her in Mebo? How long ago that was. It seemed she had lived many lives since that time.

A thin wail rang in her ears. It was a night creature, but she thought it was Kajinsha calling her. Maybe he was dying of hunger! I'm coming, she wanted to shout. I will find food and we will live! Her heart thudded so loudly she thought the trees were breaking and crashing all around her. She began striking the earth harder and deeper. Mother earth, I know you. Give me food! Her hand flung earth and leaves skywards until she touched something. Her knife grazed a yam. She recognised the scent and she was tender, concentrated, smiling in the darkness when her hands eased out a full, round tuber.

One evening when she was returning to the house carrying a basket of yam she heard voices. Kajinsha was sitting with someone in the manthang. She entered and saw it was Chowsa! An old friend's presence in hard times can brighten the darkest hour and Gimur felt Chowsa's sudden arrival was godsend. He handed her a packet of dried fish.

'Welcome!' she cried. 'What news?'

Chowsa's big, beaming face gave no indication of the grave news he had brought. First, he said, there was word from Lendem in Mebo village. The British sahibs had visited Mebo recently. They had camped there, met the village elders, looked at the surroundings and and then gone away. Nothing there, except that Lendem had overheard them talking about something. It was about the murder of the two priests, and Lendem said that they were planning to send soldiers into the Mishmee hills to catch the culprit. Lendem did not know the full story but he had known Krick and he wondered about Gimur and Kajinsha. He had sent word to Chowsa to warn them about this development. The other news was that the British sahibs had sent someone to his house in Chunpura to find him. The messenger was a kinsman. Chowsa had found out that another priest had come from Assam to meet some tribesmen to find out what had happened to his two friends.

'Something is afoot,' said Chowsa. If the hills were quiet the border towns in the plains were bustling with activity. He had seen the arrival of soldiers carrying guns and torches and wearing hunting boots. He had told his kinsman that he would meet the sahibs and then he had quickly moved out into the hills to bring them this news.

Gimur heard the conversation but she heard it like a story that had nothing to do with their lives here. Just yesterday Awesa had managed to snare a squirrel. The aroma of cooking filled the house and all her focus was on the strips of roasting meat.

'Maybe you should move north,' said Chowsa.

'No,' said Kajinsha. 'The white men will never come this far.'

'They will, if they want to. They are the rulers.'

'Bah! We'll see about that.' Kajinsha could not imagine travelling north again. He knew Marpa would give them shelter if he asked for it, but that was something he would never do. Better to stand here and face soldiers than fall into Marpa's trap and become his subordinate. 'This is the first time I'm hearing you call the kah klamflung rulers,' he said to Chowsa.

There was a silence. Chowsa poked at the fire. 'You are far away from them,' he said. 'I feel them around me every day. Their boats are moving up and down the river. They bring salt and pieces of coloured cloth and our people rush forward to receive the petty gifts, stretching out their arms like beggars…' He stopped.

Kajinsha sat quietly, listening. Then he said, 'Come, you have brought us gifts. You are my brother. Let us eat!'

Chowsa left early the next morning. Kajinsha did not say anything more about what had been spoken and Gimur did not ask. They continued each day as they always did, rising before dawn, washing their faces in icy water and feeling the sharp wind on their skin. One morning, when the cold made them wince, Kajinsha said, 'I remember my father's words. "This is how it is," he said, "one day the wind blows snow from the mountains then the next day it is warm and dry. One day there is food enough to break the smoking rack and another night the rack is empty. Our lives are like this. We don't know how long anything will last. Even the sky changes colour. But there are more things to be afraid of than dying."' Gimur understood. The days were slipping out of their hands and perhaps this was but a moment to catch their breath, but it was enough. Their hearts were beating for the same thing, still eager to love, and they both knew nothing would change this. They were living in a hut like a fortress surrounded by ravines and waves of hills and jungle. If strangers came then they would fight to keep their land and die here if it was so destined. This was their unspoken pact. And though nothing of this period is recorded anywhere it is likely that these brief days in a village in a quiet valley by a stream were the happiest in the life of Kajinsha and Gimur.

One evening Awesa brought a bamboo tube full of millet beer. His mother Auli was visiting and she had sent one of the younger boys to bring the entire stock of maize and barley from Sommeu, and he had brought this back too. Gimur ate a bit of the fermented millet mash and felt drowsy immediately. Kajinsha and Awesa spoke in low tones and she felt happy seeing them sitting together by the fire. 'At last, all is well, all is well…' she repeated to herself and dozed. She had barely closed her eyes when a short, sharp whistle ringing in her ears startled her. It was followed by a loud shout. A strange light was filtering in. Is it morning already? What is it…? Kajinsha was shaking her wildly. She felt her eyes were stuck together. 'Wake up! Gimur! Get up, get up. The men are here!'

She stared at him. He was holding his spear and in his other hand his sword was unsheathed. He dropped everything and began lifting her up and dragging her towards the small window at the back of the house. 'Quickly! Quickly!' She heard men shouting and something banged hard and reverberated like thunder. A woman screamed. Gimur clutched at Kajinsha. He saw her staring eyes. 'Jump!'

'No!'

'I will find you,' he said. 'Jump!' Gimur struggled but it was no use. Kajinsha pushed her roughly through the opening. She fell with a thud and Kajinsha stopped only for a moment to peer out and see her tumbling down over the edge of the hill into the void below. Then he turned around to face the men who had crept up the hill to hunt him down. Out of the corner of his eye he saw the thatch on the side of his house burst into flame and he ran out with his spear poised straight above his shoulder.

'Run! Pai!' he heard Awesa shouting and turned around to look. Something struck him hard. A white cloud covered everything and he did not know what had happened. The spear fell from his hand. A figure was approaching and he thought it was Lamet. He let out a loud roar and charged forward straight into a sepoy. Kajinsha snatched at his rifle and clawed at the man's tunic and tore off the buttons. A stinging blow hit him on the back in between his shoulder blades. A woman screamed again. He felt heat creeping up his body. Someone was pulling him down. Had he fallen? He felt drugged. His eyes fluttered and he thought he heard the drum of the shaman calling him away on a long journey.

'I leave the mark of my blood on this place!' he shouted, struggling to stand with his arms lifted up to the sky.

It was the dawn of a cold grey morning referred to in documents of the time when a punitive expedition under the command of Lieutenant F. G. Eden reached Kajinsha's hideout deep in the Mishmee hills. A few weeks ago Eden had accompanied Captain E. T. Dalton on a survey mission into the Abor hills and visited Mebo village from where Lendem had sent Kajinsha and Gimur the warning message about a possible raid on their territory. The British authorities in Assam could not ignore the reports of the murder of two French priests and immediately on his return from Mebo, Eden and his troops of twenty Assam Light Infantry and forty Khampti volunteers and porters had marched up from Suddya across the patch of dense forest towards the hills. It had taken them eight days of forced march—crossing rivers and climbing, climbing in the bitter cold across range after range of mountains towards the high ridges overlooking the Dau River. This was the first punitive expedition against the Mishmee and no doubt Eden and his men were able to achieve this feat with the assistance of some villagers who showed them the way perhaps under pressure or due to local rivalry amongst the different clans. It was a great show of British might and authority. The silence of the towering mountains was shattered and that morning saw the end of solitude and the beginning of war and sorrow in a land where the inhabitants had refused right of way to every stranger until now, with the exception of Father Krick and Bourry passing through into the Zayul valley of Tibet. With the ambush in the wilderness it was felt that the murder of the two priests was fully avenged and the matter closed.

According to British expedition accounts many of Kajinsha's 'relatives and sons' were killed in open combat, his people dispersed and Kajinsha was taken to Debrooghur jail. A son of Kajinsha's who was too young at the time and escaped capture was reportedly seen years later, in 1871, attending the annual Suddya mela that attracted tribesmen from all the hill regions bordering Assam. These are the words, recorded on paper, of the officers leading the first British punitive expedition into the Mishmee hills. But on that morning when Kajinsha thought he heard the drum of the shaman and lifted his eyes there was only Awesa clinging to the branches of a tree. The sky was slowly falling down on all the men below. Awesa was shouting. He was shaking the branches like a thousand spears but no one one heard him or paid heed even when Kajinsha closed his eyes and fell, and Awesa wept loudly like a howling beast for his feared and beloved father.

In another account a young woman present during the raid reportedly told the soldiers that her brothers had killed the priests but whoever she was it was not Gimur. No one knew Gimur and her name is not mentioned anywhere in the records.

Gimur was invisible lying under a pile of leaves at the bottom of the ridge. There was no movement, no sound and when her eyes fluttered open, she saw a bird perched on a tree. It is another dream, she thought. The bird moved and with it something dark and warm moved close to her face. Someone was bending over her. Her eyes traced the outline of the nebulous shadow with a painful effort and slowly she delineated the face of Awesa's mother, Auli. The woman was whispering something. Then she pressed something warm into her mouth. Gimur coughed and Auli put her hand over her mouth making her swallow the bitter medicine. Perhaps it was opium, or coptis root, or a potion of something that Auli had concocted in her pursuit of a cure for her own ailments, Gimur did not know, but it had the effect of waking her, and later, she realised, of treating concussion and restoring her back from the brink of death. All this was not evident now as Gimur steeled her body to recover from her injuries and Auli moved back and forth like a furtive shadow ministering to her in the shelter of trees and stones.

One morning she whispered, 'I will go back to Sommeu. Awesa will help you now.' Her words startled Gimur. In a dream she had seen fire and smoke and heard the dying cries of men and women. She thought everyone was dead. 'No,' said Auli. 'Awesa is not dead. And Kajinsha is alive!'

That night Gimur looked up towards her house on the ridge and felt a cry rising up from her soul. What had happened while she had been lying asleep? She remembered her last image of Kajinsha and his wild eyes staring at her, pushing her away from him. As she fell she had caught a glimpse of a white man and thought it was the dead priest come back to life. She tried to focus her mind on what had happened. She did not know how long she had been lying under the pile of leaves—maybe a day and a night, maybe two days…She only knew that she must find Kajinsha now. Auli had said he was alive. Where had they taken him? The approach to their house lay on the other side of the ridge but she could not be sure if soldiers were lying in wait for her. There was no other way to reach the top except to climb up from where she was. She listened carefully. There was no sound, no movement anywhere around her. The sun was already losing its strength and long shadows were spreading along the side of the mountains. She could not wait for Awesa. She felt for her knife tied around her waist and found it was still there. She stood up straight and felt the blood flowing beneath her skin, flowing into her heart, cleansing it of all sorrow, and then her soul lifted and burst free, soaring above the earth, the wilderness of mud and trees and mad rivers, up into the platform of the sky. Free! She was an eagle. She would find Kajinsha. She tied her wrap tighter around her waist and began the ascent.

Awesa found her on her knees crouched at the top of the burnt, black hill. There were no words to exchange. For once Awesa had failed in his duty. He had fallen asleep and had not heard the approach of the soldiers. It was Auli who had heard them. The world was still covered in darkness when she heard a cock crow and then she had heard the stealthy breathing of strangers creeping up the hill.

'They are here, quick! Awesa!' she shouted. Awesa jumped up and immediately started running towards his father's and Gimur's hut. He whistled and shouted loudly as he ran. But it was too late. The sepoys were over the hill. Awesa sprinted up the slope and flung himself onto a tree. His mother who was running with him jumped down the ravine. Awesa watched everything from the top, looking down through the branches. Through a pall of smoke and thick morning fog he saw men running into each other and fighting with their bare hands until a young white man gave a long shout. The sepoys cried 'Oojur! Ojur! Yes, yes sa'ab!' And suddenly the air around him was blazing and crackling with streaks of fire. He saw the two men who had been with his father by the stream where the priest died, jumping up high and then suddenly buckling and falling backwards flat on their backs. A woman was screaming. Someone was pointing to Kajinsha and Awesa shut his eyes as the babble of voices suddenly stopped. Everything was hushed in that moment of great silence when Kajinsha lifted his spear and fell to the ground. Awesa stayed up till long after he had seen the attackers moving quickly down the slope, taking Kajinsha and eight other men and women away with them.

'It is what I saw,' said Awesa.' The soldiers will not come back now.'

Gimur looked around. Yes, what man would come back here now? What man would dare to step on ground strewn with ash and blood? All that was left of their home was charred wood and black, broken sticks of bamboo. The flat stone of her fireplace were overturned and all the half burnt logs thrown to one side. She struck the ground with her fists. 'Let the jungle cover up this bleak black hill and let it become the dwelling place of spirits forever!' she cried. 'I spit on the murderers!'

Awesa stared at her, helpless.

'We must find Kajinsha,' she said. 'We must go to Chowsa. Only he can help us now.'

Awesa mumbled something. 'There will be sipais... he said,' gurgling his words in agitation. He was afraid for Gimur. 'It will be dangerous.'

Gimur silenced him. 'We'll travel east,' she said. 'Then we cut across the river and reach Chunpura from the southeast.' She had a map in her mind and her heart was set like a sharp stone with but one purpose—to find Kajinsha. She knew that news of the attack would have reached every home and village. Kajinsha's clan would mourn the dead but it would be a while yet before the outrage committed on their people in their territory could be fully avenged. The success of the expedition had shocked everyone, and now, every one knew that the hills would be full of armed soldiers watching their every move. She alone among them could travel immediately because no one knew about her.

There is only one way to do it, she thought. She would have to set out alone with Awesa. There was no time for planning, no tactics to think about. The moment would decide everything.

She looked into her granary and found her baskets of grain and tubers spilled and strewn around. She picked up the tubers and and grabbed all her bead necklaces that were her only possession from Mebo, and put them into a bag. There was no need for any other preparation. They travelled as they were, Gimur with her knife tied around her waist and her bag across her shoulder and Awesa carrying his bow and sword and a bag with two strips of dried yak meat strapped across his shoulders. A soft rain began to fall as they left the high peaks of enormous fir trees and struck south. They met no one on the way. The other men and women had been freed after the sepoys reached their first camp but Kajinsha had not been released. The sepoys had retreated quickly because they were afraid of the jungle, the terrifying silence that had descended on the hills, and they did not want to be trapped in this terrain where they knew everyone was now their bitterest, sworn enemy.

They don't know us, thought Gimur. We will never forget. And we will survive. And she turned eastward, Awesa, sturdy and tireless, walking ahead of her. The landscape changed into forests of giant Dipterocarpus trees. They were at home in the jungle and they walked swiftly. Sometimes Gimur thought she heard the voices of children. Halfway through their journey the loud call of gibbons startled her. Awesa smiled at her. 'Those are Ulu monkeys,' he said. 'They are far away...' He pointed eastward toward the Patkai hills. One day Gimur saw a tagat tree in full bloom. Her heart overflowed with memories. These coral trees would be blooming in the hills of Mebo too, she thought. How sad it is... I loved them once. Now they bring me no delight. Instead the flowering tree reminded her that time was passing. They had set out when the moon was on the wane, now Gimur saw it was waxing full again. She began walking faster and faster, snapping twigs and breaking leaves and branches with her hands.

It was after more than a month of travel, crossing mountains and streams and pushing their way through swamp grass and reeds that one evening they knew they had reached their destination. They emerged into the clearing and saw several men sitting around a fire. Chowsa came forward to receive them. 'They are friends,' he said quickly. He had been expecting their arrival. The men looked at them silently as they entered and then perhaps with a signal from Chowsa they began to take their leave. Chowsa walked them to the edge of the forest where they stood together for a while, speaking in low tones. The news of the raid on the Mishmee hills and the capture of Kajinsha had spread far and wide. In the last decade since the attack on Suddya garrison and the murder of the British Colonel by Khampti and Mishmee tribes in 1839 the hill tribes had remained peaceful, but for a few skirmishes in the Abor hills. With the capture of Kajinsha this uneasy calm was shattered and the latent hatred and distrust of outsiders among the tribes had been stirred up again.

'Kajinsha is in Debrooghur,' Chowsa told them. Gimur closed her eyes. She had heard the name of this place since the days of her childhood in Mebo, and Kajinsha had pointed it out to her once, when they stood on a rock near this very place. 'There, on the banks of the dark water is Dibru,' he had said. 'Don't forget this route.'

'He's locked up. No one can see him,' said Chowsa. Then he added, 'Lendem is also on his way.'

This piece of news brought some consolation to Gimur. Now, more than ever, she needed a brother.

But it was a fortnight before Lendem arrived. 'There are police guards all the way from here to Mebo,' he said. 'More British sahibs are coming by boat and everyone is afraid that these migluns are coming to kill them and take their lands. All the village chiefs are meeting to prepare to defend themselves.'

For the British officers who were serving in these outposts on the north bank of the Burhampooter River it was also a crucial period of stocktaking. The question was whether they should establish more frontier posts or even military battalions to deal with acts of aggression by the tribes. Currently the strength of the police force was broken up into dry weather strength and rains strength (when the number of personnel was increased slightly), though generally the total strength of troops consisted of some six hundred men between Suddya and Debrooghur, the latter being the station headquarters of one of the four Native regiments in Assam province with a jail and treasury office. It was a turbulent, anxious time. The borderlands between Assam and the hills were seething with rumours and men moved in and out of Chowsa's house under cover of darkness. Chunpura was a strategic frontier post and more soldiers had been rushed here after the Mishmee expedition. Gimur knew Chowsa was also meeting the British sahibs. As a chief of the Khampti nobility who knew the border he was in a position where they, the sahibs, relied on him for assistance to negotiate with the tribes whose names and villages they did not know, while the tribes living close to the border towns relied on him to shield them from a British attack on their villages, and she, Gimur, now relied on him to arrange a meeting for her with Kajinsha.

'Take me to Debroogurh,' she said to him one day.

'Hai! That is impossible,' he cried. 'The station is guarded by armed police. It is not safe to go there at all!'

Gimur turned to Lendem. 'No one knows me. If you can show me the way I have a plan,' she said. 'I have to see Kajinsha again.'

Chowsa remained silent. Lendem looked at her. He had known Gimur since childhood and he knew that once she had fixed her mind on something she would never give up. He had a premonition of something terrible about to happen—a big mistake, another death, but seeing her set face he knew no power on earth would deter or change the course of events that she was preparing to set off by her actions. 'Let us see,' he said. 'We don't know what the migluns are planning to do with Kajinsha.'

As yet there was no outcry from the Mishmee hills. Debrooghur was a distant and impregnable place and even if Kajinsha's clan members travelled the distance down to the plains to rescue him it would prove futile. They would be stopped and subdued with force. Sometimes Gimur felt she had been totally abandoned. She thought Lendem and Chowsa were afraid and perhaps they were right. The might of the migluns had frightened everyone. Chowsa said he was going to Debroogurh to see what he could find out and if they could do nothing to alter things she knew Lendem would ask her to return to Mebo. It was his duty. But she could not give up. Her duty was to keep hope alive.

One afternoon Gimur was sitting outside when she saw Chowsa returning. She quickly followed him into the house in anticipation of news. He was carrying a big bag and she saw him going into the house hurriedly. He said something to Lendem and they began talking excitedly. What had happened, she wondered, when Lendem turned and met her gaze and she saw fear and desperation in his eyes. Gimur braced herself. Chowsa was seated on the small cot wiping his sweaty face. He sighed and kept his head down as he spoke. The news was like a blow to her heart. Kajinsha had killed a prison guard.

'No!' she cried. Oh gods! What was happening?

Chowsa said a sepoy who had been appointed to guard Kajinsha had said something to him. Maybe the sepoy had heard about a letter that everybody was talking about at the time, a letter that the masters of the dead priests—for they had masters too, who served the same gods—had sent to the British sahibs. The letter said something about murder and pardon…

And it is recorded that there was, indeed, a mercy plea from Father Louis Bernard on behalf of the Foreign Missions. When news of the death sentence for Kajinsha reached him, Bernard had persuaded the Directors of the Paris Foreign Missions to send a letter to the Governor-General Lord Dalhousie, pleading not vengeance but the mercy of God, and for the punishment of the killer to be commuted to life imprisonment.

Perhaps it was this letter that the sepoy was talking about. He was pointing at Kajinsha and making a cutting motion with his hand, perhaps taunting him, or merely telling him that he would be pardoned and that he would live. Who knows what it was that he said, for no words were spoken. He was standing very close to Kajinsha, who understood not a word of what the sepoy was saying, and then he thought the man was telling him that soon he would be hanged to death. When the sepoy made a gesture again, pointing up, perhaps to the mountains that were the prisoner's home, Kajinsha had pounced on him and before anyone could do anything he had grabbed the man by the throat. They had fallen to the floor and Kajinsha had strangled the man with the iron chains around his wrists. A miglun officer had pulled out his gun and almost shot Kajinsha there and then, but then refrained. The jail was in uproar. A crowd had gathered outside and Chowsa who had been standing there all the time saw sepoys running in and heard men shouting, and thuds and curses until an eerie silence fell on the place and Chowsa knew that Kajinsha had at last been overpowered, beaten and dragged away to a dark place.

'Now they will surely hang him,' he said. 'He cannot escape.'

A hush fell on the room. Awesa broke the silence. 'There must be a way!' he cried.

'What way is there now?' said Lendem.

Chowsa sat with his eyes shut tight and rubbed his face wearily. Then he said, 'I returned the next morning hoping to see Kajinsha, but the guards on duty would not let anyone enter.' He said he was still standing outside when he had spotted a young man who was a relative of his being summoned inside. His name was Yong. When the man came out Chowsa approached him. 'What is happening now?' he asked. Yong was surprised to see him, but told him that the sepoy was dead and the sahibs would show no mercy to Kajinsha. They had called Yong to replace the dead sepoy. That was all. Yong's face was pale and tense. Chowsa had understood his predicament. No one wanted to serve the white man like this by fighting against their own people. Yong had seen Kajinsha, he knew the Mishmee was a friend of Chowsa's, and being his guard was not a proposition that he would have wished, but it was a time of British rule and the sahibs were engaging local men to serve in the armed frontier police to man the frontier outposts, guard the jails and treasuries and furnish escorts. The Khampti were among the first of these recruits. They knew the terrain, they were hardy, fighting men and once chosen they were sworn to loyalty, to protecting British interests in the region. For this they were drilled, received musketry instructions and were armed with rifles. In an emergency like illness or death young recruits like Yong were immediately called in and assigned replacement duty.

For Chowsa, it had been a fortunate meeting. He had talked at length with his kinsman and then come back to Chunpura. 'I have some things here,' he said now, opening his bag. He pulled out a blue shirt and two sarongs. 'You can use these clothes,' he said. 'It will help if you appear as Khampti. There is a boatman I have talked to. He's a friend of Kajinsha's. His name is Lasong. He knows the water routes better than any man and he will take you to Debroogurh, and from there, god willing, on towards Mebo, if you are lucky.'

Gimur and Lendem stared at Chowsa, speechless. It was a great risk he was taking, helping them to reach Debroogurh right under the noses of so many sepoys. And what would they do once they were there? 'Yong will be on duty. He will be on the lookout for you. The other guards are Cacharees and Mataks. I don't know what may happen but with Yong there it is worth a try. They have nothing against Kajinsha, we are the same people and they should not stop you from seeing him. Why should they? Before the arrival of the British, before all this—' he opened his arms in a wide arc, 'we were friends!'

Chowsa began talking rapidly. It was the outline of a rescue attempt but how they would achieve this goal was unclear. He was only creating a space for things to happen. Everything else would depend on what happened when they reached Debroogurh. What he worried about now was ensuring secrecy and anonymity. So Awesa was staying back with him, until such time when they could meet again.

All this time Gimur had been aware of Awesa's eyes shifting back and forth, back and forth from each of their faces, listening intently, but he did not speak.

There was no time for farewells. The boatman was waiting, said Chowsa. He clasped them hard. 'Go! May the blessing of Lord Gautama be with you!' Awesa pressed his face close to Gimur's. 'Tell my father…' He gulped and stood back, blinking rapidly. Then he bent down again and whispered clearly and tenderly, 'Tell my father we are here.'

Gimur felt breathless. It was the end of a long journey together. Stage by stage she had travelled this strip of forest from west to east and north, and back again. It was here that she had met men and women of other tribes and found her life in the high, northern mountains. Now there was no knowing what might happen to the tenuous network of friends. There were many things she wanted to ask Chowsa but all her questions were brushed aside in the urgency of the moment as she followed Lendem out of the house and into the forest. She saw Awesa's face one last time looking at her with the same devotion and love that she had seen so many times before. 'I want to carry that face with me,' she thought. 'Help me God! Help me to be strong!'

◆

The Woman and Her Love

The boatman, Lasong, stood on the prow of the boat in a relaxed, patient manner as if they were about to set off on a journey to reach an island that might be his home in this maze of sandbars and channels.

No sooner were they on board, Lasong and another oarsman began to pole the boat away from the bank strewn with boulders. The wind was biting cold and the sky was grey. Gimur was surprised to see a couple and a young boy in a blue shirt already seated in the boat.

'It is a cover,' said Lendem. 'The boat must appear to be ferrying passengers to Debroogurh…keep your head down.'

Now and then the boy dribbled spittle and bent over and picked at a sore on his knee that had begun to bleed. Gimur pretended not to see anything. They, the couple, in turn, did not look at her. The man looked straight ahead and the woman bent forward a little every time the boy twitched and touched his knee but she did not say anything to him, nor to the man. Once she raised her hands to her head and smoothed back her hair in a slow, dreamy, gesture. Gimur glanced at her quickly and saw her staring ahead sternly. Sorrow…the gesture made Gimur think of sorrow. She felt the heaviness of the sky, so dark and secret, and her heart like a stone deep under the water that flowed so swiftly and silently without once stopping to think about what was there, buried underneath. Lasong and his friend poled and then picked up the oars and rowed strongly without a break into the middle of the river. They were afloat in the whirling current of the river. The world seemed to rock and sway as if the boat was but a piece of paper. We will die in water, Gimur thought when suddenly they were across and gliding silently towards a dark, sandy shore. It was one of the numerous ghats known to Lasong and his friend. The couple and the boy got off as soon as the boat scraped against the pebbles and walked away quickly without looking back. Where is their village? Gimur wondered. She thought they were taking the boy to a doctor and had expected to see buildings, but all she saw before her was a flat, empty expanse of sand.

'Dibru is very near. We will have to get into another boat,' said Lendem.

'Come!' Lasong signalled for them to follow him and they walked a short distance along the bank to a canoe hauled up on the sand just like the one Gimur had been in when she had travelled on this river with Kajinsha a long time ago. It was a narrow dug-out barely able to hold two but Lasong said it would bring them very close to the central buildings of Debroogurh. The light vessel tipped and lurched under their extra weight, but Lendem and Lasong perched on the extreme ends and with Gimur crouched down in the centre the boat soon rode smoothly with the current. No one knew what would happen in the next few minutes. In a short while, thought Gimur, I might see Kajinsha again. She shut her eyes tight. 'Oh gods! Kabom lanka! Protect us, look after us!' The canoe curved around a projecting sand bar and Lasong said, 'We are here. Quickly, quickly!' He had already jumped off the boat and Lendem was with him holding the boat steady in the shallow water. A man emerged from the shadows. It must be Yong, thought Gimur. Her heart was pounding. Many thoughts were whirling in her head. She wanted to prepare herself to appear calm in front of Kajinsha. She wanted to be cautious and fearless, and she wanted to put on ornaments and change her dress, but there was no time. She scrabbled in her bag and put on her necklace over the Khampti cloth that she was wearing. Lasong said he would wait until just before dawn—another two hours from now. After that he would be gone. Gimur nodded and threw down her bag into the boat. Lasong raised his hand. 'Till we meet,' he said.

'This way, this way….' Yong hurried them on. In the darkness they were stick figures sprinting over the sand straight into a brackish channel of foetid water that trickled into the river. In front of them

Gimur saw the outline of a building that loomed up like a gigantic grey stone. The channel widened into a pond choked with weeds, a putrid green moat that was the southern periphery of the jail. To the left, along the western part of the wall, Gimur noticed an open space eerily lit up by what looked like a small fire. Perhaps that is where the jail sa'ab lives, she thought, trying to remember everything. 'This way… this way…' Yong swerved to the right and ran along a crumbling brick wall that led them to an arched opening in a black wall. The entrance!

Now that they were inside, the place appeared cavernous. Lendem stopped. 'I will wait here,' he said. Someone had to keep watch. He looked at Gimur and said, 'Go, quickly! Don't linger.'

Yong walked in a little way and pointed. 'There.' Then he too was gone. Gimur's eyes searched the darkness. A dim lamp was flickering in a corner and she moved towards it. The place appeared bare. There was no sound. She felt her breath shaking the thin light. 'Kajinsha!' she called softly. And suddenly she saw his face. He put a hand to his mouth and stood there facing her in silence. Gimur wanted to scream seeing his broken face. She was not prepared for this. She had planned for speed and action and tearing down a door or a house. Now she stood staring, falling forward against the iron bars. She did not shed tears but her heart thudded because she knew he was weeping to see her again. She could not bear it.

'Oh my love,' she cried. 'What have they done? What have they done to you?!'

In that terrible moment Gimur saw everything that had passed since that fateful morning on the Dau when their hill had crumbled and they had perished: Kajinsha is caged in a small cement hole. He is a leopard, turning his back on everything. No forest. No shade. The world has disappeared. The iron bars are terrible, the heavy locks twisted into the latch for eternity. But his eyes are burning darkly, looking at her with love. That look! He is stronger and lovelier than he ever was, than she ever remembered. He is standing right up against the iron bars and clasping her hand.

It is only a few iron rods, she thought. So what? What were a few rods against their hearts? One more obstacle, another stone in their path, but it would be rolled away. They had overcome much more, oh! much, much more than this. She smiled foolishly at him. She stared into his eyes. She was travelling with him again across the mountains. The wind was whipping the land and they were bent against the biting cold like two animals determinedly ploughing through the snow… there was a swift-flowing stream to cross. She felt stones crunching under her feet. She was slipping. He steadied her. Go on. Go on. Don't stop now. She clung to his shoulder. He heaved her forward. No one will find us, he said. We are safe here, you and I. The high pass loomed up right in front of them. One more obstacle. It was trying to block their escape. So what! They were together and no adversity could defeat them. The wind shrieked in her ears and through it all unexpectedly she heard the sounds of a flute.

'You saw it. I did not kill him.' Kajinsha had said.

Ah, yes! He was stronger and lovelier than she ever remembered him to be. She lifted her chin to look at him as she had always done, with her eyes half closed, and it struck her like a sharp pain in her heart that his eyes were wet and he was looking at her with tenderness. For the first time she felt the agony of tenderness. Her eyes were blurring. What would happen now? Through the rush of sound in her ears, she heard the music of the flute again. Her thoughts were wandering. That poor dead priest crumpled up in his strange clothes lying by the cold stream. It was his death that had brought this curse on them. Why did he have to die? What did he come here for, so far away from all that was his? What did he know of their lands, their lives and thoughts? What had he gained? He had died looking at her with a tenderness that had pierced her soul.

There is no greater love…The man had said so many things like that. He had looked at her to see if she understood what he was saying and she had secretly felt that she did. But she really hadn't understood anything at all, until now. Now she thought she understood something of what the priest had been trying to say. It was a story of love, all life was only about this feeling that was now welling up in her heart until she thought it would break into pieces and she would be left with nothing except this wondrous glow that suffused her whole being.

Long before dawn Gimur heard the sound of footsteps. Someone was trying to take her away. A man was pulling at her, and she was fighting bitterly. She would kill someone, she knew that, and the thought gave her great strength. It was one man struggling with her. In the dim light she had seen him coming towards her and Kajinsha and she had thought it was Lendem or Yong coming to call her. But he was another prison guard. Gimur did not know if his appearance was expected and the man said nothing as he approached her. Instead, he smiled. Gimur realised something was wrong. Perhaps the man had come in from the west entrance of the building. She stood against the bars, blocking Kajinsha from his view and faced him with no expression on her face. She raised a hand. The gesture was so imperious the man stopped, but only for an instant. A woman! My God! What was a woman doing here? His smile was false and he gripped his rifle nervously as he came up close. He was a short, thickset man with a wide mouth and black, slanting eyes that stared at her silver necklace, her short blouse, her face. Beware, beware, these woman have no shame! What brings her here? He saw Gimur's hand slide down to her waist. At this moment he jumped forward. He was trying to pin her arms back and force her down on the ground. He was shouting at the top of his voice but Gimur knew no one would hear him in this godforsaken place. She locked her right leg around his thigh and pitched her body against his in a silent, deadly struggle. The man's back slammed against the iron rods. She heard the clink of metal and she could not see Kajinsha anymore. The man was breathing hard. He was very strong, but he was still pressed up against the rods as if fixed there by some unseen force. Kajinsha had grasped the man by the hair and was holding him there in a vice like grip. His eyes were mad with anger. 'Run!' he shouted at Gimur. 'Run!' But she did not heed him. She had the sepoy now. What am I? Am I not one of the chosen, she thought. Am I not God's creation? A woman is God's creation! Which God? What did it matter? Here she was standing inside prison walls and staring at the man she loved more than life and god. Too many words. She had no need of all these words after all. Who was this man trying to pull her away? Her wrap fell open and she let it. Her knife was attached to her waist string. She contorted her arm and yanked at it so hard the string snapped with a ping. Let it, she thought. My life is gone too. She had no time for gentle love, tears, soft words, obedience. These are not for me, she thought. This is love. My love draws blood. Now! She did not hesitate a second. The man looked at her stunned when she turned with all her strength and plunged the knife into his throat. There. She was snarling like a beast as she held the knife firmly against the guard who was staring at her and trying to claw her face. Kajinsha cried out and put his hands up to his head. Released from his grip the man began to fall forward. Gimur pulled the knife out with a jerk and the man's blood spurted on the floor. She jumped sideways as he fell, and she grabbed her skirt and wrapped it hurriedly around herself. She wiped the knife against her hips. She saw Kajinsha pressed up against the bars with sweat streaming down his face. Her own face was cold and wet. What would happen now?

'Run for your life, go!'

'No!'

'You must! Go!' he shouted. He stretched his hand through the bars and tried to push her. 'Go, go! Live for me! Live!'

She touched his face, her fingers trembling, unable to utter a word.

This was the moment when Gimur would stop speaking forever. Instead she was uttering sounds like unintelligible prayers. There was something the priest used to say about prayer. 'Kumsinam—to pray…' Lendem had explained it to her in Mebo. It is what you communicated with the universe, just as the shaman spoke to the spirits. It was the same. You uttered words in your head and god heard them. 'You will never be alone like this.' That was what the priest had always been saying, clutching his cross and smiling at her. Prayer…

Someone was pulling her again and she was struggling furiously.

'Come! We must leave!' Gimur heard Lendem's voice and Kajinsha saying, 'Capmi! Brother! Leave quickly!'

Lendem was dragging her away. Gimur was running and words like prayers were racing through her head never to be spoken aloud again. Dimly she heard shouting, the sharp sound of a whistle, the voices of men. A dark figure appeared and she leapt back. 'This way, this way…' Yong was running ahead and they were all running down the path skirting the prison, leaping over the brick wall and across the dark moat towards the broad, sandy banks of the Burhampooter.

The boat was still there. Lasong saw them coming and immediately jumped into the water, ready to push the boat into the deep current. Lendem pushed Gimur into the boat.

'You can travel faster without me. The boat is too small,' he said. 'I will meet you again later.' 'No!' Gimur struggled bitterly. 'I will not leave this place without Kajinsha,' she cried. But Lendem was firm and with one push Lasong's boat had been propelled into the river. There had been no escape. The river narrowed as they moved upstream, hemmed in by mountains, and Gimur felt nothing as Lasong rowed, leaning forward with his hands curled around the oar and pulling it back into the pit of his stomach. He did not utter a word. He let her weep, and he did not say goodbye when he left her at the foot of the pale hills hidden behind a curtain of mist. It was the same spot where her people had first met Captain Vetch in 1848, and Father Krick had first set eyes on the tribe called the Abor and wondered about the meaning of the tattooed cross on their faces while Gimur and Lendem were on the cliff overhead asking, 'What is beyond?'

At daybreak the sky was clear and calm over the town of Debroogurh. A streak of red tinted the sky in the east and a soft light beamed down on the prison and extended over the moat of weeds and water lilies. No one knew about the night of terror that had passed within its walls and no one saw a dark canoe float away on the river like a piece of driftwood. For the residents of the town at the time Debroogurh was a charming and salubrious place that had grown from a small settlement on the left bank of the Dibru River, a little above its confluence with the Burhampooter, into an important frontier station and commercial centre of Upper Assam. Its transformation had begun with the discovery of tea as an indigenous plant growing in the surrounding hills in 1823, when the spot was marked for commercial growth. In 1839 the Assam Tea Company was formed and gardens opened in and around the town. Marwari traders made their entry and started a lively bazaar on the banks of the Dibru that also attracted tribes from the surrounding hills, giving Debroogurh the air of an adventurous border town. On a clear day it was a beautiful stretch of country with its proximity to river and mountains and the dark, shadowy jungle that grew right down to the water's edge on the opposite bank.

In his prison cell Kajinsha was trying to look towards the hills. A man was standing in front of him, standing very close to the bars and saying something. Idly he wondered what the man was saying. Where had he come from? After the noise and the beating, this man had come in quietly and stood staring at him in silence. He was a white man. At first Kajinsha had thought he was a priest, he resembled the dead priest in the way he stood and looked, sad and eager at the same time, and in the way he held his hands in front of him as if he was going to pray to another unknown god. But Kajinsha felt no sorrow or fear. A few minutes ago a fat, angry jailor had rushed in and banged his gun against the iron rods threatening him in pidgin Assamese. 'You are finished! You are defeated, savage! Now you will die!' Kajinsha had laughed at the man showing his teeth and his broken mouth. 'Hah! Sepoy! Dog! Tell me, what is defeat? I do not know the meaning of this word. If I am standing like this, even if I fall down, I am still alive—and stronger than you! As long as my heart is beating there is no defeat. Do you want to see how I die? Come closer you coward! You are afraid. It is *your* defeat!'

He had grasped the bars of the cage and the man had retreated yelling at him all the time: 'You are finished, savage, you are finished!'

And now there was this white man. What does he want? Kajinsha could barely see anything now—his eyes were closing up and he was afraid of falling. The man raised his hands and the meaning of his presence suddenly dawned on Kajinsha. He was here to prepare the way to send him on his final journey. A line of soldiers were coming towards him. Kajinsha tried to stand up straighter, gripping the iron bars with all his might. He was being dragged and pulled. He did not want to fight anymore. All he wanted was to see the mountains of the Dau valley again. A strange feeling of eagerness stole over him, as if light would break on the horizon and something, someone, a new life would reach him.

He felt he wanted to start again. There on the black hill, in the same place, as the same person. Not anyone else older, or younger, better, more rich or strong. He just wanted the chance to start again. Time had flashed by. And now it is too late to save myself, he thought. He could still see the steep hill. It was so black it pulled his gaze into memories of what once was, of how he longed to be, and what had been lost. It was the place where his hands and feet had struggled up the steep side to reach the top, to look beyond the rim of earth and face the open sky. Deep in his heart he had always wanted peace. Like his father he too had dreams. But it was too late now.

He heard the men grunting and panting. They were prodding him on and hitting him, but he did not care. He was outside, under the open sky. He struggled to look up. To see the mountains! That was all he wanted, a shred of mountain peeping through the mist. No one shouted for him, no one begged for him to stay alive. There was no glory in dying before strangers in a hollow space surrounded by grey walls. But his soul was a bird in flight. You will not come back again to earth till the small stones grow into great rocks and the feathers of the crow turn grey. The words of his forefathers flashed through his head.

A man cannot return to earth after his death… But I can look up, and the sky is limitless.

He was free! He could feel the cold water from the stream near his house. He could see the beautiful dawn—such a calm morning! A fresh breeze was flowing down on him and he was splashing cold water on his face from the water point. Gimur was coming out of the house, smiling. She was sending him her thoughts. How strange a thing was sound! Can you hear the sound of her thoughts? He tried to turn his head and heard shouts and curses…And then he heard the voice of the priest, his gentle cry of surprise, a shout, his fingers lifted to play the flute…No, no, everything was getting mixed up. What would the sepoys and the white sa'abs say of him now? Sinner, shaman, priest, lama, legend, all mingled together with the secret that no one would ever know, that all he had ever wanted was the desire to feel love.

It is so cold… an icy wind is sweeping down and I can see the tracks of tala, the musk deer in the snow before the storm erases them. My father and I live in a cave. His arms are clasped around me. It is the happiest day of my life…

The moment, stretched taut as a coiled spring. The soldiers, the jailor, the priest, Kajinsha, his father and Gimur were frozen together in a silence that stopped time until it was broken when Kajinsha bared his teeth and suddenly he was alone and naked as a stone in the water that swung down, fell and exploded with a burst of sunlight into a deep gushing stream.

At that exact moment a cry went up in the hills. Kajinsha is dead! Kajinsha is dead! No one knew whose voice it was that was calling out so loudly nor by what magic the news was travelling so mysteriously over the treetops and sinking down into every house and fireplace and into the rocks and trees.

High up on a hill Gimur heard the cry and stopped.

From where she was the river and fields and everything on that flat landscape that had been so impregnable and oppressive appeared like tiny dots. She sat down and lifting her necklace over her head threw it on the ground. She lit her pipe. She placed one foot on a protruding rock and blew out a plume of smoke. The sun was following her. It rose higher, higher than the mountains and the puny prison walls and the mud huts and the flat, weeping river, higher than the tallest trees and the summer grass where she now sat on a high rock looking back at the plain below. A boat had taken her once to a distant hill and another had brought her back to the same river bank of sand and stones where she had set out from. She was ceaseless, like water, a gleaming, flowing world with a hidden language and secret journeys. 'Live!' Kajinsha had said. There must be some meaning to her being alive, she thought, but that meaning eluded her. She wanted to throw herself down the mountain and be with Kajinsha again.

All those who heard the terrible cry that morning knew that Kajinsha's death in a Debroogurh jail was the beginning of war and turmoil. It would provoke a string of attacks on settlements along the border in Upper Assam.

It began with a raid in 1855 by the Idu Mishmee clans, who swept down through the dense forests between the hills and Suddya and captured three of Lieutenant Eden's servants. More atrocities followed, provoking the British to prepare for military operations to punish the tribes but a full-scale expedition had to be put aside as more urgent matters claimed their attention with the outbreak of the Sepoy mutiny of 1857. However, this was not the end of hostilities between the tribes and the British authorities. The Abor raid of 1858 on a Beeah village of gold washers called Sengajan, just six miles from Debroogurh station on the north bank of the river, set the stage for the Anglo-Abor war that would last another fifty years and engulf so many Abor villages, including Gimur and Lendem's home village of Mebo and bring British troops deep into Abor territory.

Perhaps Lendem would fight in those wars and die like Kajinsha. Perhaps Gimur too would fight and perish, or move to another village. And many years later she might hear, perhaps from another villager, that Kajinsha's relatives had killed all Lamet's family in a war of revenge for betraying Kajinsha to the British. No one among them knew what the history books would say. Perhaps everything would be forgotten and people and names disappear, with Gimur's name lost, even in memory, for Gimur had turned her face in another direction.

Whatever has been, the victory, the defeat, she thought, I know only one thing. I was there at the heart of the tumult that has blown like dust and leaves swirling around me. I was there carried by the pure light of the heart's fire. There is no turning back. What is fate? It is all but what I have chosen.

'Tell them about us,' Kajinsha had said to her that night in the jail. 'Tell them we were good. Tell them we also had some things to say. But we cannot read and write. So we tell stories.'

Stories…words…I too have words…

She pursed her lips, puffing out more smoke. God, love, mercy, faith—story words—now she knew all the words, even though she would never speak them again. Green words. Bone words. Green, crunchy words. Painted sky words. Rain words, and water words, like stories from the lakes of the sun and the lake of stars. Bitter poison words. Words like sweet waters of honey from the lakes of beautiful spirits. Words like dreams of love that men dream to overcome the sad dreams of destruction. Poppy seed words. Disappearing, unhappy words. Wolf, nightmare words…

What have they done, these words that fill the air? I breathe in, I breathe out—breath words. Words are extra…

She puffed a little harder.

Ah! Blue words, the priest's words—now, if I move my hand like this it is to say this is all there is—blue, green, white, black…I have eaten them all… Ox blood words, abyss words…

She moved the pipe deftly to the other side of her mouth. Puff…

The sky above shone with a soft, clear light. She could inhale the grandeur of the sky. Her soul was returning to her. Beyond this spot the true forest would begin. So much death and waste… A strong wind was blowing everything away. Now for miles around there would be no people. She was returning alone, deeper and deeper into the wilderness that was her home. She had loved and lost, but she knew they would be together again. If one road had ended another was opening. There are doorways—what is life if not a dream of doorways?' she thought. A blue mist swirled down. She heard the cry of a bird and her breathing slowed. She wanted to be that bird with glinting yellow eyes gliding over the trees.

Feel the wind…hear the air rustling through my body like the murmur of centuries. Nothing is changed since the world began. There was fire, water, air. And I am fire, water, air. All that was is mingled in my blood, dripping in my marrow, crusted into my bones. It is what keeps my heart beating.

She thought about this thing called aith, the soul of man. The shaman sang songs about it. The dead priest had talked about it all the time. She remembered the look in Kajinsha's eyes. That, she knew, was his soul. Her soul and Kajinsha's had connected the moment the fierce gaze of those eyes had touched her when they first looked at each other. It was a movement, a cry, a fastening of untold strength. Now nothing on earth could destroy it. It could not be untied, not even by death, for what was death? Who died? No, nothing had ended. She stretched her legs out straight in front of her. The hillside was cold. The ground seemed to tremble beneath her body. She gazed up at the sky. In the gathering darkness a smile stretched her pale face.

Look at that, she thought. Listen to my heart drumming. The gods have played a game. They tossed something down—a piece of soul, maybe, she was smirking now and their toy broke in two. One piece was found by Kajinsha and the other—I swallowed it! Now they cannot find the way to undo what has happened. The gods are bystanders. And I am earth and Kajinsha is the sky and we have looked at each other and will look at each other like this for a million years.

Author's Note

The 'Mishmee Hills' in the novel is that part of Arunachal Pradesh that was the Lohit Frontier Division in the erstwhile North East Frontier Agency (NEFA). Prior to the Agency all the Frontier Divisions of NEFA were Frontier Tracts with the Mishmi and Abor Hills forming part of the Sadiya Frontier Tract of North Upper Assam. The first recorded contact of the British with the Mishmi tribes was in 1825 when Lieutenant Phillip Burlton, exploring the upper course of the Brahmaputra River, returned with a report of the 'Mismah Hills', claiming that its inhabitants 'were very averse to receiving strangers'.

Today the area covered in the book is the district of Anjaw that was bifurcated from Lohit District in 2007. The word 'Anjaw' means 'hill' in the Kaman language. The town of Oualong (now Walong) is a circle headquarters, with a mixed population of the Mishmi tribe and the predominantly Buddhist Meyor tribe. It is still as scenic as Father Krick first saw it in 1852, surrounded by pine clad hills, but it is now a place of historical prominence as the scene of some of the fiercest fighting in the Indo-China war of 1962. A few kilometres beyond Walong the road leads to Kibithoo, Kaho and Dichu close to the McMahon line. This is India's easternmost road that ends in the wall of mountains delineating the country's international border at the tri-junction with Tibet, China and Myanmar.

The other places in the book—the village of Sommeu (Sama)

and Rima, the seat of the governor, lie on the other side of the border in Zayul (Chayü) county. Chayü in Tibetan means 'a pile of rocks'. This was once the Tibetan Kongpo area, now referred to as China's Nyingchi prefecture of the Tibet Autonomous Region.

As also mentioned in the book the origin of the word 'Mishmi' is unclear. The three Mishmi groups in Arunachal Pradesh are known as the Kaman (Miju), Taraon (Digaru) and Idu (Chulikata). Similarly the nomenclature today for the Abor tribe is Adi. There is no chieftain system among the Mishmi though I have left the term in the book following its usage in the first records of the region. As is the case of many families who once lived, traded and moved freely in the Himalayan borderlands, the demarcation of the border separated the Mishmi people. Today, there are Mishmi families still living in some nine villages located deep in the mountain forests of Chayü County. Although largely outnumbered by the different nationalities and ethnic groups inhabiting the Tibet Autonomous Region, they continue their cultural traditions, surviving on slash-and-burn agriculture and speaking their own language. But they are known not as Mishmi but as Dengba, the Deng people of Nyingchi prefecture.

About the story of the priest—I came upon Father Krick's name when I was working on my first book. He had visited 'Mimbo' (Mebo), just across the river Siang from my hometown of Pasighat, and had left a written record of his observations of the place and its inhabitants, with the closing line: 'They seem to possess much of the child's simplicity, and Mimbo is undoubtedly less corrupt than Paris...' I wanted to know more. But in Mebo they tell me there is no one now who remembers the visit of the priest. *It was such a long time ago, how can we remember? Father Krick... who...?* Some other names from the past ring a bell, but faintly, and those who would have remembered the stories of war and how the tribes fought the British attackers have passed on. Today, everyone is immersed in work. There are houses to be built and crops to be planted. The children are growing up and that is all that matters. The past is gone. It is only people like me, who look back. And maybe some stray ghost of love who thinks the past is alive. And it is speaking to me, telling me, 'Dig deep. Search. Don't give up. It may be my brother's story, a sister's, a friend's, or my own...'

In 2009 I visited the Paris Foreign Missions. It was a brief visit, a fleeting glimpse of a green oasis in the heart of Paris, the bookshop, crypt, the matyrs' room, the seminary. In 2010, more than a century-and-half after the journey of Father Krick I was travelling on the road to Walong. It was October—not a bad time to travel, but one route was cut off by a flooded stream. By the new bridge over the Lohit River a warm gust of wind seemed to blow out of nowhere, making me sit up in surprise. Where was this wind coming from?

I thought I would note down everything but the effort was too much. Despite the fact that this Walong route was the favoured route of explorers, soldiers, naturalists and surveyors throughout the nineteenth and early twentieth centuries it is still a narrow road with the jungle creeping in on every side. Trees with straight, white trunks tower above us. It is hard to imagine how the French priests could have walked in this jungle day after day, and in the case of Father Krick making not one, but two journeys; so determined, so faithful. When you see these forests what the missionaries achieved seems unbelievable. Perhaps the journey never happened, perhaps it is not true?

The past is a mysterious place. The shaman chants his songs remembering everything. How is memory so intricate with colour, image and scent, where there are no paths visible in this green and luxuriant cover? I had come in search of another story—about the Mishmi chief who had roamed so independently in the Tibeto-Mishmi border, and who was hung in Dibrugarh jail for the murder of Father Krick and Augustine Bourry. Perhaps it is still all there, I thought. It must be there—a place of meeting. It is the same jungle, the same jagged pile of rocks on the roadside and the same immoveable mountains rearing up around me. But here too rapid developments are taking place and it is not easy to find out anything more about the enigmatic chief. Even in official versions the spelling of his name varies. The records are also unclear about whether the condemned man killed one or two prison guards while awaiting his sentence. The ravages of time, flood, fire, have destroyed many important government documents of the time, especially those that were housed in Sadiya and Dibrugarh. The great earthquake of 1950 with its epicentre in Rima tore through the Mishmi and Abor hills, gouged out mountains, changed the course of rivers, destroyed towns in Assam (including parts of Dibrugarh on the banks of the Brahmaputra) and buried the famous town of Sadiya forever.

There is no restitution here. Perhaps some stories will always elude the historian. Perhaps some things are better left unexplained.

About the Abor woman, Gimur—there is not a trace of her in any record of the period. Nor is there anything about Lendem of Mebo, or the boy Awesa, or Chowsa, the Khampti who might have escorted the British through the Mishmi villages up to Rima in the years following the Eden expedition of 1855, and ultimately helped the authorities to fix the country's extreme north-eastern boundary between the territories of China and India.

And about the men who came from a different world, the missionaries—what happened to their endeavour, their very presence in these mountains? In their lifetime they could not convert a single soul. The south Tibet mission was abandoned, forever, it seemed, until one day in December of 1997 the first Mishmi Catholic converts were baptised in a makeshift church in Tezu, the headquarters of Lohit district, by a French priest of the Society of Foreign Missions of Paris. Today there is a Krick and Bourry

Memorial school, and in Tezu market I saw a shop sign: Krick & Bourry Cyber Cafe.

Perhaps nothing is as it seems and everything can be explained the other way round: that lives are ended, but a story—never.

Acknowledgements

I am deeply indebted to many people who have inspired and nurtured the idea for this book. I thank: Fr V.M Thomas, SDB, Founder Director, Don Bosco Institute, Guwahati; Fr Andrew, SDB, St Xaviers School, Harmutty; The Don Bosco Centre for Indigenous Cultures (DBCIC), Mawlai, Shillong; Fr Walter Fernandez, SJ, Jesuit House, Guwahati; Ms Leila Lounici, Librairie de L'Asie Culturelle et Religlieuse, SDME, Paris; Tinlay Choedon Dewatshang, my friend who so kindly gave her time and helped me find 128, Rue du Bac; Bruno Philip, *Le Monde*, who first gave me a translation of Father Krick's writings.

For many reasons this work turned out to be quite a complex exercise. I thought I had the middle, beginning and end; but most of it was in-between, a striving for kinship with the past, if only in passing, in between the pages of a book. I was fortunate to be able to travel and meet many people who gave me advice, support, and answered my questions. I am indebted to Kalikho Pul, politician and minister from Anjaw district, for his encouragement and generous hospitality when I was travelling through the district; my kind hosts Kayowlum Towsik and Khope Thaley who sacrificed their time to undertake the journey together and introduced me to the nuances of the Kaman language; noted author Hakraso Kri; the people of Hawai, Wembreylum Pul and Kambring elder Alolno Pul; Dy. Commissioner, C.S Jeinow; the people and officers of

Walong, Kibitho and Kaho; S.Minin, EAC Hawai; Kabang Apum, CO Kibithoo; Anchal Samiti Chairperson, Smt. Meyor and her family ; Redi Pul in Hayuliang; Sokhep Kri, state editor (Gazetteers); Jotem Borang, Director, Public Libraries and Mukge Tayeng, Donyi Polo miri of Mebo.

I also express my appreciation of travel companions Sanjit Shah, Nicolas, Ozing Dai, Gung Dai, and of Otem Dai who lent support for my travels with a sturdy back-up vehicle.

There are many journals and books I have delved into for information and inspiration to imagine the period that the book covers. Most notably I acknowledge Françoise Fauconnet-Buzelin, MEP (*Mission unto Matyrdom);* Hakraso Kri (*The Mishmis: An Introduction);* Fr N.M Krick (*Relation d'un voyage au Thibet en 1852;* and *d'un voyage chez les Abors en 1853*—the latter translated by Rev A. Gille, SJ as *An account of an Expedition among the Abors in 1853*, and published in the *Journal of the Asiatic Society of Bengal,* 1913). The territories, routes and geographical features covered in the book are spelt as in the journals of Fr Krick and R.Boileau Pemberton—*The Eastern Frontier of India,* 1835.

As ever I remain humbly indebted to my parents and family for their love and support, and to my friends and colleagues who have given me courage and inspiration. My sincerest gratitude is also owed to David Davidar of Aleph Book Company, for his steady support; and as ever to Ravi Singh, for all the years he has invariably supported me with good advice, painstaking effort, understanding and patience.